The Reporter Wore Petticoats

To Karen —
all the best

Dr. Abigail Elizabeth Reynolds

by

Dr. Abigail Elizabeth Reynolds

INFINITY
PUBLISHING.COM

ISBN 0-7414-5785-7

Published by:

INFINITY
PUBLISHING.COM

1094 New DeHaven Street, Suite 100
West Conshohocken, PA 19428-2713
Info@buybooksontheweb.com
www.buybooksontheweb.com
Toll-free (877) BUY BOOK
Local Phone (610) 941-9999
Fax (610) 941-9959

Printed in the United States of America

Published January 2010

I wish to thank Carol Crawford Rowe, my sister, friend, companion, housemate, and editor, for her loyalty and collaboration on this novel.

I wish to thank Dr. David Foote, along with all my fellow Bohemians and Civil War Reenactor Friends, for their encouragement and support of the project.

I wish to also thank Laura Pearce, educator extraordinaire, for her assistance with the Student/Teacher Guide.

In addition, a special appreciation to the following for contributing letters of correspondence in their "first person" personas:

Mister Allan Stone as General Robert E. Lee
Miss Hannah Opdenaker as Miss Tillie Pierce
Mister Nick Korolev as Brigadier General William Averell
and Captain Henry Bingham
Missus Sue Sodomin as Miss Clara Barton
Dr. David Foote as Mister David Foote

This book is dedicated to my family, especially my children.

I also dedicate this novel to Doctors Kenneth May and Christopher Spizzieri, my cardiologists, who work diligently and continually to assist in maintaining my quality of life.

"To God be the glory, for great things He has done"

"Clouds and darkness surround us, yet Heaven is just, and the day of triumph will surely come, when justice and truth will be vindicated."
                    - Mary Todd Lincoln

"There were angry men confronting me and I caught the flashing of defiant eyes, but above me and within me, there was a spirit stronger than them all."
                    - Antoinette Brown Blackwell

"Because men and women are a complement to one another, we need women's thought in the national affairs to make a safe and stable government."
                    - Elizabeth Cady Stanton

"I freed a thousand slaves. I could have freed a thousand more if only they knew they were slaves."
                    - Harriet Tubman

"There is a time for everything,
and a season for every activity under heaven:

a time to be born and a time to die,
a time to plant and a time to uproot,

a time to kill and a time to heal,
a time to tear down and a time to build,

a time to weep and a time to laugh,
a time to mourn and a time to dance,

a time to scatter stones and a time to gather them,
a time to embrace and a time to refrain,

a time to search and a time to give up,
a time to keep and a time to throw away,

a time to tear and a time to mend,
a time to be silent and a time to speak,

a time to love and a time to hate,
a time for war and a time for peace."

- Ecclesiastes 3 (NIV)

Book ONE
a time to be born...

CHAPTER ONE

The year is 1865. My name is Elizabeth Grace Fitzgerald, **MISS** Elizabeth Grace Fitzgerald, to be more precise. I am a War Correspondent for the New York Tribune newspaper out of New York, New York. I emphasize the Miss part because I have never married and now, going on my sixth decade in this world, it would seem to most that it is unlikely I shall ever have the opportunity to truly enhance the life of one of the opposite sex, not that I would particularly want to. I have enough trouble enhancing my own life, let alone taking on that responsibility for someone else. And thus begins my story, as I shall endeavor to tell how I came to be a War Correspondent at the New York Tribune during this time of national tribulation.

I was born in the small town of Cranbury, New Jersey, on December 30, 1808, to Maggie Jo and Benjamin James Fitzgerald, the first of two children. My younger brother, William David, would die at his birth, along with our mother, two years later. My father would never remarry, but instead dedicated his life to my care, education, and upbringing.

Father was a self educated man and worked hard in the local carriage shop. He loved to read, and firmly believed that everyone, including his daughter, should be educated to the greatest extent possible.

I began to read, so I have been told, before I could walk. My love affair with the printed word has been long and enjoyable. However, my love of investigation and discovery has been even more enjoyable, a passion, as it were, and a powerful driving force throughout my life.

I would read local news stories to my father and would exclaim that they did not tell us all the details. I wanted to know why someone behaved as they did, what motivated them to such behaviors, how did it affect the victims and their lives afterward. My questions, at times, seemed almost endless to my father. He would laugh and suggest that when I was old enough, I could write my own stories and share what I thought was important. I vowed at age ten to become a world renowned reporter. And so I did.

In the fall of 1824, at the age of sixteen, my father made it possible for me to attend Wilson's School for Women, in Chambersburg, Pennsylvania. Miss Clarissa Poffenberger was the

3

teacher who inspired and encouraged me in my endeavors. Early in my time at Wilson School, she discovered my love for reading, investigation, discovery, and writing, and she learned of my desire to become a great reporter.

She introduced me to Mister Oliver Jones, the editor of the Chambersburg Democratic Tribune. Mister Jones was a larger-than-life man who told of great adventures when he was a younger lad. He had been in the newspaper business since age six, first as a press apprentice, then a type setter, reporter, editor, and finally editor and owner of the local paper. He shared many adventures with me in that first meeting, and took me home to meet his wife and to have dinner with them.

Missus Prudence Mary Jones was a petite and lovely lady. She had borne no children, and now was well beyond her age to do so. She seemed not to mind, and was content to assist Mister Jones in any of his adventures. She shared how they had travelled together over many miles, and now was more than willing to stay at home and care for the shop as needed in the times Mister Jones was absent with his duties.

That first meeting was a mystical, enchanted evening for a young woman just beginning her journeys outside the safety of her father's home and small village. As we talked throughout the evening, comfortably seated in the large parlor, I became more aware of the deep stirring inside me to truly become what I had always dreamed, a reporter. I asked Mister Jones for a position at his paper.

At first, he choked on the warm rum drink he had been nursing for some time. Then he laughed so hard that I thought the room itself was going to join in with his amusement. Tears from the laughter filled his hand rag, and finally, after all the entertaining spasms he endured at my request for a reporter's position, he calmed himself and asked Missus Jones how she felt about my desire to work for him.

During this entire display of amusement on the part of Mister Jones, Missus Jones sat quietly, arms folded, face as straight and unrevealing as any I have seen. She would have been good at playing cards, should she have ever decided to. She waited patiently for Mister Jones to complete this show of disapproval, as I had interpreted it.

After several moments of silence, Missus Jones finally, with a glaring look at her husband, spoke.

4

"First of all, Mister Jones," she began in a stern, almost matronly way, "I do not appreciate the way you have just treated our guest. You have filled her head and her heart with grand visions of romantic flight in your chosen profession, and have given her to believe there is no other love for you but this paper of yours.

"Now, when she dares to open her vulnerable heart and ask for your help, you act as if she is some absurd and childish thing that needs to be placed back into the box, only to be taken out and played with at another time."

"But my dear…" stammered Mister Jones.

"Don't 'my dear' me, husband, for you know that I am strong willed enough to take you on in this matter. But never mind to us, for we shall discuss your behavior later, in private."

And with that, she smiled and made a flirtatious look in her husband's direction, before continuing.

"Now, back to your question, my Dear. Miss Fitzgerald, is it for me to understand that you desire to work at the newspaper and for my husband as a reporter, while you complete your studies at Wilson School?"

Missus Jones spoke with such calm, care, and tenderness at this point. I was not at all sure this was the same person who had just spoken up to Mister Jones.

I suddenly felt a little girl again and for the first time in many years, longed for the touch of my own mother. Missus Jones was much as I thought my mother would have been, had she lived. She would have been strong but tender, educated but humble, loving yet firm, gracious while protecting her loved ones, adventurous, yet stable.

As I looked into her eyes, I could almost see her growing fondness for me, perhaps even her own desire to have such a daughter as me for her own. At that moment, I knew we would become forever friends, if not family. Thus began my journey toward journalism.

CHAPTER TWO

My apprenticeship as a reporter and writer began at the Chambersburg Democratic Tribune that following spring, under the stern mentoring of Mister Oliver Jones, Editor and Proprietor, and the watchful and loving care of his wife, Mamma Jones, as I had come to call her. I was now seventeen years old, and the year was 1825.

The work was hard and long, which I did not mind so much, with the exception that it made the studies at school more strenuous. "Mamma Jones" had insisted that I continue my lessons at Wilson School for Women, as part of the condition for my apprenticeship. Of course, Miss Poffenberger, my favorite teacher at school, along with my father, heartily agreed with this condition of employment.

My day often began before five o'clock in the morning, and lasted well into the evening. The exception was always Sundays, in which I would rise at six o'clock, review my assignments for the coming week, and prepare for Church services at the local Methodist Meeting House.

Mister and Missus Jones would stop for me at the School Boarding House on their way to the services, and we would ride together in their well appointed surrey. Missus (Mamma) Jones always made certain that both her husband and their transportation were in immaculate condition for Sunday meetings.

After the services, we would always venture to the home of the Jones', along with other guests, for a lovely meal and time of relaxation, story telling, reading, and music. Ever present on these Sunday gatherings were the Methodist Preacher, Reverend Hobart Young, along with his wife, Suzanne, and their three children, Kathryn, age nine, Samuel, age eight, and Micah, age six.

Micah was, by virtue or nature, no one knew for sure, the most mischievous of all little boys I had ever met. He would torment Kathryn until she was in tears and ignore Samuel to the point of constant complaint. On more than one occasion he would attempt to "hide" under my petticoats, although I am sure his motive was to seek a better glimpse into the underpinnings of a lady's attire.

In addition to the Reverend and his family, there was always an additional room full of invited guests, some repeat customers, but mostly out of town dignitaries and acquaintances just passing through. These were the ones I always loved to engage, as they had tales to tell of life beyond the little, sleepy hamlet of Chambersburg.

On one occasion, Reverend John Blake came for a visit, along with his friend, Missus Sarah Hale. Reverend Blake was attempting to raise funds to start a Women's Magazine in Boston. Missus Hale had been a writer and was already published at the time. She had been recruited by Reverend Blake to assist in this new publication. Sarah was to be its first editor.

Sarah Hale had already pursued a literary career with her first husband, an attorney, who had died of fever only a couple of years prior, leaving her with five children of her own. Thus, Missus Hale launched her full-time literary career, and now found herself proposed as the first woman editor of a publication specifically directed to the interests of women.

Reverend Blake was a true visionary, realizing the power of women to change the world and affect the outcome of political causes through their feminine ways and wonders. He believed in the fullest possible education and participation of women in all the affairs of men.

The honorable minister was also an avid abolitionist, who saw that the way to bring an end to the cruel practice of slavery was to set the women free first. Thus he began his enterprise, and employed the services of Sarah Hale, author, abolitionist, mother, widow, and friend, to bring about this great endeavor.

Missus Hale was explaining on this particular Sunday, to those of us gathered at the home of Mister and Missus Jones, that women are indeed "capable of engaging the intellect and of expressing in a most logical way the formulas of human nature".

"But, Missus Hale", Oliver Jones was saying, "is it not a total offense to societal rule to have a woman so blatantly engaged in the affairs of men? How will you encourage advertisers to your publication, engage good writers, hire and oversee printers, distributors and a whole host of other necessities, as a woman? It is utterly impossible, and should be left to men to care for."

"Are you suggesting that women are not capable of such things, Mister Jones? I have met your wife, and she is more than capable of running your entire publication without your assistance. Is that not true?" Sarah countered.

"Of course it is true, Missus Hale, but not without the oversight of a loving and thoughtful husband such as myself. I have, and do, give my wife a free hand in the daily operations of the paper, but I am there to insure her safety and the safety of the paper. Without the oversight of a capable man such as myself, women would be naturally taken advantage of. Don't you agree, my dear?"

Mister Jones was speaking through Missus Hale, at this point and directly to Mamma Jones.

Now, Mamma Jones was not one to belittle her husband in front of others, unless of course the situation demanded that she intervene on behalf of her guest, and quiet her husband before he became too involved in the heat of the moment, thus embarrassing himself in the process. Mamma came and stood slightly behind her husband, and, with her hands resting ever so gently on his left shoulder began to speak freely with her guest.

"I believe what my husband is trying to say, Missus Hale, is that he is a strong and opinionated member of his unique class known as the male species. As for his need to give male oversight of the paper, in order to protect both me and the paper, well, I have learned that it is all right to allow him to believe certain partial truths for his well-being."

"Yes, yes, Prudence, you are indeed quite correct in allowing me my illusions of maintaining control of every situation. Otherwise, how could I face my friends? Never let it be said that you have been the source of my disillusionment."

Mister Jones now addressed his guest directly, since Mamma Jones remained behind her husband, thus forcing him to direct his conversation toward Missus Hale.

"It is not my desire to discourage you, my dear, only to point out that there may be obstacles to your endeavor that could be easily avoided, if there were a managing editor as well as a literary editor. Perhaps if you could find someone, a male counterpart, to assist Missus Hale, Reverend Blake, in the day to day management of the publication, it would go easier for both of you. That is all I am trying to suggest."

Reverend Blake had been sitting quietly, observing the exchange that had been taking place for some time between these two literary colleagues.

8

"I believe you are quite right in your thinking, Sir", Reverend Blake began. "I know Missus Hale to be very capable in her literary skills, as well as her managerial abilities. She has already proven that she can care for her household following the death of her husband, and, of course she has managed to write significantly on several of the current moral situations facing our nation and world, quite elegantly, I might add. So I have no doubt that she could certainly do it all.

"But I am concerned that the tasks will take away the time I would like to see Sarah devote to her writing, attracting and recruiting other writers, and her general editing oversight of the materials to go into print and publication.

"And that is precisely why we have made this trip to see you. Sir, by reputation, you are an excellent managing editor. I know that you surround yourself with talent, encouraging them to achieve the best they can produce for publication."

"Your words are too kind, Reverend Blake, but I thank you for them."

Oliver Jones spoke with that air of pride and sophistication that comes when one truly knows of his ability, and is not afraid to show it.

"Yes, I have been successful in hiring talented reporters over the years, as well as craftsmen who do the daily and laborious work of putting out the paper each week, but it really has been Prudence, who over the past couple of years, has found the truly good writers. It was she, after all, who convinced me to hire Miss Fitzgerald."

Mister Jones was obviously proud of his wife, and of course, his paper and reputation. What Reverend Blake was not aware of, though, was that Oliver Jones would not in any fashion give away his trade secrets or insight to attracting good people. For Mister Jones knew that at any time, he might be in need of the very talent he had passed on to some other editor. Mister Jones continued to keep his thoughts very close to his vest.

"Now I suppose you would like to know if there is some small way that I could assist you in your new enterprise with Missus Hale. Am I quite correct on this assumption, Reverend Blake?", Mister Jones stated.

Reverend Blake also held things close at hand and revealed only what was necessary in order to maneuver his opponent into a position from which there was no retreat, only surrender.

"Quite right, my dear friend", Reverend Blake commented. "I know you often will not release information to help a competitor, but as you know, we are starting a Lady's Magazine to be published monthly out of Boston. I have no concern that we will be in any type of competition, and am sure that whatever advice and counsel you may pass on to us would not hurt you in the slightest. In fact, we may be able to be of mutual assistance, once we have begun production."

Reverend Blake was beginning to lay his own trap to corner Oliver with the use of flattery, kindness, gentle speech, and the most powerful of all aphrodisiacs, the possibility of financial gain.

Reverend Blake continued, "You see, my dear Oliver, once we are in production, I would be happy to forward for consideration in your publication, those materials which have been submitted to Sarah that we might find inconsistent with our goals of publication. Perhaps, together, we would find a talented writer who could contribute to both of our successes.

"There, of course, would be no charge for this from us, and the only financial considerations you would have to contend with would be with the author of the material."

"I see your point and thoughts here, John. May I call you John? Reverend is so formal when we are discussing a business relationship of this sort, don't you agree?

"Yes, by all means, call me John and let us suspend with the formalities. So, Oliver, what I really need from you is the name of someone who could become our Managing Editor, who would work closely with Missus Hale on the day to day activities of the paper. Would you offer any suggestions for me at this time?"

Missus Jones, along with Missus Hale, Missus Young, and a few other visiting ladies and, of course me had been carefully listening to the conversation between these two business men, as they thought themselves to be at the moment, wondering when, or rather if, they would include any of us in their plotting. It was, I must admit, amusing to watch these two peacocks strut around the room as it were, showing off their feathers and attempting to flatter one another into submissive return.

10

And so the maneuvering and repartee continued well into the evening, with neither gentlemen appearing to have gained the upper hand in the process.

The other guests of the day had already returned home, or retired to their lodging for the night. Reverend and Missus Young, along with their three children, had promised, as they always do, to return for more lively discussion following next week's services.

As the hour was late, and I had to be up early in order to begin my activities for the day, I excused myself to retire. As I was leaving, I overheard Mister Jones state that he would like Reverend Blake and his traveling companion to stay on for a few days, to enjoy the local offerings as well as to further discuss possibilities for the future.

My spirit seemed to leap inside my very being, as I heard the Reverend agree to the offer. I was not sure why, but at the time it seemed as if something truly wonderful, perhaps even magical, might be ready to unfold, and I did not want to miss any of it.

As I lay in my bed back at Wilson School, sleep would not come, for I was still excited at the prospect that a Lady's Magazine in Boston was about to be launched under the watchful eye of a woman, not a man, for the first time in my limited knowledge of historical fact. It was all just too exciting and full of promise and possibilities. I even began to think that I could someday possibly be an editor, or a manager, or even an owner of a renowned publication. I finally drifted off to sleep, with thoughts of being a world renowned reporter traveling around the globe for the most elusive stories.

On to the future!

CHAPTER THREE

I am here in the warm, sun-drenched park in the spring of 1828, seated on the grass pavilion, waiting for my name to be called so that I may go forward to the podium and receive my diploma. I find myself reflecting upon the past four years.

How did I come to this point in my life so quickly? These past four years went by so fast that it seems just yesterday that I arrived at Wilson School, was introduced to Mister Oliver Jones under the tutelage of Miss Poffenberger, went to work as a reporter apprentice at the Tribune, and now have come to my graduation day. Where did the time go? And, oh, the experiences I have already had!

My first reporting assignment was to be a simple story about Charles Mason, who had been accused of stealing a horse from his neighbor. I was to cover the trial, the anticipated guilty finding, and the eventual hanging of Mister Mason.

According to Mister Jones, this was a straight forward project, well within the abilities of any young and inexperienced reporter to handle. So off I went to meet Mister Mason, at the jail for a one-on-one interview. After a brief meeting, I was convinced that he was neither a horse thief nor a terrible man, but that he had been wrongly accused by his neighbor.

I ventured into the Franklin County, Pennsylvania, country side to speak with his wife, Lottie. She told the same story as her husband. She explained how their neighbor, Mister Gideon Smith, had tried on many occasions to buy their property for the water and fertile soil. She further stated how her husband had continued to resist the sale and the intimidating tactics of Mister Smith.

Mister Mason one day had the need of a new horse, as his had taken ill and needed to be put down. Mister Smith heard of this news and sought to take advantage of the situation through other than honorable means.

Mister Smith contacted Mister Mason and informed him that he had a mare that he no longer needed. He was sure that she would meet the needs of Mister Mason, and, just to show there were no hard feelings over his failure to purchase the Mason farm, he would offer Mister Mason the mare at a most fair and reasonable price.

Missus Mason told how her husband and Mister Smith had agreed on the price, and that Mister Smith sold the horse to him, promising to provide a bill of sale at a later time. Mister Mason, a trusting and honest man, believed him. Two days later, the local Sheriff arrived and arrested Mister Mason for the theft of Mister Smith's mare.

Missus Mason went on to explain that, because there was no bill of sale Mister Mason could provide, the sheriff had to act on the word of Mister Smith and arrest her husband. She also explained that, if convicted, her husband would be hanged, and she would be forced to sell their property to Mister Smith.

Since they were not particularly wealthy folks, there was little they could do in order to defend themselves, except to tell the truth, and hope that in the end that would be sufficient.

Being a young reporter at the time, and this being my first assignment, I knew that I would have to dig deeper. My job was to find out what was really going on and to get at the truth, not merely report the fact of the court proceedings.

I went to see a young man whom I had met through the Jones' at their home on a Sunday after Church. His name was Isaac Stoltzfus.

Isaac was a handsome, intelligent young man, with strong features and thick, bright, red hair neatly groomed upon his head. His full rich, rusty red beard was also neatly trimmed and immaculate. The young gentleman was studying at the Theological Seminary in Gettysburg, and was spending the present year as an intern with the Trinity Lutheran Church in Chambersburg.

I arrived at his office in the church rectory around noon, two days before the trial was to begin. Mister Stoltzfus welcomed me at once, for, as I later learned, had been smitten with me at our first meeting during dinner.

He had spoken to Mister Jones about me, asking if I would consider attending a concert with him at some point, stating that he had never met anyone with my ability to ask so many questions, especially a young woman. Reportedly, Mister Jones laughed and encouraged the young preacher to continue his studies first, and then, if he was still interested in making further my acquaintance, he would explore the idea with his wife.

"Please, please, come in, Miss Fitzgerald", Isaac began. "I am so glad you are here. I have not stopped thinking of you night and day since our first meeting last month. How have you been? What brings you here today? May I offer you a cup of tea? Let me look at you. You are as beautiful as I recall you in my thoughts as I go to sleep each night. Please, where are my manners? Sit down and let me be still while you tell me your business. I am so glad you are here. Can you stay a while?"

Mister Stoltzfus was acting as if he were a school boy in love for the first time, giddy, blushing, and talking on without taking even a single breath. It was delightful and even a little flattering, and did cause even my heart to blush somewhat.

"Thank you, Mister Stoltzfus. I would love to sit and visit, and, yes, I would enjoy a cup of tea, but I must outright confess that my visit is not purely social. I need your assistance. I came with the hope of appealing to your sense of moral duty and fairness, and in the hope that you would be willing to assist me in proving the innocence of a wrongly accused gentleman."

"Of course, of course, Elizabeth. May I call you Elizabeth, and please call me Isaac. I would like to put aside the formalities as we talk, if that is all right with you."

"By all means, Elizabeth is certainly appropriate, Isaac."

I felt myself blushing under Isaac's careful watch and considerate ways. He was well mannered, most delightful, and, of course, abundantly handsome. Isaac would undoubtedly make a wonderful husband for some fortunate woman in the future.

I sat there pondering if I was such a woman and could I be happy with Isaac, as Mamma Jones has been with Mister Jones all these years. It was then that I knew that I could never marry, for the work I wished to do would not leave time for care of husband and home. I had drifted off into my own world briefly, before I realized that Isaac was back with the tea and already speaking once again, going on about how delighted he was that I was there.

"There, I trust that the tea is just right for you. I am not very good at brewing a fine tea. I make it either too strong or too weak. Would you like some sugar? Milk? Lemon? Perhaps some cakes? What else may I get for you, Elizabeth? Your every wish is my command."

And with that he offered a slight bow, with his hand graciously extended. We both laughed, and Isaac settled in to make himself comfortable next to me on the divan.

I continued in my silent assessment of this fine young man. He was so very thoughtful, and I was certain he would work beside any wife he might eventually take for himself, not expecting her to do all things for him, but would, I suppose, share equally in as many responsibilities as possible.

"Isaac, the reason for my visit is that I have a story to tell and a favor to ask."

I went on to explain the situation of Mister Mason and his wife, and how I had only two days to find out the truth and be able to prove it. I shared how the Masons would lose their farm to Mister Smith, and how Mister Mason would hang for this crime, if convicted. The thievery, I explained, was not on the part of Mister Mason, but on the part of Mister Smith.

After sharing my concerns and my desire to prove Mister Mason innocent, Isaac began, "Elizabeth, first we must pause and pray for guidance in this matter."

"Pause and pray. Is that all you can think of? I thought you were a man of action. Or at least that is what you led me to believe in our first meeting. Defend the rights of the poor and disadvantaged.

"Gain the freedom of slaves and all peoples. Correct injustices as you may find them. Take up the just causes. Was that all just fancy talk, Mister Stoltzfus? Are you merely a pacifist who believes that God will take care of everything in His own time, and we are to do nothing but PRAY?"

"Please Elizabeth, let me..." Isaac stammered.

"Please Elizabeth nothing, Sir. If you do not intend to help me, then I shall be on my way, and we will speak no more of this situation."

"I will help you", Isaac almost shouted. Then with such tenderness, "It is just that I always pray for guidance before designing a plan. If nothing else, prayer seems to help me focus. That's all. Now, may we pray?"

Isaac took my hands into his, holding them ever so gently, and began to pray for guidance and direction. He interceded on behalf of the Masons and asked for divine intervention to make right a wrong. After Isaac had finished praying, we devised a plan to entice Mister Smith into making a confession.

Isaac knew of Mister Smith and that he enjoyed his drink most evenings at a nearby establishment. He also knew that Mister Smith enjoyed boasting from time to time of his business successes in obtaining that which he desired. As Isaac pointed out, pride always comes before the fall. It was Isaac's intention to exploit this weakness in the man. The plan was for Isaac, along with one of his fellow clergy friends, to attend to the pub and get Mister Smith to talk about how he intended to acquire Mister Mason's property. With two of them present, they would be able to witness the deception, for out of the mouth of two witnesses, is a man condemned.

It is hard to believe that was almost four years ago. Mister Jones was so impressed with my work, how I was able to get someone to help me prove the innocence of the accused man, and turn the table on the accuser. Isaac Stoltzfus later said that it was as if "the Lord Jesus himself had turned the tables on old Lucifer, the accuser now being the accused".

As for Mister Smith, it was later discovered that he had lied and deceived many business men in the community. He was forced to sell off his holdings, make restitution, and move out of the area. It was said that he went to the west and was eventually killed in an Indian attack in Ohio.

I went on to cover many more events, and to tell the story of unique individuals and their families. Mamma Jones said that I had a wonderful way of telling the human side of a story, not just the facts, as most men do. Mister and Missus Jones, Missus Sarah Hale, Miss Poffenberger, Isaac Stoltzfus, Reverend and Missus Hobart Young and their three children, the men and boys at the paper, along with their families, and many at school had all become dear friends, and many, like Mamma Jones, were more like family.

As my name was now called to come to the platform to receive my diploma, my thoughts turned toward my father, who had traveled from New Jersey to be present for this occasion. I looked out upon the crowd and saw his wonderful, proud, beaming face, glowing with pride as his only daughter and living child was about to graduate with honors and from here, go off into the world to write and report on the affairs of men.

He knew that he would not have to worry after his death whether I would be all right and cared for, for he saw that I had matured into a self reliant and independent young woman, ready to take on the world. I was as proud of him for raising me in this fashion, counter to the societal norms of the day, as he was of me at that moment.

I also thought of my own mother, and how much like Mamma Jones I was sure she would have been, had she lived.

Over the past four years, I had come to appreciate and love Prudence Jones as if she were my very own mother, and she had come to love me as if I were her own daughter.

As I reached the podium and received my diploma, I saw Father, Mamma Jones, Mister Jones, and a host of other friends stand and let out a thundering cheer, which was contrary to all decorum, not unlike my life to that point, and ever to be in the future.

Book TWO

a time to build...

CHAPTER FOUR

Upon graduation from Wilson School, I continued to work for the paper with Mister Jones. Mamma Jones insisted that I take a room with them, so Mister Jones converted the attic into a comfortable living space for me, complete with all the furnishings I would need or desire. Mamma Jones made sure that I was always warm and comfortable, and saw to it that I had the finest bed linens and comforters money could buy.

Oliver complained to his wife that the bed coverings they slept with were not nearly as fine, but he, like Mamma Jones, wanted me to stay and be as comfortable as possible. Even if he would never admit it publicly, he shared with his wife privately that he thought of me as much as a daughter as she did.

During that year, Sarah Josepha Hale, or Jo as I had started calling her, was a visitor on two separate occasions. Jo and Reverend John Blake had formed the *American Ladies Magazine and Literary Gazette* in Boston and she came to seek the counsel of Mister Jones.

I loved Sarah Hale and her spirit of adventure. Over the course of time that had passed since I first met her in 1825, we had become friends and communicated often. Jo had followed my early career and was impressed, as Mamma Jones was, with my ability to share the human interest side of a story. She often stated in her letters how I had the most obvious ability to see into the very souls of people, and to tell their stories with dignity and fairness.

Mister Jones had given Reverend Blake the name of a gentleman from Philadelphia, Mister John Norvell, a very distinguished and honorable man, for consideration as the Managing Editor of the publication they were about to launch. As it were, Mister Norvell was already gainfully employed and was looking to start his own daily newspaper in the near future. He seemed not at all interested in giving up his dreams in favor of assisting a woman in achieving hers.

Against the advice of Mister Jones, and the objections of Reverend Blake, Sarah Hale had assumed the responsibilities of both Managing and Literary Editor of the Ladies Magazine. She had proven that she was well up to the task, and the start of the publication had been most successful.

Missus Hale had begun to build the reputation of her magazine by attracting both local and national materials from talented writers, most of whom were women. She insisted on original works that clearly benefited the female reader.

Her monthly circulation was already at an impressive forty thousand subscribers, after only eighteen months. Reverend Blake attributed this success to Missus Hale's marketing of the magazine to the interest of the fathers, brothers, and husbands of her readers, by encouraging them to purchase a subscription. She assured these gentlemen that their daughters, sisters, and wives would not only be grateful for the subscription, but that the women would also be in a better position to please the men in their lives as a result of having read the magazine.

In November of 1829, Jo once again ventured to our small community. She came this time for the sole purpose of seeing me. I was, to say the least, flattered by this visit, especially from such a mature, sophisticated, and accomplished woman, author and publisher. But why would she want to see me? After all, I was just a small town reporter and did not have the kind of experience or type of counsel that Mister Jones was able to offer.

Mamma Jones knew well before the visit, that Missus Hale was coming with the expressed intention of visiting me and not Mister Jones, as she usually did. Mister Jones was surprised, as I was, for she had said nothing to him of the possibility.

Sarah had already shared with Mamma Jones that she wanted to talk with me about writing for her publication, and that she was willing to offer me a position in Boston. She also intimated that she had even further news of importance that I would surely want to hear and eventually be a part of.

Mamma Jones did not want her husband to know about this particular visit, as she was sure that he would try to talk me out of whatever Missus Hale had to propose. In order to keep me from hearing about the proposal, he undoubtedly would have sent me off on some assignment to the state capital or elsewhere, just to get me out of town for a few days.

So it was that, when Missus Hale arrived, we were able to speak freely together on the subject of her visit. After settling into the guest room at the home of the Jones', Mamma Jones, Missus Hale and I sat down to a cup of tea and some fresh cakes that Marilla, the Jones' housekeeper and cook, had made.

Missus Jones had us sit in the library where a warm fire was blazing and Mister Jones had his most comfortable, overstuffed leather chairs for us to enjoy. Typically we would have gone to the parlor, but this room afforded more privacy, and was, on this frosty November day, more warmly heated than any other part of the house.

"Elizabeth, it is always so good to see you. I have been following your career with great delight, as you already know from our correspondence. What you don't know, as of yet, is that I wrote to Prudence, and asked for a meeting with you and her, to talk about your future."

My future? That sounded so far away and why would she want to discuss it with me? Did I not have my own thoughts about where I wanted to go, what I wanted to do, how I wanted to write? And why was she involving Mamma Jones? Were they going to conspire against me? And what about Mister Jones? Did I not work for him, as well?

"I can see that your head is already beginning to swirl with questions, Elizabeth. That is one of the things I love about you. But before we go too far and your head explodes, let me explain why I am here on this occasion. The first thing I ask, though, is that before you make any decisions, ask any questions, come to any conclusions, you will hear me out."

Hear her out! Don't I always listen and hear people out before jumping to conclusions? Well, almost always, except when someone is about to tell me what I will or will not do, or how I should or should not act. Then my independent, rebellious spirit begins to show itself, and I usually just speak my mind and walk away.

"All right, Jo, I promise to hear you and Mamma Jones out before I jump to any conclusions about this visit. But I will confess, I am always excited when you come for a visit or when your letters arrive. I love to hear of your adventures and successes. All I ask is that you don't try to box me in or steal away my dreams."

At that we all laughed and breathed a sigh of relief, for we knew that we could talk as friends and not expect more than a wonderful exchange of ideas. If something beyond that emerged, then so be it, but for now, we would talk.

CHAPTER FIVE

Sarah Hale shared her news with Mamma Jones and me. It was indeed exciting, as she told how she had met Mister Louis A. Godey of Philadelphia, and how he had made her and Reverend Blake a sizable offer to purchase their Ladies Magazine, providing, of course, that the required funding could be secured.

Reverend Blake was still somewhat hesitant about the offer, but Sarah saw it as a wonderful opportunity to make a significant profit, in addition to expanding the publication. The agreement was contingent upon four issues.

The first issue was raising the necessary funds to complete the transaction. Mister Godey had stated that most of the funds had already been acquired, but that the final piece still needed to be arranged. He was certain that the financial matters would be easily resolved within the next few months.

The second issue was that the name of the publication would be changed from the *American Ladies Magazine and Literary Gazette* to *Godey's Lady's Book*. At first Sarah had felt as if her child were being taken away by a stranger and given a new name, but, as Mister Godey explained, the name, being somewhat shortened, made it easier to remember. Additionally, in consideration for the change of name, location and ownership, she was being offered a sizable sum of money, which would put both her and Reverend Blake in a comfortable position for the remainder of their lives. Sarah also saw this as an opportunity to pursue other interests at a later time, if she was so inclined.

The third was that Sarah Hale would eventually relocate to Philadelphia and remain with the publication as its Literary Editor. Mister Godey would assume all matters of managing the publication, but would allow Sarah to maintain a fair amount of influence over the material content.

When Sarah inquired as to how long she would need to continue at Godey's, and what would be the compensation for her services, Mister Godey replied that he would ask for her continued service for one year. Anything beyond this period could be negotiated on an annual basis. As for compensation, Missus Hale would be offered a sizable salary, as well as a percentage of the magazine's profits.

Her only other concern was the issue of relocating her family and finding adequate accommodations, as well as fine schools for the children to attend. Mister Godey assured her that all of this would be cared for, and that she would find Philadelphia to be a marvelous city, with wonderful opportunities for both her and the children.

The last issue was that Reverend Blake would surrender his influence and ownership of the publication, and would no longer be involved. This was not a major obstacle, in that Reverend Blake was still active in his pastoral duties at the First Christian Church of Boston and had no desire to leave his post. The major objection, however, which remained largely unspoken, were the feelings that Reverend Blake had for Sarah.

Unlike Missus Hale, who was a widow, Reverend Blake had never married, instead devoting himself entirely to his work for the Church. Over the past few years, he had begun to question his decision, and now found that he loved Sarah quite completely and desired to make her his wife and, with her five children, make a home for them all. Reverend Blake was, however, a shy man when it came to matters of romance, and had never had the courage to openly share his feelings with Sarah, until now.

He had always been fond of her, but this fondness had grown to an immense love that for the most part had gone unrewarded, if not completely unrecognized, by Missus Hale. Reverend Blake finally was able to admit to Sarah over dinner one evening in Boston, shortly after Mister Godey had made his offer, exactly how he felt toward her and inquired if she had the same or similar feelings.

Sarah shared with us how she was at first stunned, then flattered, and finally somewhat amused at Reverend Blake's expressions of romantic sentiment. Sarah never saw his interest in her work or his devotion to her projects as any more than a business adventure on the part of the good Reverend. And here he was now, proposing a romantic interest, with the possibility of marriage.

Sarah admitted that, at first, she gave some thought to the matter, but then quickly recognized that she had no romantic interest in the good man. She told him so, and he gracefully resigned himself to his ministerial work, agreeing to the settlement terms for the sale of the magazine. In the future, Sarah would make certain that her mourning for her late husband would be evident as long as she lived and that she would, forevermore, wear only black.

"This is all so exciting, Jo" I exclaimed, with almost the giddiness of a school girl.

I could no longer hold my excitement or joy at her good fortune.

"So when will all of this take place, and how soon do you have to move to Philadelphia? And what will ever happen to poor Reverend Blake?" I inquired.

Sarah continued, "Well, this is the good part. The sale should be finalized within the next few months, providing Mister Godey is able to secure the funding, and the *Godey's Lady's Book* will begin its monthly publication sometime this coming year. Mister Godey hopes to have his first edition out by June. In the meantime, we will continue to publish the current magazine, until we are ready with the new publication."

"But Jo", I interrupted. "When will you move? Where will you live? What about the children?

"Slow down, Elizabeth, and be patient. Let Missus Hale tell the story."

Mamma Jones often felt it her responsibility to remind me to allow others to speak in their own time and at their own pace, and to not hurry them in their tales. She often said that if I would be more patient in this endeavor, I would find out more than I probably would care to know.

"Yes, Mamma Jones. You are right, as usual. Please, Jo, tell us more. Tell us all about everything. I shall be more patient."

Sarah went on to explain that she would stay in Boston for at least another year, to finish the work of the current magazine and to allow time to transition to the Godey's Book. She also said that Mister Godey agreed that she could edit the new publication from her home in Boston for the first year, until they decided if she were to stay with "Godey's Lady's Book" beyond that.

"And now, Elizabeth, I want to share with you part of the reason for my visit that only Missus Jones knows about. I would like you to come to work for me at the new publication."

I was beyond myself in excitement, as she spoke of this possibility. I had for some time thought how wonderful it would be to work with Jo and to learn from her. I loved what I did at the paper with Mister Jones, but I wanted to be able to report on bigger stories, especially those that had a national interest, rather than just the local happenings of Franklin County, Pennsylvania, and Chambersburg.

"I realize", Sarah continued, "that the writing we will engage in at Godey's is not the same journalistic endeavor you are accustomed to, but this will give you a chance to meet others who are engaged in the literary field, and to meet writers from many walks of life."

Jo tried to help me see how all of this could advance my career. She said that with my abilities to see the human side of a story, and then communicate the heart and soul of the matter to the reader, that expanding into the realm of story telling for women would be a logical next step for me. She also believed that I could write articles that would encourage the work of women in the home and further establish the necessity of the female presence in maintaining the good order of family life.

"But, Jo, do you not see what you are asking of me? I agree that to work for you has been a dream of mine for some time. I appreciate much of what you have already accomplished in your life and what you have done for me in promoting my work."

Sarah Hale had been instrumental in introducing me to many fine reporters and editors throughout the region over the past couple of years. She had encouraged me in my writing and reporting. For all she had done and given me, especially her friendship, I would evermore be grateful.

"But please understand that I can not go to work for you or Mister Godey. It is not that I would be able to write and learn even more than I have. It is a wonderful opportunity for any writer. The problem is that I am NOT a writer. I am a reporter who then writes the stories of my reports.

"It is the investigation, discovering the truth, and communicating that truth to the public in a way they can see and understand that is important to me. I want to know the what, when, where, why, how of the story and convey it to the public. I want people to feel the story, as much as read it, and enter into the conflicts, victories, sorrows and joys of my subjects."

I went on, "It is not just story writing, or promoting a particular position or policy that excites me. It is the hunt. It is the ability to dig into the lives of people and find the truth and then report that truth. That is what matters to me."

"Yes, but what about your future?" Mamma Jones interrupted

"What about my future? Am I not a good reporter here? Have we not seen good results from my work at the paper? Have you not told me that I am the best at what I do here? When the time is right, have you not told me that other doors will open for me to advance my career?

"This is such a door, my dear." Mamma Jones spoke with a hint of a tear.

I knew she wanted the best for me and saw this as an opportunity to advance my career, while at the same time keeping me safe. She had hoped for awhile that I would find a romantic interest, especially in the young Seminarian, Isaac Stoltzfus, marry, have a family of my own, and engage in a writing career much as Jo had done.

Such was not to be for me. I was too fiercely independent to be tied to a husband and a home, as Jo and Mamma had already come to understand.

We talked more as the evening wore on, and Jo understood my desires and dreams. She admitted that she, too, had dreams and that it would come to no good if I, or anyone, should attempt to settle for anything less. Finally, Jo admitted that I, of all people, was probably least qualified to tell women how to run a home, since I had never learned how myself, leaving that task to others.

With that, we enjoyed a good laugh and retired for the evening.

CHAPTER SIX

By May of 1832, I had completed nearly seven years at the Chambersburg Democratic Tribune, along with my schooling at Wilsons School for Women. These had been exciting years, as I had begun to learn the newspaper and reporting business under the wonderful and watchful eye of Oliver Jones, editor, publisher and owner of the Tribune, and his wife, Prudence.

Isaac Stoltzfus and I had also become good friends, as he completed his seminary work in Gettysburg. With Mister and Missus Jones, I went to see Isaac as he graduated from the Seminary in Gettysburg that spring, and was present for his ordination.

How exciting it was to watch the Bishop lay hands on the head of Isaac and ordain him a minister of the Gospel of Jesus Christ. Isaac was so proud, and often stated how he wished his parents and sister had been alive to witness this occasion in his life. He knew, however, in his heart that they were indeed present in spirit and watching the proceedings of his life from their heavenly home.

Isaac's older sister, Mary, had died, along with her first child, during the birthing process two years ago. Both his parents had died of fever early in 1832, just a few months before he was to finish his seminary work.

Isaac still had his younger brother, James, who was also at Gettysburg in his first year at the Seminary. James, like his older brother, felt called to the work of the ministry, and was just as adventuresome.

The three of us, Isaac, James and I, were good friends and came together as much as time and distance would allow. Isaac's earlier infatuation had given way to sincere affection and friendship, as he recognized that my independent spirit could never be tethered by the bonds of matrimony.

Isaac and James would often travel together to Chambersburg and the Jones' home on special occasions and holidays. Mamma Jones had adopted them, much the same as she had adopted me, and made them a regular part of the family traditions.

Isaac and James had also traveled to their home in Lancaster, Pennsylvania, for summer breaks and at Christmas time, to assist their father and mother with the work of their small family farm. Isaac often shared how he enjoyed the warm days in the fields growing up, and how it was that in the fall of his fifteenth year, while harvesting the wheat, he heard the voice of God calling him to the work of the ministry. Now that he and James were the only surviving members of the family, Isaac decided to sell the farm and use the proceeds to assist James in his studies and future ministry.

Isaac said that he hated the thought of selling, but he was called to the work of God and could not care for the farm alone. James had never enjoyed the farm, and was only too anxious to leave and move to the city. James dreamed of one day becoming a minister at a large church in New York City, or even possibly Washington City, and becoming the pastor to the President of the United States.

Following Isaac's graduation and ordination, he accepted a position as the second assistant pastor at the prestigious Saint Mark's Lutheran Church in Hagerstown, Maryland. We were all excited for him, as Hagerstown was still close enough to Chambersburg to be able to make the journey in a day. Also, he would be at one of the largest and most influential Lutheran Churches in the east.

Isaac was always interested in helping the less fortunate, and had grown increasingly more supportive of the Abolitionist movement over the past few years. His new appointment would give him opportunity to become even more involved with the work of freeing the slaves and ending slavery in this country.

Isaac had been in correspondence with Lord Harry MacBride of the British Parliament, and was excited to hear that Great Britain was in the process of abolishing the practice of slavery throughout their empire. Lord MacBride had shared in a letter with Isaac that this would most likely go into law in 1833 or 1834 at the latest. Isaac had hoped that the same would occur in the United States as well, once Great Britain had acted on the matter.

Shortly after Isaac assumed his post in Hagerstown, he wrote:

18 August, 1832
My Dearest Elizabeth,

I write to you with so much joy and excitement that I can hardly contain it all. We have been such good friends over the past few years, and you know how fondly I think of you. The adventures we have already shared in together go beyond description. Remember our first, when we turned the tables on old Mister Smith when he tried to falsely accuse Mister Mason of horse theft in an attempt to gain his property? We have been quite a good team on these escapades of yours, haven't we?

And now I write to you, my dearest Elizabeth, in the desire for you to visit with me and explore the work I am doing, endeavoring toward the freedom of the slaves. I have met a wonderful group of people, Quakers, who are most involved. I want you to hear their stories and, if possible, to share them with your readers.

Please say yes, and that you will come at the first opportunity. I have made arrangements for you to stay with one of the Quaker families upon your arrival. I can assure you that you will be most comfortable and safe in their care, modest though it may be.

I will look for your reply with great anticipation.

Most fondly, your friend,

Isaac

I spoke with Oliver and Prudence Jones upon receiving Isaac's letter about his request. Mamma Jones thought it would it be safe for me to travel and stay with the Quakers. She knew some Quakers and found them to be simple and honest folk who loved life, the land, their faith, and others. She said that I could expect my accommodations to be fairly simple and sparse to say the least, nothing at all like the comforts I had come to enjoy at the Jones' home.

Mister Jones was more hesitant. He was not sure he wanted me to travel so far on my own, without a proper male escort.

"Now, Papa", as Missus Jones sometimes called her husband, "There is no need to be concerned about Elizabeth. You know she is quite capable of taking care of herself, as she has already proven, and is very resourceful when the situation demands, to get out of a tight scrap."

"Yes, my dear, I agree. But this is different. She will be traveling to a large city, and you know I can not spare one of my workers at this time to accompany her on her travels, as I have always done in the past."

Oliver Jones had been protective of me when I went on an assignment, and always sent one of his workmen to accompany me for my protection. Often I would have to plot my escape from the workman, so that I could gain the information I needed for the story.

This was usually not difficult, as I would offer to let them wait for me at a local pub, and then give the workman a few dollars to spend on his libations. This worked well for me and kept the men out of my way, as I went about the work of investigating and reporting.

"Perhaps, Elizabeth," Mister Jones was saying, "You could wait until later in the fall for this adventure. Then I should be able to send someone with you. Besides, I am not at all sure we want to take on this assignment and become involved in this particular battle."

Mamma Jones at once picked up on that last statement and immediately launched into one of her speeches on the role of the paper to not only report the news, but to also make social commentary when appropriate.

"And" she said, "is it not appropriate to make commentary on the plight of suffering Negroes who are held against their will in the bondage of others?"

Mister Jones at once saw his mistake and relented in his objections. He agreed that I could go to Hagerstown on this assignment, if Mamma Jones would accompany me on the journey. He also expected me not only to write a story on my findings, but also to begin to write an occasional editorial for the paper. He insisted that this would be a good place to start, upon my return.

Mamma Jones and I were excited at all of the possibilities Mister Jones had just offered. To be able to write my own editorials was beyond something I could have imagined. It was, after all, only the editors who wrote these pieces, and now I was being given the chance to do so. And Mamma Jones would be traveling with me for the first time. Mister Jones had never before allowed that, even when we had asked him nicely.

I went off immediately to write Isaac of the news:

26 August, 1832

My Dearest and Most Trusted Friend,

I was so excited to receive your letter and to hear of the possibility of coming so soon to Hagerstown to meet your new friends, and to hear their story. I at once went to Mister Jones to discuss the possibility. You can well imagine the discussion that occurred in this matter, with Mamma Jones always at my side and in defense of any cause I should endeavor to engage.

After much discussion, Mister Jones finally agreed to allow me this opportunity, and that, in addition to writing a story, I should also write an editorial to be published in the Tribune for all our readers to ponder, regarding the state of the Negros held in slavery.

There is one condition, my dear friend, to my coming. Missus Jones must accompany me on the journey. Do you think it possible to find accommodations for both of us at the same home? Mamma Jones and I have agreed that we will travel to you as soon as you are able to make arrangements for our accommodations.

Until then, I remain your trusted friend,
Elizabeth

Early in October, Mamma Jones and I boarded the coach for Hagerstown, leaving Mister Jones to care for himself and the paper. Mamma had instructed her husband to treat with kindness their servant, Marilla, who now was increasing in her years as much as the Jones' were. As of late, Marilla had grown a bit more fragile and weary, along with a tendency to be forgetful, especially about those issues she no longer wished to care for.

Marilla had been acquired by Mister Jones several years ago, in the settlement of a debt owed to him by one of his advertisers. Shortly after he had taken ownership of Marilla, Mamma Jones made certain that Oliver had executed her freedom and made it a matter of public record.

The former slave had stayed on with the Jones', and was provided adequate quarters and a fair wage for her services. Both parties agreed that this was a good solution at the time, and Marilla was now as much family as she was servant.

Mister Jones agreed to look out for Marilla in the absence of his wife and promised not to take advantage of her excellent care and service, but would, instead, take his meals nightly at the local pub during the absence of Prudence.

The ride to Hagerstown would take about ten hours by coach, with a short stop in Greencastle, Pennsylvania, to rest and change the horses. This was a good time of year to travel, as the temperatures were once again fairly moderate and the weather usually was sunny and bright, with little rain. Such was the case for our travels. The roads were dusty but smooth, not having been washed out lately by the rains of the late summer storms.

The Inn Keeper at Greencastle, Silas Hollinger, and his wife, Flora, were ready for our arrival, along with the other four passengers who were to be our traveling companions this day. Missus Hollinger invited us into the Inn and seated us at a long table, already laid with plates and silver, and heaping bowls of deliciously made breads, hot steaming vegetables and the most wonderful fried chicken anyone could have imagined. She had also prepared a large serving of freshly made mashed potatoes and gravy to top off the fare.

We at once settled into the routine of indulging ourselves upon her hospitality, overeating to the point of exploding our waistlines beyond any hope of future recovery. To top off the extravagance of the meal, she rewarded our hearty appetites with a large, freshly made peach pie from the year's harvest. Mamma Jones and I quite agreed that, if we were to go no further in our travels, the trip would have been worth just this meal.

Before long, the coachman was calling for us to once again board and continue our trip. It was now well past noon, as we began the second leg of our journey. I was growing more excited as we pulled from the Inn, waving goodbye to Mister and Missus Hollinger and shouting over the rumble of the coach our thanks and goodbyes. We would be in Hagerstown by nightfall, if all went as planned, and, before evening came, would be comfortably settled with my dear friend, Isaac Stoltzfus.

Isaac had made, so I had been told, arrangements for us to stay with a Quaker family in the area and to hear their stories of the Abolitionist movement in Maryland. I was excited for the opportunity to hear first hand accounts of the cruelty and suffering of those slaves who managed to make their way north in search of freedom and a better life.

I drifted off, as we continued our travels, rocked to sleep by the swaying movement of the coach and the ever pounding hoofs of the horses as they pulled and strained under the weight laid upon their backs. My dreams became ever more fitful as we traveled on, dreaming as it were of the burdens which the Negros must suffer.

The horses in my dreams were now black men, stripped naked with their bare skin glistening in the sunlight. The whip of the coachman ever so cruelly lashed at their strained muscles, buried under the tremendous loads they were required to bear in servitude and slavery.

I awoke from my restless slumber, to find that we were nearly at our destination. Missus Jones had been knitting a new scarf for Isaac as we traveled, and had been observing me quietly as I slept.

"My dear, you fell deeply asleep some time ago. I trust you are well enough rested."

Mamma did not speak what she really was wondering. She had observed my restlessness, but did not know what was at its source.

35

"Yes, thank you. I am afraid I am not a very good traveling companion, Mamma Jones. I seem to always fall asleep on these types of journeys."

We arrived at the station just before six o'clock in the evening, and Isaac was waiting for us on the platform. He assisted the coachman as he unloaded our belongings, and immediately escorted us to his waiting carriage.

"My dear Elizabeth and Missus Jones, how wonderful it is that you are finally here", Isaac stated. "I am so excited you have been able to make this journey and I have so much to tell, and show you. But first, we must get you settled, and then some dinner."

We boarded the waiting carriage, and Isaac began to drive us to our quarters.

"I have made arrangements", Isaac began, almost at once, "for you to stay at the home of Reverend and Missus Christopher McKenna, a prominent Presbyterian minister in town."

"But Isaac, I thought we were to stay with a Quaker family, and to hear their stories?"

I was at first very disappointed at this sudden change. I wanted to hear first hand of the struggles of the abolitionists and their charges. I had come all this way for the story; I did not want to be denied.

"Yes, dear Elizabeth", Isaac continued. "You will most definitely meet many of the Quakers, and others, who are working for the end of slavery, I promise. But for now, lodging has been arranged with the McKenna family. After you meet them, you will understand better why I have made this arrangement for you both."

Mamma Jones was always easy to please on these matters, and assured me that all would work together as it should, and to just be patient. It seemed as if she were always telling me to be patient.

The carriage suddenly came to a stop in front of the most beautiful and stately home I had ever seen. Isaac announced that we had arrived and immediately escorted the two of us from the carriage to the front door of the house, where, with great pride and fanfare, he announced our presence to the occupants.

CHAPTER EIGHT

Reverend and Missus McKenna immediately welcomed us into their home, and invited us to sit comfortably in the drawing room.

"Robert, please attend to the ladies' luggage, and take their belongings immediately to their rooms."

Robert was the chief servant of the McKenna household, and had been retained by Reverend McKenna when he assumed the post as the senior pastor two years earlier. Robert had been purchased by a former minister of the parish some years earlier, but had been granted his freedom shortly after the McKennas arrived. Both Reverend and Missus McKenna were Abolitionists and found the situation of having a slave at the church appalling.

At first, Reverend McKenna had some difficulty with the Presbyters of the Church over his actions, but soon, those who still held to the belief that slavery was God's ordained institution had left the church and found others of like-mindedness in another faith community. Robert Smith, as he was known, had agreed to stay on for wages and a place to lay his head, for he really knew no other way. Missus McKenna had also taken on the task of teaching Robert to read and write, so that, in the event he desired to move elsewhere, he would have the skills to do so.

"We are so very delighted to have you with us for the next several days, and trust that your visit will be both rewarding and enjoyable. I must say, Isaac, Miss Fitzgerald is every bit as lovely as you have said."

Missus McKenna was a delightful host, and I could tell that this would indeed be a grand visit.

"And now, my dears, let me show you to your rooms, so that you may freshen from your travels. Then we shall dine for the evening and get better acquainted."

Missus McKenna showed us the accommodations that would be our home for the next several days. Our rooms were large and bright, full of life, as I would imagine a church parsonage to be.

In my room, there were bowls of flowers and fresh fruits neatly arranged on a table near the center of the room, and at the far end, the largest four cornered poster bed I had ever imagined.

The mattress was thick with fresh bedding, and a gas fire had been lit to take off the evening chill for our comfort.

Mamma Jones and I retired to our quarters to refresh from the long journey. I was much too excited to take long, so within a short time, I was heading down the stairs to the parlor and the sounds of laughter and conversation. Mamma Jones was still upstairs, caring for her needs, when I arrived at the parlor.

As I entered the room, I immediately saw Isaac standing next to the most beautiful young woman I had ever seen. She was petite and graceful. Her long auburn hair flowed gently across her shoulders and down to her waist. It was neatly tied by blue ribbons that perfectly matched her dress. Her eyes were a rich, velvety green and reflected the fire from the candles lit about the room. Her smile was alive and bright. In every way, she was perfect.

Isaac came to my side and escorted me to the center of the room, where everyone had gathered. Constance McKenna rose to her feet and immediately came to my side and embraced me.

"I am so glad to have you here, and to finally meet you, Elizabeth. I am Constance, and, of course, you have already met my parents."

Her speech was as perfect as she was in form.

"Please forgive me for not having been here upon your arrival. I trust that your journey was pleasant and uneventful."

Isaac suddenly appeared to be somewhat uncomfortable at having both Constance and myself in the same room. I was a little amused at his apparent sense of awkwardness.

"Isaac, you did not write and tell me about Constance or this lovely family. How simply unforgiveable of you."

I was going to enjoy poking at Isaac, if for only a little and, of course, all in fun.

"Constance, I can see by the way you are looking at Isaac, and by his slight blush, that there is more than currently meets the eye. Please, do tell me. Is there good news to be shared?"

Reverend McKenna had been observing with his quiet manner the introductions and apparent embarrassment I had suddenly caused Isaac.

"Yes, my dear", the Reverend began. "We have good news for us, but I am not sure exactly how good you shall find it. Reverend Stoltzfus has asked permission to marry our Constance. Her mother and I have given our consent. Constance, on the other hand, has refused to accept until you have had opportunity to meet her, and us, and to also give your approval. You see, Isaac has told us what good friends you are, and how you are really more family, brother and sister, as it were. So we are glad you have come, and we await your answer."

We all enjoyed a hearty laugh over Isaac's blush and slight embarrassment. Isaac apologized for his failure to tell me about Constance, but justified his behavior by assuring me that he knew that as soon as we had made our acquaintance, I would readily approve and give my blessing. By now, Missus Jones had joined in the party and was rejoicing with the news as I, and all present, were. We retired to the dining room for an evening meal and more lively discussion.

"Isaac, I am delighted for you and Constance. She is absolutely wonderful; and I know you both shall be so happy together. And, Constance, we shall indeed be good friends from this day, until forever. I shall be at the Christening of every one of your children and shall always be known by them as Auntie Liz, the FAVORITE Aunt."

CHAPTER NINE

Early the next morning, Missus Jones and I began our journeys. Missus Jones, along with Missus McKenna, decided that going to the town market for fresh vegetables and fruits, and to check on some of the new fabrics that had recently arrived, would be to their liking. Reverend McKenna was going to be at the Church office most of the day, preparing his sermon for the coming Sunday's service.

Isaac and Constance had decided that they should escort me to the Quaker family that Isaac had written about in his letters, so that I could begin my work and report on the plight of the Negro slave. We arrived shortly before ten that first morning, at the home of Elder Cyrus Van Allen and his wife, Hannah.

The Van Allens were charming and simple people who had an obvious love for God and their fellow man. Isaac introduced me to them, and they readily invited me in to their humble abode. Their home was small and comfortable, lacking any particular adornment. It was in stark contrast to the McKenna home, plain and bare.

"What would thee have us speak to thee, Sister Elizabeth?"

Missus Van Allen had spoken in her simple and quaint Quaker language. Isaac and Constance had both warned me before hand of the manner of speech accustomed by these simple and honest people, assuring me that I would quickly pick up on the language and that they would not be offended if I did not speak as they did.

"I have come, at the request of Reverend Stoltzfus, to meet you and to hear of the plight of the slaves you are assisting in finding their freedom. So what I wish for you to speak of is your adventures in this matter, and how I may be of assistance to you."

Missus Van Allen and her husband spent the better part of the morning and early afternoon sharing how a trail north, as it was called, had been established, as a means of helping the runaway slaves find their way to freedom. They also explained the great difficulties the slaves faced, of their hardships and beatings, their lack of resources in finding freedom, and the cruelty that awaits them back in the south, should they be caught and returned.

Missus Van Allen also told how they could be arrested and jailed in Maryland, if they were caught assisting these run away slaves. I assured her that I would not reveal their identity in anything I wrote, and would do my best to protect them from attack.

Elder Van Allen then escorted me to his barn and, after moving some hay from the floor, revealed a trap door that led to a dug out cellar beneath the barn floor.

"Here, this is where we protect our fellow souls as they journey toward the promised land of thy fathers and thy freedom."

The place was nothing more than a dirt hole in the ground, not more than a few feet wide in any direction, with a wooden door over the opening to the ground level of the barn floor. "How many do you sometimes have here?" I inquired.

"As many as God will send us, dear Sister. I fear too many at times. Last month we had four men, three women and seven children in all." Elder Van Allen spoke with such tenderness and compassion, and I could see that he was filled with great sorrow that the accommodations had to be so meager for his charges.

"It is not that we wish to do so little and no more. It is that we must not risk discovery, lest we be put to the gallows for assisting in this endeavor. I am not afraid to die, but what will happen to these poor black children of God, if we should all perish in this struggle before freedom has been attained for all?"

Yes, what should happen indeed? Am I not my brother's keeper? And who is my brother?

I could not, must not, become emotionally tied to this struggle, if I was to report the efforts and the situation in a proper way. But how could I not become involved after hearing of the stories of the suffering?

Over the next few days, the Van Allens shared several more stories of the sufferings of men, women, and children, ripped from their homes in the night, beaten by an angry master, separated from families and sold, made to mate with who ever the master determined, and on and on, until I thought I could stand no more.

Late the following Saturday evening, as I was drifting off to sleep in the comfort of the McKenna home, Constance came for me. She was dressed in men's clothing and told me to put on some of the same things she had brought with her. She commanded me to not make a sound, but to dress quickly, hiding my hair in the hat and pulling on the boots she had provided.

We quietly stole away into the night air, not saying a word until we were safely away from the house.

"What is going on, and what are we doing?" I demanded to know as soon as I felt it safe to ask.

"Father must not know that I am on my way to assist a family in need this very night. Isaac and I have agreed that, if I should assist any family in need, that neither he, nor my father must know, should they be questioned. That will protect all of us much better, should anything go wrong."

"But I don't understand. Who are you assisting this night? And why the secrecy?"

"Just come with me, Elizabeth, and be as quiet as a mouse, and you will see more than enough to write your story, and a good editorial, I pray."

We arrived in a small meadow just south of town and there, in the shadows, were a group of six people huddled together, as if they were afraid a ferocious animal might be lurking nearby, ready for an attack. As we drew near, I could see that these were, indeed, some of the contraband, as they were known, who had made their way to this small island of perceived safety.

Constance spoke to the small band of runaways, and instructed them to follow her. As they went cautiously with the woman dressed in men's clothing, I could make out now that there were three men, two women, and one child about five years old. They were barely dressed, having only the remains of thread bare clothing attached to their backs.

Within the hour, Constance had taken them to the home of another Quaker family, the Van Wyck family, to be cared for and prepared for the next part of the journey north. Missus Van Wyck and her husband took the visitors into their home and immediately set about tending to the needs of these frightened refugees.

One of the men, a large black man of about forty years of age, was in serious need of medical attention. His back had been beaten severely just before his escape, and now showed signs of infection. He was weak, fevered, and somewhat disoriented. The others appeared to be in relatively good shape, given the condition of their flight from hardship and slavery.

I watched as Missus Van Wyck carefully cleaned the wounds of the poor soul, and then applied a salve made of various herbs and spices. Missus Van Wyck said that the ointment she applied was a biblical remedy that she had learned as a child, and that it indeed would draw the infection out in a few days.

No sooner had Missus Van Wyck finished the dressing of the wounds that her husband announced that the sounds of barking dogs were growing near. Immediately, the runaways were moved to the "safe" room, as they called it, in the attic of the home, with instructions that they should remain there until they were retrieved by one of the family. They were also instructed not to make a noise, until they were told that it was safe.

Missus Van Wyck also gave Constance and me plain dresses to put over our clothing. Then we were instructed to gather around the table for prayer and Bible reading.

CHAPTER TEN

It was nearly four o'clock in the morning when the local sheriff arrived, with a group of men and their dogs. There was a sharp knock at the door, and the voice of the sheriff demanded that we open the door and let him in. Mister Van Wyck went to the door and opened it, inviting the sheriff and his men inside.

"Good morning, Sheriff. On what business does God have thee to attend to this day?"

Mister Van Wyck spoke in his gentle way, with the simple speech of his religion and piety.

"Don't 'good morning me', you pig farmer."

The sheriff was in no mood to be deceived, and I soon found myself afraid, as I had never been afraid before. There had been many times, while going after a story, that I had been trapped, confronted, attacked, and even beaten once, but never had I been afraid as I was now. And what was even more troubling for me, is that I did not know why.

"We know that you help those run away niggers whenever they come by, so don't lie to me now. Where are they? We know you have 'em here."

The four men with Sheriff Adams were slave catchers from the south, and they had every right to search the property without cause, if they felt it would aid in the capture of the runaways.

"The dogs led us right here, Van Wyck, now, fess up, where'd ya hide 'em? Come on, now, we don't mean you no harm, we jest want our bounty money from them niggers, that's all."

The little, fat, greasy man who was holding the dogs had now spoken. He carried a large whip with him, as if he intended to use it on anyone who stood in his way.

Mister Van Wyck was obviously becoming somewhat annoyed at the intrusion and language of his guest, but continued to keep his mild ways.

"We have no one here but our own brethren, as we prepare for the labors of the day. Search the grounds if you care to, or join us in scripture and prayer if you wish. Our home is available to all God's children, even if they are instruments of hatred and suffering."

One of the men standing off to the side of the door and holding chains and shackles suddenly sprang forward and struck Mister Van Wyck to the floor, while at the same time spewing such vehement filth from his mouth that I am not able to repeat the language.

"Now, Horatio, we'll have none of that. These people are not violent in nature, just a bit uppity with their religion, that's all."

The fat man spoke to the other as he laid his whip gently across the face of Mister Van Wyck.

"I trust you ain't hiding any niggers here, but if we do find out that you are, we will burn the place, and hang you for the fun of it, preacher man."

With that, the five men left the house and went out into the dawning light of the early morning sun. Missus Van Wyck quickly went to the door to bolt it shut, while Constance and I assisted her husband.

"Now don't worry, dear ladies. Our God is on our side and He shall guide us in all these matters. Now let us attend to the scriptures and prayer, and then we will care for our guests as soon as I believe it safe to do so."

And with that, Mister Van Wyck shared a scripture reading from Romans 8.

"What shall we then say to these things? If God be for us, who can be against us? He that spared not His own Son, but delivered him up for us all, how shall He not with Him also freely give us all things?"

And then, "For I am persuaded that neither death, nor life, nor angels, nor principalities, nor powers, nor things present, nor things to come, nor height, nor depth, nor any other creature, shall be able to separate us from the love of God, which is in Christ Jesus our Lord."

Mister Van Wyck added, "Let us now, my beloved wife and my dear sisters in Christ, attend ourselves to His most divine inner light for guidance in all of these matters."

CHAPTER ELEVEN

As the dawn broke into morning, Constance and I assisted the Van Wycks with their morning tasks of feeding the animals, preparing food for the day's gathering of worshipers for Sunday Meeting, as it was called, and the eventual preparation of preparing the contraband for the next part of their journey. Mister Van Wyck had insisted that both Constance and I should stay and continue to work and worship with them until he was sure no one was watching the house. He felt that, should we leave too soon, suspicion would be raised and we, along with the entire community as well as his charges, would be at great risk. Constance quite readily agreed to this, and so arrangements were made for our continued visit.

"Constance, I am, however, concerned that your family should miss us and worry", I finally shared with my escort.

"Please, my dear Elizabeth. I have been through this before, and Father knows not to worry, unless the sheriff should arrive at his door-step and announce that I have either been detained or kidnapped."

Constance spoke with an air of abandonment that I was sure only I had acquired by reputation at the paper.

"Now, let us set about as farm hands, to continue our disguise, and then we shall enjoy the meeting of the Quakers. Have you ever been to a Quaker Meeting? If not, then you are certainly in for a truly different experience. Elder Van Allen and his wife, Hannah, you remember them, of course, will be there to lead the services as they do each Sabbath."

Constance so enjoyed these adventures. Her spirit was as free as any I'd known. As I watched her working along side Missus Van Wyck, I began to imagine what kind of wife she would make for Isaac, and the life they would enjoy together. Isaac had been correct in one of our recent conversations, that Constance and I would surely become the best of friends over time.

He went on to say that he was sure we would have him in trouble more times than not over the coming years. He pondered whether he would turn prematurely gray because of the two of us.

As the morning wore on, Missus Van Wyck continued to worry about her guests hidden away in the attic room. She was most concerned for the older gentleman with his wounds, infections and fever. She was hoping that the salve she had applied earlier was working and felt it necessary that she should repeat the application every few hours, for it to be effective. Her husband had refused her permission to go to the attic, for fear that they would still be discovered.

Mister Van Wyck knew that these slave runners often would remain for some time near a property they suspected, just out of sight, waiting for the family to make a mistake. This had happened too often in the past, but now the Abolitionists were becoming more cautious and aware of the dangers they faced in their work. It would not be until after the Meeting that Missus Van Wyck would be able to attend to her guests.

We arrived at the Quaker Meeting shortly before nine that Sunday morning. As we gathered around the tiny room set aside for the Meetings, I noticed how simple and plain everything was. The men sat on one side of the hall, while the women sat together on the opposite side.

Elder Van Allen began, "Let us now, my brethren, attend to thy inner light and seek the most holy and divine presence for guidance in all matters."

At that, the members of the Meeting sat quietly, with their heads bowed in contemplative prayer. I was so exhausted from the night's work and lack of sleep that I fell fast asleep.

It seemed as if I had just drifted off when Constance was shaking me and commanding that I "wake up, you silly goose", as she had begun to call me.

"The Meeting is over and, we are to return to the Van Wyck farm. Come, we must be on our way, or we shall have to walk all the way home."

Somehow I had managed to sleep through the entire service, while the others worshipped. I felt so embarrassed, and immediately began to apologize to everyone in attendance, but especially to Elder Van Allen and his wife and, of course, to the Van Wycks.

Elder Van Allen was most gracious and simply said that if rest was what I needed, then it was God who had provided it, so they should not be offended or concerned. Missus Van Wyck had assured me that I was not the first who had fallen quickly to sleep at Meeting, nor would I be the last.

We arrived at the Van Wyck home shortly before three in the afternoon, and immediately set about with some chores and tending to the farm animals. Mister Van Wyck still was not certain that we were free of last night's invaders and continued to be watchful. I asked about feeding the poor souls in the attic and Missus Van Wyck assured me that there had been more than sufficient stores of food and water placed in the attic before hand. She stated that they could easily remain there for several days before being attended to, if needed.

As nightfall came, Mister Van Wyck felt it was now safe for his wife to venture to the attic to check on her charges. He also said that he would go outside to the barn and watch there for any movement from intruders. If he should spot any, he would ring the dinner bell that hung at the door of the barn, to sound the alarm.

Missus Van Wyck had me accompany her to the safe room, to assist in the care of the poor souls, and put Constance to work boiling water and preparing more salve for the older black man. As we went into the attic, I could see the fear-filled eyes of the six slaves hidden away in the tiny space above the kitchen. They all seemed to move as far away from the opening as possible, the men shielding the women and child in their midst, ready to defend to the death if necessary from attack. Missus Van Wyck spoke gently to them, announcing that it was she and I who had come to care for them.

As we entered the tiny space, I could smell for the first time the decay and infection that was attacking the older man's body from his wounds. I felt for a moment that I would vomit, and wanted to turn and run away from that place.

Missus Van Wyck must have sensed my desire, for almost as soon as we entered the room, she took me tightly by the hand, as a mother would to prevent her child from running into danger.

"My dear Elizabeth, this is why I brought you here with me. You MUST see this and write about it. But now I need your help in tending to these poor souls."

We set to work offering fresh linens and bandages, assisting with removal of the human waste and helping the women and child dress in better clothing for the next part of their journey. Missus Van Wyck explained that they would have to stay in this place for a few more days, until they were sure it was safe to move them on up the trail to the next stop. She also explained that a "guide" had already made contact with them and would give them the final details within the week.

As Missus Van Wyke was finishing replacing the bandages on the slave's back, one of the women spoke for the first time.

"Missus", she said to Missus Van Wyck, "My name be Nettie, and that my man you be caring for. His name be Jonah. This 'un be our boy Jesse. My man, he gonna live?"

I saw Missus Van Wyck look up from her work with tears in her eyes. Run away slaves rarely spoke, and even more rarely told their names to anyone, lest they be discovered and returned to their owners.

"Yes, my dear, dear Nettie. I believe he will live. But we must keep these bandages in place and change them several times a day. If I give you some of the ointment, do you think you could change them for me, in case I can not get here in time?"

"Yes 'em, I knows how. I done it before at Master's house, only we got no bandages, jest rags and salve we make from the marshes. Master said he don't need waste no money on nigger medicine. He can get one good buck for what medicine cost, so we jest make do wit our own medicine."

"Well, Nettie, we are going to get you to a place where you can have good medicine in the future, and no master will tell you what your life is worth. We are going to get you to your freedom. I promise."

After Missus Van Wyck was certain that her charges were cared for, and that there was adequate food and water for them, as well as more ointment and bandages for Jonah, we retired back to the bottom of the ladder, and the door was closed to the attic home of the refugees.

It was well after dark when Mister Van Wyck came into the house. He shared that he had walked around the perimeter of the farm that could be seen from the house and found no signs of the previous night's intruders. He suggested that we stay another day or so before venturing home, but Constance felt that it would now be safe for us to return to her parents, well after the night had set in.

It was shortly after midnight when we said our farewells to the Van Wycks. We were once again dressed in our men's clothing, for as Constance reminded me, it was easier to travel on foot in pants, shirts, and boots than in a dress with layers of starched petticoats.

Also, as she was happy to say, "We shall be less conspicuous dressed like this, than in womanly attire. After all, my dear Elizabeth, we would not want to be mistaken for ladies of the night, out, unescorted in the night air, would we?"

We spoke barely a word to each other as we traveled home that night, for fear that someone might overhear us. Constance knew the way, and easily maneuvered through the woods toward the city lights. It was nearly dawn when we arrived back at the safety of her home and the warmth of our beds.

I quickly fell asleep, exhausted from our adventure. Constance and the family allowed me to sleep well into the day, before waking me for tea in the late afternoon.

It was several days later that word arrived through Isaac that the runaway slaves at the Van Wyck's home had been transported by the trail north, on to their next stop in Pennsylvania. They were now safely north of the Mason-Dixon Line and would, in all likelihood, be safe on the remainder of their journey, though no one ever knew for certain.

Mamma Jones and I had already been away from home for three weeks, and began to talk about making the return trip. Reverend McKenna assured us that we were more than welcome to stay as long as we wished, and Constance was not at all eager that I should go back north.

"Is there some way you could remain here in Hagerstown with us? We have just begun to get acquainted, and I know we have so many more adventures ahead of us. Isaac and I want you to stay. Please say that you will."

Constance was almost convincing in her arguments that we would make a great team in helping establish the freedom of slaves and establishing the rights of all peoples in the days to come. I had begun recently to feel the need to move to a bigger paper and more responsibilities, but I was not sure this was the time.

Mister and Missus Jones were now well into their fifties, and Mister Jones had of late talked about retiring in the next few years from the newspaper business. They had been so good to me, and Mister Jones had recently offered to allow me to write editorials and hinted at my taking on some editorial responsibilities.

"I would love to stay and be a part of your life here, Constance. But that would not be fair to you and Isaac. No, you must begin your family with him and establish your own home first. Then, perhaps someday, I will be able to live near you. In the meantime, we shall remain the best of friends, and I do promise to be here for you whenever you need. Besides, my responsibilities are still with the Chambersburg Democratic Tribune."

I filed my story of the "The Trail North" with Oliver Jones at the Tribune, leaving out certain specifics, to protect all the parties involved, and reported extensively on the plight of the African slave. I wrote and published an editorial on the advantages of a free society and the atrocities of the slave trade. I even wrote how other civilized nations were already abolishing slavery, and that even Great Britain was about repeal the slavery laws in their entire empire. I dared to suggest that we should do no less. That was in the late fall of 1832.

CHAPTER TWELVE

Isaac and Constance were married in December of 1832. Mister and Missus Oliver Jones and I had attended the affair. The wedding had been a great celebration, and I was sure that Isaac and Constance were going to be very happy together over the coming years.

Isaac's brother, James, had also been present, and had returned with us to Chambersburg to visit over the holidays, before returning to his Seminary studies. Over the course of the next four years, James would often visit us in Chambersburg before venturing further south to Hagerstown for visits with his brother and sister-in-law.

Isaac and Constance were blessed within the first year of their marriage with a son, whom they named Amos. He was growing quickly into the very image of his father, with bright red hair and a strong will.

A little over one year later, their second child was born, and Abraham also began to grow, demonstrating a stronger will than had been known by their first child. Isaac said that this was more in tune with the disposition of the child's mother than his, and from every appearance, he would seem to be more the likeness of her as well. As promised, I had been present at both of the children's christenings.

James graduated from the Gettysburg Lutheran Seminary in the spring of 1836. After his ordination, James was assigned to work in a parish in Baltimore, Maryland, the Church of the Holy Spirit Lutheran Church. He was to be the third assistant pastor, in charge of visitation and compassionate works.

Life seemed to be going well for all of us. I had been taking on more editorial responsibilities at the paper, and that had given me opportunity to meet other editors and publishers. Mister Jones was now into his early sixties, and Mamma Jones had encouraged him to slow down a bit and to permit others to do some of the work. He had agreed, and those additional responsibilities fell to me.

Although I appreciated all that the Jones' had done for me and certainly enjoyed the expanded role I had at the paper, I was still feeling somewhat restless for a new adventure. The war in Texas with Mexico was winding down. Texas had declared its independence from Mexico in March, and then Santa Anna had defeated the Texans at the Alamo.

The defeat served only to solidify the resolve of the Texans, and they went on to finally achieve independence. The Texans approved their constitution on March sixteen and the following day, March seventeen, abolished slavery in the new Republic. Sam Huston had been elected president of the Republic of Texas on September 5 of 1836, and the inauguration was scheduled for October 22nd.

I spoke to Mister Jones about the possibility of traveling to Texas for the event but was told that it would be entirely out of the question. There was the consideration of cost, as well as who would take on my duties during my long absence. Mister Jones reminded me that we were able to pick up stories like this from other services as needed, and we would be content with the news that affected our local community.

It was on October the third that I received word that my father had suffered a major heart attack and was dying. Mamma Jones immediately made arrangements for me to travel home by way of Philadelphia and Trenton, New Jersey, to attend to my father's needs. She announced that she would travel with me and would hear no argument to the contrary.

We left the next day and traveled by train, arriving on the fifth, to find that my father had passed only a short time before our coming. Missus Jones assisted me in making all the arrangements, and we laid my father to rest five days later, next to my mother and baby brother.

Mamma Jones and I stayed on for the next month, to tend to the affairs of my father. I was able to sell his carriage business to one of his employees, as well as the family home.

Missus Jones was not sure I should sell the house, since it was the only property I had and had been my home since my birth. I assured Mamma Jones that it was not the house, but my father, that I adored. Now that he was safely in the arms of God, I could let go of the property and move on to other places. I assured her that home would be wherever my friends were. I also reminded her that she and Mister Jones were as much family to me as anyone had ever been.

After settling the estate and my father's affairs, we returned home to Chambersburg and my duties at the paper. I was alone now, with no other living relatives and little time to grieve.

The customary mourning period would have to be waived. I did wear black for the next year, but refused to go into hiding.

My father's estate had left me with a considerable sum of money. Mister Jones was concerned that some would take advantage of me in this situation, and encouraged me at once to make wise investments. His idea of wise was to place the money in the care of the bank and use only what I needed from time to time, but I had other ideas.

Sarah Hale and I had continued our friendship over the years. Mister Louis Godey had approached her a few years ago about a Lady's Book he wanted to start in Philadelphia. Unfortunately, the funding had not been arranged, and the project did not come to pass.

Sarah and Mister Godey had remained in contact with each other, and the possibility of the publication was once again being discussed and explored. Sarah had written me after my father's death and encouraged me to reconsider coming to Boston and working with her on the "American Ladies Magazine and Literary Gazette". Of course, she reminded me that if the project with Louis Godey ever came to pass, I would be welcome there with her, as well.

I decided that, rather than work for Sarah, I would invest in her magazine. She had already demonstrated that she knew how to attract readers and was making a profit. I spoke with her about this, and she was receptive and assured me she could help my money grow through her publication. Her partner, Reverend Blake, also agreed to allow me to invest with them and to be a partner, with a small share.

I then invested all but a small sum of the money with Sarah, to the disapproval of Mister Jones.

"Elizabeth, my dear child," Oliver began. "I don't want you to be disappointed or to lose your inheritance on some foolish investment. The paper business is not always fair or profitable."

"Yes, Papa Jones, I do understand your concerns. But I am sure that Sarah will be honest in her dealings with me."

"Yes, quite right, Elizabeth. It is not Sarah I fear, but the volatile nature of this nasty business. What if her publication suddenly fails and you lose everything? What then?"

I knew that Mister Jones had only my best interests at heart and try, as I might, I would never be able to ease his thoughts. On many issues he was just as stubborn and strong willed as I, and he was also very tight when it came to money, spending, and investing.

Oliver had made considerable money with the paper and was well off financially. He and Mamma Jones would be comfortable in their aging years. Papa Jones agreed to let me do as I wished in this matter and assured me that, if I needed help, he would be there for me.

CHAPTER THIRTEEN

By early 1841, I had assumed most of the literary editorial responsibilities from Mister Jones at the Tribune. Mamma Jones had insisted that Papa Jones allow me these added duties in order that, if needed, I would be able to assume the complete run of the paper. Oliver Jones was now into his sixties and beginning to show signs of his age, moving a little slower, and complaining a little more about his general aches and pains.

Mamma Jones had been trying to encourage her husband to sell the paper and move into retirement but, as always, he insisted that he would rather die at the helm of his publication than watch someone else destroy his work. And so it was that Mister Oliver Jones stayed on as Manager, Editor, and Owner of the Chambersburg Democratic Tribune.

On January six, 1838, Mister Samuel Morse had introduced his telegraph machine to the country, with the first public demonstration of sending a message over wires with a series of dots and dashes. This invention promised to revolutionize how information was passed from place to place, and would allow the reporters in the field to file more timely reports with their editors.

Since I had assumed the majority of literary editing responsibilities, my ability to escape, as it were, from the office and cover stories in the field had been greatly reduced. I enjoyed the editing responsibilities, but did miss the excitement of getting the story first hand. However, on occasion I was given leave for special events by Oliver Jones. On March first I left for Washington City, to listen to the closing arguments of former President John Quincy Adams before the United States Supreme Court, on behalf of several Negro slaves.

The story had evolved over the illegal slave trade of Spain at the time, and several reports that Negroes had been taken from West Africa in mid 1839 to Cuba. The Cubans had detained the Africans, and later sold them as Cuban slaves.

These slaves, some fifty men and four children, were then boarded on a ship, La Amistad, to be sent to other parts of the island. Shortly after setting sail, the Africans took over the ship and killed its Captain. The men then ordered their captors to sail for Africa. The ship was seized off the coast of Connecticut and salvaged.

The Africans were tried and convicted of murder. However, they had won an appeal through the United States Supreme Court, and John Quincy Adams was to be their representative before the court.

I was most excited at the prospect of this adventure, for I had been closely following the efforts of the Abolitionists and knew that this would be a historic decision. Should it go well for the Africans, it could eventually lead to the abolishment of slavery in the United States.

England had taken a similar step in 1834. The British Parliament had ruled slavery illegal in all the empire, late in the fall of 1834, and, since then, several other empires and kingdoms had followed suit. Spain had been the most recent addition to the list of nations declaring slavery illegal.

It was thrilling to be in Washington City in the spring time. The flowers and trees were beginning to show new signs of life and giving evidence that summer was not far behind.

It was also thrilling to visit places that I had been before, and to meet with editorial colleagues and reporters who were also in the City for this historic event. Of most interest was the opportunity to see an old acquaintance, Senator John Norvell from Michigan.

Senator Norvell and I had been acquainted since May of 1829, just as he was starting the Pennsylvania Inquirer in Philadelphia. He had not been very successful, and was forced to sell the paper in its first year. We had, however, remained corresponding friends from time to time, and my coming to Washington had given opportunity to spend a little time over dinner with the good Senator.

John was a kind man who, I believe, enjoyed practicing law more than anything else. During our brief time together, he indicated that he would probably serve only one term, and then return to Michigan to do that which he enjoyed most.

Over dinner, I asked him about the current debate in the Courts, and if he thought the justices would agree with former President Adams in the Amistad Case, and grant the freedom of the slaves. I also inquired whether he thought that the United States would follow the trend of Europe in abolishing slavery. The Senator was most gentle as he reminded me that the Federal government, unlike the parliaments of Europe, had little power over the affairs of the states, and that states rights' in the matter of slavery would undoubtedly prevail in this instance. He said that if the Abolitionists really wanted to affect change, they would have to do it state by state.

As I took my seat in the gallery of the Supreme Court on March nine, 1840, my heart seemed to beat out of my chest with excitement as I saw the former President, and now legal counsel for the Africans, take his seat on the floor across from the bench. The quiet in the room was almost deafening. No sound at all was heard, except for the gentle rustle of the justice's robes, as the nine entered the chambers and took their seats, high above the lawyers and in the front of the small crowded room that housed the Court.

The oration of the Court was long and deliberate. But in the end, the justices had awarded freedom to the Negroes and declared they were indeed not slaves, in violation of trade agreements with Spain and Cuba. The surviving members of the African group, thirty-four in all, were immediately released and ordered returned to Africa. It had been a moral victory for the Abolitionists, and sparked a fire of controversy that would rage for years into the future.

CHAPTER FOURTEEN

In June of 1845, the United States was preparing for war with Mexico. President Polk had sent General Zachary Taylor, along with 3,500 armed men, to the Texas border with Mexico, in preparation if Mexico should invade the new republic.

Mister Oliver Jones, my friend, mentor, publisher and father figure of nearly twenty years, lay upon his death bed. Mamma Jones had died the previous year, and now the sorrow of her passing was taking its toll on both Papa Jones and me.

I had taken over most of the managing and editorial responsibilities at the paper, as Oliver had been too depressed at the loss of his wife. I, too, suffered great sadness from Mamma's departure from this life, but had managed, as with the death of my father, to put aside my feelings and continue the work that I believed God had laid before me many years before.

During the past year, Mister Jones had also cared for me, with a considerable sum for my labors and had arranged that in the event of his death, I would become the sole heir of his estate. The Jones' had no children of their own, and some time after my arrival at Wilson School for Women many years before had adopted me as their own daughter.

Mister and Missus Jones had been wonderful caregivers and providers during all these years, and my love for them was equal in nature. Mister Jones made certain that I had learned every aspect of the newspaper business, and had been responsible for my achieving a place of recognition and achievement in the publishing world.

Over the past several years, I had been sought by other editors to leave the Tribune and work at larger and more prestigious papers. I was, however, never able to leave this family that had given me so much and the paper that allowed me to truly become a reporter.

Late on the evening of July first, Marilla, Mister Jones' old house servant, came to my room to announce that her charge needed me at once. I hurriedly dressed in my evening wrap and immediately went to Papa Jones' bed side.

"Elizabeth Grace, is that you?" Papa asked.

"Yes, my dear old friend, I am here. Let me hold your hand."

I took Mister Jones' hand into mine and pressed it close to my heart. He looked so frail and tired. Tears came to my eyes, but I refused them, for fear that Papa Jones would catch sight of the moist drops and be in distress. He always said he could never stand it when either Mamma Jones or I shed tears, and that he always found it necessary to give in to our will, when ever we displayed such feminine emotion.

"My dear Elizabeth, I need you to hear my last wishes."

"Please do not speak this way Papa, your time is not yet."

"No, Elizabeth, my time is drawing very close at hand, and it is all right as I am ready to join Prudence, even this very night. But I must tell you some things first."

Papa went on to explain that he had updated his will in the past months and that everything was to be left to me. I could not hold back the tears as he shared how he wanted me to care for the paper, but that I was free to take on new adventures as I needed to. He said that if it was my desire, I would be able to sell the paper to the employees, so that they could continue his work.

Papa Jones also went on to explain that Marilla was also old and needed to be cared for. He asked that I make provision for her care in the days ahead, with some of the funds that were available.

I promised Mister Jones that I would see that all was done according to his wishes. I knew that Mamma Jones also had been concerned for the care of Marilla and had made her husband promise to make provisions for the faithful servant prior to his passing.

Early the following morning, Oliver Jones drew his last breath. Marilla assisted me in making the final arrangements and, after the mourning period, he was laid to rest next to his beloved wife, Prudence.

The funeral had been one of the largest I had ever seen. Dignitaries from all across Pennsylvania, friends and publishers alike, and many whose stories had been told in the Tribune, came to say farewell to their respected colleague and friend.

During the service at the Methodist Meeting House, many spoke of their friend with fondness and tenderness. Most spoke of how fair he had been to them in business and community matters. Several reported how he was a gentleman to the ladies, a friend to the men, a father to many of the children, and a task master to the politicians.

Francis R. Shunk, the Governor of Pennsylvania, traveled from Harrisburg to speak of his old friend. Governor Shunk shared how Oliver Jones kept the politicians honest with his investigative and fair reporting, along with his heady editorials. He also reminded his listeners that Oliver had been a great supporter of the Democratic Party, the rights of all Americans, and a promoter of individuals based not on the color of their skin or their gender, but rather on their abilities and virtues.

Isaac Stoltzfus, Constance, and their four children also traveled to Chambersburg to be with Marilla and me during this time. Isaac was invited, along with Reverend Josiah Young, to conduct the service of Death and Resurrection. Both Isaac and Reverend Young spoke eloquent words from the scriptures, as Oliver was lowered into the ground.

As was customary, both Marilla and I took a hand full of dirt and tossed it onto the casket after it had been placed in the ground next to Mamma Jones. I stood there for a few moments and for the first time, allowed myself to shed tears of sorrow at the loss of my dear friend. Constance came to my side, and together we walked to the waiting carriage that would return us home.

Later in the evening, Isaac shared how they would be traveling back to Hagerstown in the next few days, unless I needed him to stay on. I assured Isaac that I would be fine, and that Marilla and I would care for the household needs together. I did ask Isaac if he would accompany me to the attorney's office in the morning. I shared that I had several items of business surrounding the affairs of Oliver Jones that needed immediate attention, and that I had no time to mourn.

Both Isaac and Constance reprimanded me in this, and insisted that I should take at least the next month off to mourn the loss. Constance said that she would not leave me for that period and would look after my needs as she was able. I assured them that this was not necessary, and that I was quite capable of caring for the matters of the moment that had presented them to me. Isaac knew from many previous encounters that, once my mind was made up, the only course of action was to go along and try, as best he could, to keep me out of trouble.

Early the next morning, Isaac and I went to the office of Mister John Appleton, Esquire, Oliver Jones' attorney.

"Good morning, my dear." Mister Appleton greeted me with his usual pleasantness. "I am most surprised by your visit so early. I only assumed you would take a period of mourning before concerning yourself with the affairs of our dear friend Oliver."

"Yes, I am sure you are surprised by this early visit. This is my dear friend Isaac. I believe you have met before…"

"Yes, I have, and it is a delight to see you again, Reverend. I only wish it were under more favorable times than this. How are things at the parish in Hagerstown? I believe that is where you are still serving?"

"My work in Hagerstown goes well, but, please, I am here for Elizabeth's benefit and not mine."

"Quite right", Mister Appleton continued. "I am most sorry for your loss, Elizabeth. So please, continue where I so rudely interrupted you."

I went on to explain that I was there to execute the last will and testament for Mister Jones. Mister Appleton explained the provisions that Oliver had set in the will.

The first provision was that his entire business, which included the paper, a small transport company, and a hardware and mercantile company Mister Jones had purchased a few years ago as an investment, along with all material possessions and holdings, including all real-estate holdings, which included several houses, stables and business buildings, had been left to me. He also shared that all bank accounts with the First State Bank of Pennsylvania, and whatever may be held at the bank in terms of material possessions, were mine.

Mister Appleton indicated that the value of the holdings was in excess of five hundred thousand dollars, and they were mine to do with as I wished. The only exception was that Mister Jones had made it known that he wished for me to see to the care of Marilla, and that I would need to set aside some funds for this, if I were to honor Mister Jones' last request.

In a fashion that was totally unlike me, I nearly fainted at the magnitude of the inheritance that had been given to me by this dear old friend and his wife. Isaac had to at once gather the smelling salts and apply them, to help me steady my body and mind.

After a few moments, I shared with Mister Appleton that I had no need for all this fortune, and that we would talk more about it later. For now, I needed time to think through the needs of the paper and my work as the manager and editor of the Tribune. Mister Appleton agreed that there was no hurry to make changes or decisions in these matters, and that, for the time being, I could access all the funds I needed from the bank. I thanked him and promised that I would return in a few days to discuss how I wished to proceed.

Isaac and I then went to the Bank to verify the contents of the safety boxes Oliver had maintained there. I also wanted to verify the amount in reserve for the coming payroll and other expenses at the paper.

We met with Mister Joseph Bailey, the bank president, who, as others had already done, offered his sincerest apologies and regrets at our needing to meet under these circumstances. He assured me that the Bank would cooperate with me in every detail.

Mister Bailey, like most of the people in Chambersburg, had already learned years before to accept me as an equal in all business matters. I had built a reputation of strong will, sound thought, intellectual ability, and business savvy. Most of the business men also knew that I, like them, enjoyed a fine cigar and brandy from to time and was not shy from joining them on occasion, when success had been mine in gathering an important story.

Mister Bailey opened the contents of the safety deposit box and there revealed a tidy sum of gold, worth nearly a hundred thousand dollars. There also were bonds, with an additional value of nearly twenty thousand dollars. In the cash accounts were a little over seventy five-thousand dollars, more than enough to keep the paper running for the next five years if no additional revenues were to come in.

Isaac and Constance returned home with their children the following week. It had been wonderful having them near, but I needed to get on with living and caring for the paper, and as it often is with guests, Constance knew that they were standing in the way of the tasks that were of importance to me. Marilla and I were also accustomed to having the home a little quieter than it was with four children running through the house. Isaac left for Hagerstown, with the promise to return should I have need of him.

Over the course of the next several weeks, Mister Appleton had all of the buildings, houses, and businesses appraised for me. The estate of Oliver and Prudence Jones turned out to be close to one million dollars.

I met with Mister Appleton, to begin the work of settling the affairs of the paper and the property. As I had little need for the entire wealth, I began to distribute the assets to various members of the community.

My first priority was to care for Marilla. Negroes did not typically own property, so I wanted to make sure that the Jones' faithful servant and friend would not have to worry about the prejudice of the day. Unfortunately, slavery had not ended in the United States, as many had hoped. Although Pennsylvania no longer endorsed slavery and was a free state, there were those who did not see the African as a citizen.

I had Mister Appleton draw papers making Marilla the owner of the Jones' home and file the deed with the county court house. I then set a trust fund of $75,000 for the care of Marilla and the home. The trust was placed at the Bank, with Mister Appleton as the executor. Mister Appleton knew Marilla and was as fond of her as he had been of Oliver and Prudence.

Together, we found a young woman by the name of Megan Mahoney, who had recently emigrated from Ireland. Megan had been in need of employment, and Mister Appleton was able to arrange for her to work and stay with Marilla. Megan was most happy with the arrangements and appreciative of the employment. She quickly settled into the daily routine of caring for the elderly African woman.

It was at first difficult for the old servant to allow another person to care for her. The one who had been servant was now mistress, and had her own servant. But with the advance of years and arthritic joints, Marilla settled into the care of this competent, able, and compassionate young woman.

I then decided that it was time for me to pursue other avenues for my work. Over the course of previous years, I had been invited to join various publications and newspapers, and this seemed a good time to branch out.

Sarah Hale and I had remained friends over the years, and she was now working for Mister Louis Godey at the Lady's Book in Philadelphia. Mister Godey had been able to finally arrange the funding necessary to purchase Sarah's Gazette in Boston late in 1837, and began publishing the "Godey's Lady's Book" in 1838. Mister Godey, as Sarah had before him, often invited me to join his publication.

I had invested funds into Sarah's magazine after my father's death some years earlier, and she, in turn, had made a sizable profit for me. These funds had been reinvested with Mister

Godey and others, and now were worth over a hundred thousand dollars on their own. I was, by anyone's standard, a wealthy woman, and now, at the age of thirty-five, considered by some a "rich old spinster". Little did most people know, however, that I had many suitors who still came to court me.

I arranged with Mister Appleton to transfer the paper to the current employees, with equal shares in the publication. Jeremiah Smith was acting managing editor at my request, and was made the overall editor and executor of the paper, to see to the day to day operations. This action made each of the new owners of the Chambersburg Democratic Tribune fairly well off, and they were grateful that they would be able to continue the work they had enjoyed with Oliver Jones for so many years.

I also made the same arrangement with the Chambersburg Hardware and Mercantile Company. Nathan Kelly had been managing the business over the past four years for Oliver, and had increased the operation considerably. Much of the business growth and profits were directly related to the work that Mister Kelly had invested in the business on behalf of Oliver.

I met with Nathan early one morning and, over breakfast, shared with him my proposal to assign the business to him, if he would be willing to hold a fifty-one percent share and give the other forty-nine percent to the seven employees that had been with him for the past several years. Mister Kelly was most surprised and pleased at the prospect of owning the business.

He, at first, could not understand that this was a gift to him and the other employees from me, on behalf of Oliver Jones, and insisted that he should buy the business. I explained that this was my desire, and that Mister Jones would have wanted the same thing.

The remainder of Mister Jones' holdings were sold, and the proceeds placed into trust for my use at some future date. With the proceeds from the sale of the remaining houses, buildings, and businesses, along with the bonds and gold in the bank vault, I now had over three hundred thousand dollars left from the estate. My fortune had now increased to well over five hundred thousand. Both Mister Appleton and Isaac reminded me that I could retire if I desired, and not go running all over the country-side reporting on the stories that interested me. Of course, they both knew better than to believe that I should ever stop, at this point, and retire. I was still much too young for the rocking chair, and too old to take on the project of a husband.

After everything had been settled, I decided to move to Hagerstown, to take some time to write and visit. Marilla reminded me that I would always have a home with her in Chambersburg, and that she would leave my room as I had it, for my return. I promised her that I would write often and come to visit as often as I was able.

James, Isaac's brother, had moved from his church in Baltimore to the prestigious First Trinity Lutheran Church in Washington City. I also had wanted to visit with him, but had not had the time until now. His assignment began in January, and he had been called to be the First Assistant Pastor of Compassion.

This was also the church where President James Polk, along with his wife, Sarah, had recently begun to attend worship. Although President Polk was a Presbyterian, he commented that he appreciated the depth of the sermons by the Reverend Doctor Edward Johnson, the senior pastor, and the work that Reverend James Stoltzfus had engaged in.

James had continued to work for the compassionate care of the Negroes who had fled to the north, as he was able, and often lobbied for the abolishment of slavery both in Maryland and in the entire country. On one occasion, James had been beaten, tarred, and feathered for his outspoken remarks on the ills of slavery.

James had met a man by the name of Frederick Douglass at an anti-slavery meeting in Philadelphia, during the spring of 1843. Mister Douglass had spoken so eloquently of his own captivity that James had been moved to step up his activities in attempting to win the freedom of slaves everywhere.

It was during one of the anti-slavery meetings held in Baltimore the following year, that James had stood to suggest that the Church as a whole had failed its moral obligation to defend these poor souls who had no voice of their own. Several Baltimore clergy and churchmen were waiting for James after the meeting, and dragged him to a waiting buckboard. He was quickly and quietly rushed off into the night country-side, where a group of men were waiting with the tar barrel already prepared.

James was stripped to the waist, and flogged. Then tar and feathers were applied to his head, back and chest. He was left alone, to make his way back to town, if possible.

He managed to return to the church parsonage the next day, where the senior pastor, who was anything but antislavery, greeted him without any compassion or mercy. James was taken to his bed by the housekeeper, who was herself a slave. She tended to his wounds.

It was several days later that James recovered enough to resign his post, at the encouragement of his bishop. The Bishop sympathized with the young minister, but tried to help James see that there was little, if anything, he could do to rectify the situation at this time.

As soon as James was able, he left Baltimore for the last time and went west to be with his brother Isaac and his family, to recover. It was a few months later that the Bishop called on James to offer him the position in Washington City. His new Senior Pastor was more in tune with James, and had promised to work along-side of and with him, whenever and wherever he could, to relieve the sufferings of the Negro.

Book THREE

a time to search...

CHAPTER FIFTEEN

Early that fall of 1845, I left Marilla and her new caregiver, to go to Hagerstown. Isaac and Constance had insisted that, for the time being, I should stay with them, to allow me the freedom to venture on visits throughout the region as I desired, without the burden of caring for a home of my own. I was, as always, most appreciative of their hospitality, and felt that it would be good for me to be with them and the children for period of time.

All four of the Stoltzfus children referred to me as Auntie Liz and, although she was only five, Caroline insisted that she was my favorite, and I hers. Whenever I was with the family, Caroline would attach herself close to me and remain by my side everywhere I would go. She often said she wanted to be just like "Auntie Liz" when she grew up.

The boys, on the other hand, would torment the child and remind her that she was only a girl and had to do what she was told by the men. Both their father and mother would reprimand the boys at this point, for Isaac and Constance were independent minded and strong willed individuals who regularly defended the rights of all. Constance would cuddle her daughter and share that Caroline, as well as her three sons, could become anything she desired in life.

As Christmas approached, James had written to say that he would be coming to spend the holidays with Isaac and the family, and that he would arrive on the train from Baltimore on the twenty third of December. Everyone was always excited when James came for a visit. He always had interesting news to share about his work and had, of recent times, become regarded as an ecclesiastical hero, for his work with the antislavery movement.

The Stoltzfus children, especially the boys, loved to be with their Uncle, who told wild and adventurous tales of helping run-a-way slaves make it to their freedom. He often told of narrow escapes and the sounds of hounds trailing the contraband, along with the angry insults of the slave trappers.

James arrived as planned, and shared a wonderful holiday with us. I had continued to investigate and write stories that interested me and would file them with the Chambersburg Democratic Tribune. Jeremiah Smith would always pay me for the articles, though I had requested no such reimbursement. I would always place the funds I received from Jeremiah in a special bank account, and called it my "Rainy Day Adventure Fund". There was now well over five hundred dollars in the special account.

After the Christmas Day festivities were behind us for another year, James sat one evening before his return to Washington, to share news that he was sure would be of interest to Isaac, Constance and me. Bishop Hiram Barlow, the Stoltzfus' resident Bishop, had contacted James about traveling to London on August of the New Year, to attend the World Temperance Convention.

James went on to explain that Frederick Douglass was currently in England and would be speaking at this event. He was excited, as he shared about the opportunity to travel to England. He felt honored to have been chosen by the Bishop to be the delegate and representative from the Church in the greater Baltimore and Washington area to this prestigious conference.

"Isaac, do you know that I will undoubtedly be the youngest minister there?"

James went on to exclaim with great enthusiasm.

"What an opportunity for me. And here is the wonderful part of it all. The Bishop has informed me that I can take along one other person of my choosing to assist me in this work."

I could see on the face of Isaac that he would like to go, but that he knew his work at the Parish could not be suspended at this time. Isaac had recently earned his Doctor of Ministry from the prestigious Yale School of Divinity and had been promoted to the Senior Pastor position at Trinity Lutheran Church in Hagerstown, following the death of his mentor, friend, and pastor, the Reverend Doctor Thaddeus Mitchell.

Reverend Mitchell had liked Isaac from their first meeting, and had treated him as much as a son, as a colleague in ministry. He had been grooming Isaac for this appointment for the past three years, and now the mantle of leadership had fallen to him.

"James, this is wonderful news for you. We are so very proud of the work that you have been doing, even though it has cost you at times your health and very nearly, on more than one occasion, your life."

Constance now spoke for the first time, contemplating her response, should her husband decide to join Isaac on this adventure.

"Now, my dear brother, have you thought who you would like to take with you, or is this subject still open to discussion?"

"Yes, Constance, I have given much thought to this. I would love to take all of you, but I know that this is quite out of the question. I want very badly to invite Isaac to go with me, but I have spoken to Bishop Barlow regarding Isaac's responsibilities here, and he has suggested that this is not a good time for Isaac to venture abroad."

I could almost see the relief on the face of Constance, as James spoke of the Bishop's hesitance of Isaac going to England. She knew that if the bishop had said no, then Isaac would certainly submit to his authority and decline any offer James might make. It was not that Constance did not want her husband to make this adventure his own, it was simply that she knew how important the work of the parish was to Isaac at this time. She also knew that Isaac would be torn in between loyalties to his ministry and to his brother.

James finally shared his thoughts, "Constance, as much as I would like to take all of you, as I have already said, I know that that is not possible at this time. Therefore, Elizabeth, I am asking you to go with me."

I was surprised by the invitation. James had always respected me and my work, and we had, over the years, become good friends. Yet James always remained somewhat distant to me when it came to including me in his adventures. He always said that I was reporter first, and friend second.

Only on one other occasion had he invited me to go with him, and that was to hear Frederick Douglass speak in Philadelphia a few years earlier. At that time, I was already involved in a story and could not go, but had promised that I would take him up on his offer, should he ever make it again. And now he had.

"James, I would be most honored to accompany you on this adventure. I have desired to report on the Temperance movement, and now this will give me an opportunity to do so. And who could ever pass up the chance to go to Europe?"

Isaac was immediately concerned with the protocol and appropriateness of a single minister traveling abroad with a single woman.

"James, do you think that the Bishop would approve of Elizabeth going with you? After all, neither of you is married."

"I think there is little to be concerned with here, dear brother", James began. "Elizabeth is a few years older than I and she has often traveled alone, or in the company of a gentleman. Did not old Oliver Jones often send one of his workmen with Elizabeth when she was on some assignment?"

"Yes, indeed, that was often the case", I immediately stated.

"But as you know Isaac, there were many occasions when you would travel with me as well, before your marriage to Constance. And how many times have I traveled alone in recent years, when the opportunity availed itself?

"I do, however, see your concern and we would not wish to do anything to give the appearance of impropriety, for the sake of James' reputation as a minister."

"Then what choices do I have? I want someone to go with me who would enjoy the adventure, and I really do not have any other thoughts regarding another choice."

I could sense that James was beginning to experience some frustration over this concern that he perceived as unnecessary.

"Do you really think there would be scandal if Elizabeth accompanied me to London for this Convention, Isaac?"

As the four of us sat together to ponder the dilemma, a thought occurred to me. If Isaac could not go, then perhaps Constance and the children would be able to accompany James. I immediately proposed the possibility.

"That would be a wonderful idea," James expressed, and I could see the joy in his eyes and hear the excitement in his voice as he concurred with my proposal.

"The only problem is that the Bishop will pay only the passage and expenses of one other person."

"I realize that, my dear James", I shared. "But what if I were to pay the way for the children and Constance?

"The Bishop would then have to care only for my needs, and we would have the propriety of a female escort with me on this grand adventure. This would give Constance an opportunity to

74

see London as well, and who knows what other sites we may take in."

Constance was as excited about this possibility as any would have been. She shared how the trip would be wonderfully educational for the children. Isaac also saw this as a grand plan, as he was often encouraging Constance and me to take trips together as time would permit.

"Constance, we will have a magnificent time, so let us do this together with James", I suggested.

After additional discussion around the expense, which I assured my friends would be no bother for me, only delight, it was agreed that we would make the adventure together. The only unhappy part of the decision was that Isaac would remain by himself in Hagerstown, while the family was an ocean away.

Isaac assured us that he would be quite content in caring for the parish, and that the housekeeper would see to his meals and other duties, as she regularly did now. Constance said that she would inform her parents, and they would also look after Isaac.

Isaac chimed in, "All of you are acting as if I am still some incapable young lad who might not find his way home if left unattended. I assure you that I shall be quite all right in your absence. Besides, we have several months yet in which to prepare for your departure."

With that, we all enjoyed speculating on the adventure that would be ahead of us in the coming year. James would return to Washington City immediately at the start of the New Year and would, he promised, make all necessary arrangements for us. I would make funds available to him, as well, to finalize the arrangements as needed.

I decided that I would take some time to study the emerging Temperance Movement, to better acquaint myself with the goals and values of the coming Convention. I also wanted to make contact with a few editor friends, both in New York and Philadelphia, before our trip, to see if there was interest in the story I would file from the Convention.

CHAPTER SIXTEEN

Spring came quickly in the year of 1846. James was busy with his work in Baltimore. Isaac had settled into the routine of his ministry in Hagerstown as the Senior Pastor. Constance and the children were all excited about the coming trip to Great Britain in the summer. And I was researching the Temperance Movement, in preparation for the coming convention in London.

Through my good friend, Sarah Hale, and her editor, Louis Godey, I was introduced to Mister Jason Gamble, the news editor at the Philadelphia Inquirer. Mister Gamble was already familiar with my work at the Chambersburg Democratic Tribune, and was most interested in my ability and willingness to cover the coming Convention in London.

He had received word through his contacts in England that the whole English countryside was electrified with enthusiasm for Frederick Douglass as he travelled and lectured, speaking about the ills of slavery in America. It was even being rumored that Mister Douglass was considering accepting an offer to remain in England as a citizen, and would perhaps abandon his work in the states.

Mister Gamble wanted the full story of the eloquent black man, and agreed to hire my services for this event, if I would write about the reception and remarks of Mister Douglass at the Convention. He also agreed to assist with my expenses as well, which was, of course, a welcome addition to the financial arrangements. My only other obligation was to make the story an exclusive for the Inquirer, to which I heartily agreed.

Sarah and Mister Godey were both excited for me at this assignment and the sponsorship of the Inquirer. Louis Godey also said that he would make contact on my behalf with an editor he was familiar with at the London Times, who would be able to assist me with filing my story and caring for any additional needs I may have while in Great Britain. I thanked Mister Godey for his kindness, and assured him that I would some day return the favor.

By June, final arrangements for our travels and accommodations, once we arrived in England, had been completed. Passage had been booked for James, Constance, the four children, and me aboard the *Cambria*, a British steamer.

The *Cambria* was the same vessel that had transported Mister Douglass to England the previous year. Due to the fact that Frederick Douglass was a black man, he was denied first class passage, and instead was relegated to the lower decks in the steerage compartment and second class accommodations.

This action had outraged many sympathizers in Great Britain, and a demand was made from the Canard Line for an immediate apology. Mister Canard issued and published an open apology to Mister Douglass, and assured both him and the British people that this type of behavior would no longer be tolerated aboard his ships.

Mister Douglass would later write that Mister Canard had been faithful to his word, and that he was not aware of any further denial of any person aboard a Canard Line ship from first class passage, if they were able to pay the fare.

James told us that it was expected that the crossing would take approximately twenty-five days, and we would be traveling first class. James and I would each have a room of our own, while Constance and the children would share a room.

Caroline, upon hearing this, expressed her immediate disapproval.

"But Mamma", she stated. "I want to stay in Auntie Liz's room with her. The adventure will be much more fun in her cabin than with my brothers. Please say that it is all right with you, Mother."

Constance often found it difficult to refuse her daughter when she would look at her with those large, beautiful, wide, green eyes and pure, angelic face.

"My dear little one, I can not commit to your request until I first speak with Elizabeth about the matter."

Before Constance had the chance for us to speak, I entered the room to hear the child issuing her appeal of the matter to her mother.

"All right, now what is the fuss about, Caroline? You have some great desire you are pressing your mother with, so out with it, what is your wish?"

I looked to Constance with just the slightest hint of an amused smile. I could not help but to interject my voice upon the discussion, knowing that I would undoubtedly add fuel to young Caroline's fire, which her mother was probably attempting to extinguish.

"Oh Elizabeth, Caroline is just expressing her displeasure at having to share a room with her brothers on the voyage before us. She would much rather room with you. But I have assured her we will discuss this later, in private."

"My dear Caroline, I believe your mother is quite right in this. She and I must first discuss the matter privately, and then we will make a decision that your mother feels is best for you and all concerned. So now, you run off to play and let us talk."

Caroline left the room with a demonstration of her displeasure at having to do so, to find her favorite doll, while Constance and I began to discuss our travel plans.

Once in London, we were to stay at the Parliament Hotel, which I was told was very near to Buckingham Palace and Exeter Hall, where the Temperance Convention was to be held.

James also informed us that William Lloyd Garrison, a significant leader of the Abolitionist movement and close friend to Frederick Douglass, would also be aboard the *Cambria*. This would give us further opportunity to engage in lively discussions regarding the state of the Negroes' existence in this country, according to James.

CHAPTER SEVENTEEN

Our merry band of travelers departed in early July, from New York City, for Liverpool. The voyage took twenty-three days, and crossing the Atlantic for the first time in my life was indeed an adventure I shall never forget.

Caroline, of course, won the day with her mother and spent the entire trip with me, sharing my cabin, and escorting me around the ship throughout the days and evenings. The boys also had their own adventure with their Uncle James.

James adored the boys as much as they adored him. He spent hours taking them to the various parts of the ship often restricted to passengers. Of course, he had the permission of the Captain.

Constance was able to enjoy the voyage with a room to herself. She enjoyed much time for relaxing and reading, which she thoroughly enjoyed and took advantage of.

The weather had been fairly calm and sunny for much of the trip, with only a day of rough seas with wind and rain. I enjoyed standing at the bow of the ship to feel the salt laden waters of the briny sea spray across my skin, gently stroking my cheek as if to say that I was welcomed upon her breast. The wind filling the sails sang a song of joy, as the large vessel was guided toward her destination, echoing their melodic tunes within the very being of my soul.

I felt alive and ready for whatever adventure might come my way. It was as if I was in love, not with a man whom I had had the pleasure of knowing, but with a mystical and enchanted lover, yet to be identified and embraced.

We arrived in Liverpool, to be greeted by Mister Alistair Abercrombie from the London Times. Mister Abercrombie had been assigned by the Times to be our escort to the Parliament Hotel in London, and to see to our needs. He also had a letter of introduction for me to present at the Temperance Convention, to assure that I would have no problems covering the story as a member of the press. Alistair was a delightful gentleman ,and I would look forward to becoming better acquainted with him and his paper.

We immediately settled into the new quarters that would be our home for the next several weeks. Because of the

Convention and crowded conditions in London, Constance, Caroline and I would share a room, while the three boys and their Uncle would share another room. The arrangements were quite satisfying and enjoyable, and I did not mind in the least the accommodations as they were set forth.

James set off, soon after our arrival, to meet with other delegates to the Convention, and to see if Mister Douglass had arrived in town. He also wanted to find out if there would be ample opportunity for visiting the London theatres and museums.

Constance and the children set off as well, to discover the attractions that interested them, and to begin to make arrangements during their stay. Constance had decided that this was to be an educational adventure for the children, as well as a holiday.

As for me, I decided to take a brief rest before setting out. The journey had been wonderful so far, but the constant attention from young Caroline had practically exhausted me.

It was mid-day when I lay down to rest. I was awakened by the noise of the children upon their return late in the day. Caroline decided that it was time I should arise, and began to tell me all the wonderful sights they had already seen within a short distance of our hotel.

Constance shared that they had taken some afternoon tea and crumpets at a local shop and enjoyed feeding the pigeons in the square just off Buckingham Palace. James, she informed me, had run into them as he was strolling through the yard of the hotel and had informed her that we should all be ready to dine at half past eight that evening.

We were to be the guests of both Mister William Garrison and Mister Frederick Douglass at the Lion and Lamb Inn, just a few blocks away. Mister Garrison told young James that he would send his carriage for us shortly before our meeting time.

James was extremely excited about this opportunity to meet these two men. We had briefly encountered Mister Garrison on our crossing of the Atlantic, but for the most part, he had kept to himself. He said that he was busy writing a book about the Abolitionists movement, and he was taking advantage of the solitude aboard ship to accomplish much of his work.

I, too, was most excited about this first meeting with the former slave, Frederick Douglass. I had heard a great number of stories about his abilities to speak before a large crowd, pleasing them with his tales of captivity, moving his listeners to positive action in ending the cruel and peculiar institution.

As the hour was already late, we had little time to prepare ourselves for the evening gathering. We quickly dressed and arranged ourselves as to be most presentable to these distinguished gentlemen. The children were gently reminded that this was to be an official dinner, and that only the very best of manners would be acceptable.

Mister Garrison's carriage arrived shortly after eight, as promised, and carried us toward our rendezvous at the Lion and the Lamb. As I stepped from the carriage, I had my first glimpse of the stately and handsome Frederick Douglass. I could immediately understand how, by his commanding and stately presence, he was able to excite to action those with whom he had opportunity to speak.

If his speech was as commanding as his presence, he would be either a powerful ally or an overwhelming enemy. My desire, upon meeting him for the first time, was to make this man my friend and ally.

CHAPTER EIGHTEEN

Mister Garrison and Mister Douglass immediately greeted us.

"My dear James, how good of you to be able on such short notice to come and dine with Mister Douglass and myself."

"Thank you so much, Mister Garrison..."

"Please, feel free to call me by my first name, William, if that would not offend you. And please, introduce us to your lovely company. Ladies, and young gentlemen, first allow me to introduce my distinguished friend, Mister Frederick Douglass."

Introductions were immediately made by James of all his traveling companions. By the look upon his handsome face, I could easily see how proud he was of his sister-in-law and his nephews and niece.

"And finally, gentlemen, allow me to introduce my dear friend, Elizabeth Grace Fitzgerald. Miss Fitzgerald, as you may already know, is a reporter covering the Convention for the Philadelphia Inquirer."

Mister Douglass took and gracefully kissed the back of my hand, with the slightest bow.

"How delightful to finally meet you, Miss Fitzgerald", the stately black man declared.

"I have heard much about you and have read, with great delight, many of your articles, particularly those regarding the plight of the slaves as they attempt to make their way to freedom and safety from the slave hunters of the Deep South."

"Thank you, Sir," I responded with some blushing under the eye of this significant man. "My work as a reporter is as passionate to me as your work in striving for the freedom and justice of your people."

"My people? I am afraid you have me quite wrong, my dear. These are not my people, but God's own people. It is His work that I do, in striving to assure the freedom of all people, regardless of the color of their skin or the sex they were born."

"My humblest apologies, Sir. I meant no disrespect. I am aware that you are also striving for the rights of women, as well as the person held in bondage and slavery."

"No apology is needed, my dear Miss Fitzgerald. Now, let us go in to our table for the evening. Would you do me the great honor of sitting by my side, so that we can share in lively discussion together? I know by your reputation, and now in the meeting, that you are indeed a person with the lively ability to engage and banter."

With that exchange, we all laughed together and entered the Lion and the Lamb for a wonderful evening of dining and discussion. I sat to the right of Mister Douglass, and Caroline, also taken by the handsome gentleman, insisted that she should sit on his left. He was most flattered by her request and immediately granted it, with the permission of her mother.

As the evening wore on, both Mister Garrison and Mister Douglass shared many tales of their work in winning the freedom of slaves and attempting to abolish slavery, altogether, in the United States. Mister Douglass and Mister Garrison were of different opinions regarding the Constitution of the United States in condoning or condemning slavery. Mister Garrison felt that the Constitution was used to keep slavery as a practice, and Mister Douglass felt the Constitution could be used in supporting the freedom of the slaves and ending the practice.

Mister Douglass also stated that he was looking forward to the Convention and having the opportunity to speak out against the use of alcohol in the treatment of slaves.

"So you see, my dear Elizabeth, the slave holders often force liquor upon the slaves to keep them under alcoholic influence, making it even more difficult for the poor souls to think enough to make their escape."

Mister Douglass and I had, by this point of the evening, given to calling each other by our first names. This was certainly a sign of the growing fondness between us, as well as Frederick's trust of me as a reporter to share correctly what I would be told in an interview. Mister Douglass was an easy man to like and to listen to. It was effortless to see why so many women, as it had been rumored, were without difficulty attracted to him.

The hour was late and the children, as well as Constance, were exhausted. Caroline had fallen fast asleep upon the lap of Mister Douglass, and had remained there as he gently stroked her thick, auburn hair. Mister Douglass remarked earlier in the evening how he missed his own children, who were still in Massachusetts, along with his wife, Anna. He went on to share that his daughter, Rosetta, was about the age of Caroline, and that he hoped both children would have the opportunity to meet someday.

Mister Garrison called for his carriage, to return all of us to our lodging for the night. As James escorted Constance and the boys to the waiting coach, Mister Douglass carried the sleeping Caroline in his arms with such tenderness. He gently kissed her cheek as he placed her in her waiting mother's arms, and quietly spoke "goodnight, little one" to the child.

Frederick turned to me before I boarded the coach, "Elizabeth, this is how it should be for all God's children. Not one should ever be stolen, or sold from the arms of their mother or father. Not one should have to be placed in the servitude of another, placed in bondage to do another man's bidding. Neither slavery nor poverty, nor any other thing on the face of this earth, should be allowed to rob a child of a parent's love. Can you understand this, my dear?"

As I looked into the eyes of this distinguished gentleman, with his soft, yet powerful speech, his broad and strong shoulders, his stately appearance and gentle ways, I caught a glimpse of a tear in the corner of his eyes, telling me of the deep suffering and longing for his own mother and familiar love.

I wanted to take him into my own arms and hold him close, to assure him that indeed I understood. I wanted to let him know that he was, at this very moment, loved by many, his wife and children still in Massachusetts, his many readers and the listeners of his words, by children everywhere, and by me.

I took liberty that I rarely take in times like these. I reached for the dear man's hand, held it to my breast and kissed him ever so gently on his cheek.

"I understand, my dearest Frederick, I understand."

We then bid a good night to one another. I would not see him again until he was on stage before the Temperance Convention several nights later.

CHAPTER NINETEEN

At breakfast the next morning, James informed us that Mister Garrison had requested a meeting with him later that day, and had asked if I would be willing to accompany James as well. Constance and the children had plans to tour the London Museum of Art and to see the changing of the Guards at Buckingham Palace.

James and I arrived at Number Five Whitehead's Grove, London, and the home of Mister George Thompson. Mister Thompson had been a long and faithful friend of Mister Garrison, and had also become a friend and a supporter of Mister Douglass.

Mister Garrison was waiting for us, and immediately made introductions of all parties.

"Elizabeth, I am so glad that you were able to accompany James on such short notice to our meeting. Do come in and make your self at home."

Mister Garrison was as charming this day as he had been the previous evening.

"Elizabeth, please allow me to introduce you to my very dear and old friend, Mister George Thompson."

"It is my delight to meet you, Miss Fitzgerald. I have read much of your work. You are indeed a gifted reporter and writer. I am often amazed at how you bring to life the very essence of the subject of your investigation and tell with such vivid expression their story of triumph and victory, or agony and defeat. Tell me, my dear, how did you ever come to such a place as to be a reporter, especially as one of the fairer sex?"

I thanked Mister Thompson for his kind words and shared some of my story from childhood, through meeting Mister Oliver Jones and his wife, Prudence. I was not at all offended by his referral of me as the fairer sex, but took the comment simply as a compliment and affirmation of my achievements.

Both Mister Garrison and Mister Thompson had attended the Temperance Conference of 1840, in London, where Elizabeth Cady Stanton and Lucretia Mott had been refused their seats as duly elected delegates. The Conference had refused to acknowledge the right of women to hold delegate positions, and denied official standing to all women.

The women were forced to sit in an area behind closed curtains, out of sight of the men, and behind a roped barrier. Mister Garrison and Mister Thompson had arrived just after the discussion and vote, and could not offer their objection to this action. In protest of the exclusion of the women delegates, both Garrison and Thompson joined the women behind the curtain in the roped off area for the duration of the convention.

Both of these well known and distinguished gentlemen were supportive of the rights of women, as much as they were of the rights of Negroes. Both had taken active roles in the Anti-Slavery Movement, the Women's Suffrage Movement, and the Temperance Movement.

"Mister Thompson, I am well aware that both you and Mister Garrison are actively involved in many of the social issues facing the United States, as well as Great Britain. But do tell me, sir, how do you find the time and energy to be involved in so much?"

I asked my question with the hint of a smile and flirtatious glance, demonstrating to both that I was impressed with their commitments and work and respected the men for it.

"You toy with me, Miss Fitzgerald", Mister Thompson countered. "I do what I can and where I can and encourage others to do so likewise, my dear."

Mister Garrison began, "Mister Thompson is one of the leading members of Parliament to bring about the repeal of slavery laws in Great Britain and its empire.

"His work, along with many others, has served Great Britain well, for, as you will discover, the need for slave labor was proven to be a myth. England has prospered well since slavery ended here.

"Also, my dear, I believe the next time you have opportunity to speak with Mister Douglass, he will affirm that the treatment of the black man here is far better than in the States", Mister Garrison concluded.

Mister Garrison went on to share that there was increasing desire on the part of Frederick Douglass to remain in England, and that he probably would do so if his family could be brought here and provided for. Mister Douglass had expressed his longing for his family and how much he missed them. He also shared that when he walked down the street, he was not greeted as a black man, or fugitive slave, but as a man, a free man, free as any other, and respected as a learned man.

James shared, "Yes, this is so true, Elizabeth. I have heard people speaking already in the shops that they are looking forward to hearing the great orator, Frederick Douglass, speak at the next possible occasion.

"People love Mister Douglass and so want him to remain in England. Many have expressed a fear for his life, should he return to America. There is also discussion that, if he must return, then his freedom must be purchased at all cost, to insure his safety."

James further explained that Mister Douglass was still considered a fugitive slave, after his escape from Hugh Auld of Baltimore in 1838. Publishing his autobiography and becoming well known as an orator had put Mister Douglass at great peril of arrest and reinstatement to slavery.

"So you see, Elizabeth, Frederick had to flee to England out of fear for his very life. He is still considered the property of another man in the States, and as such, can be returned to his owner, should Mister Auld decide to pursue him.

"Yes, James, I have heard similar tales since our arrival here, as well as in Philadelphia in preparation for our coming to the Convention. So, Mister Thompson, do you think that in the end, Mister Douglass will remain, or shall he return to the States?"

Mister Thompson was not sure at this point what the black statesman might do.

"All I know is that we have raised sufficient funds to bring Anna and the children to England, but she refuses to come. And we have sufficient funds to purchase his freedom, but so far he has refused. I suspect that in the end, Mister Douglass will return to America and his family. Let us only hope that he will consent to the purchase of his freedom before hand."

Mister Garrison, Mister Thompson, and James continued to discuss the politics of the coming Convention. Neither Mister Garrison nor Mister Douglass had been elected delegates to this event but the Convention had graciously given them tickets to be seated as honored guests. Word had already been sent out that both gentlemen would be speaking during the seating of the American delegation on the platform.

CHAPTER TWENTY

August four, 1846. The Temperance Conference was officially called to order in the main auditorium of Exeter Hall in London. The room was large and well appointed, accommodating the approximately four thousand persons who were in attendance.

As I entered the hall, I was immediately stopped by a burly looking attendant who held the responsibility of insuring that only properly credentialed delegates and officials were permitted to enter the main auditorium. I presented him with my press credentials, and politely asked to be directed to the press balcony.

"Now there, Missy," he started with his patronizing speech. "What you want to be goin' to the press box fer? That ain't no place for a lady like you. No, you want to go to the visitors section at the rear of the auditorium. This here entrance is for the officials and members of the press. That is, my lady, male members of the press. There ain't no such thing as a lady reporter. It jest ain't right, you know."

I was about to express my objection when Mister Alistair Abercrombie appeared by my side.

"Good morning, Miss Fitzgerald. Hello, Mike, I see you are at your job controlling the lot of us this fine day."

"Good morning to ya, Sir. Yes, Sir, that be my job all right. How 'bout a wee bit of a pint later round the corner, after this busy body nonsense is over. Whata ya say, Mate?"

"That would be fine, Mike, but first, Miss Fitzgerald and I have a job to do."

"Yes, Governor, I was jest explaining to the little lady that this is reserved for you press boys, an' ladies ain't allowed in the men's room, if ya know what I mean."

"Now Mike, Miss Fitzgerald is not your usual London type lady, she is an American lady. And she happens to be a first class reporter, come all this way to tell the story of these teetotalers. Now she can come with me, and I'll make sure she behaves herself like a lady should."

"But Mister Aber..."

"Now Mike, you want me to make a favorable report about you and spell your name correctly in the paper, don't you? So you just turn the other way, while Miss Fitzgerald and I take our seats. And afterwards, we will all go out for that pint."

With that, the doorman looked away to others who had begun to gather, and motioned for us to proceed to the press area. Alistair seemed to be amused with his actions and his ability to get us both beyond the doorman.

"He can be rather difficult at times, Elizabeth. I have learned that if I promise not to spell his name wrong and to say something nice about him in the paper, he usually grants my wish. I hope you did not mind my coming to your defense?"

"No, not at all, Alistair. I quite appreciate the fact that you were able to get me past him. I am afraid I would have put up a much fiercer fight if left to myself in this matter."

"Well, I will warn you that he may have done you a favor by keeping you out. The men in the press box sometimes can be somewhat rowdy but perhaps, with the presence of a lady, they may behave a little more civilly. They may not like it, but they will probably be on their best behavior for you."

"That's quite all right, my dear friend. I have been around some fairly rough characters over the past several years. I am sure I will not be offended. I only hope they will likewise not be offended by my independent and somewhat feisty ways."

We both enjoyed a laugh together all the way to the third floor balcony, where the press had been set up. This was a wonderful vantage point from which to see and hear all the proceedings of the Convention.

Mister Abercrombie introduced me to the other Correspondents who had arrived before us. There were about twenty in all, including Mister Alfred Waud, a young sketch artist for the London Times.

Mister Waud was just learning the art of being a correspondent, and was already a gifted artist. He stated that he would prefer to draw and paint with pencil and charcoal than to paint with words.

Over the course of the next few days, Mister Waud would ask me copious numbers of questions regarding the United States. He said that it was his dream to one day travel to the States.

I guaranteed that, should he have that opportunity, he was to look me up and I would assure him the same professional and courteous treatment his editors and reporters had extended to me in London. He confessed that if we were to ever have the opportunity, he would certainly take advantage of our meeting and subsequent friendship.

The first day's proceedings went as expected, with little interruption and fanfare. The delegates were seated according to country of origin and position. This Convention had allowed women to also be recognized and seated as official delegates of their respected countries.

As the evening session came to a close, Alistair invited me to accompany him and several others to a small pub close to Exeter Hall, with the promise of good food, lively discussion, strong drink, and a coach ride back to my hotel when I had my fill of the noise, clamor and boasting of the other reporters. I immediately accepted the offer and went off with my new found friends of the London press. James left with Mister Garrison and Mister Douglass.

Constance and the children had spent the day sightseeing, and by the time I returned to my room, were fast asleep. Constance stirred as I came in and inquired as to whether or not I had a good time of it all. I told her that, indeed, I had a wonderful day and evening and we would talk in the morning. She immediately drifted back to sleep.

I sat at my desk for a few moments, collecting and writing my thoughts and impressions of the day. I pondered how far I had come since I first met the abolitionists in Maryland, through Isaac and Constance. I remembered those early days at the Quaker farms, hiding run-a-way salves, and the encounters with the slave trappers.

What a different world this was, here and now, in Great Britain. If only we could end slavery as the British had already done, and work for the equality of all people, regardless of the color of their skin or the sex to which they were born. What a different and more productive world this would be.

I closed my journal and put to rest my pen and ink. As I lay upon my bed, I could not help but feel excited for the days yet to come. I began to contemplate my own destiny and the possibility that the whole world now lay before me. I began to consider remaining in Europe and not returning with Constance, James and the children when they would sail for New York the first week in September.

As I drifted off to sleep, my dreams came as peaceful glades of wildflowers, strewn upon rocky fields. Where once lay only barren soil upon the craggy, rock hewn landscape, now rose wild, passionate gardens filled with beauty and sweet fragrance. Is this how my life had been, and now was becoming?

CHAPTER TWENTY ONE

The next day I met Alistair Abercrombie at the entrance to Exeter Hall, and we went in together. Mike was present at the door, caring for his responsibilities and taking great care to insure that only properly credentialed individuals were allowed in.

"Good morning, Mike." Alistair greeted the man as we entered.

"Good mornin' Sir, and, me lady. How'd you like the accommodations for you press boys? I been told they the best seats in the whole blooming hall."

"Yes, Mike, you are quite correct. The seating is perfect. And Miss Fitzgerald thanks you as well."

"Never you no mind. I am jest glad that you and the lady were accommodated. Did the other boys behave themselves, Miss, or were they the rude lot that they usually is?"

"They are a delightful and entertaining group of gentlemen, Mister Mike. And thank you for your kindness in allowing me access to the press balcony. I shall be sure to say nice things about you and spell your name correctly in my report to the Philadelphia Inquirer."

"Oh blimey, Miss. That be awful kind of ya. The missus likes to see me name in the paper on occasion for something nice. She says it is better when that happens than when me name shows up on some Constable's list. And to be reported in the American paper, why that would jest be the 'bout the best thing ever happened to me."

As we entered into the hall and took our seats in the gallery reserved for the press, I asked Alastair how it was that someone who appeared more to be a bouncer at the local pub than a doorman at the Parliament came to be at this Convention. Alistair explained that Mike and two others like him had been hired by the organizers, to protect the Convention against the possibility of disruption by some who did not quite agree on the issue of Temperance.

The day was filled with speeches and rhetoric regarding the ills of drink. Many gave testimony to the destructive power of alcohol and the need to ban the substance from public consumption. Others gave witness to some of the restorative properties of alcohol and suggested that moderation was needed in this, as with all things.

The American delegation was to be seated at the evening session. Both Mister Garrison and Mister Douglass would join the distinguished group on the platform. While Mister Garrison did not intend to speak, Mister Douglass had been invited and strongly encouraged to share his thoughts. He had hesitated, stating that he did not wish to cause anyone distress at their own Convention, and that he was not a delegate but merely a man who was honored to be invited to attend.

As the evening wore on and the hour growing late, Mister Douglass was, at last, introduced to the assembly. The entire floor of the Convention stood in ovation to the man who represented the struggles of slavery in America. Cheers and shouts of affirmation were given. The applause was thunderous and continued for over ten minutes.

When the crowd finally yielded to Mister Douglass, he began, "Mr. Chairman, Ladies and Gentlemen, I am not a delegate to this Convention."

Douglass stood as a tall and eloquent statesman, his stature that of a nobleman. His voice was deep and strong. As he spoke, his words reverberated throughout the Hall. There was a hush over the entire assembly, as if everyone present were about to hear from the divine at any moment.

Mister Douglass continued, "Those who would have been most likely to elect me as a delegate, could not, because they are tonight held in the most abject slavery in the United States. Sir, I regret that I cannot fully unite with the American delegates, in their patriotic eulogies of America, and American Temperance Societies.

"I cannot do so, for this good reason, there are, at this moment, three million of the American population, by slavery and prejudice, placed entirely beyond the pale of American Temperance Societies.

"The three million slaves are completely excluded by slavery, and four-hundred thousand free colored people are almost as completely excluded by an inveterate prejudice against them, on account of their color."

At this the crowd erupted with cries of "Shame! Shame!" The Chairman had to call order to the assembly, to allow Mister Douglass to continue.

"I do not say these things to wound the feelings of the American delegates. I simply mention them in their presence, and before this audience, that, seeing how you regard this hatred and neglect of the colored people, they may be induced, on their return home, to enlarge the field of their Temperance operations, and embrace within the scope of their influence, my long neglected race."

There arose great cheering from the audience at this point and, at the same time, appeared to be some confusion on the platform. It was becoming more and more obvious that the American delegates had not bargained for these words from Mister Douglass and were now more than willing to dismiss him from further speech.

Mister Douglass had recently accused some of the American Clergy, both in the North and the South, as being, if not pro-slavery, then, at the very least, indifferent to the issue of slavery. In meeting with James, Mister Douglass had encouraged the young minister in his work, knowing that James Stoltzfus was not among those whom he cited in this belief. Mister Douglass had been told of the suffering Reverend Stoltzfus had endured at the hands of Baltimore Clergy only the previous year, over his Abolitionist stance.

Mister Douglass continued, "Sir, to give you some idea of the difficulties and obstacles in the way of the Temperance reformation of the colored population in the United States, allow me to state a few facts. About the year 1840, a few intelligent, sober, and benevolent colored gentlemen in Philadelphia, being acquainted with the appalling ravages of intemperance among a numerous class of colored people in that city, and finding themselves neglected and excluded from white societies, organized societies among themselves, appointed committees, sent out agents, built temperance halls, and were earnestly and successfully rescuing many from the fangs of intemperance.

"The cause went nobly on till the first of August, 1842, the day when England gave liberty to eight-hundred thousand souls in the West Indies. The colored Temperance Societies selected this day to march in procession through the city, in the hope that such a demonstration would have the effect of bringing others into their ranks. They formed their procession, unfurled their teetotal banners, and proceeded to the accomplishment of their purpose. It was a delightful sight. But, Sir, they had not proceeded down two streets, before they were brutally assailed by a ruthless mob. Their banner was torn down, and trampled in the dust, their ranks broken up, their persons beaten, and pelted with stones and brickbats. One of their churches was burned to the ground, and their best temperance hall was utterly demolished."

More cries of "Shame! Shame!" arose from the delegates on the floor of the assembly, while the gathered delegates on the platform, becoming increasingly more annoyed by their speaker, called for silence and for the assembly to be seated.

In the midst of this commotion, the Chairman tapped Mister Douglass on the shoulder and informed him that the fifteen minutes allotted to each speaker had expired. The audience, upon hearing this, began immediately to cry out "Do not silence him. Let him speak." They then began to shout "Don't interrupt. Don't dictate."

Following this, the assembled crowd began to shout "Douglass, Douglass, Douglass." This show of acceptance and love by the people continued on for several minutes.

Finally, Mister Douglass was able to continue.

"Kind friends, I beg to assure you that the chairman has not, in the slightest degree, sought to alter any sentiment which I am anxious to express on the present occasion. He was simply reminding me, that the time allotted for me to speak had expired. I do not wish to occupy one moment more than is allotted to other speakers. Thanking you for your kind indulgence, I will take my seat."

As he proceeded to sit down, there arose loud cries for him to "go on and speak". The gentle statesman stood for a few moments more and spoke kindly to his audience, saying no more of the condition of the colored people in America.

Upon taking his seat, The Reverend Kirk of Boston stood and accused Mister Douglass of unintentionally misrepresenting the Temperance Societies of America. He further stated that Mister Douglass' remarks may have produced the impression on the minds of the public that the temperance movement in America supported slavery, which according to Reverend Kirk, was not the case.

As the evening was drawing to a close, a note was passed to me by a young page. It read,

"Elizabeth. Meet me at the main entrance following the closing prayer. We are going to a party. James"

CHAPTER TWENTY TWO

I met James at the main entrance to the meeting Hall immediately after the closing prayer. Alastair Abercrombie was with me, as he wanted to assure my safety, should I not meet with James as expected.

"Elizabeth, I am so glad you received my note. I have the most exciting news. We are to be the guests of the Ambassador and his wife at the American Embassy this evening."

"James, that is wonderful, but I am not dressed for a meeting with the ambassador."

"You look just wonderful, as you always do. This is not a formal affair, but an informal gathering of a few friends." James noticed for the first time that Alastair was standing with me.

"Mister Abercrombie, my apologies. I did not see you with Elizabeth. How nice it is to meet up with you once again."

"Thank you, Reverend Stoltzfus. It is indeed my pleasure to see you. I have thoroughly enjoyed the company of Elizabeth these few days. Thank you for bringing her with you from America."

"It is Elizabeth you must thank. She was the one who was able to make this trip possible for all of us together. I only wish my poor brother Isaac had been able to join us, as well. We will have wonderful tales to tell when we return home, won't we, Elizabeth?"

"Yes, James, indeed we will."

"Mister Abercrombie, would you honor us with your presence in tonight's gathering at the American Embassy? I would be honored if you would say yes." James extended the invitation as if it were his party.

"I am afraid, my dear Sir, that it would not be proper protocol for me to attend without an invitation from the Ambassador himself. I have met Ambassador Bancroft and can assure you that he is a most capable representative of your country to the Court of Saint James."

George Bancroft had been appointed the Ambassador to Great Britain, formerly known as the Court of Saint James, mid year, following the return of Louis McLane, earlier in the year, to the United States.

"Yes, I fully understand, but I have been assured by his Charge de Affairs that I may bring with me any who I believe would enhance the evening." James offered a most compelling invitation, but, at last, British formality and protocol ruled the day for Mister Abercrombie.

Alistair and I bid good evening with the promise that, if possible, we would dine together at lunch. He was to arrive at my hotel around half past eleven in the morning. We would dine at the hotel restaurant, before going to Exeter Hall for the final day of the Convention.

James and I arrived at the American Embassy, and were immediately escorted to the library, where several others had already gathered. Mister Thompson, Mister Garrison and Mister Douglass were present. Several members of the British Parliament and their wives had joined the merry group. Ambassador Bancroft and his wife, Elizabeth, were at the center of the room, along with other representatives of the American Government.

Mister Thompson immediately came and took my arm to escort me to be introduced to the Ambassador.

"Mister Ambassador, may I have the honor of introducing to you and Missus Bancroft one of your more respected journalists, Miss Elizabeth Grace Fitzgerald."

Ambassador Bancroft took and kissed the back of my hand.

"Miss Fitzgerald, it is an honor to finally meet you. I have read some of your reports and editorials over the past few years. I admire your rhetoric, even if I disagree with some of your assertions."

"Thank you Mister Ambassador. And thank you for welcoming me into your home this evening. It is indeed an honor to be surrounded by such a group of distinguished and important guests. I do promise not to report anything I may overhear tonight, as I am not here on official business."

"Not to worry, my dear. I am certain most of the evening's discussion will be quite dull. Allow me to introduce you to my beloved wife, Elizabeth."

"How do you do my dear? I am so glad to have you here with us this evening. As you can see, we women are far outnumbered by the men."

Missus Bancroft was a delightful, petite woman with a smile and gentleness that disarmed one immediately. As I met her,

I was taken that she was the exact opposite of her husband in appearance and, I assumed, disposition.

The Ambassador stood tall and had the appearance of a well weathered sea captain. His speech, although finely trained, gave the impression of one who could cause a mad dog to retreat at his command.

Missus Bancroft continued, "I do hope, Miss Fitzgerald, that you will do me the honor of sitting next to me at dinner this evening, so that we may become better acquainted."

"I would be honored to sit with you. Thank you for the invitation."

Mister Thompson excused us from the Ambassador's presence and began to introduce me to other members of the evening's gathering. We finally arrived back to the group with Mister Garrison and Mister Douglass.

"Yes, my dear friend", Mister Garrison was speaking to Mister Douglass. "I believe you caused a rather unforgivable strain at tonight's meeting."

"It was not my intention to do so, William. You do understand, though, I had to speak about the plight of the colored people, and have to make known that there are those who still would harbor ill for us, as well as turn back what small advances we may have already achieved. It has been over two centuries now of bondage."

Mister Douglass had the appearance of exhaustion and frustration over the evening's events.

"Yes, Frederick, I do understand. But that is all the more reason not to alienate the very persons we need to achieve the ultimate freedom of the slaves."

"No, William, we do not need these thugs who disguise their intentions in societal politeness over issues that will never result in the freedom of people, white or black, held in the bondage of slavery or drink.

"No, we can no longer stand by and say nothing, while the Negro suffers day and night in bondage, while so called good men of the cloth promote, by action or inaction, the slavery we can no longer tolerate for ourselves."

Mister Douglass watched as we approached and changed his discourse with Mister Garrison.

Frederick Douglass directed his remarks to me, "Elizabeth, it is good to see you once again. James, thank you for bringing your Elizabeth with you tonight."

The next several hours were spent in dining and discussing the politics of the times, with specific regard to the ending of slavery in America. Ambassador Bancroft reminded his listeners that he did not support the peculiar institution and that many had tried over the course of the past ten or twenty years to bring about a referendum in the Senate, to end slavery.

The Ambassador went on to say that both the Congress and Senate were composed of as many representatives from the slave holding states as from the free states.

"As long as there is this equality in vote, my dear friends, we will never be able to pass a Constitutional Amendment to end slavery."

"That is exactly my point, Mister Ambassador."

Mister Garrison was responding to the remarks of Ambassador Bancroft.

"That is exactly why we must do away with the present Constitution, for it encourages slavery by its very existence."

"Remember, William, that I am a representative of the United States Government, and your words come close to speaking treason. Of course I can not endorse your point of view, even if I may agree with you."

At that, the Ambassador let out a hearty laugh.

"Ladies, if you will excuse us, the other gentlemen and myself shall retire to the drawing room for a night cap of brandy and a fine cigar, thanks to our friends in Havana."

With that, the men retired for the remainder of the evening, James with them, to the Ambassador's private drawing room, while the ladies and I remained together for a glass of Sherry and relaxing conversation.

I thought for a moment of objecting to the relegated role of domestication, but decided that, in the best interest of future stories, I should remain somewhat polite to my host. I would much rather have joined the men in a good cigar and brandy, along with the political discussions that surely would take place. Instead, I would endure for a brief time the mundane banter of household responsibilities and the trivial talk of pleasing one's husband.

As the final hours of the evening waned on, I grew more bored with the feminine company and sleepy to the point that I felt

I must return to my hotel for the night, lest I embarrass myself by falling asleep in the presence of the Ambassador's wife. I excused myself, and Missus Bancroft escorted me to the waiting coach that would return me to my quarters.

The Ambassador's wife had offered to retrieve James for me, but I assured her that that would not be necessary.

"I am quite sure, Missus Bancroft, that James can find his own way home at the proper hour. In the meantime, allow me to thank you for a wonderful evening."

"It is I who should thank you, my dear. It has indeed been a pleasure to meet you. I do hope that in the future you will feel free to visit us again, and perhaps we should even become good friends."

Elizabeth Bancroft was a charming host, and I was sure that if the circumstances presented themselves accordingly, we would indeed become friends. But as anyone knows, a good reporter does not have good friends, only good sources.

As the carriage plugged along the cobblestone streets in the thick London fog, I drifted off to sleep, not to awake until the driver opened the door to assist me out at the hotel entrance.

CHAPTER TWENTY THREE

I met James and Alastair Abercrombie for lunch in the Hotel restaurant the last day of the Convention. James had scolded me for leaving him at the Ambassador's home the previous night.

"I was so bored and was ready to leave hours before, when I realized that you had already returned without me to the hotel, Elizabeth. How could you do such a thing to me?"

James, of course, did not mean it when he declared he had been bored. He loved these discussions, and was always glad to be around men of importance who believed in the causes he supported.

I was enjoying our little banter, and Alistair was delighted to see that James appeared somewhat put off by my independence of him.

"It would appear, Reverend, that you seem to have some thought that Elizabeth should look after you?"

"Not at all, it is just that she usually does. And then when she doesn't, I become concerned for her safety and well being, thinking something nasty may have happened to her. Sometimes Elizabeth can be so, well, so damned independent."

James went on to share that lively discussion had occurred the previous evening, with Mister Douglass being at the center of it all. Douglass was pressed toward the end of the evening as to whether he would return to the States and, if so, would he first attempt to purchase his freedom.

Mister Douglass, as James understood it, was still undecided, but since Anna had refused to move to England with the children, he was inclined to return to the States sometime in the next year. He also was inclined to allow for the purchase of his freedom, to insure he would have the ability to pursue his cause without further interference from the legal authorities.

Mister Abercrombie inquired as to when we were to return to the states. James had said that we were scheduled to take the *Flying Liberty* from Liverpool to New York on the third of September. In the meantime, Constance, the children, and James had several sights they still wished to see, and had talked about taking a trip to Dublin for a few days.

I had decided to stay in London while the family took holiday in Ireland, to catch up on some writing and file my stories with the Philadelphia Inquirer. Alastair had stated that he would be most happy to assist me in any fashion possible and would insure that the dispatches to Philadelphia would occur in a timely fashion.

That evening was the closing session of the London Temperance Convention of 1846. Frederick Douglass was still the talk of the convention floor, over the previous evening's remarks. Several delegates were amused at the reaction of the American delegates to Mister Douglass. Many stated that they understood why America had not yet ended slavery, if the response of the American people were matched by the response of the delegates.

More than a few of the delegates from Great Britain, Denmark, and Sweden came to the side of William Garrison, and encouraged him to take a stronger stand in support of his friend in the days ahead. Garrison assured them he would continue to do all that was possible to protect his friend, and to work toward the freedom of all slaves.

These same delegates also encouraged Mister Douglass to remain with them in Europe, assuring him of his continued freedom and liberty. All attempted to bring comfort to Mister Douglass, by stating that they were sure his wife in due time would see the merit in this course of action, and would most certainly join him in England at some future opportune moment.

Douglass graciously thanked all those who spoke words of kindness and reassurance, but simply stated that he was not yet sure of his future course of action but would, he promised, investigate every avenue and pursue the most favorable for all.

As the Convention came to a close, Alastair invited me to join the other Correspondents, along with Mike, the doorman, for a final evening of refreshments and conversation.

"I am sure that we will not be as sophisticated and proper as the American Ambassador and his wife were last night, but you know we shall have great fun. Do join us, Elizabeth."

"I would be delighted to, my dear friend."

And with that we were off to the "King's Ransom Inn", the favorite pub of the British press.

After enjoying a fine meal of mutton stew and a pint of ale, Alfred Waud offered me a cigar. The others, who did not already know of my delight in a fine smoke, looked on to see if I would be offended, or take him up on the offer.

I reached for the well made Havana, cut the tip, and allowed Alastair to light the end for me with the strike of a match. I drew in and savored the rich, deep, buttery hue of flavors that enriched the Cuban tobaccos.

All at once, the men around me burst out in applause, cheers, and laughter at my ability to embrace some of the finest tobacco in the world. One of the correspondents from Russia gave me a hearty slap on the shoulder and invited me to come and drink his Vodka and dance with him.

Mikhail laughed and said, "You are better than Ruskie women. You dance, drink, and smoke with best of all men. Come, my little bushka, we be best friends, and maybe even make love, what say you, my little wildflower?'

At that, we laughed and made light of his flirtatious behaviors. Mikhail was a fine man with strong features, but I was not interested in making intimate acquaintance with him. He would depart in two days for his homeland, along with the Russian delegation, and return to his wife and seven children.

As the evening wore on, one by one, the correspondents returned to their hotels or homes for the night. Alastair and I were the last to leave, and decided to stroll the several blocks back to my hotel in the damp, thick, silent London Fog.

"Alastair, I can not quite get over all the fog in London."

"I am told that it is much the same in your town of Boston. I am sure it has to do with the proximity of the sea,"

We walked slowly along, without saying much. I had my arm securely locked into his.

Alastair was a handsome man, tall, with dark brown, tussled hair showing the ever so slightest hint of grey at the temples. He was nearly forty, as was I, and not married.

He had shared, shortly after our arrival in London, to my question of whether he had a wife and family, that he had married several years before. His wife, Margaret, had died, along with their only child, during the birth of their daughter. He had never remarried, finding the thought of potential loss again too painful. Instead, he dedicated himself to his work as a reporter, and had developed a strong reputation for being tenacious, fair, and accurate.

I knew that there was an attraction between Alastair and myself, but was not sure what, if anything, I wanted, or would do, about it. We both had our careers, and I was not about to end mine to be a wife.

That thought did not, however, satisfy my longing to be loved, intimately loved by a man of my choosing, at a time of my choosing. Were the feelings I had for Alastair merely human passion, or was it something more? Was I willing to explore them, or should I leave them alone?

I was still pure and had known no man. Yes, I had been kissed many times, and held close by many. Nothing more had occurred, and it always ended with my pulling away and refusing the encounter further.

We arrived at the door of the hotel lobby as I pondered these thoughts.

"Elizabeth, I feel you are trembling. I am afraid that this night air and fog has chilled you. I am so sorry. We should have taken the carriage."

"No, Alastair, it is not that at all." I looked deep into his eyes, and he saw for the first time what I had been thinking, but not saying.

"My darling Elizabeth, how could I have been such a fool?"

"You are not the fool, Alastair, I am. I can not, should not, choose not, to belong to any man. I made that decision long ago. I desire my work over all else. And I have seen too much distress, loss, pain, and sorrow on the part of those who marry, to wish to experience it for myself."

"I, too, have seen such sorrow and pain, but I have also seen much joy and happiness", Alastair stated with a hint of protest in his voice.

I knew that Alastair was feeling what I had begun to feel. He was as much taken by me, at the moment, as I was by him. But the question still tugged at my mind, was this only basic human passion, or was it the beginning of love? Either way, I felt as if I wanted to abandon myself to the calling of its adventure, and the pleasure I was sure was to follow. But at what cost?

At that moment, Alastair took me into his arms and pulled me close.

"Elizabeth."

He pressed his lips to mine. The effects of the alcohol, tobacco, and walk in the night air caused my head to swirl. I felt limp and helpless in his strong arms. I wanted to succumb to his every command and submit myself to his pleasure.

His hand began to gently caress my bosom as his tongue slipped between my teeth and danced around and around on mine. I suddenly stopped and pulled back, wanting to regain control of the situation.

"I am so sorry, Elizabeth, I…"

"Please, Alastair, don't. I want you, too. I want to be with you. I want you to hold me. But this is not the place or time, and I have no privacy of my own here."

I went on to share, "Alastair, do you love me, or is this simply the drink of the night and the exhaustion of the day, taking us places we may later regret?"

"My dearest Elizabeth, I feel that we may both have come to a place that we may not wish to be, but are not able to pull away under the night's influence. Perhaps we should say goodnight and talk of these matters when we are both rested and fully in control of our thoughts."

I agreed with my friend's suggestion, although I did not want to at the moment. I wanted him to love me, there, that night, that moment. We, however agreed to meet the end of the week, over lunch, to discuss what, if any, future we might have, or wish to have.

CHAPTER TWENTY FOUR

By the end of the week, James, Constance, and the children were off for a few days of sightseeing in Dublin. They had taken the early morning train from London, and would arrive late that night. I had the entire hotel suite to myself, for the first time since our arrival, and it was a wonderful feeling to be alone again.

I truly enjoyed the company of Constance and Caroline, but at times the desire to have my privacy from both the watchful eyes and inquiring mind of the child was, well, overwhelming.

Alastair called on me shortly before noon, as promised. We went by carriage to a small Inn outside London for lunch and a chance to talk freely about our feelings, hopes, plans, dreams, and any other topic we felt important to share on this occasion.

The day was sunny and bright, with the warmth of the August air blowing gently through the windows of the Inn. Along with the sounds of birds singing, the fragrance of the flowers growing just outside the open windows of the Inn made for a most intoxicating and romantic get-a-way.

Alastair escorted me to my seat at a prepared table, set with fine china and glistening silver. The waiter laid a napkin across my lap and asked if I desired a glass of wine at this time. I thanked him and said no, that I preferred simply a cup of tea, for the moment.

Seated across the table, Alastair looked absolutely charming and handsome in his finest attire. His soft, dark brown beard had been neatly trimmed, while the hair upon his head remained in its usual bushy, unkempt fashion. He always appeared with his hair tussled as if he were a boy coming in from play. This only added to his charm and delight, which he often used to easily disarm his prey.

And was I now his prey? I mused over the thought as I watched Alastair fidgeting with his waistcoat. He had spoken little on our journey to the Inn, saying only that he was enjoying the day and looking forward to his next assignment.

I could sense that he was somewhat nervous over our meeting. My only uncertainty was why. After we had parted a few nights ago, I was sure that we would both fully recognize the impulsive nature of our embrace, and the effects that the alcohol and night air had on our emotions.

Alastair at once started, "Elizabeth, I must apologize for my behavior of the other evening. I took advantage of the situation. Please forgive me."

As I watched him, almost squirming as if he were a small lad caught behaving in a most inappropriate way in church, I almost began to laugh.

"My dearest Alastair, you owe me no apology. I desired you as much as you desired me. And trust me, my dear friend, if I had not wanted you to take me in your arms as you did, I would have made my protest quite noticed."

Alastair immediately began to relax, for he suddenly realized that he was not the only culprit in this scenario. I, too, had freely joined into the plot of the previous evening and had, by all accounts, enjoyed the moment, even desiring for more. I felt that if I had not had the presence of Caroline and her mother in the hotel suite that night, Alastair and I may have ended the evening together locked in each other's arms.

I reached across the table and took his hands into mine. "Alastair, we must talk about this, however. I must know your feelings for me. I must know if I am just prey that you wish to conquer, or is there more to this than simply passion?"

Alastair looked into my eyes, and I felt as if he were about to pierce my very heart.

"Elizabeth, how could you even think that I would see you as prey? I know we have only known each other for a short time, but I know that I am falling in love with you. I could only hope that the same were true of you."

"My darling, the truth is that, I too, am falling in love with you, but how could a romance ever work between us? We come from two different parts of the world. You have your career, and I have mine. Are you willing to give up your life, anymore than I am willing to give up mine, for the other? Is that not what love demands?"

"Yes, Elizabeth, you are quite correct on every issue. No, I can not leave my work, anymore than you. And I do not expect you to leave your life, your work, your home, to make me happy. But it still does not change the longing I have for you, the desire I have to hold you in my arms..."

"The desire to make love to me", I finished the thought for him.

"Yes, Elizabeth, the desire to embrace you in every fashion."

"Alastair, do you not think that I, too, may have those desires? I have passions, as well, but have never met a man that I was willing to submit those passions to, until now."

We continued expressing our feelings for some time, over our late afternoon meal. We talked at length about our work, the stories we had covered, the people we had met along the way, and our desire, though placed out of sight and thought for the most part, of finding someone with whom to share life's journey.

I told Alastair of Isaac's desire for my hand many years before, and of my decision never to marry, when I was but twenty or so. I shared how, despite those initial feelings, we had become, and remained to this day, good friends.

We spoke of the people we knew who were happy and strong and in love. And we spoke of our own need for intimacy and experience.

Alastair shared that he knew only his wife and one other who had come before her, but of no other in the past several years. I confessed that I had known no man and had vowed to remain pure.

As the hour grew late, Alastair suggested we should take the coach back to London. We had enjoyed the gardens of the Inn for the better part of the afternoon, into the evening. It would be dark soon, and Alastair did not wish to keep me out late. He suggested that we could return to London and have a late dinner at the hotel. I agreed.

We arrived back at the hotel shortly before nine that evening. Alastair went into the hotel restaurant to order a table for us, while I went to my suite to freshen myself from the day's adventure and the coach ride back into London.

We sat together and enjoyed a light supper, followed by a sherry. Our conversation was soft and gentle, as we spoke of love, romance and passion. Deep inside me was still the stirring and longing for Alastair to take me into his arms and sweep me into places I had never gone before.

As we finished our evening dinner, Alastair escorted me to the lobby of the hotel. As he was about to speak goodnight, I touched his lips with my fingers and asked him if he would escort me to my room. I took his arm, and we began to climb the stairs to the third floor suite.

Alastair took the key from my hand and opened the door. He stepped into the darkened room and lit the gas lantern upon the mantle. As he turned to face me, I moved into his embrace, freely giving myself to his strong arms and caressing mouth.

This time, it was Alistair who pulled back. "Elizabeth, are you sure this is what you want?"

"No, Alistair, it is not. You are indeed a most honorable gentleman. And have become a true friend. Perhaps if the time and day ever become right, we will be together in a proper fashion. But for now, my dearest, I should bid you goodnight."

Alastair left the room, leaving me alone in the emptiness of both the hotel suite and my heart. I fell upon my bed and wept tears of loneliness that I had never known. Love had found me once again, and I had denied the cruel master, as I had come to see love.

I would see Alastair at the offices of the London Times only once more before our return to the States, less than a month later. We spoke briefly, and he offered his best wishes for a safe and uneventful return across the Atlantic.

As I looked deep into his eyes, I wondered how many more times I would have to deny love for the sake of my work. I thought of the joy Isaac and Constance shared, the love between Oliver and Prudence Jones that endured for more than fifty years, of my own father's and mother's love that brought me into this world.

Had I been willing to pay too high a price for my own desires of recognition as a reporter? My goal had been achieved, but was it now worth it all?

CHAPTER TWENTY FIVE

I went to see Alastair at the offices of the London Times, the day before we were due to leave for America. I wanted to see him one last time and talk about what had occurred between us. I still was not sure I had made the right decision, and wanted to meet with him once more, in an attempt to sort out my feelings.

Mister Hiram Burnham, the managing editor of the Times, informed me that Alastair had been sent on assignment in Ireland, to cover the riots occurring in Dublin. He had departed only five days ago, but was expected back in London on tomorrow's morning train. As soon as he checked into the office, Mister Burnham assured me he would give word to Alastair that I wished to see him, and would send him right over to the *Flying Liberty* docked in Liverpool.

Early the morning of September third, we left our hotel and set off for Liverpool and our ship home. I prayed all the way to the docked steamer that Alastair would receive word that I wished to see him before we departed. I stood alongside the entry way on board until the last possible moment, in hopes of seeing the man I was in love with, yet had denied.

As the ship pulled from its moorings and began to make way, I strained with the last fleeting hopes of seeing my beloved running toward me on the dock. At last, it was not to be.

As I slowly made my way to my cabin, a page came through the decks bellowing, "Page for Miss Fitzgerald, page for Miss Elizabeth Grace Fitzgerald." I immediately alerted the young man that I was Miss Fitzgerald. He handed me a note that had been passed to the Captain just moments before sailing. I thanked the young man and handed him a small coin.

The note read,

"Miss Fitzgerald. Alastair killed in train accident on return to London. Our most sincere sympathies. Mister Hiram Burnham, London Times."

I could not believe the words I had just read. James and Constance, along with the children, came around the corner of the deck just then, to see me standing motionless, holding the paper note in my hands. James asked at once what was wrong, as Constance took the paper from my trembling grasp.

As she read the note, she took me into her arms and held me close, as I began to weep uncontrollably over the loss of Alastair's life and his love forever. She escorted me to my room, where Caroline had already taken her things as well. Constance instructed her daughter that she would have to stay with her mother on the voyage home, as Auntie Liz needed some time to be alone.

I remained in my cabin for the duration of the voyage, with the exception of going upon deck to the dining room to take what few meals I desired. I would see no one and refused to be comforted by James or Constance. I ate alone at dinner, and then quickly retired to my cabin.

On several days at open sea, I contemplated ending my own life. I thought of jumping overboard as the most expedient manner, but in the end could not bring myself to the deed. I felt as if I needed to live, for some reason yet to be discovered.

Constance tried for several days to comfort me, but then realized that I was unable to receive her words of encouragement. I needed time to mourn and heal. Constance understood that. James felt at a loss of what to do for me, and pledged to maintain a watchful eye on me, lest I should do something rash and impulsive.

We arrived in New York on the eighteenth of October, forty-three days after our departure from Liverpool and word of Alastair's death. The arrival was greeted with enthusiasm by Constance and the children, and with concern by James for what I might do at this time. I assured James that I was going to be fine, and just needed to get back to work as soon as possible.

We left for Philadelphia on the afternoon train. I was going to spend a few days there with Sarah Hale and file my final reports with the Inquirer. James was to escort Constance and the children home to Isaac in Hagerstown, and then proceed to Washington City to resume his duties.

The next day, we arrived at the train depot in Philadelphia. I bid farewell to my dear friends, and assured them that I would travel, as soon as possible, to rejoin them in Hagerstown.

I took a carriage to the home of Sarah Hale and arrived late in the afternoon. Eliza Mary, Sarah's housekeeper, was at home and greeted me. "Why Miss 'Lizabeth, it is mighty fine to be seein' you again. You come right on in. Miss Sarah says you be coming today. She is at the office doing some last minute work and tells me to make you at home as soon as you git here."

Eliza Mary was a former slave from Maryland. Sarah had met her at a home of a mutual friend on one of her visits in 1837. Upon hearing that she was a slave, Sarah asked if she could buy Eliza Mary, and the friends sold her for a small price. As soon as Sarah was safely in Boston, she had papers drawn to free her.

Eliza Mary asked if she could stay on as Sarah's housekeeper. An agreement was reached on fair wages, and the young woman remained with the Hale household.

Over the past few years, Eliza had become as round as she was tall. She was one of the jolliest individuals I had ever met, and ended almost every conversation with her laugh as she would exit the room. Today was no different.

Sarah came in to the house an hour after I had arrived. As soon as she saw me, she started, "Elizabeth, what has happened to you? You are skin and bones and look as if you have been in mourning for weeks."

Before I could say a word, I broke down in a heap of mournful tears and shared my sorrow at the loss of Alastair. We spent several hours together, as I told how we had met and how I had fallen in love with this man so unexpectedly.

I shared about my physical desires for him, as well as the emotional pulls of my heart. I then told how I had left him, in order to pursue my own career.

I explained how I had second thoughts and wanted so to talk with Alastair one last time before leaving for America, in the hopes that perhaps I would be able to resolve my inner conflict and either stay in London with him, or depart for the States free of his bonds of love. The final hope was dashed as Alastair failed to show at the docks, only to learn that he had died in a tragic train accident.

It seemed as if I sobbed on for hours, while Sarah sat patiently listening to my story of sorrow. At last she spoke, "My dearest Elizabeth, you have been through quite enough for the day. We will talk more later, perhaps tomorrow, if you are ready. In the meantime, you are to stay with Eliza Mary and me until you have recovered from your losses and are ready to face a new day."

Sarah called for Eliza Mary and had her take me to my room for the night. Fresh linens had already been placed on the guest bed in preparation of my coming. Eliza was then instructed to brew me a cup of tea for bed.

I went to my room and prepared for bed, even though it was still light out. The window had been closed and a small fire had been set in the stove, to take the autumn coolness from the room.

I crawled into the bed, and covered myself with the bed sheets and warm quilt that had been placed at the foot of the bed. I propped myself up on the four large pillows set just for me.

Sarah entered the room with the tea and encouraged me to drink. She had added some lemon, honey, and a small amount of whiskey to the brew. She said that it would help me to sleep better, and that she kept some Kentucky Bourbon on hand for such an occasion as this.

Sarah left the room for a few moments and returned shortly, herself ready for bed. We sat and talked for a few more minutes until I had finished the last of the tea.

She took the cup from my hands and placed it on the stand next to the bed. "There, now, Elizabeth. That should help you feel better, and perhaps sleep will come tonight for you, my dear."

I thanked her for her kindness and hospitality. Sarah pulled back the covers and slid beneath them alongside of me. She pulled me to her bosom and stroked my hair.

Once again I began to cry as she held me. She whispered that she understood loss as well, and that she would stay close, until I no longer needed her.

She whispered tales of her husband from long ago and the joy they had shared, even though it had been brief. She spoke freely of love and discovery and that indeed, the sun would rise in the morning, as it had every morning since the birth of creation. I drifted off to sleep with her beside me, still stroking my hair as a mother does with her hurting child.

I woke late mid-morning the following day. The sun was coming through the open window, and the day was bright and warm. The smell of fresh falling leaves and dying flowers permeated the air.

Eliza Mary entered the room and immediately spoke, "Why Miss 'Lizbeth, I was thinking you might jest sleep all day long. How you be feelin' this morning? Miss Sarah sez you had a fretful night with your nightmares and cryin' an' all. Twas after midnight before you finally settled in to sleep."

"I am fine, Eliza Mary, and thank you for asking. Where is Miss Sarah?'

"She done left for the office early. Says she be back after noon and then she be home the rest of the day. She tells me to look in on you regular like and don't wake you unless you already up. I put fresh water on the stand for you if'n you want to freshen up a bit. I can fix you some breakfast in a hurry if you don't want much fancy. How 'bout eggs, bacon, toast, and some fresh coffee? You like that, wouldn't you, Miss 'Lizabeth?"

"Thank you, Eliza, that would be splendid, but I can come down to the kitchen and help you."

"No Ma'am, that be my place down there, and I don't let no one in my kitchen, you knows that. Beside, Miss Sarah tells me that she left a special present for you on the writing table, along with some writin' things for you to use if you need them. You jest freshen yourself up a bit an' I be back soon as possible with your breakfast."

"Thank you again, my friend. You are most kind to me."
With that, Eliza Mary hurried off to her kitchen with her usual laugh and mumbling something about "white folk".

I slipped from the bed and put on my house wrapper and slippers. The water had been heated ever so slightly, to take the chill off and yet remain refreshing to the face.

I sat at the desk where Sarah had laid a lovely, leather bound journal with my name engraved in Gold on the cover. Inside, Sarah had written,

My Dearest Elizabeth,

I had intended to give you this journal for Christmas but have decided that you need it more now.

Over the years I have discovered that I learn more about who I am as I write out my feelings, emotions, desires, hesitations, joys, sorrows, victories and frustrations. I have discovered more about who I am as daughter, mother, wife, friend, author, abolitionist, and a host of other descriptions, as I have written my thoughts and reflected upon them in my own daily journal.

Perhaps if you would enter into this exercise as well, you may discover some of your own truths about love, career, life, and a host of other issues only you can define.

I shall remain here for you, and shall forever be your
friend.

With all admiration, love and acceptance,

Sarah
Twentieth of October, 1846

I picked up the pen, opened the ink and began to write.

CHAPTER TWENTY SIX

I spent the next several weeks reflecting and writing. Sarah was a most gracious host, and Eliza Mary made certain that my daily needs were attended to.

Early one November day, I made my way over to the offices of the Philadelphia Inquirer. Mister William Pryor, Managing Editor of the Inquirer, had been waiting for my visit. As I entered his office, he stood and, with a warm handshake, greeted me and invited me to stay for tea and a visit. I accepted his kind offer. It was good to be out of the house on this crisp day.

"My dear Elizabeth, how good to see you once again. Your reports from London were absolutely marvelous and well received by our readers. We are all impressed by your ability to have received such wonderful interviews with Mister Douglass and Mister Garrison, along with your reports from the Convention itself."

Mister Pryor was most sincere in his remarks. Many of his readers had written to the paper, expressing their pleasure with the reports. Pryor had forwarded many of the letters to me at Sarah Hale's home, prior to my arrival.

"I appreciate the opportunity that you gave me to cover the story. It was indeed an experience I shall never forget."

"I should also state how sorry we all were to hear of the death of Mister Abercrombie from the Times. I understood that he had been quite helpful to you in gaining access to the Press Balcony in the early days of the Convention."

"Thank you for your kind words. Yes, he indeed had been most gracious with me and assisted me throughout my stay in London. I have been told that Alastair, I mean Mister Abercrombie, died in a tragic train accident returning to London. I am afraid I did not have the opportunity to say a proper goodbye before sailing home."

I held back my tears as I thought lovingly of the man who had briefly won my heart.

"We received word from London", Pryor continued, "that his death was the result of protestors tearing up the tracks just prior to a river crossing. The tracks gave way as the train began to cross the bridge, and the passenger cars plummeted into the ravine and river below. In all, twenty-three persons died."

"Has there been any word as to the capture of those responsible?" I inquired.

"According to our friends at the Times, two men have been apprehended, with the authorities searching for as many as five others. They will be caught and put on trial for their crime, my dear."

Mister Pryor gave me the look of a father who knows of his daughter's heart ache.

"If you wish, we will send you back to London at the appropriate time, to cover the trial."

"Again, thank you, Sir, for your kind offer. But I feel it best to leave the past where it is, for the time being. Now, I have compiled a list of my expenses for reimbursement, as we agreed. I have already noted that payment has been deposited in my bank for the articles submitted for publication."

I changed the subject as quickly as possible, to avoid the shedding of more tears in the presence of the editor.

William Pryor assured me that the funds for reimbursement would be deposited within the week. Should I have any further concerns, or wish to change my mind about returning to London, I was to call on him.

Before departing his office, Mister Pryor offered once again his sincerest condolences at the loss of Alastair. He also assured me that if I wanted to remain in Philadelphia, I would always have a position with his paper. I was, and would remain, most appreciative.

As I left the Inquirer, I spotted Sarah Hale walking toward me, accompanied by Mister Louis Godey, her editor.

"Elizabeth, I am so glad to see you out and about this beautiful winter's day. Louis and I are off to lunch. Please join us."

"Thank you Sarah. Mister Godey, it so nice to see you again. Sarah, I would love to join you for lunch, but you must allow me to care for you this time. Sarah has been much too gracious toward me, Mister Godey, over these past weeks, and not allowing me to contribute anything of value to the household."

Mister Godey responded, "I have been told by Sarah that you have been enjoying time for yourself, to recover from the long and eventful trip to London. I have read your reports of the Temperance Convention in the Philadelphia Inquirer, and I must confess that I am most jealous of your reporting skills and ability. You, my dear, have turned a master craft into an art form."

"You are much too kind, Mister Godey. If my writing and reports are enjoyable to read, it is only because I enjoy my work so."

We ventured to the Venetian Restaurant, a favorite dining establishment in the city market area that Louis Godey often visited. We ordered and enjoyed a cup of tea, while waiting for our meal to be properly served.

Throughout the course of our light repast, Godey was full of questions regarding my trip to London. He was most interested in any details I could give him regarding the latest fashions of London.

"I understand that you dined at the American Ambassador's resident. Can you share what Elizabeth Bancroft was wearing?"

I did my best to share in great detail what each of the ladies had been wearing when I arrived at Ambassador Bancroft's residence. I shared that I had gone directly from the Convention to the Ambassador's home and was not entirely dressed according to the standards of the evening occasion. Elizabeth Bancroft had made sure, however, that I was treated with every kindness, and no notice had been drawn to my attire.

"Louis, I almost forgot, a package arrived for me this very morning, from London. It is a most beautiful dress of at least ten shades of pink, layered over and over again in the richest silk I have ever seen."

Sarah was most excited in telling of this story.

"And who, may I inquire, sent this marvelous dress to you?", Louis countered.

"Why it came as a gift from our dear Elizabeth."

Sarah went on to explain that, shortly before my departure from London, I had ordered the dress to be made for her at a most elite dress shop in London. The dress maker had assured me that it would be an original, and no other of its likeness would ever be produced.

"Elizabeth, I can not thank you enough for thinking of me while you were on your adventure."

"My dearest friend, it is I who thanks you. The dress is the least I was able to do for you. I do hope that you will enjoy it and, please, if it must be altered, allow me to care for that as well."

I was undeniably delighted to see how excited Sarah was with the gift. Mister Godey promised to have the dress sketched and placed into the magazine, with Sarah's permission.

As we finished our meal, Sarah and Louis returned to their office, while I decided to stroll through the market for the remainder of the afternoon. It had been a little more than two months since I learned of Alastair's tragic and sudden death. It seemed that I had used those months to grieve all the losses of my life – my mother – brother – father – Mama and Papa Jones – , and now Alistair. Now it was time to return to living. The time had come for me to begin contemplating my next adventure.

CHAPTER TWENTY SEVEN

4 December, 1846

My Precious Elizabeth,

How I, how we, have missed you, and have been in constant worry of your fragile state of mind upon our return from London. Sarah Hale has been a wonderful friend to all of us, writing often to tell us of your ever present resilience and abundant tenacity in the midst of suffering and loss.

Isaac has been most concerned, as well, and expresses daily his thought that perhaps we should have traveled to Philadelphia and returned you to us here for a time of recovery. I have continually reminded him that you are with a most capable, loving, and longtime friend, and that Sarah will always see to your needs and best interests.

The children especially ask each day when Auntie Liz will come to be with us again. I have told them only that you are in Philadelphia tending to business and your work, and that you will join us as soon as possible.

Caroline wants me to tell you that she has a new dress and can not wait for you to see it. The boys are growing ever so tall and even more adventuresome, as if that would be at all possible.

James has written to say that he will be traveling to be with us for the Christmas Season and will depart Washington City the morning of the 25th. He has responsibilities in the Church on Christmas Eve, and will not be able to take the train until early Christmas Day. He promises that he will arrive in the late afternoon and remain with us until after the New Year.

My Dearest Elizabeth, I do hope that you will find it in your heart and spirit to also join us for the Christmas Season. You have been with us every Christmas since Isaac and I first met and wed. Could this be the first time you will not be here? Say it is not so. We would all miss you terribly, should you not come.

I also know that Sarah's household has grown, married, and moved away. Although I am sure she has many friends and family who will attend to her during this festive time of year, she is, of course, always welcome to our humble home and we dare invite her to join you now, this Christmas, with us in Hagerstown. Please ask her for me.

So please say you will come and bring Sarah, if at all possible. I will wait anxiously for your reply and pray that it will indeed be favorable to all of us.

Forever, your loving sister in Christ,

Constance

I received Constance's letter the second week of December and was pleased to hear from her. I had been thinking of traveling to Hagerstown for Christmas to be with the Stoltzfus family, as I had for nearly fourteen years now.

My only concern was how I would be received after my depressing voyage across the Atlantic. I was not at all sure that they would have forgiven me for my display of weakness. Isaac, Constance and all my friends saw me as a strong, resilient, tenacious woman, who rarely gave into feminine emotional displays. This time had been so unlike me.

I had refused to mourn the earlier losses of my own father and Oliver and Prudence Jones. Sarah, not surprisingly, had comforted me that their lives had been lived long and well and their deaths had not come as a particular surprise or shock.

Alastair's death, on the other hand, had come suddenly and violently, without warning. She also gently reminded me that I had fallen in love with Alastair, and that made all the difference in the world. She gave me permission, should I have decided out of necessity, to take the customary mourning period of a year for Alastair.

Constance's letter took away any fear or reservations I may have had about reentering into the life of this dear and precious family of mine. Constance and I grown to love and view each other as sisters, and were as close as any family tie could establish.

I spoke that evening with Sarah about the invitation for her to join all of us in Hagerstown.

"I know that you will have a wonderful time with the children, as well as Constance and Isaac. Please consider the possibility, Sarah."

I went on to share that Eliza Mary was to accompany us, and would be warmly welcomed as part of the family.

"I have no fear that the Stoltzfus' would make us all very comfortable and we would have a grand time of it, Elizabeth. But I am glad this has come now, for I was going to speak of Christmas to you, as well."

Sarah went on to explain that she and Eliza Mary had been invited to Boston for the holidays, to the home of her oldest son, David, Hannah, his wife, and their three children. Sarah and Eliza Mary were to leave on the twenty-first, and would not return until mid January. I was welcome to join them, but she understood, if my desire was to spend the time with my dear friends in Hagerstown.

After some discussion, I expressed my longing to be with Isaac and Constance. I thanked Sarah and her son for their kind invitation. Sarah was assured that I would have a good time, and that I was now capable of caring for myself once again.

I would to travel to Washington City the same day Sarah and Eliza Mary would go to Boston, and spend the few days with James. From there we would travel together by train to Hagerstown, arriving on the twenty-fifth in time for Christmas Dinner.

All was agreed upon as we had discussed, and the final plans for our holiday adventure were finalized. I now had much shopping to attend to before my arrival in Hagerstown on Christmas Day. My, oh my, where to begin, and what gifts to purchase?

The day of our departure for the holidays arrived. The weather had turned cold and overcast, with the threat of an early winter storm approaching. Perhaps this year we would have a white Christmas. Undoubtedly, the children would have been praying and hoping for such an event.

Sarah, Eliza Mary, and I were taken by Mister Godey in his carriage to the train depot. We shared farewells, as we prepared for departure to our respective destinations. Mister Godey waited with us until we were safely aboard the train and on our way.

Sarah's and Eliza Mary's train departed first, as we shared a tearful goodbye.

"Now Elizabeth, promise me that you will take good care of yourself and do not let the children wear you down as they most always do, especially that precocious little daughter of theirs, Caroline."

With a laugh, "Now Sarah, you know that the child absolutely adores me. I would not be at all surprised if she grows up to be just like me, in every way, with the exception that she will undoubtedly have her mother's beauty and charm."

"Don't put yourself down. You know that you have stolen many a man's heart by your own charm and beauty. It would do Caroline well to acquire some of yours, as well."

"So I have been told. But only one has ever truly stolen my heart."

As I spoke, a moment of melancholy came upon me. I, however, immediately went on.

"Oh, well, let us not start down that path any more. Have a good trip, dear Sarah. Good bye, my dear friend", I spoke to Eliza Mary.

I gave both Sarah and Eliza an embrace and the usual kiss upon the cheek as we bid farewell.

"Oh, I almost forgot. Here is a small token of my love for you, Eliza, and one for you, dear Sarah. I love you both and shall always be in your debt for the kindness you have shown toward me."

I handed each of my friends a small package wrapped in fine gold colored paper with a magnificent bow wrapped around.

Both Sarah and Eliza profusely thanked me, stating that they thought we had agreed on not purchasing gifts for each other this year. I simply laughed and bid them to hurry, lest they miss their train.

I stood on the platform alongside Mister Godey as the train began to pull away from the station toward Boston. Tears filled my eyes as I watched them go, thinking how wonderfully blessed I was to have them, and many others, to count as my friends.

Louis Godey accompanied me back into the terminal to wait for my departure time.

"Mister Godey, it is good of you to wait with me, but I still have a little more than an hour before my train departs for Baltimore. You do not have to wait here, for I know you are most busy and have much to do."

"Nonsense, my dear, I promised Sarah I would not leave you alone in this miserable place, until you were safely on the train. And besides, the publications are all out and I, too, am making merry the next few days."

"My dear Sir, if you insist on staying with me, you must allow me to purchase a cup of tea and a biscuit for each of us."

I took Louis Godey's arm and we went into the depot restaurant. Once seated, we enjoyed a cup of tea and a lovely dessert from the chef's daily selection. We talked for the passing hour of hopes and dreams. He told of his desire to expand the Lady's Book to include more fashion, along with patterns that any woman would be able to use to produce fine clothing.

I spoke of my desire to begin reporting regularly again, as I had for many years with Mister Jones in Chambersburg. I thought back on those years with great fondness.

"That is all well and good, Elizabeth, but, as I recall, the last few years with the Chambersburg Democratic Tribune you worked as much as an editor as you did a reporter."

"Yes, I did, and must confess that I found that part of my work, well, laborious at times."

"Sarah tells me that you were very good at your position of editor, and that you were especially gifted at writing editorials. I have some of your work from those days and I must agree with her assessment. You do have a wonderful way with words."

Mister Godey was often complimenting me on my writing style and literary abilities. Louis, on more than one occasion, requested that I come to work for him. I had, of recent days, given some thought to the prospect, but was not ready to be confined to the desk of an editor in a small office. I enjoyed my freedom to travel and investigate stories more, and was not ready to surrender that part of my life, not yet, at least.

By the time we had finished our tea and dessert along with our conversation, it was time for me to board the train to Baltimore and then on to Washington City. I assured Louis that I had to wait only a little over two hours in Baltimore before traveling on, and that James would meet me upon my arrival in Washington.

As soon as I arrived at my destination, I would wire Sarah in Boston, and she, me, that we had both arrived safely. Mister Godey made me promise that I would include him in that agreement.

I stated that I would wire him as soon as I had received word from Sarah. With that, Louis Godey handed me an envelope with one hundred dollars in it.

"I promised Sarah I would give this to you if you would telegraph me of the safe arrival of both parties as soon as possible. This should cover any expense you may have in the assignment."

I chuckled lovingly at his need to care for both Sarah and me, and assured him that I would not need the money, as I was well enough off on my own. Nevertheless, he insisted I take the envelope and use the money for the children, if nothing else. I thanked him, boarded my train and waved goodbye as he stood on the platform, watching the train pull from the station.

By the time my train pulled into Baltimore, a light snow had begun to fall. The streets were fresh with the white frozen moisture, and the air had that fresh smell that comes only with the first snowfall of the season.

I went by carriage the ten blocks from the Baltimore Street Station to the Saint Charles Street Terminal, where I would board the late afternoon train to Washington City. I had debated walking the distance as I still had over two hours before my next train but decided against it, due to the falling snow. My luggage was already being cared for by the porters, and would be waiting for me upon my arrival in Washington.

I sat alone in the dining room of the train station, finishing a light meal, when the station master began calling my train.

"All aboard the Washington Flyer, all aboard. Departing for Washington City in fifteen minutes, all aboard", the tall, handsomely groomed station master boomed above the noise of the crowded station.

I paid for my meal and thanked the young black waiter for his kindness and service with a generous tip. He tipped his hat with a slight bow and held my chair for me, as I stood to leave for the platform.

As I walked to my train, I spotted a friend whom Sarah had introduced me to only a few months prior. Sara Jane Lippincott had submitted a children's story to Sarah for consideration in the Lady's Book. At the age of twenty-three, Sara was already regarded as one of the foremost women authors of the day, with her beautiful and challenging poetry and winsome children's stories.

"Sara, is it really you? How absolutely marvelous to run into you here."

I took her into my arms and gave her a loving embrace. Although we had not known each other long, we both felt an immediate friendship on our first meeting. She had written to me in London, congratulating me on my wonderful assignment. We had corresponded frequently and enjoyed the lively letters that we exchanged.

"Miss Fitzgerald, Elizabeth, what on earth are you doing in Baltimore? I had no idea you were coming this way. The last letter I had from Missus Hale, she shared that you were spending some time at her home, recovering from your journey to Europe for the Temperance Convention. She let on that you had not been well. I was so afraid for you that I was not even able to write to you these last few weeks."

"Well, my dear, as you can see, I am fully recovered. I am on my way to Washington City for a couple of days and then to Hagerstown, to the home of my good friends for Christmas. What brings you here, Sara?"

"I, too, am on my way to Washington City, to join with Father and Mother for holidays. How fun this part of the journey shall be. May I travel with you?"

I instantly agreed that the journey would be more pleasant, having familiar company for the last few hours of the laborious and boring train ride. We boarded the Washington Flyer for the City, and settled in for the remaining three hours of the trip.

Sara Lippincott was full of questions regarding the trip to London. She asked every imaginable question about the Atlantic crossing, the fashions of the day, the Convention, any interesting, eligible men I may have met, and of course about Mister Frederick Douglass.

"I have heard that he enjoys the ladies of the Irish and English society, and they him", she offered.

"I am afraid that that particular claim is overly exaggerated", I responded. "Mister Douglass at all times acted in a most gentlemanly way and never once, to my knowledge, made any impropriety that would discount his devotion to his wife and children. I do think, however, he is a lonely man without them."

Sara went on to ask about the dear Mister Abercrombie. She had heard that he had been most helpful to me during my stay, and that he had lost his life the day of our departure, while on assignment.

I shared how Mister Abercrombie and I had become dear friends in a very short period, and that, indeed, he had been most comforting and helpful. I then changed the subject to lighter conversation, refusing to be taken in by youthful, romantic inquiry.

The time passed quickly, and we arrived in Washington City. The snow had subsided, leaving only a trace of the white glitter on the grass and roof tops of the Washington landscape.

As we entered into the Washington Depot's main lobby, Sara's father was waiting for her as she ran to his arms. James was near by, and he immediately came and greeted me. Sara came to us with her father and introduced the handsome gentleman, not much older than me.

Mister Lippincott thanked me for traveling with his daughter and invited both James and me to his home for dinner. We thanked him, but made our apologies as we had other plans, not yet decided, for our few days in Washington.

Saying our goodbyes to the Lippincotts, James handed me a telegram from Sarah Hale.

"Arrived in Boston shortly after noon (STOP) Uneventful (STOP) Good to be home (STOP) Sarah (END)"

I smiled at the note and its brevity. It was so like Sarah to get right to the point.

"I must stop before we leave the station and return this message", I explained.

James escorted me to the telegraph office located in the station. I sent the following message to Sarah.

"In WC (STOP) Good Trip (STOP) Love, E (END)"

The word count was just six and the cost was less than a dollar. I, too, could be brief.

I then wired Louis Godey to inform him that Sarah, Eliza Mary, and I, were all safe at our destinations, and wished him a most blessed and merry Christmas.

CHAPTER TWENTY NINE

James and I arrived on the afternoon train in Hagerstown, that Christmas day of 1846. We were in time for the splendid dinner that Constance and Greta had prepared. Greta was their new housekeeper, who had recently emigrated from Sweden and spoke only broken English.

"Elizabeth, what joy it brings to all of us at your being here. It would not have been Christmas at all, had you been unable to join us."

Constance was making every attempt to welcome me once again, and to make me feel as comfortable as I had in the past.

"Thank you, Constance. I have been so looking forward to being here."

Caroline, followed by the boys, came running through the house. "Auntie Liz!" shouted the children, as they raced into my arms, nearly knocking me over with their excitement.

"Auntie Liz, I thought you might never come to see us again. I was almost sick to my death over fear."

Caroline at times could be as melodramatic as any seven year old was prone to be.

"And you did not even write me for my birthday. How could you?"

Caroline always melted my heart when she would speak this way and look at me with her large, green eyes and pouting lip.

"Now, Caroline, you know that I could never forget you and your brothers. And I did not forget your birthday. I have brought a gift with me, along with Christmas presents for all."

Caroline immediately recovered and wrapped me securely in her arms.

"I shall never let you go away again for so long."

It felt good to be here.

Isaac and James, assisted by the boys, carried my trunk and packages into the house and placed them in the room I always occupied when spending time with the Stoltzfus family. Greta took my wrap and hung it in the hall closet, along with my muff and hat.

"Elizabeth, do come and join me in the parlor, so we may talk of your past few weeks in Philadelphia."

Constance led the way, and we took our seats across from each other in the warmth of the glowing fire.

"Tell me, how you are feeling these days? And be honest with me. I can always tell when you are holding something back, so do not try and hide anything from me. Let us be direct with each other, as we usually are."

I knew better than to attempt to deceive Constance. She had been able to read me from our very first meeting, and I her.

"Honestly, Constance, please do not go on so. I really am fine and ready to move on to more adventures. I am just not certain at this point what I plan to do next."

We spent the next hour catching up on all the news. I shared how Mister Pryor from the Inquirer had discovered the circumstances surrounding Alastair's death and made the offer for me to return to London to cover the trial at the appropriate time.

"Do you think you will go?" Constance asked.

"No, I do not wish to go back. I have put that part of my life into the pages of history and do not wish to return to them."

I sensed the relief that Constance almost immediately felt at my decision not to return to England. She and Isaac had heard of the possibility through Sarah Hale, and both were extremely concerned for my well-being, should I make the journey.

Greta came into the room to announce that dinner was ready to be served.

"Ve have de food on de table, if please you it does" she spoke with her lilting Scandinavian accent.

Isaac and James had kept the children entertained in the library, allowing Constance and me a few moments of uninterrupted conversation.

"Thank you, Greta", Constance spoke. "I will inform the Reverend and the children, and we will join you in the dining room momentarily."

Greta curtsied and returned to the kitchen.

"Constance, how did Greta come to be with you and Isaac? She looks as if she is not more than the age of Amos."

"Actually Liz, she is only sixteen. She came to America to be with an Uncle and Aunt in Minnesota, arriving in New York late in September. She had stayed with friends, waiting for passage to her family, when word came that they would not be able to support her at this time and she would have to return to Sweden."

Constance went on to explain that Greta had no money for the return, and that she was about to become homeless when she went to see the Lutheran minister in New York City's Bronx area. The minister had been a friend of James in Seminary, and thought of Isaac and James as possible helpers in finding her work elsewhere.

"And, of course, you know Isaac", Constance went on.

"Our old housekeeper, you remember Missus O'Connell, retired and moved to Harrisburg to be with her family. We were in need of a new housekeeper, so Isaac wrote and sent money for Greta to come to us."

Greta had arrived in early November and immediately assumed the chores assigned to her. Isaac had promised her that she would be well treated, and if she wished, would be as one of the family in no time.

"Liz, she is just wonderful with the children. She is practically a child herself, and I do feel sorry for her. She is so far from home and not very good with the language yet. She is a fast learner, though, and I am sure will be quite capable in mastering the English language in short order."

We sat down to the table prepared with wonderful delights. The traditional Turkey with all the trimmings was present. Greta had dressed in her native attire. She looked absolutely charming in her traditional Scandinavian costume.

In addition to the usual Christmas meal, Greta had prepared a grand dessert called a Krumkake, filled with strawberry jam and whipped cream. There also were Kringla, a cookie-like treat made with finely crushed almonds.

"Greta, you are indeed a wonderful cook and talented young woman. Where did you learn to make such wonderful desserts?" I inquired of her.

"Tusen takk, Miss Elizabeth. That mean 'tank you'. My Mamma teach me to cook, but I not so good as her."

"Well, your Mother must be a marvelous chef, if she has taught you so well", I replied to the shy young girl from Stockholm.

Greta was invited to join the family at the table, to enjoy the meal. Constance and I, along with help from the men, assisted Greta in serving the fine courses of Christmas dinner. After the meal was finished, we all pitched in to clear the table and clean the kitchen. Constance had promised the children that, as soon as all the mess from dinner had been cleaned and everything put back into its proper place, we would exchange the presents that Uncle James and Auntie Liz had brought with them.

The thought of more presents and gift exchange was all that was needed to solicit the assistance of the children in the task at hand. Amos briefly objected, stating he was now too old to be doing women's work, until his father and James reminded him that if they were to help in the work, then he was to assist as well, or be left out of the present exchange which would commence shortly.

In short order, the table was cleared, with the exception of some dessert items, and the kitchen was returned to its orderly state, in preparation for the next day's breakfast. Constance commanded the entire family to the front parlor, for the purpose of exchanging presents.

CHAPTER THIRTY

Christmas evening had been filled with the laughter and joy of the children, as they opened their gifts and danced around with their new found toys. Caroline had displayed her new dresses and the coat that I had given her, made in London during our trip.

Alastair had introduced me to a well known seamstress who had designed clothing for the royal family and many in the British Parliament. I commissioned her to make Caroline a winter's coat of fine wool and velvet. She had designed a most stunning garment, with a matching muff to keep her hands warm. In addition, I had discovered, on one of our walks through London, a magnificent bonnet for her head that would go nicely with her new coat.

Amos, Abraham, and Andrew were also equally excited with their new suits that included long trousers. The two older boys insisted that their youngest brother was still too young for long pants and would have to wait at least another year. Andrew's mother, as she most often did, came to the rescue of her youngest son, and said that he could indeed wear the long pants, but only on special occasions, as these were very expensive clothes that I had bought for them all.

There was the usual protest, but, in the end, the children relented and seemed happy to have received such fine gifts.

"But what did you bring for Mother and Father, as well as Uncle James, Auntie Liz? You never forget them."

Caroline was always concerned that no one should be left out. She would also, before long, remind me of both her birthday present, and that I should have something for Greta.

For Isaac, I had purchased a new preaching collar with white tails, like those worn in London. Although more formal than he was accustomed to in his present parish, he was appreciative and assured me that he would wear it at the next service.

James received a devotional book written by John Wesley toward the end of his life. I had found this particular copy at a wonderful book store on a side street in London that catered to works by famous people. It had cost a tidy sum, but I knew that James would treasure it as much as he treasured life.

Constance had received her gift some days earlier. I had commissioned the same dress maker who had created the dress for

Sarah Hale to also make one for Constance. It had arrived before Christmas, as I had hoped, but she had not yet shared it with anyone in the family.

"Mamma, do show us the new dress Auntie Liz got for you", Caroline begged.

Constance went to her room and shortly came down in the most stunning dress, made of rich wools and velvets. The dress was made for both day wear and traveling, with an over jacket design. The main body of the fabric was a deep forest green and black plaid, and the velvet trims were the darkest green I had ever seen. The front closure on both the jacket and dress were finished with bright gold buttons that made the dress seem to glow with a life of its own.

As Constance descended the stairs, I watched as Isaac stood and admired his wife, looking as if he were seeing her for the first time.

"My Darling", he finally spoke. "You look absolutely radiant. Elizabeth, how can I ever thank you for your generosity and love for all of us?"

Isaac always appreciated any kindness shown to his family by others. But he always felt a special bond between us and knew deep in his heart that I would always be there to care for them, should something ever happen to him.

I had, on this occasion, brought along an extra gift or two, in case there might be special need for them. Such was the case in this event. Greta was not to be left out of the gift giving occasion.

The family had already showered her with many fine items that she could make good use of. Constance had taken her to be fitted with several new outfits, as her clothing was severely limited from her passage from Stockholm to New York.

I presented Greta with a small, festively decorated package. Hidden away in the wrappings of the paper and ribbons were two books.

The first was a collection of poems by Ralph Waldo Emerson, which had been recently published. The second was a small leather-bound journal.

"Greta, I do hope that you will enjoy Emerson's works and be able to take time to journal your memories of the great adventure you are on."

The young Swede thanked me many times over, and cried as she shared how kind everyone had been to her. She promised to write of her adventures and would try, if possible, to do so in English, rather than Swedish.

At last, Caroline insisted that I had forgotten one more important gift. I played along and mused that I had no idea what she was talking of. "Auntie Liz", she said as she stomped her right foot as she often did when making a severe point. With her hands on her hips, she went on, "My BIRTHDAY!"

"Oh, yes, of course, my darling. How could I forget such a momentous moment in history? Let me see, you are now six years old."

"No, Auntie Liz, I'm seven."

"Oh yes, you are quite right. " I countered. "Here is your birthday present, my precious one. I do hope that you will enjoy it so."

Caroline tore open the gift, which had been neatly wrapped in a large box. As the top came off the package, she stared with her mouth and eyes wide open.

In almost a whisper, she said "Auntie Liz, it is the most beautiful thing I have ever seen. May I play with it at once?"

I agreed, and Isaac helped his daughter take the gift from the box, and placed in on the center table for all to enjoy. Constance and the boys, along with Greta, expressed that they had never seen such a beautifully handcrafted music box. As the dancing figures went round and round, the music box chimed out its version of the "Sinngedichte" by Strauss.

Caroline would often say in later years that this had been one of her most treasured gifts, for it often reminded her of my free spirit and love for life.

CHAPTER THIRTY ONE

Shortly after the first of the New Year, I purchased a small house on Washington Street, a few blocks from Isaac and the family, and close to the center of town. It was good to set up housekeeping in my own home for the first time. I enjoyed the privacy this residence afforded me, although I would have frequent visits from both Caroline and her mother.

Constance had been able to locate Hetti, a former slave from Virginia. She was a caring and capable older woman in need of employment. We met and instantly formed a companionship that would continue for the next several years, as she came to be my housekeeper and friend.

At the same time, I took a position as a reporter with the Hagerstown Weekly Dispatch. This small, local paper, much like the one that Oliver Jones and his wife operated in Chambersburg those many years of our association, became my new home for the work I loved doing.

Over the course of the next year and a half, I would cover routine stories of court trials, political events, and even a few of the social events of the local community. The work was relaxing and enjoyable, with enough challenge to keep me happy for the moment. The other members of the reporters' pool welcomed me into their midst, and many of the shop personnel assisted me in every way possible.

Mister David Foote, the Managing Editor of the Dispatch, had quickly come to regard my work as professional and my abilities as exceptional. We also enjoyed the benefit of becoming friends. After a few weeks with the paper, Mister Foote invited me home to meet his wife, and to dine with them. I immediately accepted. I always enjoyed meeting new people, and especially the family members of those I worked with.

Foote's wife, Florence, was also a delight to know, and often would engage me in lively conversation. I would spend many hours with Florence, as we would shop and talk together. One of our favorite pastimes was to steal away from office and home once a month, along with Constance, who had been welcomed into this new circle, and travel to Baltimore for an overnight shopping and get-away adventure.

It was on one of these trips that Florence asked me what I knew about the Women's Suffrage Movement, and if I had heard of Elizabeth Cady Stanton.

I replied, "I am sorry, Florence, I am not at all well versed on the movement, and have not kept up with the proceedings."

Constance added, "I can hardly believe you would not be familiar with the Women's Movement, my dear Elizabeth. Why, your very life is a prime example of what women are beginning to fight for in their own existence. You live daily what most women only dream of."

I offered some protest to her comments, but Florence stopped me.

"She is absolutely correct, Elizabeth. You do not know how I wish I could have grown up and been as strong as you in my younger years. I was married to David at such an early age, by the agreement of my father in his business dealings almost forty years ago. I have not known anything but the duties of a wife. How I wish my life could have been more."

Florence had expressed her feelings with such longing. She had borne seven children in all for David. There were four boys and three daughters. Of the seven, only three had lived beyond the age of five, and now the surviving children were grown and off on their own adventures.

The Foote family's three remaining children consisted of two sons and a daughter. Henry, the oldest, now thirty-nine and married, living in Harpers Ferry, Virginia, had followed his father's footsteps and was the Managing Editor of the Jefferson County Weekly.

Their second living child, Ella, was thirty-five and living in a small rural town located in the rugged, western mountains of Virginia, called Mannington, along with her husband and five children. Her husband was the local postmaster and ran a small feed supply company.

The third surviving child was Jason. Now close to twenty years of age, he was still attempting to find himself and his way in life. At the age of twelve, he had run away from home to Baltimore and signed on to a small merchant vessel, *The Queen Victoria*, as the Captain's cabin boy. He had been at sea since, returning home on only one occasion two years earlier, for a brief visit with his mother.

As our conversation continued on the subject of the rights of women, I promised I would research the issues and determine if there was anything I could do in telling the story. Both women assured me that there would be plenty to write about, and Florence committed to speaking to her husband about the issue as well.

"I shall inform David that he is to give you a free hand and all liberty in pursuing this investigation."

Florence went on, "You shall have whatever you need, my dear, from both him and me on this matter."

With the insistence of Florence and Constance, I knew that I had no choice. Women's issues such as these had always been the work in which Sarah Hale, not I, had found interest.

As for discrimination as a woman, I had not found that to be particularly true in my case. There had been the isolated incident from time to time, but I had always managed to overcome the obstacle or objection, often with the help of a gentleman. By using to some degree my feminine ways, I had always been able to achieve my desire in obtaining whatever story I had been pursuing The majority of both the men and women I had met over the years had accepted me as I was, and had allowed me into their inner circles.

I had been pursued by men in the past, who attempted to confine me to some extent to the domestic role. In the end, however, I had been able to avoid this departure from my true calling as a reporter.

As we returned home to Hagerstown from this early spring adventure to Baltimore, Constance and Florence continued to talk with great excitement of the emerging Women's Suffrage Movement. They shared their thoughts with me as to what it might mean, not only for the advancement of women, but to the end of slavery in America.

By the time we reached home, I was beginning to become excited on the possibility before me. As I entered the front door of my home, Hetti immediately greeted me.

"Good afternoon, Miss Elizabeth. Did you have a nice trip?" she inquired as she always did upon my return after a few days absence.

"Yes, Hetti, I did. Miss Constance and Miss Florence held me in lively discussion about the emerging Women's Movement. Have you heard of it?"

"Yes Ma'am, I heard of it. It do good for a woman, both white and black, to have better say of their property."

By "property", I knew that Hetti meant her very life. I was beginning to see that this was to be an important issue in the days ahead.

Hetti had prepared a light meal for us upon my arrival home, and we sat together at the dining table to discuss the Movement in greater detail. I was somewhat embarrassed that my housekeeper appeared to know more on this subject than I, or for that matter, Florence and Constance.

CHAPTER THIRTY TWO

In early June of 1848, David Foote came to my desk and asked if I had a few moments to talk about a possible story. I directly went in with him to his office.

David began, "Elizabeth, I have an invitation from an editor friend of mine in Seneca Falls, New York, to send one of my reporters to cover a small convention to take place there."

I could see by the look on his face that he was not particularly excited by this request, and that he was not sure if he wanted to send anyone in response.

David continued, "The invitation is to cover the first gathering of the Seneca Falls Women's Convention. I hesitate to ask you to take on another assignment, but my wife has insisted that I must send someone, and she has informed me that it must be you."

I started to laugh at this request, knowing how on our last two trips to Baltimore, both Florence and Constance had continued to remind me that I promised to research this movement further. As of yet, I had not produced one article in the paper regarding the issues.

"I am sorry, David, I don't mean to laugh. I just know how persistent Florence has been on this issue. When is the Convention?"

"The Convention is set for July nineteen and twenty. I also understand that an old friend of yours will be there, Mister Frederick Douglass."

My interest, if not so much in the Women's Movement, suddenly increased with the possibility of seeing Mister Douglass once again.

"I understand that you met him in London and became good friends", David continued.

"Yes, we did meet and became acquainted. I so enjoyed the time I was able to spend with this remarkable and intelligent man. I would love to see him once again. I had heard some time ago from James Stoltzfus that Mister Douglass had returned to the States and was now publishing a paper called 'The North Star'."

Mister Foote confirmed that James had been correct, and plans were made as to my new assignment. I would leave for Seneca Falls on the morning of the seventeenth of July and return around the twenty-third. David assured me that all expenses would be cared for and that he would wire his friend in Seneca Falls to make arrangements for my stay.

On the morning of the seventeenth, Mister Foote sent his carriage to my home to collect me and my baggage for the journey to New York. Florence had convinced her husband to allow her to join me on this adventure, and Constance, likewise, had convinced Isaac. Caroline would complete our entourage, as Constance felt that her daughter should be exposed to every advantage at the earliest possible moment in time. Caroline was now eight, and was growing more like her mother every day.

As we boarded the train for Baltimore, Caroline asked if she could sit by me, so I could explain all that we were going to see. Without hesitation, I agreed to the request, and we talked almost without taking a breath, for the three hours it took to arrive in Baltimore.

We then boarded a train that would take us first to Philadelphia, and then to New York City. We would spend the night in New York and complete the journey to Seneca Falls on the eighteenth.

We arrived in Seneca Falls, New York, to be greeted by Miss Elizabeth Register, a delegate from Buffalo, New York, to the Convention.

"Miss Fitzgerald, it is indeed wonderful to have you and your friends join us at the Convention. I can not tell you how excited we all are at hearing you would be in attendance. Mister Douglass has already informed us that you are indeed a most incredible and accomplished woman, breaking down many barriers that are held in defiance to us."

"Please Miss Register, I am here only as a reporter, to cover the events of the Convention for my paper."

She went on, "Oh, no, Miss Fitzgerald. You represent so much more to many of us who have followed with great interest your career and writings over the past several years. I personally just became acquainted with your work last year, but some, like Missus Stanton, have known of you for at least the last five years and had hoped in the past few months that you would become involved in our cause."

I was flattered to have some recognition coming into this convention. Miss Register had the porter and Coach Driver care for our bags and transport us to the Grand Hotel in downtown

Seneca Falls, only two blocks away from the Convention Center, for our stay. The four of us would share a two-room suite for the next few nights, allowing us adequate space to be comfortable with each other's presence.

As we traveled the few blocks to our hotel, I asked Miss Register, "How is it that some have already heard of me and my work so far north of Pennsylvania, where I have done most of my reporting for so many years?"

"Oh, Miss Fitzgerald, it was Sarah Hale from Godey's Lady's Book who has told some of the women your remarkable story. I have not met Missus Hale, but I do want to some day."

Elizabeth Register carried on in the fashion of most seventeen year old women who hold fantasies of life in their hearts. As I looked upon this young woman, I thought of my own fanciful youth, full of dreams, hope, and wonder. I thought back on those early days with Oliver Jones and Prudence, or Mamma Jones, as I called her, and how they had encouraged me, along with my father and many others, to pursue my own dreams and desires.

"Well, my dear Miss Register, I do pray that you will have all your dreams some day fulfilled, as I have had mine", I offered with a most sincere heart.

CHAPTER THIRTY THREE

The Morning of the Seneca Falls Women's convention arrived, and the Convention floor was seated with the roll call of delegates. Over three hundred women and men had gathered for this historic event, organized and promoted by Elizabeth Cady Stanton and Lucretia Mott. Among the more notable men in attendance were Frederick Douglass and William Garrison.

The members of the press were then called upon to be introduced. Papers from the region were in attendance, as was Mister Douglass from "The North Star". Few papers beyond the region, and no paper from the larger metropolitan areas had accepted the invitation to cover the story, expressing, instead, their displeasure with the course Missus Stanton and Mott were taking in their editorials.

As I was introduced as the only female reporter in attendance, the convention broke into thunderous applause. Missus Stanton immediately invited me to the platform for a more formal introduction, asking me to speak a few words to the gathering of delegates.

I expressed my appreciation to her and the other members of the Convention, and then spoke briefly.

"Ladies and Gentlemen, delegates to this great Convention, I come to you today, not as an Abolitionist, nor as one in the Temperance Convention, neither as a suffragist in your great cause for the rights of women everywhere, but as a reporter.

"I am deeply honored to have been invited, through my editor, to be in attendance here. In order to do my best to fairly report on your convention, and not to be seen as favoring one cause, one Convention, or one side, over another, I must refrain for participating in a fashion or giving any acknowledgement that I concur with your position."

At this, there were loud murmurings of dissatisfaction. "No, let it not be so" were the shouts from the assembled crowd. Missus Stanton immediately came to my side and thanked me for being present, assuring the Convention that I would be fair and accurate in my reporting.

She went on, "Delegates, we must, and do, confer agreement with Miss Fitzgerald's position as a reporter first. It is only in doing this thing that we shall all be free one day. Free from oppression in a white, male dominated society.

"For as we have seen in the power of the press, any advance in liberties and freedoms can come only if the press is able to, in itself, be free of the tyranny that befalls the powerless."

Elizabeth Cady Stanton then turned to me and said, "My dear, please report on our work here as favorably as you can, and with the same integrity that we have accustomed ourselves to expect from you."

At this point, the Convention continued, with many speaking on the difficulties women face in achieving fairness in all matters of concern. Issues such as education, health care, manners of dress, and, of course, the matters of the heart were presented.

Many called for reform among the courts regarding the right of divorce, and of property ownership when married. Several of the delegates felt that white women were no freer than the black man or woman, and called for an end to the slavery of the white woman in the bonds of her master in the home, be it her husband, father, or brother.

Many argued for the right of women to vote and hold political office. Others simply wanted the right to be their own person, aside from their husband and not subject to the husbands' abuse without recourse.

As the Convention came to a close on the next day, most of the delegates had the feeling that a strong, new movement, equal in importance to the Temperance and Abolitionist movements, had taken root. Elizabeth Cady Stanton and Lucretia Mott presented to the delegates a report entitled, "The Declaration of Rights and Sentiments".

The document closely resembled that of the United States Declaration of Independence. Constructed by Elizabeth Stanton, the Declaration went on to spell out fifteen violations of rights perpetrated upon persons of the female gender.

By the close of the Convention, only one hundred, sixty eight women and thirty two men had signed the document. The other two thirds in attendance expressed sentiments that the wording was too divisive and would harm the cause of women more than assist them. Stanton and Mott held firm, however, in their determination.

Frederick Douglass had supported the document and many of the resolutions put forth. With his voice, he was able to assist

Stanton and Mott in achieving some success in this first gathering for women's rights. Douglass wrote in the North Star that the document was the "grand basis for attaining the civil, social, political, and religious rights of women."

Following the close of the Convention, Mister Douglass and I had the opportunity to share a late evening meal together. He shared that relations with Mister Garrison had recently become strained, and that William was exhibiting some jealousy that Mister Douglass had formed his own paper in competition to Garrison's publication.

I expressed my sorrow for the rift between the two men, and promised to assist in the repair of the relationship if I could be of any service in the matter. Mister Douglass assured me that he would solicit my help if it was needed, and that in the meantime I should enjoy my work and continued success. We parted with kind words for each other. I would not see Frederick Douglass again until midway through the War Between the States.

The next day I returned home to Hagerstown with my traveling companions. Florence made me promise that I would insist that the entire Declaration be published in the Dispatch. She assured me that her husband would agree. She also made me promise to write a most favorable review of the events and share my impressions, not just the facts of the story.

"You know, Florence, that I always report the story on its own merits, without commentary", I reminded her.

"Yes, but I also know that you have in the past written many editorials as well, and in them you do express your opinion. I believe it is time for you to write an editorial on the Women's Movement for the Dispatch."

I had a difficult time trying to convince the editor's wife that it was the editor, not the reporter, who wrote editorials. I was not sure I really wanted to enter into this debate with her or her husband. I had enjoyed my achievement and success as an unmarried woman.

I was not about to enter into a marital disagreement on any issue, regardless who might try to draw me in. I had learned to stay clear of these lively discussions that often are a part of marital bliss, while living with Mister and Missus Jones. Now was not the time to take a different approach.

Shortly after our return home, I filed my story, with the complete copy of the Seneca Falls Declaration. The article was received with much appreciation by the readers for having covered the event, and for sending a woman to do so.

Mister Foote did ask me if I would be interested in writing an editorial piece for the paper and I suggested that he would probably do a better job of pleasing his wife if he were to write the piece himself. He agreed and took on the project.

In later years, General Thomas Francis Meagher of the Union Irish Brigade of Civil War fame, would say, "If the women ever get the vote, it's because they are the ones who tell their politician husbands where they can really sleep at home, if the men refuse to obey these feminine creatures. As everyone knows, it is really the women who are the boss."

CHAPTER THIRTY FOUR

Over the course of the next two years, the women's rights movement would gain significant momentum and advancement. Many significant members of the male society joined the early advocates for women's rights, thus lending even more credibility and authority to the cause. Such men included William Lloyd Garrison, Reverend William Henry Channing, Stephen Symonds Foster, Samuel Blackwell, and Wendell Phillips, along with Frederick Douglass, who had persuaded the Seneca Falls Convention to adopt suffrage as part of the process for women's rights.

Among the many members of the female gender were Lucy Stone, Harriot Kezia Hunt, Ernestine Rose, Antoinette Brown, Sojourner Truth, Abby Kelly Foster, Abby Price, Elizabeth Cady Stanton and Lucretia Mott. These strong and independent women formed the nucleus of the advancement for women's rights, and through their efforts, such conventions would regularly occur.

The First National Women's Rights Convention was held in Worchester, Massachusetts, on August twenty-third, 1850. Unlike the previous convention two years earlier, many members of the press from New York, Philadelphia, and other large metropolitan communities attended. Horace Greely was one such editor. As Lucy Stone spoke to the Convention, Greely was so moved by her manner of speech that he wrote a favorable account of the Convention in the New York Tribune.

The crowd reportedly exceeded a thousand attendees, with one delegate coming from California. Many additional delegates had been unable to enter the Convention Hall, due to lack of space and the overflow attendance.

The Convention, by every standard, had been a success. It was later reported that Susan B. Anthony had been so moved by Greely's article that she decided to join the women's movement.

Two years later, following the success of Lucy Stone and the others with subsequent Conventions, I had the opportunity to meet Stone, along with Antoinette Brown, her close friend from Oberlin College. Both Miss Stone and Miss Brown were dressed in attire I had briefly read about through Sarah Hale, from an article that had been submitted to her for publication in the Lady's Book.

Miss Amelia Bloomer had submitted an article, along with drawings, of a new outfit to be worn by women. It gave them modest covering as well as freedom of movement from the traditional clothing women were forced to endure by societal norms. The dress called for freedom from the whale bone corset of the day and the long, encumbering length of the dress.

It also freed the wearer from the necessity of starched petticoats to create the fullness for the dress. The attire thus had a shorter skirt, under which a pair of bloomers, or breeches, was worn. The bodice of Amelia Bloomer's dress gave the wearer more fullness across the shoulders and freedom of movement for the arms.

"Miss Stone and Miss Brown, how delighted I am to meet you at last. I have heard so much about you from my friend, Sarah Hale, at Godey's Lady's Book, and of course from the wonderful correspondence I regularly enjoy with Missus Stanton and Missus Mott.", I began at once.

Both Stone and Brown seamed delighted to meet me as well, sharing that Elizabeth Cady Stanton and Lucretia Mott had both spoken favorably of my work and of our first meeting four years earlier.

"Miss Fitzgerald", Stone began. "We do so wish to thank you for taking time to travel and meet us on such short notice."

Lucretia Mott had contacted me, asking if I would meet these two ladies in Baltimore during a speaking engagement they would be attending. I had responded that I would be most delighted to meet with them, and so plans had been made.

As we sat in the lobby of the Baltimore Hotel on Charles Street, the ladies began to share their stories with me. Lucy Stone told how she had come to this place of fighting for the rights of women. Antoinette Brown talked about her desire to be ordained and serve the ministry of Jesus Christ, but that she had been denied because she was a woman.

As I listened to them, I could feel their frustration at the restrictions that these women, like most women of the day, often experienced. I had been fortunate in many ways because I had never married. Single women, although they faced some ridicule and often were referred to as "spinsters", managed to enjoyed greater freedom and liberties, along with fewer restrictions, than married women experienced.

Lucy Stone pointed out that, once a woman marries, she loses what rights and privileges she has to her husband, and becomes nothing more than his additional property.

"This is one of the reasons, as of this date, I have chosen not to marry", Miss Brown went on.

"I can understand much of what you say, although I myself have not experienced as much discrimination as a female as many of my acquaintances and friends have. I believe it is because those who would offer such conduct would find a rather unpleasant article published in the paper regarding their performance", I stated in a light hearted manner.

We went on discussing many additional issues and the fight for equality and freedom of all peoples, white and black, male and female.

"I would like to ask about your manner of dress and hair style, Miss Stone. I see you and Miss Brown are both wearing Amelia Bloomer's new outfit.

"Miss Stone, I have also noticed your hair is cut to a short length and that you wear it down around your neck. How is it you have come to dress this way?" I inquired.

Both Stone and Brown elaborated on their manner of dress. Lucy Stone assured me that if I was to wear this new apparel, I would discover how much freer my movements would be, and my increased ability to engage in my work.

I confessed that I was looking forward to the age when I would no longer be required to adorn the corset, but expressed that I was not certain I was independent enough in my thinking to attempt to change my attire entirely.

Miss Stone also explained that she decided that wearing her hair shortened and down was not any less attractive or feminine.

"I truly believe, Miss Fitzgerald, that the consignments of society upon the manner of hair and dress placed upon me, and all women, is constructed sorely for the purpose of the enlivened male fantasy of the ideal woman.

"Do men conform to our ideas of manliness? They most certainly do not, so why should we continue to indulge their whimsical fantasies?"

I understood the position that both women had taken and, in my thoughts, admired both for their courage and open defiance to the constructs of society. I promised that I would give the matter of dress some consideration.

I went on, "Now for the purpose of my meeting you at your request, is there some reason you have desired this meeting, other than becoming acquainted?"

"Yes, we have a great request that Missus Stanton has assured us you would consider. We wish to invite you to cover our activities and to report regularly in "The Liberator". Are you familiar with the publication?" Brown asked.

"Yes, I am. I have been privileged to read several issues of the paper. Mister Garrison has done a fine job over the years of putting together a most informative and accomplished publication."

I was friends with Mister Garrison, although not close. He had never before invited me to write for him, although he had, on more than one occasion, admitted to being an admirer of my work.

"Does Mister Garrison know of your desire to have me contribute to his paper?"

Miss Stone continued, "Yes. He has endorsed our request with great enthusiasm. He is willing to offer you a regular commission for your work as a full-time reporter, or if you wish, to pay you a fair sum for each submitted article."

"I am flattered for this consideration and will have to give it some thought. Is there a deadline by which you must have my answer?"

We continued to discuss the possibilities for some time, with much excitement on the part of these two women as to my participation in their cause through my reporting skills. I was assured that I would have full autonomy as to how I would report their activities.

The next day I returned to Hagerstown, after bidding my new friends a fond farewell. Upon my return to the office, I met with my editor, David Foote, and Florence, his wife, to share my interview with Stone and Brown.

Before mentioning any possibility of a new assignment, however, with the Footes, I would take time to discuss the offer with Isaac and Constance. Isaac would respond with his usual, "Before we begin discussing the matter, Elizabeth, let us pray." I was sure that their counsel would be good, as it had always been in the past.

CHAPTER THIRTY FIVE

Constance and Isaac agreed that to write for the Liberator and Mister Garrison would be a wonderful opportunity to cover many areas of social interest, including the Temperance Movement, Women's Rights, and the Abolitionist stand.

Constance went on to say, "Up to this point, Elizabeth, your career has focused on a wide range of subjects, but mostly you have covered only the local and regional news worthy events. This would give you an opportunity to cover significantly larger events on a national scale."

I had thought of that as one of the real benefits of this assignment. I knew Mister Garrison well enough that I was sure he would continue to give me the same liberties in reporting as I had enjoyed in my career to this point.

"You have already met some marvelous people and have been exposed to the national scene on a limited basis. Why not take this advantage and engage in furthering your career to the next level?" Isaac insisted.

As we discussed the matter well into the evening, it became more evident by the moment that I should pursue this opportunity and lose no time in making my decision.

"Very well", I submitted. "I will send a telegram to Mister Garrison first thing in the morning and begin to make the necessary agreement for my employment with his publication. As soon as the details are arranged, I shall inform Mister Foote and Florence of my decision.

"In the meantime, Constance, we must keep this to ourselves. I do not wish even the children to know that I will most likely leave the Hagerstown Weekly Dispatch."

The next day I sent a telegram to William Lloyd Garrison at "The Liberator", informing him that I was open to the possibility of reporting for him, and requesting that he send me the contracts for my review. I spoke with my editor, and asked for some time off to rest and recover from several projects I had been working on and recently completed. I did not wish to take on another assignment, should I decide I would leave the paper.

I purchased a copy of Harriett Beecher Stowe's book, "Uncle Tom's Cabin", and proceeded to read the newly published work. This would occupy my time for the next few days.

Two days after sending the telegram to Mister Garrison, a response was received and delivered to me at my home. The telegram read,

"Contract on the way (STOP) Excited to have you on board (STOP) Will make arrangements for your visit to Boston (STOP) Garrison (STOP).

Within the week, a package had arrived from Mister Garrison, with the necessary documents and contracts for employment. William Garrison had once again been generous with his offer and had assured me complete autonomy in my writing. He further stated that there was no need for me to relocate to Boston and that I could easily continue my work from my present home.

Garrison did request that I come to Boston and meet with him and his editors to finalize the agreements. He promised he would make all necessary arrangements for my transportation and housing needs. He also invited both Constance and Sarah Hale to join me.

That evening, I invited David Foote and his wife to dine with me at my home. Hetti prepared a wonderful Lamb's Stew for our dining pleasure. We gathered around the table and enjoyed lively conversation, the company of one another, and the delicious meal Hetti had provided.

The conversation centered primarily on my recent assignments and the quality of my reporting. Florence was full of questions concerning my visit with Lucy Stone and Antoinette Brown. She was particularly interested in the information regarding the new manner of dress proposed by Amelia Bloomer.

"I have heard of this dress and have thought how delightful it would be to have the attire for myself. David, however, is quite against the matter".

Florence shared her thoughts with an air that she was determined to have such an outfit, despite her husband's objections.

Florence also asked, "Elizabeth, David tells me you have taken a few days off to rest. I do hope that you are all right. I should have checked on you sooner, but David insisted that I needed to leave you alone for a few days."

"I am quite fine, Florence", I responded to her question.

"But there is a matter that I wish to discuss with both of you. That is why I have invited you here tonight, and also the reason for my being absent for a few days from the office."

I went on to share how, upon meeting Stone and Brown, they had invited me to write for William Garrison. I then explained that I had been in contact with Garrison and that he had indeed offered me a position with the Liberator.

Mister Foote immediately countered, "But you must not leave the Dispatch, my Dear. You have built a wonderful following here, and you are one of the most gifted reporters I have. What, may I ask, shall I do to keep you at your present position?"

"Now, my Dearest Husband", Florence at once interjected. "You must not try and stop Elizabeth. This is a wonderful opportunity, and she shall gain much national recognition from this new assignment. Elizabeth, I whole heartedly support you in this decision. You must not think twice about accepting."

Florence went on to say that she was excited for me to be able to devote my full attention to the matters of women's rights, as well as other social issues. David continued to argue, without success, with his wife, stating how he needed me at his paper.

"Nonsense, David" she said, with a hint of irritation at his continued debate. "The paper ran before Elizabeth came, and will do so after she is gone. I agree that you will not find anyone as creative as she to take her place. But you, and your cherished paper, will survive, my Dearest."

With that, David and Florence gave me their blessings for my new work and encouraged me to remain in Hagerstown as Mister Garrison had suggested was possible.

"Though we may not have you at the paper, dear Elizabeth, we still wish to have you as a dear friend", both David and Florence shared.

I assured them that I would indeed remain in my present home and would continue our friendship as long as they both desired it. I also expressed to David that I would be willing to cover local stories as he had need and my time permitted. He was appreciative and Florence delighted that I would continue to remain close.

"And we must continue our tradition of going to Baltimore with Constance the first of each month for shopping. Promise we will still do this great thing together, as we have all along."

With that, we enjoyed the remainder of the evening. The next day I would formally submit my resignation and prepare to travel to Boston to see Mister Garrison.

CHAPTER THIRTY SIX

By the time of the Christmas Season, I had begun work for William Garrison and "The Liberator". Lucy Stone and others working for the cause of women's suffrage consumed most of my time, as I traveled to report on many of their meetings.

Constance had made me promise that I would take time off during the holidays, to spend time with the family. She promised that all three of her sons would be home from school, and all were most anxious to see me and report on their latest adventures.

The week before Christmas, I arrived home in Hagerstown, along with James. James had most recently accompanied me to New Bedford, Connecticut, to meet with Mister Garrison. Garrison had been able to secure an interview with Harriet Tubman, and expressly requested that I should conduct the meeting and subsequently write her story.

I invited James to attend the meeting with me, suggesting that he would enjoy the opportunity as much, if not more than, I. He was elated at the possibility, as he had supported Miss Tubman in her daring escape almost three years prior, from a Maryland slave holder.

As we joined Isaac and Constance at their home upon our return, James could not stop talking about the remarkable Tubman.

"She is a large woman, full of the most marvelous grace and affection for life as any I have ever met", explained James to his brother and his sister-in-law.

Harriet Tubman had indeed been most excited about her life as a free woman, and was looking forward to the ability to assist others to make their way north toward freedom of body and spirit. Miss Tubman explained that the underground railroad that had been in existence for many years had collapsed in the past decade and was in immediate need of revival.

She had gone on to explain that she was relying on persons like James, and others who had assisted in the past, to join the cause once again.

James went on, "The wonderful news, Constance, is that we are to assist once again."

Constance had previously been a part of the process in her earlier years, but had not actively assisted run-a-ways for some time. Her last escort had been nearly twenty years earlier, during her time of waiting with Amos.

"Do you not think I am getting too old for this, James?" Constance asked, with the hope that he would assure her that she was still much in her youth.

James assured her that there would be much she could do, and that it would be like the early days of the Abolitionists' work. Caroline, ever listening to the conversation, joined in.

"Mother, you know that I could help, too. I am thirteen now, and growing more capable each day."

Constance was well aware of her daughter's growing charm and ability, as she watched her youthfulness mature, as her own youthfulness seemed to be fading.

All agreed that we would once again do what we could to assist any who attempted to make their escape from slavery to the freedom of the north. The old network had all but faded away, with stricter laws and enforcement. In those earlier days, several of the Quaker families had been arrested, some had been put to death, and most had been forced to move away.

Constance and James had both narrowly escaped several times with their lives in the previous activities, and this was on the mind of Constance, as she saw her daughter preparing to take over the work she had once committed to.

James left the next day for Washington City, with the promise to return following the services at his church on Christmas Eve. He would again take the first train from Washington to Hagerstown, arriving in time for Christmas dinner, as he had for many years now.

On the evening of the twenty-second, I had dinner with my friends, and answered the endless questions Caroline asked about Harriet Tubman and our trip to Connecticut. She was also filled with curiosity regarding the early days of the fugitive slave work that her Mother and Uncle James had engaged in.

I inquired as to when the young men would be home from school. Isaac said that Amos and Andrew would arrive the next day, and that Abraham had decided to attend services with James on Christmas Eve and travel home with him on Christmas Day.

"You are going to be surprised at how grown all three boys appear these days" Isaac commented, with the proud look of a father pleased with the direction his sons had taken in life.

Amos was now in his third year at the United States Military Academy at West Point. I had visited with Amos on two previous occasions, during trips to New York to cover previous stories, while I worked for the Hagerstown Weekly Dispatch.

At each visit, Amos showed increasing maturity as he grew taller in stature and assurance of his abilities. He would always be certain to escort me through the campus and introduce me to his professors and the Commandant of the Academy.

Abraham was in his second year at Gettysburg College, studying rhetoric, with the intention of following his Uncle and Father into the work of the Church. He was still much like his mother in appearance and disposition. His commitment to life and the fair treatment of all persons was much like the men in his life had modeled by example.

Isaac's and Constance's youngest son, Andrew, had insisted that he, too, wanted to enter a military academy, but refused to follow his brother to West Point. He, instead, went off to the Virginia Military Institute, located in Lexington, Virginia, and had just completed his first semester. VMI had been celebrated as one of the best Military schools in the East, and it was considered a great accomplishment to be invited to attend.

Andrew, like his older brothers, had grown tall in stature. With his red hair and beard, he looked much like his father earlier in life. Some said he at times looked more like a Norske Viking than a minister's son.

All four of the children were well liked and loved by the Congregation at Isaac's Church. Several of the more distinguished and influential members of the Congregation had written letters of petition and support for both Amos and Andrew to attend military schools. The same was true for Abraham in his acceptance to Gettysburg College.

It would be wonderful to once again gather for the Season as had become the custom for over twenty years now between Isaac, Constance, James, and me. The addition of the children had only added blessings upon blessings too numerous to count.

CHAPTER THIRTY SEVEN

We enjoyed a wonderful holiday season together at the Stoltzfus home. All three of their sons had been present, along with James. Amos and Andrew both looked very handsome and distinguished in their military grey uniforms.

Caroline and I spent many hours together, talking about her future and reminiscing about the days when her mother and Uncle James had been involved in helping the run-away slaves find their freedom in the north.

As the New Year was underway, Amos and Andrew returned to their respective Academies and Abraham returned to Gettysburg. During the holiday visit, Andrew had been especially excited about a new professor in Mathematics and Military Strategy. His name was Major Thomas Jackson.

"Auntie Liz, you have never met such a brilliant mind as his", Andrew had declared. "He is a wonderful teacher, as well as a soldier. And he has such a faith in God that even Father would admire him."

Of course, Amos would ague back and insist that only the most brilliant teachers and military men were allowed to teach at West Point and that any teacher at VMI would only be considered second rate. Andrew countered that Major Jackson was indeed a West Point man himself and could teach, if he so desired, at his former school. The rivalry between these brothers had started early in life and appeared as if it would easily continue on for many years yet to come.

Abraham had enjoyed spending time with his Father and Grandfather, the Reverend Christopher McKenna. Both men were equally proud of Abraham's desire to follow in their footsteps, and encouraged the young student as much as any possibly could. The young novice minister even enjoyed the opportunity to preach at both his father's and grandfather's churches during his winter break from school. Many of the parishioners of both congregations had commended the young Abraham for oratorical abilities.

One early, cold, snowy February morning, a letter arrived for me from Mister William Garrison. He simply stated that he would be in Baltimore on the twenty-fifth of the month and would arrange for me to meet with him there. The Baltimore Hotel was the prearranged meeting place, determined shortly after I began working for The Liberator.

It would always excite me to receive these invitations, as they usually meant an assignment which Mister Garrison did not want to trust the mail system to deliver. Such was the case for this meeting.

As I entered the hotel lobby on the afternoon of the appointed day, Mister Garrison rose from his chair and welcomed me with his usual genteel manner, taking my hand and kissing the back of it, as was his custom.

"My Dearest Elizabeth, how marvelous to see you again. You grow more beautiful with each passing day."

I thanked him for his kindness and his compliments. I was beginning to feel my age, even though I was barely forty-five. The intensity with which I had pursued my profession at times seemed to be taking its toll.

My Doctor had suggested that I might wish to slow down, stating that he was concerned for a slight irregularity of my heart. I had countered that the only thing wrong with my heart had been the disappointment of love that engulfed me with the death of Alastair Abercrombie several years prior.

"It is always good to see you, my old friend", I stated as I greeted William Garrison. "I can hardly wait until I hear the purpose of our meeting. I assume it is to be some task of importance."

Over the course of the afternoon, Mister Garrison shared how Harriet Tubman had made final plans to begin the Underground Railroad again, having already "laid" some of the tracks. The start of the new movement would begin in April.

"I want you to accompany Miss Tubman on her first trip and report, with as much discretion and anonymity as possible, the events and success of her work", William had finally stated.

I inquired as to whether James had been contacted as well, and if he was working with Miss Tubman. Mister Garrison assured me that, indeed, my old friend was closely involved with the work, and that he, too, would be along side Miss Tubman on the first journey.

He went on to further share how Miss Tubman was to escort several slaves from the Lexington, Virginia, area. As I heard where the first route was to start, my heart gave way to fear for a brief moment. Virginia Military Institute was located in Lexington, and Andrew was there.

Harriet Tubman had insisted that it was necessary for her to make the first trip. This was to ensure that the route had been properly planned and would work according to the time table of the railroad.

James had also insisted that he would go with Miss Tubman, to cover for her and the run-away slaves as best as possible, should there be a problem. He would be traveling as an itinerant preacher, with a letter of introduction from his Bishop.

I was to go along simply as an observer, with proper press credentials in the event we were stopped and arrested. Should I be detained, I was to have the authorities wire Mister Garrison, who would see to my immediate release.

I left Baltimore the next day for Washington City, to meet with James, as instructed by Mister Garrison. William had assured me that James would fill me in on the remaining details.

James met me at the platform and took me by carriage to his home at the Church.

"I am glad you are here, Elizabeth", he began. "This is just as exciting as the old days. I can't wait for you to hear what is planned.

"We are truly hoping to assist as many, if not more, slaves to escape their burdens as we did those few years Constance and I worked together, when she was first married to Isaac."

James went on to explain how the new rail system had been organized, and the routes to be taken. He stated that his old mentor and friend, Reverend Schumacher, was still to be involved as well, and had made his home at the Seminary in Gettysburg one of the stations along the route. Abraham had also agreed to help in Gettysburg, and would act as a conductor on the next leg of the trip north.

"James, I remember a few severe beatings you took along the way, the last time you became involved. I am not sure that you have ever fully recovered from them. Is it wise for you to take on this added responsibility?" I spoke with tenderness and concern for my friend.

In 1845, James had suffered a severe beating, had been tarred and feathered, and left for dead after an abolitionist meeting in which he had spoken out against the clergy of Baltimore for supporting the cruel institution. As a result of the incident, he still walked with a mild limp and, on occasion, suffered from intense headaches.

"Now, Elizabeth, how can I do anything less? You know that this is as much a calling for me as your work of reporting."

I understood his position. I offered my support as I was able, but reminded him that I went as an observer and reporter. I promised I would assist in any way possible, should he or Miss Tubman be arrested, but reminded him that there was most likely little I could do in such a case. He agreed.

James promised that he would contact me as soon as the final plans had been made. He would send a telegram with the words,

"Now (STOP) Alastair (STOP) JS (END)."

This was the code for me to proceed at once to Lexington. Alastair had been used to mean that I should meet James at the favorite pub of the young cadets of VMI.

There were other code words to be used to indicate various locations. During our time in London, Alastair and I would often meet at the favorite Inn of the press corps for times of lively interaction. Thus the reason Alastair was used for the pub at this time.

Once we arrived at the agreed meeting place, James and I would proceed to the rendezvous spot that Miss Tubman had previously arranged. From there, we would pick up the passengers and begin the journey north.

I left James the next day in Baltimore, with the assurance that I would comply with his instructions and be ready on short notice to begin the trip south. The train ride back to Hagerstown seemed to take no time, as I had spent most of the trip deep in thought of the adventures that lay ahead.

CHAPTER THIRTY EIGHT

Late in the day of April twelfth, I received a telegram from James.

"Now (STOP) Alastair (STOP) JS (END)".

The Underground Railroad was to begin, and I was to meet James in Lexington Virginia at the "Queen Anne", a favorite restaurant of the cadets from the Virginia Military Institute.

The Queen Anne was a small Inn at the heart of town, just a few blocks from the Academy where Andrew attended. Because Andrew was a freshman at VMI, he was restricted from attending the affairs of his senior classmates at the Inn. I prayed that he would be obedient to this requirement of the institution, and would not be present upon the arrival of James and me.

I left by train from Hagerstown the next day, for Lexington. The trip would take little more than a day. I would spend the night in Harrisonburg, and would travel on the next day to Lexington.

As my train pulled into the station on the afternoon of the fourteenth, I held my breath, watching the cadets marching through the town in smart order. They were carrying their rifles, perfectly balanced upon their shoulders. The heavy black packs, with neatly formed bed rolls, lay squarely on their backs.

I looked with a strained intensity, hoping that I would not see Andrew in this mix of men training for war. Relief came over me as I witnessed these bright young men, clad in their grey and white uniforms, continue the brisk march towards the Institute, with the realization that Andrew was not among them.

I gathered what few things I had carried with me on the journey, and proceeded to the Queen Anne. I registered with the attendant and took a small room at the top of the stairs, leading toward the attic.

Later that evening, while I was enjoying a meal of beef and stew, along with some freshly baked corn bread, James entered the Inn. He looked my way, and acknowledged my presence.

As he approached my table, he opened his arms and said, "My Dearest Hannah, how good of you to meet me here. I trust your husband does not know you have come?"

I was somewhat perplexed at the greeting, for neither was I Hannah, nor did I have a husband. Knowing James as I did, I assumed he was protecting our identity for the moment, so I responded, "Yes, darling, he knows nothing. But we must not waste any time, for I must be off in the morning, before first light. Come now, I have a room for us."

I escorted James to my room for the night, and he took care in sharing the plan for the next day. He asked if I had clothing acceptable for the journey north, as most of it would be by foot, and we would travel for several nights until we arrived north of the Mason-Dixon Line.

"Yes, James. I have traveling clothes I think are appropriate and should serve me well. I have purchased a "bloomer" outfit, which will serve me as a reporter's attire, should we be stopped along the way."

I had purchased just such an outfit at the encouragement of Lucy Stone, to be used on special occasions when a dress and petticoats would be too difficult to maneuver in.

As we talked, I thought back to earlier times, when Constance had me put on men's clothing for such an adventure. I had often thought, since those days, how much easier it would be, should women be allowed to dress in similar fashion to men.

The "bloomer dress", as it had come to be known, was not readily accepted by either gender. It was the men, however, who had expressed the most displeasure with the garment.

"What about your other clothing? What will you do with your present dress?" James asked.

I assured him that everything I had would be put into the small haversack, and could easily be carried on my shoulder. Anything that would not fit or was too heavy, was to be left behind.

James insisted that I sleep in the bed that night, while he would sit in the chair. I objected, reminding him that he was a perfect gentleman. He could join me in the comfort of the bed, remaining, of course, on his side of the sleeping arrangement.

Early the next morning, we arose to the smell of fresh bacon, eggs, coffee, grits, and an assortment of other fine foods cooking in the kitchen below. We dressed for the day, packed our belongings, and proceeded to the breakfast table.

As I walked into the room, wearing my new outfit, several men commented on the attire, expressing amusement as well as a few remarks best left unsaid in the presence of a lady, or gentleman, for that matter. The Inn keeper was gracious, and reprimanded his other customers.

"Now, boys", he stated. "This lady is from the north, and they are wearing things like that up in the big cities. Let us show some respect and courtesies to our visitors."

With that, several of the men apologized for their rudeness and offered us a seat at the main table. They immediately began passing the plates, heaping with food, in our direction.

After finishing our meal, we settled our account with the Inn keeper and made our way into the sun filled morning air. The streets were already busy with shoppers and merchants alike. Several cadets were seen roaming about.

James and I had been fortunate the previous night at the Inn. Only a few cadets had been present, and Andrew had not been among them. It appeared as if we might make this journey without encountering him.

James commented that if we saw Andrew, we were to avoid him, if possible.

"We do not want to risk his involvement or curiosity at our reasons for being here", he had warned.

We began to make our way past the Institute, to the north side of town. We had been instructed that we would see a small brook just outside of town and were to follow it for approximately one mile, to a clearing where a tall oak stood.

Harriet Tubman instructed James that it would be here that she would meet us. If she had not arrived by the time the moon was overhead, we were to assume that the plan had failed and were to make our way home at first light.

It was still day light when we arrived at the spot, as instructed. James suggested that we should try to rest and perhaps get as much sleep as possible. I realized that my haversack was too heavy and decided to empty some of the contents.

I buried most of my clothing except for what I was wearing and an extra shawl. I also kept a few undergarments in case there were women in the group who might have need of the items. If that proved not to be the case, then I would dispose of the clothing when Miss Tubman arrived.

I lay down on the grass, and fell quickly to sleep. It seemed as if only a few minutes had passed, when James began to quietly wake me. It was already beginning to grow dark, as the sun settled behind the mountains of Virginia.

"Be quiet, Liz. Someone is coming", James warned.

Before long, we saw the tall, familiar figure of the Negro woman who was going to assist others to achieve their freedom as she had done. I thought of her courage in this undertaking, knowing full well that, should she be caught, it would mean, at the very least, her return to slavery and, at worst, her death.

Tubman greeted us with her usual warmth and appreciation for our involvement. James reintroduced us once again, and Miss Tubman acknowledged that she remembered our first meeting three years prior.

She and James walked a few yards away from me, as she filled him on the next part of the plan. Throughout the conversation, Miss Tubman would look my way, and I could tell she was questioning James on the validity of my appearance and clothing.

Harriett Tubman had dressed in men's clothing and looked as if she were indeed a man herself. She had not cared for the new bloomer outfit, and had suggested that if women wanted to dress like men, then they should simply do so.

James defended my dress and presence. He stated that my manner of attire gave more credibility to my work as a reporter, should we be apprehended. He went on to state that at least I would be able to get back north and continue to tell the story of the difficulties that Negros, and those who helped them, faced, should arrest occur.

Miss Tubman finally agreed that I could continue on with the clothing I had, and that she would make no more fuss about the matter. It was now deep dusk, as we began making our way further up stream.

CHAPTER THIRTY NINE

It was nearly midnight when we reached a small clearing, barely visible through the thick briars and brambles we had been passing through for nearly an hour now. In the glow of the moon light, there were several figures visible, huddled together against the cool night air.

Although I had seen this scene before in my earlier days with Constance and James, I had never grown accustomed to the frightened faces and the wretched condition of these poor souls searching for their freedom. Tonight's passengers would include four men, seven women, and five children, the oldest child appearing to be not more than eight or nine, the youngest, an infant in the arms of her mother.

As had been the condition of most run-away slaves in the past, their clothing was minimal and torn, at best. They stood together in protective fashion against the three of us, as we entered their small camp.

Miss Tubman greeted them and introduced us as her traveling companions who would assist her with this journey. The fugitives acknowledged our presence.

One of the younger black men questioned the presence of the white woman with her fancy clothes, stating that she looked as if she were half man and half woman. Miss Tubman assured him that I was appropriately dressed for this journey, and that he should take no more thought to who was with them, or what they were wearing.

At that, we helped gather their belongings, such as they were, and began to make our way north. We traveled by night and slept through the day, with the men taking turns guarding the small company of Negroes with their white angels, as they had begun to refer to James and me.

The first two days went without incident or concern, although the night travel was at times challenging. Miss Tubman kept us close to strong overgrowth and streams. She stated that it was easier to hide in the briars and underbrush if necessary, and that wading through the streams for a mile or so would lose the scent for the dogs in the event of an attempt to capture these fugitives in our possession.

It was on the third night, near Harrisonburg, Virginia, that we encountered the authorities. Near day break, I heard what I thought were dogs howling. We stopped and listened. Harriet agreed that they were indeed dogs on the scent, but was not sure if they had picked up theirs or another's. She estimated they were at least half an hour behind.

James instructed Harriet to proceed with her passengers, while he would stay and make it look as if he were attending to camp. He promised that, if possible, he would rejoin them at the earliest opportunity.

I insisted that I would remain with James, to add creditability to his story, should he be questioned. Tubman was to enter the stream with her passengers and continue toward the next station, yet several miles north.

James set to work at once, building a small fire, to give the appearance of one who had been present over night. I unpacked what bedding I still had and lay down, pretending sleep.

As the sun was making first light, six men, along with their hounds, entered into our quickly made camp. James was preparing coffee and making ready a small meal for us, to add to the illusion.

"Howdy, stranger, mind if we warm ourselves at your fire?" the lead man asked James.

James invited the men to come and warm themselves and rest by the fire. "What brings you to these parts, stranger?" the man asked.

James explained that he was an itinerant preacher visiting the farms in the area, looking for new converts. He went on to explain that I was his sister, helping with his work.

"That so?" the man continued. "Where's your horse? Ain't ever known a preacher not to have a horse."

James explained, "He went lame two days ago and I had to him put down. My sister and I were sharing the same mule, and we do not have enough funds left at the moment to purchase another one."

"That too bad, Preacher. Wish we could help. Perhaps if I take a look at your belongings I might find enough money to buy one for ya", the lead man stated. The large man ordered two of the men with him to search our belongings.

They made fun of my attire, and ripped open my haversack. My journal fell to the ground. One of the men picked it up and took it to his boss.

The man began, "Thanks Jim. Now Jim don't read too well, so I'll jest have a look in this yer book and see what it says."

As he flipped through the pages, he found my press credentials.

"I thought you said she was your sister helpin' you. She is a northern reporter for one of them Abolitionist papers. Ya know what I think, Missy? I think you and this man of yers is helping run-away niggers. That's what I think"

James immediately protested, stating that he knew nothing of the kind, and was indeed a minister of the gospel. He produced the letter from his bishop, but to no avail.

"You know what we do with nigger lovers down here, boy? We string 'em up."

The man ordered another man to get the rope out and place it over the nearest tree strong enough to hold it. They tied James' hands behind his back and placed a noose over his head in preparation.

I protested at the actions, declaring that James had nothing to do with helping the slaves, and was indeed a minister on an assignment from God. I was with him to report his success and to tell the story of the poorer farmers in Virginia, as they struggled to earn a living off the land.

"Well, if that be true, then when you enter the pearly gates, Preacher, God will have his reward for ya. But if it be a lie, then you gonna burn in HELL!" he said as he spit a wad of tobacco juice into the face of James.

The man commanded, "Now boys, jest pull the rope tight enough as to make our new friend stand on his toes and be a little uncomfortable."

With that, the rope was pulled tight, still allowing James some room to breath, but causing pain to his neck and tension throughout his body.

"Now I am jest going to ask you one time, Preacher. Tell me the truth and I will let you down easy. Lie to me and I will see you hang. Which way did those niggers go? Upstream or down?"

I spoke up at once.

"Let him go. He was not helping them, but they did pass through last night. They went a few yards down stream, and then headed west toward the mountains."

"Now that's better, Missy. I wouldn't want you to write about how unfair we are here in the south, so I'll let your little man go without a hangin", the leader stated. "Let him down boys."

His men complied but grumbled that they always loved a good hanging of "nigger lovers".

As James was released from the noose, his hands still bound, the man took his pistol from his holster and shot James, wounding him in his shoulder. James fell to the ground with a moan, and lay unconscious in a bloody heap.

I screamed, and accused the man of barbaric behavior.

He responded, "Now I promised I wouldn't hang 'im. Besides, I only wounded him. If he lives, he won't feel like helpin' no more run-away colored again, that's for sure."

After taking what money we had and the little food left, the man ordered his followers across the stream, with the hope of picking up the scent once again. He had stated that it was probably doubtful, but he would try.

The sounds of the hounds drifted off to the west, as I attended to James. He had regained consciousness and was asking what had happened after he was shot. I told him the full story of the group's departure to the west and that they felt they would not have the trail back.

"You know that you were brilliant in thinking to tell the story of our passengers going west", James commended. "It will at least buy Harriet some time to get further north. I do pray that she and her passengers will make it to Pennsylvania all right."

"Yes, my dear James, I pray, too, that they will make it. God help them, though, if they don't", I stated with sadness.

How cruel this peculiar institution was. I could not understand how reasonable men were able to allow it to continue. If only we in America could embrace the freedom and equality of the black man and woman, as Great Britain had. We would be so much the better for it.

CHAPTER FORTY

I bandaged the wound in James' shoulder the best I could, with the limited materials available. I tore bandages from my undergarments and stuffed the gaping hole with cotton.

It was nearly ten miles into the nearest town. We had decided that we should try for Harrisonburg, with the hope of finding a doctor who could, and would, assist us. From there we would be able to take the train north. The men had taken all the money we had, but I knew I could wire Mister Garrison for funds and he would immediately send them.

We had been traveling slowly for the better part of the day, going only a mile or two. James would regularly pass out, and I would have to wait until he recovered before continuing on.

More than once, he had insisted that I should travel ahead and return for him, after procuring a horse and carriage in Harrisonburg. I refused, stating that I would stay with him, and we would make the journey together.

Toward the late afternoon, I spotted a small house with smoke rising from its chimney.

"James, do you think we could make it to that farm, and perhaps find help there?" I asked with some excitement and hope in my voice.

James agreed that it was worth a try. After all, he said with a slight laugh, how much more damage could anyone do to him?

We approached the front of the house. I was supporting James once again, as he was on the verge of collapse, as he had done so many times already that day. I helped him take a seat on the top step of the porch and knocked on the door.

A small, elderly woman looked out through a crack in the door and asked what we wanted.

"If you please, ma'am", I began. My companion is badly hurt, and we are in need of medical attention. Could you be so kind as to offer some assistance?"

The woman opened the door further to get a better look at James.

"Looks as if he been shot to me", she said after a long gaze at the shoulder of James.

"Bring him in here, and be quick about it", she commanded.

I helped James to his feet and into the tiny house. It appeared as if the woman lived alone and, in spite of her stature, seemed more than able to take care of herself. I noticed a shotgun mounted over the door opening, and wondered if she had trained its sights on us as we walked to her home.

"Sit him there in that chair, Missy. What's his name?"

"His name is James, and I am Elizabeth." I responded.

"He your man?" she asked.

"No, we are brother and sister."

I did not want her to think unkindly of us, if I were to tell the truth that we were just good friends. Some people had often misinterpreted our relationship when we introduced ourselves as such, and James had been accused on more than one occasion of having me as his mistress.

"Well, Miss Elizabeth, most people around here call me a witch. They think I have magical skills to turn people into frogs. But those that know me, they know I can heal most any ailment. Now let's look at your 'brother'", she stated with a certain amount of skepticism that showed she was not sure James really was who I had said.

The old woman tended to James' shoulder, cleaning the wound and applying a salve made from roots and herbs. She packed the wound with fresh lint, placing a layer of green moss over the site. She then tightly wrapped the wound in fresh linens she had taken from her cupboard. It was obvious she had tended to these types of injuries before.

"There now, Elizabeth. That should take care of his wound. The bullet went clean through, and the moss will draw out any infection. We will change it in the morning."

James thanked his care giver for her generosity and said that he doubted she was a witch. She was more like an angel to him.

She said that he was delirious from the injury, and that the tea she had made for him would help him sleep. Shortly after finishing the strong brew, James drifted off on the bed the old woman had prepared for him in one corner of the room.

"Now, my dear, let us have something to eat, and you can tell me of the adventure that has brought you to my home. I suspect it has something to do with some of those slave trappers that came through here two days ago. They can be a nasty bunch. Killed more than one man who tried to stand in their way."

The old women directed me to a small rocking chair near the fire, where I was commanded to sit and wait for my meal. I protested, and offered to help in anyway possible, but she would have only her way in the matter.

I drifted off to sleep, listening to her singing ever so softly an old John Wesley hymn. Her words floated though the air with a hypnotizing effect upon my spirit.

As she sang, "And can it be that I should gain an interest in the Savior's blood? Died He for me, who caused His pain? For me, who him, to death pursued? Amazing love! How can it be, that thou, my Lord, shouldst die for me?",

I no longer could keep my eyes from closing. I dreamed briefly of home and the comfort of my own bed.

The old woman woke me with a piping hot stew of lamb and vegetables, along with fresh bread. A hot cup of coffee was set along side of my plate. I made my way to the table at her bidding and glanced in the direction of James, still sleeping on the bedding.

"He's all right, sweetie. He has hardly moved and is breathing easy." She assured me of my friend.

"If it pleases you, what is really your name?" I inquired.

"Well, when I was a child, my mamma called me Ella. But for the last several years, people call me either granny or witch, as I've already told you. I do like Ella, though, since no one ever calls me that."

"Well then, it would do me a great honor to call you Miss Ella, with your permission."

"Granted", she said with a slight curtsy and smile of delight.

Throughout the remainder of the evening, I shared how we had indeed encountered the slave trappers, and what they had done to James. I reported that they took our money as well, and we were left without funds.

Ella said, "Now don't you worry about money. We don't need any here. Did they violate you, my dear?"

I shared that one of the men had made suggestions to having his way, but that the leader had stopped him, stating there was no time for foolery. The others chided him, saying that they would be quicker than it would take for James to die by the rope. But the leader had insisted that they were not about to violate a northern woman from the papers, unless they were prepared to kill me as well. The men had backed away.

"You were lucky, my dear. They usually aren't so generous in their ways. Of course I doubt they had ever run into a newspaper woman before, and they don't take to killin' women in these parts too well."

"I am grateful they spared me the humiliation, but I find it hard to think highly of them for their behavior to the slaves and to James." I protested.

As the evening wore on, I came to learn that Ella had at one time owned three "bucks", as she called them, but had given them their freedom several years back.

"One of the men, old Sam, lives on the south edge of my property and brings me fresh produce from time to time. I will fetch him tomorrow and have him take you into town to find some proper clothes and wire your newspaper for money, so you can be traveling in proper style back north."

Ella understood, though I did not tell her, that James and I had been assisting the slaves the trappers were looking for. Otherwise, she said, "why would you be in the woods, alone, without a horse and little clothing to carry?"

CHAPTER FORTY ONE

It would be the middle of May before James was well enough to travel again. Ella had made us both comfortable and taken good care of us. I had sent word to Mister Garrison regarding our situation, by telegram. He had promptly wired the necessary funds to cover all expenses.

I had also wired Isaac and Constance. Isaac returned my telegram, informing me that he would notify James' Senior Pastor and Bishop of the situation. He also offered his willingness to travel to us, if we needed his assistance. My reply was not to come at this time.

On the morning of the seventeenth of May, old Sam took James and me by buckboard into Harrisonburg, to catch the late day train to Hagerstown, by way of Winchester. We thanked Ella for her tender care, and I left funds that Mister Garrison had made available for her.

We had made new and trusted friends in Ella and old Sam. Ella made us promise that we would come and see her if time and distance ever allowed, and assured us that we would always find a warm welcome with her.

The old woman had, over the course of our stay, told us that there would be coming the day of accounting for the sins of the land.

"You know that the only way to rid the country of this terrible and peculiar practice will be through bloodshed", she had emphatically stated on more than one occasion.

Somehow, deep in my heart, I knew that she spoke the truth. If only it were not so, I would often remark to her.

James and I boarded the train and took our seats. The return trip seemed to take forever, as I thought about the slaves and their escort, Harriet Tubman. I had wondered each day whether they had made their way to freedom, or had fallen prey to the slave trappers.

I had not asked any of these questions in my telegrams to Mister Garrison or Isaac, for fear that the telegraph operator would report my knowledge to the local officials. I had learned that it was difficult to find persons to trust in the matter of freeing the slaves. One word to the wrong person could mean the loss of freedom, and the death of both the slaves and those who assisted them.

James and I arrived in Hagerstown early the next morning. Isaac met us on the platform and assisted us to the waiting carriage.

"James, you look much better than I had imagined." Isaac spoke with love for his brother.

James went on to embrace Isaac, as we all proceeded to the Stoltzfus home. Constance was waiting at the door, as we pulled to the front of the house. She ran down the front steps leading from the porch and embraced first me, and then James.

"You had all of us most terrified for your wellbeing", she exclaimed.

We went into the home, and spent the next few moments catching up on the news of our journey and the assistance Ella had provided. Isaac reported that Miss Tubman and her passengers had arrived in Gettysburg, two weeks after their departure from us and were now safely in Canada.

James asked if further plans had been laid for future transports. Isaac assured his brother that all was in the works, and that his bishop had suggested that James travel to see Reverend Schumacher as soon as he had strength to do so.

"According to the Bishop, James, the first trip was deemed a success, and more stations have been added. Miss Tubman is to go south on at least three more such journeys to test these additional routes." Isaac shared with as much excitement as anyone.

"That is good news", James went on. "I only wish Elizabeth and I had been able to see the first journey through."

Constance shared that the Bishop had visited with them and reported on the success of Miss Tubman. The Bishop had gone on to state that the success was due to the advantage James had given her by staying behind, risking his life for the freedom of the slaves.

"He says you are to be commended, and he will do so when he is able", Constance added.

James would remain with Isaac and Constance for another month, before proceeding to Gettysburg and then on to his own parish responsibilities in Washington City.

I returned to my own home a few blocks away, and was immediately greeted by Hetti, my housekeeper.

"Miss Elizabeth, I am so glad you are home. I was so afraid that you would never get out of Virginia alive. Mister Isaac and Miss Constance kept me informed of your happenings. Is Mister James doing well?" she inquired.

"Yes, Hetti, he is all but healed now. We did have quite the adventure, and I am glad to be home. How have you been in my absence?"

Hetti was advanced in her years, and I often worried when away that she would become ill and need assistance. Caroline had taken on the responsibility of looking in on her daily during my absence, to ensure that Hetti was in need of nothing more than the daily cup of tea the young woman and old housekeeper enjoyed together.

"I already have the water ready for your bath, Miss Elizabeth", Hettie went on. "Now you take directly to getting yourself ready, and I will be in momentarily to help you."

Hetti often prepared a bath for me following my return home from assignments. It was her way of assuring me that it was indeed a welcomed return.

I sat in the hot water, filled with bathing oils Hetti had insisted kept a woman's skin soft and young. Whether that was true I did not know, but I did enjoy the sweet fragrance of oils and the richness they gave to my body as I would emerge from the waters.

Early that evening, we enjoyed a simple meal together, followed by an herbal tea that Ella had given me prior to our departure from her home. Ella shared that the tea held restorative qualities, and that both Hetti and I would enjoy its mixture. Indeed we did.

I slept well that first night home, not awaking until well into the midmorning hours. Hetti had been up some time already, and had my morning coffee prepared as I descended the stairs from the second floor bedroom. I asked how she had slept, and she agreed that it had been the best sleep she enjoyed since I left in April with Mister James.

"I believe that old witch gave you a mighty potent and rich concoction", Hetti commented.

I laughed at her statement, and reminded her that the "witch" had a name, and it was Ella.

"Calls her what you want, Miss Elizabeth. But I know of some of those mountain women and their spells and brews. And this was one of them. Had the most wonderful dreams, I did. She may be Ella, but she still a witch. I know."

There was no use arguing with Hetti. I had learned that shortly after she came to be with me, when I attempted to persuade her to some task she had no desire to engage in. It was Hetti who really was the mistress of the house, not me.

I filed my story with Mister Garrison, and spent the remainder of the year covering local stories on women's rights for the Liberator. One such story was the ordination of Antoinette Brown. Brown was a good friend of Lucy Stone, and both had attended Oberlin College.

Following her graduation, Brown attended Seminary at Oberlin, with the understanding that she would not be endorsed for ministerial standing as her male classmates would be. Brown accepted the condition, for the chance to study theology.

She entered the seminary in 1847 and by 1850 was regularly preaching and speaking, without a formal license to do so. She had no church that would accept her as their pastor, thus denying her right to ordination.

In September, that was to change. Miss Brown had received an offer to lead a small Congregationalist Church in South Butler, New York, and was given a license to preach. On September the fifteenth, 1853, Brown was officially ordained by a socially radical Methodist minister, the Reverend Luther Lee.

Lee had stated in his sermon of the day, that "if God and mental and moral culture have not already qualified her we cannot, by anything we may do by way of ordaining or setting her apart."

Lee went on to say "All we are here to do, is to subscribe our testimony to the fact, that in our belief, our sister in Christ, Antoinette L. Brown, is one of the ministers of the New Covenant, authorized, qualified, and called by God to preach the gospel of his Son Jesus Christ."

The church had been filled to capacity for the historical event.

On November fifteenth, the newly ordained Reverend Antoinette Brown would officiate her first wedding. It was the marriage of a daughter of Rhoda deGarmo, a women's rights activist from Rochester with whom Brown and others were closely acquainted.

In comparison to the events earlier in the spring, this was a joy to attend, with much celebration and fanfare. Reverend Brown had become a wonderful friend, and it had been a pleasure and privilege to cover and report on her achievements.

The year came to a close with all of the Stoltzfus family, along with James, Hetti, and myself, gathered together for our usual Christmas celebration. The boys and Caroline were all safe and maturing. Isaac and Constance were showing signs of their growing years, as well as I. And James continued his exuberant tales of the Abolitionists' endeavors to gain the freedom of slaves.

CHAPTER FORTY TWO

By early 1856, I felt as though I had accomplished all I could for "The Liberator". I resigned my position with William Garrison, advising him that I would continue to work for him as an independent reporter on specific assignments, as the occasion might present itself.

Garrison expressed his sorrow at my decision to leave the Liberator, but understood my desire for more challenging assignments and a change of direction in my career. He wished me well, and assured me that I would always have a place at his publication. He would in the future call upon me to cover some events, and to report from time to time on the work of Lucy Stone and others.

Early in April, Simon Cameron wrote, asking me if I would meet him in Philadelphia. He had shared that he was interested in hiring me for a special purpose, and that he would divulge the details of the assignment when we could meet face to face.

Mister Cameron and I had been friends for several years. Oliver Jones had introduced us many years prior, while I was still working at Chambersburg Democratic Tribune.

As my fortunes increased, first with the death of my father, and then the estate of Oliver and Prudence Jones, Mister Cameron became my financial advisor. He had made his fortunes in the railroads and banking systems. He would do likewise for me, regularly showing significant gains. With the help of Simon, I had become a wealthy woman.

I arrived in Philadelphia the afternoon of April seventeenth. Sarah Hale had invited me to stay with her during my visit, so I went by carriage to her home. Sarah greeted me with her usual air of delight at my presence.

"Oh, Elizabeth, how wonderful to see you! It has been much too long since our last visit."

I had agreed that we had been apart for a significant period, but reminded her that she had, within the past year, traveled to Hagerstown to celebrate my thirtieth anniversary in the newspaper business. In May of the previous year, several of my friends, including Sarah Hale, William Garrison, the Footes and Stoltzfus family had all gathered to celebrate my career. The gathering and celebration, organized by Constance and Sarah, had been a complete surprise to me.

I had entered my home after returning from an assignment to find Caroline waiting for me, demanding that I go with her at once to her parent's home a few blocks away. Hetti was gone, and I was sure that something dreadful had happened to her.

At once we made our way, and, upon entering the front door of the home, I was greeted with applause and affirmations of love. Over fifty people, including Hetti, had gathered for this occasion, and I had been treated as if I were royalty for the day.

"Elizabeth, that was nearly a year ago. A year apart from you is much too long", Sarah protested.

She inquired as to whether I had any thought about why Simon Cameron had requested this meeting with me. I was at a loss, but assured her that it was probably nothing more than to review my investments, and to make further recommendations as to the course of action I should take to advance my wealth.

"He has been a good friend to both of us, Elizabeth. I don't know that either of us could have done as well with our investments on our own. He is indeed a shrewd business man", Sarah continued.

"Yes, indeed, he has done well for us and yes, he is shrewd", I agreed. "He is just enough scoundrel to know when, where, and how to make money, and just enough politician to make everyone feel good about his business dealings, even when he is taking advantage of them."

At that we both laughed.

"I do believe that his earlier years in the newspaper business prepared him for his role in the economics of today", Sarah commented.

It was probably due to the fact that he had been friends with Oliver Jones in his earlier days as a newspaper man that I trusted him so now. I would always accept his advice, and gave Simon free control over the investments of my funds. He had never given me cause to do otherwise.

There had been a brief period, years earlier, when my investments took a down turn. Simon had assured me that this was normal in the course of business, and I was not to fear loss. I trusted him to do as he saw best and within the year, the funds had recovered and I was making a profit once more. After that, I never doubted him.

"When do you meet with Mister Cameron?" Sarah inquired.

"Tomorrow, at noon, for lunch. We are to meet at the Grand Hotel on State Street", I replied.

The remainder of the day we spent time shopping in the market. Sarah was working on an article regarding preparations of early spring produce for a nutritious family meal that every wife should be able to accomplish with minimal investment.

As the editor for Godey's Book, she often did not have time for her own writing and articles. However, on this occasion, Sarah thought it time for her to make an additional contribution to the publication. Her monthly editorials were rewarding, but like all reporters and writers, she needed from time to time to create an article of her own.

I met Mister Cameron the next day, as we had arranged. Simon was waiting for me in the lobby of the hotel, and rose to greet me.

"Elizabeth, my dear child, you look wonderfully youthful this fine day", he began with his usual charm.

Simon was as much politician as he was business man. I had over the years come to accept his flattery as nothing more.

"Simon", I began. "Are you sure you have never been to Ireland to kiss the 'blarney stone'?"

Simon gave his usual laugh, with a wave of his hand, and had insisted that he was, as always, speaking only the truth.

"I am glad you have come, my Dear. We have much to discuss."

At that, Simon began to introduce me to two men who had accompanied him this day.

The first was his son, James Donald Cameron. James was a handsome lad of twenty three. Tall in stature, he looked much as his father had in his youth. James told how he aspired to political life and hoped that one day he might become a Senator for the Commonwealth.

The second man was former Congressman, Thaddeus Stevens. I had met Mister Stevens once before, during a trip to Washington City. He had been a strong voice in Congress until just a few years earlier, when he lost his reelection bid to Henry Muhlenberg in 1852.

"Congressman Stevens, it is a delight to see you once again. Now, my dear Simon, to what do I owe the opportunity to meet with such distinguished gentlemen?" I inquired.

Congressman Stevens began almost at once. "My dear Elizabeth, we are in the process of forming a committee to elect our friend, the most Honorable Simon Cameron, from the Commonwealth of Pennsylvania, to the United States Senate. We want you to join our team."

Thaddeus spoke as a true politician and it was said of him, as most politicians, that he was not to be trusted.

"But gentlemen, I am not a politician, but a reporter. And if my memory serves me correctly, Congressman, we have at times had differing opinions on certain matters of state", I countered.

Stevens and the young Cameron began to discuss the process of electing a man to office and stated that we all have differing opinions at times. The former Congressman even remarked, although I doubt with much sincerity, that freedom to disagree with government was one of the great hallmarks of our society.

Simon Cameron then asked if I would join his team and help write press statements and speeches. I protested somewhat, stating that I had never engaged in this type of work before and was not sure that I was up to the task presented.

All three men assured me that I would indeed be a most valued asset, and that they looked forward to having a woman's perspective on the issues. After much discussion, I finally agreed that I would work along side the man who had been instrumental in assuring my financial well-being.

For the next year, I would regularly write press statements and releases, illuminating Mister Cameron and his achievements in the most positive light. In the elections of 1856, Simon Cameron would be elected to the United States Senate, taking office in March of 1857.

CHAPTER FORTY THREE

After the election of Simon Cameron to the Senate, I returned home to once again engage in my work. I was without a regular assignment and had been discussing the possibility with my friend and former editor, David Foote, of the Hagerstown Dispatch.

Both David and his wife, Florence, assured me that I was still welcomed at the paper as a regular reporter. I was, however, looking for something that would allow me to engage in the national political scene.

David made a promise he would contact a few editors he knew, to see if there were any who might have interest in my skills. He assured me that I had a wonderful reputation as a first class reporter and would have no problem finding a position that suited me.

I had traveled in early March to be with Simon Cameron as he was sworn into office. While in Washington City, I had the opportunity to meet briefly with Horace Greely of the New York Tribune.

Greeley was covering the Supreme Court's hearing and decision in the Case of Dred Scott vs. Stanford. The high court had agreed to hear the case. It involved first, the decision of the lower court's to recognize Dred Scott as a free black man and citizen, and the subsequent decision of the Missouri Supreme Court to overturn the lower court's decision, returning Scott, along with his wife and child, to their owner, Irene Emerson. Emerson's brother, John Stanford, an attorney from New York, defended the case for his sister.

In the end, the court had ruled that the Constitution did not grant citizenship to black men or women, slave or free. As such, the lower court held no jurisdiction in hearing the case, for only citizens were permitted to file suit in the courts.

The court had further ruled that slaves were considered property and, as such, property did not cease to belong to its owner by simple virtue of changing localities. The fact that Scott had lived with his owner for a lengthy period of time in a free state did not automatically change the status of the property in question. Mister Scott and his family were still considered the property of Missus Emerson, and had to be returned.

The final part of the decision ruled that the Missouri compromise was not valid, as the federal government could not dictate to the states whether they were to be, or remain, free or slave states. The court upheld the right of each state to make its own determination of this fact.

The court's decision and opinion had been written by Chief Justice Roger Taney, writing for the majority. Of the nine judges, only two dissented from the opinion of the court. Scott, along with his family, was immediately returned to slavery.

The decision had been heartbreaking for the Abolitionist movement. William Garrison called it the "black night for the soul of humanity". Frederick Douglass wept for the loss. Both men feared that the decision would set back what little progress had been made toward the end of slavery in the United States.

The High Court had ruled that state's rights were enforceable over the interference of the federal government. However, the court also upheld that federal laws, as spelled out in the Constitution, could not be violated by the states. Where the Constitution did not allow for citizenship, the states could not grant citizenship. Such would be the case for the Negro for many years to come.

Following the decision, Greeley, Garrison, and I had dinner at the Capital Strand Hotel. Greeley had taken just long enough to file a quick report to his paper in New York, before joining us.

"Miss Fitzgerald, are you not on assignment at this time?" Greeley asked.

"Horace, our dear friend is completing the task of seeing Mister Cameron elected to the Senate", Garrison interjected.

"That is correct, Mister Greeley. I have spent the past year working with Simon Cameron on his campaign, writing press releases and assisting with some of his speech writing."

I spent the next few moments of our conversation sharing the experience of the past year. Mister Greeley indicated that he was familiar with my work and would be in an envious position if I were to consider working for him.

"Now Horace, Elizabeth does not need your employment. She is, in the event you are not aware of it, a woman of, shall we say, significant means. She could just about buy you, my friend."

Garrison was at the time, I believed, jealous of the wealth I had accumulated over the years with the help of Simon Cameron.

"Well, William, I may have independent means of support, but that does not preclude the fact that I still enjoy working. Mister Greeley, if you are making me an offer, I am open to the possibility", I at once admitted.

Horace Greeley and I discussed the newspaper business, and the need for correspondents in the field. With the telegraph, had come the means of rapidly transmitting news from around the country.

Plans were already being made to lay a cable from New York to London, called the Transatlantic Cable. As soon as the cables were laid, sometime in mid year of 1858, the entire world would be reachable in a matter of hours, if not minutes.

"I believe that my paper with its circulation, along with your ability to cover a story and file a report from the field, could make a good team."

Greeley was most convincing with his arguments.

He shared what his vision was for the paper, and how he wanted the Tribune to become the paper of choice around the world for up-to-date news. He promised autonomy for the stories I would cover, and guaranteed my expenses. He also suggested that I stay in my present home and work from there.

I agreed to his proposal and became a correspondent with the New York Tribune. From that moment on, I was covering stories that held a national, and at times, an international appeal.

I would spend many weeks in Washington City as the primary correspondent for Greeley, covering news from the Capital. This opportunity, along with my friendship with Simon Cameron, would open doors in the years ahead to some of the most rewarding and adventurous reporting I would ever engage in.

CHAPTER FORTY FOUR

By Christmas of that year, I was well settled into my new position with the Tribune. Horace Greeley had been true to his word, and gave me autonomy as to the stories I would cover and how I approached the assignment. He had also demonstrated great generosity with expenses, as well as compensation for my work.

August had seen what was later referred to as the Panic of 1857. Several banks failed, and there was an economic crisis of unparalleled proportions. Even Great Britain began withdrawing funds from the American Banks, fearing financial loss.

Simon Cameron had assured me that my funds would be safe, and that I was not to worry. He shared that he had taken liberty to move my accounts to safer investments, and while they would not yield significant growth at the time, they would be preserved against the current economic downturn.

I was at home in Hagerstown, preparing, along with Constance and Caroline, for the festive season. James, along with Isaac, Constance and Caroline, would be present. Abraham would arrive on Christmas Day, as had become his custom.

Over the years, he had grown accustomed to traveling first to Washington City to attend the services for which his Uncle James had responsibilities. From there, he would travel with James, arriving late in the day for Christmas Dinner and the festivities of the next few days.

Neither Amos nor Andrew had been home for the past two years, as their assignments with the Army kept them away. This year was to be no different.

Amos, following graduation from West Point, had been assigned to the 1st US Infantry. He was commissioned as a Brevet Second Lieutenant. His immediate Captain was Henry Heth, a distinguished young officer, according to Amos, and a graduate of West Point, as well. Amos expressed his appreciation for the manner in which Heth treated the younger officers.

In September, 1855, Captain Heth had led an expeditionary force against the Sioux Indians, and had quelled a rebellion of the native Americans at the Battle of Ash Hollow, in Nebraska. Amos had been one of the officers accompanying Heth, and had at the battle gained the respect of his commander.

Subsequent to this action, Amos had been promoted to full second lieutenant. He was now stationed at Fort Leavenworth, Kansas. He would not have leave until late next spring.

Andrew, following his graduation from the Virginia Military Institute in May of 1856, was attached to the Second US Dragoons. Andrew was given the rank of Brevet Second Lieutenant.

The new young officer was sent west to join the forces in Kansas. He was assigned to serve with Captain John Buford. In May, he became part of the forces sent by President Buchanan to address territorial concerns in Utah. He would spend this Christmas with his men in the snow-filled and cold mountains of the west.

As we worked in the kitchen, baking fresh breads and desserts, all at the direction of Hetti and Greta, Constance read the most recent letters from her two Army sons. It was grand to hear of their adventures and the respect they had for their officers.

"I have heard from Mister Cameron that both Captain Heth and Captain Buford have very promising careers in the Army", I shared with the gathering of ladies.

Constance remarked that she was not sure, but it sounded as if both of these two young men had decided they would make the Army their life's calling.

"But Mother", Caroline interjected. "How could they not look to their heritage and upbringing? It concerns me that they have become men of violence, when they had such wonderful examples of love from you, Father, Uncle James, and, of course, Auntie Liz."

Constance reminded her daughter that every person had to decide for themselves which path they should embark upon. She, however, could not help sharing her concern for their well being as soldiers.

At one point, Andrew, early in his education at VMI, had indicated that following his military obligation, he wished to study law. James and Isaac had both encouraged him to pursue the work, and his Grandfather McKenna had assured the young scholar that he would also assist in finding the right placement for him when the time was right.

"Oh, how I do wish Andrew would leave the Military as soon as his obligation is passed", Constance had wistfully stated.

She had had recurring nightmares that her youngest son would suffer serious injury, and possibly death, in the Army. She never knew for sure if Andrew lived or died, as she would awake before the verdict in a fretful state.

"So how are your studies proceeding?" I asked Caroline.

Caroline had followed my footsteps, and was now enrolled at the Wilson School for Women, in Chambersburg. As with her brothers, I assured Isaac and Constance that her education would be paid for from my funds. It was my gift to the children and their parents, which I was grateful to have the means to insure.

Caroline, now in her second year at Wilson School, was just as excited as she was the first day of her classes.

"Oh, Auntie Liz, you have no idea how marvelous it is to study there. But of course you do. You studied at Wilson. They still talk about you and the free spirit that you always employed around the campus. Tell me, did you actually steal Missus Breckenridge's corset and petticoat and fly them from the flag pole? Everyone says it was you, but no one could ever prove it."

I confessed that I would not divulge the truth of the matter, but did state that it caused "quite a stir" on campus. That incident had taken place over thirty years ago.

The baking had been completed, and all five of us retired to the sitting room. As was the custom, Hetti and Greta always joined us, and were part of the family.

This year, we were to have an added member to the family celebration. Greta had met Peter Swenson, a Swede who had been living in Baltimore and worked for the railroad.

Peter was a fine young man, and Greta had met him as he repaired rail ties just east of town. She stopped to see the young man alone, in need of some rest and refreshment. She offered him what she had, and the two instantly fell in love.

The couple had been married by Isaac six weeks later, and the Church offered the young man a position as care taker for the congregation. He had accepted, and now was a regular part of the family.

Greta shared, "Ve have a vonderful life here in Amerika. And Mister Isaac and Miss Constance make it so."

She still spoke with a lingering lilt of her native tongue, but her English had improved significantly.

"Greta, please share with Caroline and Elizabeth the other good news", Constance implored.

"Ya, ve, Peter and me, ve are going to have a baby. In June."

Greta was obviously full of pride and love for the man she had married and the child she now carried for him.

"I pray the child is a boy and will be strong like his Papa", she went on.

Isaac and Constance had renovated the carriage house, with the assistance of the congregation, and had given the new residence to Greta and Peter to make as their home. It was a comfortable home with a spare room that would be used as the nursery.

This Christmas would be a joyful time, with as much of the family gathered as possible. The hope of new life always added to the joy of the occasion. It had been awhile since a baby had been part of the household.

We celebrated Christmas day, with James and Abraham arriving on schedule. Telegrams arrived early in the day from both Amos and Andrew, wishing us well. And the promise of a new year filled with hope and joy lay close at hand.

CHAPTER FORTY FIVE

By late summer the following year, life for all of us had settled into routine existence. Amos was enjoying the adventures, engaging the Indians from time to time, rescuing prairie families from the "ravages of the savages", as he often referred to the Indians in his letters. Due to his gallantry and leadership abilities, he had recently been promoted to Brevet First Lieutenant.

The Utah War had ended, and Andrew was assigned, along with the men of his unit, to Camp Floyd near Salt Lake City. He still had two years left of his enlistment, and would most likely remain at this post. He had written that, if at all possible, he would be home for Christmas this year. This would be his first since beginning Army life.

Greta and Peter had a handsome son, born June twenty-seven. The proud new parents named their first born Lars, after Greta's father. He had soft blond hair and large, beautiful, blue eyes. Peter suggested that his cry was as loud and ferocious as any Viking from the old days.

With the birth of Lars, Greta took time off to recover and enjoy her new child. Hetti would assist the Stoltzfus household when I was out of town, but her aging years did not allow her to work the pace a younger woman was capable of.

Constance insisted that they would look for another housekeeper, to assist her and Greta in taking care of all of them. James assisted them in this matter.

Through his contacts, James heard of a young woman in Baltimore who was to be sold at the next auction, to cover the debts of a Minister who had exercised excess in private gambling. The Bishop informed James that he thought the girl could be purchased for a reasonable sum and given to Isaac and Constance.

James went to see the clergyman about the possibility of the purchase. He was welcomed by the young Negro woman, who led him into the parlor. She was a handsome girl, tall in stature, about twenty five years of age. It was obvious that she had been raised in a proper home to perform the duties which she now carried out with dignity and grace.

"Reverend Stoltzfus", the old clergyman began as he entered the room. It was obvious that he was somewhat taken aback by James' presence.

"I never expected to see you alive, let alone here to buy my nigger woman. When did you turn from your soft nature to enter the slave business?"

Reverend Duffie had been one of the men responsible for the tar and feathering James had endured several years earlier. As a result of the brutal beating, James still suffered with health concerns.

"Reverend, I do not believe we have need of debating my opinions and beliefs on the matter of the enslavement of others. I am not here for myself, but for my brother Isaac and his wife. They have need of assistance in their home, and I understand you have need of finances." James was using all of the grace he could find, to endure the presence of this man.

"Ah yes, your brother. I understand that he may be in line for the Bishop's office in the fall. A good figure of a slave woman in the church rectory may be what you bleeding Abolitionists need.

"And to imagine that your own brother would engage a slave right before your eyes. Or is it that he needs her to satisfy, well, let us just say, his appetite when his wife is unable to do so? Now that must make your blood boil, eh Stoltzfus?"

The old clergyman was doing his best to instigate James into an assault.

James held his breath, and focused on the reason for his coming. If he could secure the price and purchase the young woman, Isaac and Constance would immediately draw the papers of emancipation and offer her the opportunity to stay, or move to another position, as she desired.

"What my brother does with the girl is his business. Now I am prepared to offer you five hundred."

The two men argued over the price. The old minister wanted four times as much, which was significantly over the current market price. Finally, the men agreed to seven hundred and fifty dollars. The girl was told to immediately pack her belongings and prepare to leave with James.

She only said, "Yes, Master", as she lowered her head and moved quietly from the room. Within a few minutes, she had returned with a small carpet bag containing only a few items of personal value. James paid the minister, and left without saying a further word.

As they walked to the waiting carriage, the minister called to James, "Tell Isaac she is damn good in bed. If she is with child, he can claim the bastard. No extra charge."

James stopped, thought for a moment, and then entered the carriage without looking back. He sat next to the young woman with tears in his eyes. He wanted to kill the man who claimed to be a representative of God and send him directly to hell where, in the opinion of James, the old man belonged.

As the carriage pulled from the house and headed for the train station, James looked into the deep, dark and beautiful eyes of the young woman. He asked her what she wished to be called.

Little more was exchanged between the two throughout their journey from Baltimore to Hagerstown. James had decided to sit with the frightened woman in the back of the train's passenger car, but spoke only to offer her some food he had in his haversack. He had not even told her where they were going, or what was to happen to her. He was still angry from the encounter with Reverend Duffie.

As they arrived at the station, Peter had been sent by Isaac to meet the train and bring the pair home. "Peter, this is Lydia Ann. She will be with us for awhile."

Peter helped the young woman into the coach, and spoke kindly to her. He told her that she would like it at the Stoltzfus house, and that Reverend and Missus Stoltzfus treated everyone just like family.

Lydia Ann spoke for the first time since leaving Baltimore except to tell James her name. "Master Peter, are you the overseer?"

Peter launched into his hearty laugh. "No, Miss Lydia Ann. There is no overseer at the Reverends' house. They don't own slaves, they just help people."

The young colored woman sat motionless, without saying another word. Could it be, she thought in her heart, that the purpose of this transaction was for the purchase of her freedom? It could not be, she was sure. Her expression began to change to sadness, as her hope of freedom faded, for fear of disappointment once again.

She had been told by an earlier master that when the old minister purchased her, he would treat her right and maybe give her freedom, if she was good to the old gentleman. When he came into her bed the first night, she had opened up to him, hoping that her obedience would be rewarded with freedom.

Instead she had been beaten for not satisfying his lustful hunger and told that he would sell her off should she become pregnant or not do as she was told. That was nearly ten years ago, and the hope of freedom was too painful to indulge for more than a moment.

The coach pulled to the front of the house and James, along with Peter, assisted the young woman to the parlor.

"Lydia Ann, would you please sit in this chair while I find Mister Isaac and Miss Constance? Peter, please stay with our guest."

James spoke with the kindness he had become known for.

Isaac and Constance at once entered the room, with James leading the way. Lydia Ann stood in their presence with her head bowed.

"My Dear, welcome", Constance spoke as she took Lydia Ann into her arms and greeted her.

"Now, please, be seated and let us become acquainted."

Hetti was at the Stoltzfus home, helping with kitchen work, and promptly brought in tea for the family and their newest guest. As she served them, she also poured a cup of the fine brew for herself, and took a seat in the center of the gathered company.

For the next hour, Isaac and James explained to the young woman that they had purchased her to secure her freedom. They also explained that they had need of help in the household, and would like to offer her a position, if she was interested.

Hetti shared that she, too, had been a slave. Through the help of many, she had gained her freedom, come to work for me, and would help Isaac and Constance as they had need.

"Dearie, they jest like family here. Treat everyone the same and helps, out too", she went on to say.

During the entire conversation, Lydia Ann had spoken very little.

Finally she said, "Miss Constance and Master Isaac, I can hardly believe what I am hearing. But you may not want me none, knowing I been with my master before and I may...", her voice trailed off.

James spoke at last. "Old Duffie violated the girl for the past ten years and threatened her that, should she become with child, he'd sell her off. It is possible."

192

Constance moved and knelt by the young woman's side, holding her hands.

"Lydia Ann, do not worry about any of that. If you want to be here with us, we will take care of you and your child, if and when your time of isolation arrives."

Lydia Ann broke down in waves of sobs at the kindness she had never known.

"Please, Master", she looked at Isaac. "Let me stay?" she spoke with pleading in her voice. "Please don't sell me off."

"My dear, you shall never need to call me Master. And, indeed, you shall stay as long as it is your desire to do so."

Isaac had demonstrated once again his love and compassion for all humanity.

Constance and Hetti dried the tears of the young woman. Greta had entered the room shortly before, with Lars, and joined in immediately, helping the girl feel as though she had come home for the first time.

Constance and Greta showed her where she was to make her quarters on the second floor. Both women also began to look for clothing that would be appropriate, and would fit her. Constance promised Lydia Ann that, as soon as I returned home from an assignment, we would all go shopping for new clothes.

The following day, Isaac and Constance took Lydia Ann to the county court house. There they executed the emancipation papers for the young woman. James went along, to ensure that Isaac would encounter no opposition, and to present the bill of sale.

The clerk, a member of Isaac's church, signed and notarized the documents. He asked Lydia if she could read and write, to which she responded she could do both. He then handed her the papers and congratulated her on her new freedom. The four stood together, along with the clerk of the court, and wept and laughed, all at the same time.

CHAPTER FORTY SIX

My work for the Tribune had been going well. I covered routine events and stories, mostly political in nature. Frequent travels to Washington City gave me opportunity to see James and many other friends, especially those on Capital Hill.

On one such trip, I spoke to James about the possibility of finding a house to buy. Isaac and Constance had suggested that, with as much time as I was spending in the City, it made good sense to have a home there and invest in real-estate, instead of renting a hotel room on each visit.

They assured me that I could keep my home in Hagerstown if I wished, or sell, and stay with them when I was in town. I shared my concern for Hetti, as she was growing in years and was well into her retirement period.

She had no family or home of her own and relied on me to provide her with income and housing. Constance at once reminded me that Lydia Ann had come to be with them, and that she, along with Greta and Peter, would always be there to help Hetti.

I had met Lydia Ann shortly after James had purchased her freedom, along with Isaac, from Reverend Duffie. She was a lovely and intelligent woman who had adapted well to her new family, instantly becoming friends with Hetti and Greta.

When she first arrived with James in Hagerstown, there had been concern for her well-being, suggesting that she may have been with Duffie's child. This had proven not to be the case. Hetti assured the young woman that she would never again have to submit to any man not of her choosing.

Late that fall, James informed me that a wonderful home was for sale near the corner of 17th and K Streets. He had requested an appointment for the two of us to visit the property, with the solicitor who was handling the sale.

As I toured the stately townhouse, I enjoyed the space, with the large, formal dining and sitting rooms on the first floor. The second floor contained four large bedrooms, each with its own fireplace.

"James, this is wonderful. I can easily convert two of the bedrooms into a suite and private study for my work", I suggested.

The asking price was well within my means, and I immediately made an offer.

The solicitor assured us that he would have an answer from the owners within the week. Shortly after arriving back in Hagerstown, the telegram arrived, telling me the offer had been accepted, and that settlement could occur at my earliest convenience.

James arranged the settlement, and on November twenty-nine, 1858, I took possession of the home that would serve as my office when on assignment in Washington City. Constance promised that she and Isaac would come and help me furnish the home and make it comfortable.

Following the New Year, Constance, along with Lydia Ann, attended to the new house. They cleaned from top to bottom. Constance shopped many of the small specialty stores, looking for the right furniture to compliment the décor and architecture of the structure.

By early March, the house had been completed, with all the adornments that made it appear as more a home than simply a dwelling. Constance stated that I should hold an open house to celebrate, and invite all my friends and acquaintances.

Invitations were sent out to over two hundred guests throughout the Washington area. The open house was scheduled for the first of June.

Constance had insisted that I should have a new dress for the occasion, and one was found to both our liking, at a small dress maker on M Street. I was told the dress maker was responsible for the attire of many Washington elite, including Missus Simon Cameron and Missus Rose O'Neal Greenhow.

As the day of the celebration dawned, guests began arriving promptly at the appointed time. One of the first was Missus Greenhow.

I had met the enchanting and manipulative "Wild Rose", as she was often referred to, at other Washington Parties. She was always part of the Washington elite and inner circles, due to the influence of her former husband's connections in the State Department.

Doctor Greenhow had died suddenly, following the birth of their youngest daughter. Rose had remained in Washington, continuing to enjoy the life she had grown accustomed to in her married life. She was often now found entertaining guests at her home, and seemed to especially enjoy the company of politicians and generals.

"Rose, it is so good of you to come. I trust that your social calendar is not too full this year as to not have time for some relaxing moments?" I inquired as Constance and I greeted our guest.

Rose was always the first to arrive at any event, to insure that she would be able to meet all the guests, especially the most important ones, as soon as they arrived. I did not particularly like Missus Greenhow.

However, she had been the source of good information regarding some of the lesser positive sides of Washington life and politics.

After all, Constance reminded me, "You don't need her as your good friend, Elizabeth. You need her only as a good source."

The late afternoon event went well, with most of the invited guests arriving and enjoying the time socializing. Simon Cameron had arrived as well, and was immediately taken aside by Rose.

"My Dearest Senator, how are you doing these days? I am told you may be in a position to run for President in the coming year. Tell me it is true."

She went on in her charming and almost profane manner, luring her prey as a spider calling its catch into the entanglement of its web.

Senator Cameron would neither admit nor deny the rumor. He suggested that Rose should remain open to any possibility. It was rumored, as with many politicians, that Rose showed special favor to the men in exchange for information and privilege.

As the day grew to an end, Simon approached me, to ask if we might speak. I took him to my study and closed the door. He began at once.

"I have been asked by some of my colleagues in the Republican Party to make a bid for the White House next spring. I may agree."

He went on to explain that, should he make the bid and be successful, he would transfer, with my approval, management of my funds to his son Donald. I had met the young man and was impressed with the integrity that his father, at most times, seemed to lack.

I agreed that Donald would be a good choice, especially if he had learned from his father the shrewd business sense which came so easy for Simon. Simon assured me that he had, and that where his son might be lacking, the elder Cameron would step in with recommendations, albeit without appearance of favoritism.

We returned to our guests with my promise not share our conversation. Simon was not ready to announce his candidacy for the Presidency of the United States. He also assured me that there was more he wished to discuss, but would make another time for the conversation.

The day drew to a close, and the last guests departed, Rose Greenhow among them.

"Oh Constance, I am always delighted to see that woman leave", I shared.

I was glad to have my home to myself and, after the flirtatious behavior of Rose throughout the day, felt as if both I and the house were in need of a thorough cleaning.

CHAPTER FORTY SEVEN

James, Isaac, Constance, and I attended the General Assembly of the Lutheran Church, held during the second week of October in St Louis, Missouri. I was there as a correspondent for the Tribune.

The Lutheran General Assembly met every four years, to set policy and statements of belief for the church throughout the years following the close of the session. The gathering also was charged with electing and ordaining Bishops, as the Church had need.

As the Convention was convened on the morning of October fifteen, 1859, Isaac's name had been given in consideration for the purpose of filling the office of Bishop in the Washington-Baltimore Convention of the Church. The current resident Bishop would be retiring at the end of the year, and a replacement needed to be named. The Washington-Baltimore Convention was considered an important entity, due to its particular relationship with the government.

As the General Assembly got underway, the tension in the air was thick with anticipation of the successor to the current Bishop. The Assembly was divided on the issue of slavery, and whoever held the office of Bishop in Washington could possibly influence the policy makers of the nation.

Additionally, there had been recent talk of secession over states' rights and slavery, by some of the southern states. The Resident Bishop of Washington would be required to take the Church's position on this issue, as well, and would indeed be called upon to assure that the Church would not divide, even if the nation did.

On the fifth ballot, Isaac was elected as the new Resident Bishop to the Washington-Baltimore Convention of the Lutheran Churches of America, Missouri Synod. James was overflowing with joy, and Constance kept saying how Isaac would be able to make a difference in the life of the Church he loved. Isaac was not sure if this election was indeed a blessing, or a curse. Either way, he would accept the position as the will of God and begin his new position at the start of the New Year.

Isaac and Constance began making plans for their move to Washington City and the residence of the Bishop. Their new residence would be less than twenty blocks from my home, and we would once again be close to each other. As Isaac and Constance made preparations for their move, I was busy on another assignment.

Horace Greeley had wired me in St. Louis, to request that I return to Washington without delay at the close of the Convention. Upon my arrival home, I would find details of an assignment to which I was to proceed immediately.

I arrived back in Washington on the evening of the twenty-fourth of October. As I read Greeley's report, I saw the need for haste.

John Brown, a radical abolitionist, had attacked the Federal Arsenal in Harpers Ferry, Virginia, with the intention of igniting a rebellion among the slaves. With little more than a handful of men, he easily took command of the Arsenal and captured the store of weapons and munitions available.

With the local militia alerted, the towns-people had held Brown and his men at bay for several hours, trapped in the Arsenal Building, until federal troops, under the command of Colonel Robert Edward Lee, arrived to secure the capture of the rebels. The trial of John Brown, on treason against the United States and the State of Virginia, would be underway in two days.

I immediately packed my bag and took the first train to Frederick, Maryland, and then on to Harpers Ferry. Arriving on the morning of the twenty-sixth, I proceeded to Charles Town, Virginia, and found lodging at the Washington Street Boarding House for Women. This was the only room available, and the Inn Keeper, a widowed woman in her late years, accepted me without hesitation.

The next morning, I found my way to the Jefferson County Court House, where the trial was to take place. By the time of my arrival shortly before nine in the morning, the court room was packed with spectators. The press had been positioned in a small area at the rear of the room, behind Brown's table.

The gentlemen from the press made room for me, and invited me to sit in the front row. I accepted their kind offer, and immediately took my seat.

Brown entered the court room, shackled at both hands and feet. Unable to walk, and too weak from his wounds, he was laid on a stretcher and carried into the court. He wore his dark suit and vest. His long flowing white beard and unkempt hair made him appear more like the figure of Moses coming from the mountain of God than a madman, as some considered him.

As the judge entered the room, Brown attempted to raise himself, out of respect to the Court. The charges of treason were read, along with other charges the state had made. The Judge asked Brown how he pleaded, and the defendant lay silent. Brown's attorney answered that his client pleaded "not guilty" to all charges.

On the afternoon of November the second, Brown was convicted of treason against the state, and sentenced to be hanged by the neck until dead. During the trial, Brown had refused to defend himself, only speaking at times, eloquently, against the evils of slavery. The sentence of death would be carried out one month later, on December the second, 1859.

I returned to Washington and filed my story with the Tribune. Before leaving Charles Town, I made arrangements with the Boarding House for a room upon my return in December, for the execution of Brown.

While in Washington, Constance visited me at my home. She was there to begin preparations for the move into the Bishop's Residence after the start of the New Year.

"I am not sure what we shall do with Greta, Peter and Lydia", she shared. "We have room for only one personal servant, as the others are already provided by the Church."

We discussed her dilemma for some time until, finally, I suggested that I would give her and Isaac my home in Hagerstown for their retirement years, with the understanding that Hetti was to remain and be cared for.

"Greta and Peter can stay with Hetti and look after her, and Lydia Ann can come to Washington with you, if that is your desire", I suggested.

Constance could not thank me enough for my kindness to them all. She was not sure, however, that she could accept the house. I assured her that I had need of only one house, and the present home in Washington was quite sufficient.

We finally agreed that this was the best course of action, and I promised we would talk further about the idea when we all gathered at her home for Christmas. This year would see both of the soldier boys home, as well as Caroline and Abraham.

I returned to Charles Town, Virginia, the end of November, to witness the execution of John Brown on December second. Cadets from the Virginia Military Institute, under the command of Major Thomas Jackson, had been sent, in the event an attempt would be made to gain Brown's freedom. No attempt was made.

On the morning of the second, Brown was bought to the gallows. He had sufficiently recovered from his wounds to allow him to walk the thirteen steps to the platform under his own power. Brown's poise and demeanor was astonishing to those who stood in witness.

He remained erect and in perfect control of self and situation. Arms secured behind his back, he greeted his executioners, and shook hands with them as best he could. The hangman's noose was placed around his neck, and a white cap was placed over his head.

After about ten more minutes of preparation, the order was given to release the trap door over which Brown had stood, patiently waiting for eternity. The door sprang open, and Brown fell the two feet to his death. His wife received his body later that day in Harpers Ferry, and returned home with her deceased husband.

The end of the slave rebellion had arrived with the death of John Brown. He had remarked at his sentencing that he was prepared to die, for he had done only what he believed right in the sight of God. No minister was present at his execution.

Following the events of the day, I ran into Major Thomas Jackson at the local Inn. He was enjoying dinner with fellow officers and instructors from the Institute.

"Major Jackson, if I might be so bold as to interrupt you in your dinner."

I spoke with simple decorum, as I was well aware that Jackson was a southern gentleman in every respect.

The Major at once came to his feet and offered me a seat at his table. The other men stood as well, and we all joined together for a few moments.

"Miss Fitzgerald, it honors me that you would recognize me after all this time."

I had met the Major while Andrew studied at VMI.

"Indeed, Major Jackson, you are a most unforgettable individual."

The others joined in laughter at my sentiment, and I noticed a brief expression of embarrassment from the Major.

"I assure you, I intend no embarrassment upon your person, Sir", I stated.

"No embarrassment received, Madam. To what do we owe the pleasure of your company this solemn evening?" Major Jackson asked.

I explained that I was covering the execution of Brown as part of my duties for the New York Tribune, and would be leaving in the morning. I shared that Andrew would be returning home for Christmas, and was then to report to the Washington War Department for a new assignment.

Major Jackson confessed he had heard that Andrew was serving well in Utah, and was delighted that he would return to a new assignment in the east.

"Andrew was one of my early students, and a fine cadet, Miss Fitzgerald."

"Andrew always speaks highly of you, as well, Sir", I shared with the distinguished officer.

We exchanged a few more moments of pleasantries regarding the health of his wife and his work at the Virginia Military Institute. I stood and excused myself from the small gathering and returned to my room at the Boarding House.

The next day I boarded the train for Hagerstown, to join the Stoltzfus family for Christmas. It would be our last in the house that had given us so many memories. It would be good to have all four of the children home this year. Though the visit would be short, it would remain in our memories for many years to come.

CHAPTER FORTY EIGHT

During the Christmas festivities, Caroline announced that, since she would be moving to Washington City with her parents after the start of the New Year, she wished for me to introduce her to the world of investigative reporting.

"Auntie Liz", she had started. "I have always admired your spirit and your work and have wanted to be like you in every way, ever since a little girl."

Caroline often had followed me on the trail of a story, when it was appropriate for her to do so. She had graduated from Wilson School for Women the previous spring, and was now more than eager to engage life.

She had been pursued by a number of male suitors, but none had succeeded in winning her heart. I prayed that she was not destined to spend her years alone, as I had been, or to experience only brief romance from time to time, thus leading the life of a spinster. I promised Caroline that I would speak with Horace Greeley and explore the possibilities.

James had been promoted to the Senior Pastor position at Trinity Lutheran Church in Washington. Although he was excited about the position, he was concerned that the new responsibilities would curtail his involvement with bringing freedom to the Negro slaves.

His Bishop had made this appointment as one of his last official acts before retirement to, as he said, "Ensure that James would realize it was time for him to slow down a bit, as well." James still suffered discomfort, headaches, and walked with his limp, as a result of previous injuries from his encounters with proslavery forces.

The exciting news at Christmas was centered on the three sons. Andrew had been given orders to report to the War Department in January for a new assignment. General Winfield Scott had requested the young lieutenant, after a meeting with James earlier in the fall. James expressed his desire to see his nephew back in the east, and Scott promised to do what he could for the young man.

According to Andrew, he was appreciative of his Uncle's influence, but reminded the family he had less than six months left to his enlistment. He was certain that any assignment now would be less than exciting, and most likely a desk job at the War Department. He would rather have remained in Utah.

Amos shared that he was extending his enlistment for another four years, and would remain in the Midwest, serving along side of Major Henry Heth. Major Heth liked Amos, and the two had become fast friends as well. Amos often spoke of the exploits of his commanding officer, who, because of his own valor, had quickly risen to the rank of brevet Captain.

The young minister, Abraham, had continued to work with James in his Abolitionist endeavors. Most recently, Abraham had been invited to teach at the Lutheran Seminary in Gettysburg, but had declined the position for fear that he would be required to curtail some of his involvement with James.

James had, therefore, offered his nephew a position as his associate at the Church. Some spoke of familial favoritism in this appointment, but James and Abraham agreed that it would afford their work the opportunity to continue, with Abraham taking over where James needed to slow down.

Everyone appeared to be pleased with the new assignments and possibilities for the future. All but Isaac.

Isaac was happy that his family appeared to be moving forward in their lives and all seemed well. However, he was gravely concerned about the future.

The newly elected Bishop had expressed that, with the raid on Harpers Ferry and the subsequent trial and execution of John Brown, more violence was sure to follow. He worried that his sons would in some way be caught in the coming conflict, and he often expressed fear for their safety.

All present reassured Isaac that he regularly worried about situations that never came to pass. Constance assured her husband that it was more the responsibilities of being Bishop, than being a father, that really weighed him down.

As the New Year dawned, Isaac and Constance moved from the rectory in Hagerstown to their new home in Washington City, and he assumed the role of Resident Bishop.

Lydia Ann accompanied the Stoltzfus family and continued in their employ, as the personal attendant to Constance. Hetti remained in Hagerstown, along with Greta, Peter and Lars, their first born. Caroline moved in with me, and began following me everywhere I went, to learn as she could and to meet the influential people of the Washington elite.

Andrew reported to General Scott for his new assignment. Scott was an elderly gentleman who had enjoyed an exemplary military career. He was both beloved by his men who had served with him, and respected by the politicians who employed him. Although known as "Old Fuss and Feathers", Scott was a respected tactician.

Following the one hour meeting, Andrew reported he was to attend to President Buchanan and serve as the military aide to the White House, representing the War Department. The young officer shared that the position was mostly honorary, without any real responsibilities. However he said that "Old Fuss and Feathers" promised that if he wished to extend his enlistment, a more challenging assignment might be found. Andrew declined.

By April, the process of electing the next President was well underway. The campaigns had begun, with several men seeking the Presidential nomination of their respected parties for the November elections. Simon Cameron had been using his considerable influence to seek the Republican nomination, and appeared to be well in the lead.

Meanwhile, the Democrats had been unable to nominate a candidate at their convention in late April, as several of the southern delegates had walked out when the convention failed to ratify the proslavery platform. Some were again calling for secession, to ensure that their peculiar institution would remain intact.

In May, the Republican Convention nominated Abraham Lincoln on the third ballot. Simon Cameron, realizing he would likely not win the nomination, conceded his support to Lincoln, and had used his influence to strike a deal with the nominee, ensuring a Cabinet position in the Lincoln administration.

In June, the Democrats nominated Stephen Douglas, and adopted a platform supporting the protection of rights for the slave states and non-interference of the federal government on the issue. The contest was now set.

In the following months of campaigning, the issues were reduced to slavery and sectionalism. Several Southern spokesmen made it clear that, if Lincoln were to win the election, secession was sure to follow. Lincoln remained a moderate on the issue of slavery, assuring the southern states that he had no intention of forcing the power of the federal government on the will of the people.

In November, Abraham Lincoln was elected as the sixteenth President of the United States. Caroline and I had been traveling extensively with the Lincoln campaign and were present with the candidate in Illinois when the results of the election were announced.

Both the President elect and his wife, Mary Todd Lincoln, looked relieved that the campaign was over. Missus Lincoln appeared delighted that her husband would be in the White House, but Mister Lincoln appeared extremely solemn at the responsibilities he had just inherited by his election.

For the first time in American history, the country had a President who was clearly anti-slavery. The Republican Party had declared that the normal condition of all the territories of the United States was that of freedom.

Within days of the election, Southern leaders were speaking of secession as the inevitable necessity. South Carolina held a state convention to propose the idea, and voted to secede from the Union.

Senator John Crittenden of Kentucky, working in committee, presented to Congress a number of proposals to ensure that secession of the Southern States was not necessary to guarantee their way of life. The nation was moving quickly toward crisis.

Andrew had completed his military service, and was beginning to study law at Georgetown. Caroline was busy writing copy for me, that was then sent to Horace Greeley in New York.

Isaac was working day and night, in an attempt to quiet the possibility of a split in the Church over the issue of slavery. He had been in South Carolina during the convention. The Lutheran Churches of the southern states announced that, if South Carolina seceded from the Union, they would join with their members and leave the Church, forming the Southern Alliance of Lutheran Churches.

Christmas came and went with little celebration. Constance had been sick for several days with fever. Amos was still in Kansas, and would not return home this year.

Isaac had returned from South Carolina, with the news of a split in the church the day before. He also reported that the South Carolina Militia had assumed control of the harbor in Charleston, and that Major Robert Anderson had consolidated his forces at Fort Sumter.

James and Abraham were working fervently, along side of Harriet Tubman, to gain the freedom for as many slaves as possible, before the issue of secession became the new reality. William Garrison and others continued to supply James with as much funding as possible to assist in his work.

The year came to a close with the possibility that several of the southern states would indeed secede from the Union, and that at some point, armed conflict to preserve the Union might become necessary. President Buchanan, and what was left of his cabinet, worked to find a reasonable solution.

Book FOUR

a time for war...

CHAPTER FORTY NINE

January, 1861, was an unusually warm month, feeling more like an early spring than winter. Yet, in spite of the warm temperatures and mild days, the cold winds of secession and war loomed on the ever darkening horizon.

Abraham Lincoln had been elected President of the United States of America, and had made it clear that he would not accept secession, declaring that he had been elected to be, and would be, President of the entire nation, including those states in the south. South Carolina had already voted toward secession, and others were quickly following suit.

Mister Lincoln had verbally advised his future Secretary of State, William Seward, that he also would not support the expansion of slavery in the new states. This position further added to the already growing hostilities with the southerners.

I had been in Washington City for almost four years now, and the city was coming to life with civilians, most of whom were refugees fleeing the coming conflict over the issue of secession. Others were additional military troops, present for the potential need to defend Washington City against an armed invasion by southern state forces. Most feared that when Mister Lincoln took office the following March, the issue of secession would escalate into armed conflict at the request of the new President.

In addition to the refugees and soldiers, there was an additional increase in the number of contraband, those run away slaves who had escaped from the south into the north, seeking their freedom. Many had arrived in this city, hoping that Father Abraham, as the President had come to be known by the Negro slave, would be able to free them and give them hope for a better future.

It was during this time that I met "Missy". She was a beautiful, young, mullato girl about twenty years old. As I came out of my home at 17th and K Streets, I saw her sitting on the street corner, huddled among her possessions, begging for food, or whatever assistance anyone would or could offer.

Dressed in rags that still bore the evidence that they had, at one time, been fine clothing, it was obvious that she had not eaten or bathed in some time. She sat staring, with blank eyes that spoke of longing and suffering.

I stopped to speak, though I was on my way to the train station to travel to a prearranged meeting with Governor Thomas Hicks, the Governor of Maryland, in Frederick. "My dear, you are so tired and hungry looking. Let me help you. Where are you staying?"

The young woman looked up at me with disbelief that I would have even spoken to her. For the most part, those who passed by either went about their business, or simply threw a few coins at her feet. No one had, to this point, taken the time to speak. "Are you able to speak, or has life taken that away, as well? I inquired.

"Yes, Ma'am, I is able to speak. Just not too good, that be all. You gonna hit me an' make me leave here too, jest like the other folks do?"

I was taken back somewhat by her speech and concern, for looking at her clothes and skin, I was certain that if she were a run away slave, she certainly would have been a house servant and better educated than the field hands of the day.

"No, I am not going to run you off and hit you. Now, where are you staying, and what is your name?"

"I be staying no place, jest where I can lay my head at night, but not with no man. They's call me Missy, Missy Stanford. That's what they call me. My Master is, was, Thomas Stanford of Front Royal. I's run away and gots no place to go now. I gonna see Master Abraham when he git here and he help then."

"What did you do for Mister Stanford, Missy?"

"I was his house servant and took care of Missus Stanford until she died. Then I cleaned and cooked for Master."

I had been living at the home on the corner of 17th and K for a little over two years now. I had purchased it with the funds I had saved from my father's estate after he died in 1836. Unfortunately, it was a large town home and I lived there, along with Caroline. I was in desperate need of a house keeper, but none was to be found at this time.

"Missy, my name is Elizabeth, and we need to get you off this street and someplace warm and safe for the day. I want you to come home with me, and I will fix you up for the day.

"You can bathe, have something to eat, and rest. I can not stay with you because I have a very important meeting to attend, but I will return tonight, and then we can talk about your future."

I helped Missy gather her belongings, and took her up the street to my home. We went inside and I showed her where she could bathe, find something to eat, and a bed she could sleep in. I also showed her a large trunk hidden away in a spare room.

"Missy, I want you to make yourself at home now. I must be off, but when I return tonight, we will talk over your situation, and you can tell me your story. In the meantime, wash yourself and go through this trunk.

"It contains several pieces of clothing and some dresses. I am sure that you will find something in here that will suit you. Whatever you find and like, you may have and keep."

"But Miss Elizabeth, how you know I won't take your stuff and run off? You don't know me."

"I don't know that you won't take advantage of the situation, but I am trusting in you and I believe you will do what is right. Now don't worry any more about this. I must be off and if you are still here when I return, we will talk. I should be back around 9:00 tonight."

It was now past 7:00 in the morning, and I needed to be at the station by 7:30 to catch my train to Frederick for the meeting with Governor Hicks. I left, and began a fast walk down the street toward the station, wondering to myself what I had just done, leaving a complete stranger, a run away slave, alone in my house.

Caroline was away for a few days attending to her mother at the Bishop's Residence. Constance had been ill with fever for more than two weeks and was showing no sign of improvement.

My thoughts immediately turned to my old friend, Isaac Stoltzfus. He would say, "Let us pray about this first, then we take action." I chuckled to myself and then decided that perhaps I should pray now. And so I did.

213

My meeting with Governor Hicks went well. We dined at a local establishment and spoke together for well over three hours.

I inquired of the Governor if Maryland would join with the secessionists of the Southern states, or remain loyal to the Union.

"My Dear Miss Fitzgerald, I assure you that if it comes to dissolving the Union to ensure the rights of each state, then Maryland will surely lean toward secession as well", the Governor had clearly stated.

The implications of Maryland joining the Southern States were disturbing, at the very least. Should Maryland secede, then Washington City, the Capital of the Nation, would be located on Southern soil.

I pressed Governor Hicks to discuss whether Maryland would take arms against their fellow country men, to gain their right to form a new nation. He refused to answer directly but offered,

"Maryland will do what it must to ensure our rights over the interference of the Federal Government. If that means taking arms, I fear I am not in a position to openly discuss the matter."

I returned home, fearing that armed conflict may be closer than anyone in Washington was willing to admit. The new President had yet to be seated in the center of political power, and President Buchanan appeared to be willing only to do what little could be done to prolong the stability of the Union until he was out of office.

Nearly all of President Buchanan's cabinet had resigned in the past several weeks. Many now sitting with the President were there only on a temporary appointment, awaiting the new President.

Those who had left the Cabinet had done so over their protest to either the actions, or inactions, of the President in dealing with the Southern States. Delegates from South Carolina had been turned away from a meeting with President Buchanan. The President had refused to meet with the delegation, out of concern that the meeting would give the impression of White House approval to the formation of a new government in the South.

By January fifth, seven states had declared their secession from the Union. Senators from the seven states had resigned from the House. President Buchanan ordered the "Star of the West" to transport two hundred and fifty additional troops to support and reinforce Fort Sumter in South Carolina.

I returned home from my meeting in Frederick, Maryland, wondering if this would be the last time I would venture to see the Governor of Maryland. Should Maryland leave the Union, I would surely be called back north of the Mason-Dixon Line, to continue my work with Horace Greely and the New York Tribune.

I arrived home well after ten in the evening, to find Missy still there. She had bathed and found a dress to wear, which gave her the appearance of a well educated and refined young woman. A light meal was already prepared and ready to be served.

"Missy, I do appreciate your preparing a meal for me, but really, that was not what I intended for you to do."

I offered her some mild protest and tried to explain that she was not responsible for taking care of me, or anyone else, for that matter.

She insisted that I sit and eat a small portion before deciding if she had really done me a favor by preparing food. The meal of fresh trout and vegetables with a side of rice was exceptional. I complimented her on her abilities in the kitchen.

"But now, Missy, let us retire to the sitting room and talk about your future", I instructed.

With a cup of tea, we sat in the two overstuffed chairs near the fire.

I began, "I would suspect that you have been known by another name at some time or other, and Missy was probably given to you by your former Master."

Missy explained that she had been taken from her mother when she was about six or seven and placed into the home of the caretaker. The caretaker's wife taught her how to speak and act in a proper way, so she could be sold as a house servant. Before that, she had been called Rebecca by her mother, and missed the name.

"Then we shall call you Rebecca, if that pleases you", I said with sympathy and understanding.

How many times, I thought to myself, have I heard these stories in the past, through James and others.

215

Rebecca went on to explain that she had been sold about two years later and had not seen or heard from her mother in over ten years.

"I don't know where she be now, perhaps dead or sold off to another master", Rebecca stated with some sadness.

"And what of your father?" I inquired.

"Don't know nothing about him. Told by my Mamma that he was the Master of the plantation where she was at. After I was born, she says he sold us both off. I been sold four times now, three before I was ten or so. Was with Master Stanford for nearly twelve years before I run away."

Rebecca went on to say that Mister Stanford had been kind until his wife died, and then he started to beat her regularly and wanted to sleep with her. She shared how he often came into her room late at night, under the influence of drink, and would lie with her.

"That's when I decided to run away, when he forced me to himself. I didn't want no white man's baby to be treated like me, a slave. I better than that."

Rebecca spoke with a pride and rebellious spirit that told she had had enough of the cruel treatment, and would tolerate no more.

"Yes, Rebecca, you are better than that", I affirmed.

We spoke on for some time longer, with the promise that we would talk more in the morning.

"In the meantime, Rebecca, you may stay here with me until you decide what you would like to do. You may sleep in the spare room and tomorrow, you may decide what is best for you."

We parted for the night. Rebecca thanked me for my hospitality and kept asking why I was doing all of this for her. I simply said that it was out of a heart filled with love for humanity, and the influence of my dear friends, that allowed me to take this course of action on her behalf.

The hour was now well past midnight, and I was exhausted from the day. Sleep, however, was restless and short lived.

CHAPTER FIFTY ONE

At four o'clock the morning of January six, there was a knock at the door. Persistent and loud, the knock continued, until I arose to see who was clattering at this hour. I took the small revolver I kept in my writing desk with me, as I went to investigate.

As I opened the door, Lydia Ann stood in the cold night air, still dressed in her night clothes and wrapped in her cape. A carriage was waiting by the street.

"What is wrong, Lydia Ann?' I immediately inquired, as I invited the poor girl inside.

Rebecca had heard the commotion as well, and stood in the hallway, just out of sight of the night's intruder. She had feared that somehow she was to be caught and returned to her former Master, and was preparing to run from the house.

"It's Miss Constance," Lydia Ann began at once. "You must come quickly. Doctor says she may not live much longer."

I turned to see Rebecca and told her that my dear friend was very ill, and I needed to go at once. She said she would help me dress and come with me, if it were all right to do so.

Lydia Ann waited, along with the carriage, while we prepared. Within the half hour, we were off to Isaac's and Constance's home. Caroline met us at the door, and shared that her mother was currently being attended to by Isaac, along with the Doctor, in the upstairs bedroom. James, Abraham, and Andrew had been sent for as well, but she did not know when they would come.

I entered the room where Constance lay near death. She spoke to me as I entered, and asked me to draw near. She then ordered everyone else from the room so we could speak in private.

"Elizabeth, my Dearest friend", she began. "There is much to tell you and little time left."

Constance went on to ask me to continue to look after Caroline.

"She is so much like you, and I fear that without your guidance and friendship, she may find herself in more trouble than she might be able to handle."

I assured Constance that she and Isaac had raised a fine daughter who needed no one's help. I, however, pledged that I would do all that I could to care for Caroline, as well as Constance's three sons, in the days ahead.

"And one more promise, Elizabeth", she continued.

"Care for Isaac. I know he has loved you for a very long time, even before we met. His love for you never died. I am not asking you to be his wife, but please stay close to him when I am gone from this world. He needs a woman to care for him. Promise me."

I knew Isaac had continued to love me even after Constance had entered his life. He had, however, been a faithful and true husband to her, and we had all been great friends.

"Constance, I could never take your place in his life." I continued, "I may have been Isaac's friend, but you have truly been his love.

"Think no more on these things, my Dearest Constance. I will do all in my power to look after your family until you are well enough to resume those responsibilities yourself."

"No, Elizabeth, I will not recover to look to the care of my family." Constance offered in brief protest.

"God has been gracious to all of us, but now I am ready to go into His eternal presence and to wait, along with all the saints, for His final victory over death and suffering."

I sat with my friend for a few more moments, holding her hand and brushing the hair from around her face. We talked of brighter days. I assured her that her children were coming to be with her and should arrive soon.

"All but Amos", she reminded me. "He will not be here before I am gone, Elizabeth. But please, do give him my love for me."

There was a light knock on the door and Isaac, along with James, Andrew, Abraham, and Caroline, entered the room. The Doctor came to her beside and checked her pulse.

Constance insisted that we should all stay with her, and asked for Lydia Ann as well. She commended her family for their faithfulness to God over the years and promised that she had no regrets and was prepared to meet her God and Savior.

She spoke to the children and asked that they not mourn her death, but to instead celebrate her life. To Isaac, she required that he continue in his work and remain faithful until the day his Lord should call him to once again join her around the throne of God's love. She thanked Lydia Ann for her faithfulness to the family, and for the friendship that had grown between the two women.

Constance's breathing was becoming more labored, and everyone, including the Doctor, advised her to rest. In her usual strong willed way she insisted that she would rest when she entered glory, but was going to speak to the last, as she had strength to do so.

Caroline on one side of the bed and I on the other, continued to sit and stroke her hair and refresh her face with cool water. The others remained standing around the bed, listening to their mother and wife as she shared her last thoughts.

As the sun sneezed its first breath of a new day and broke into the morning air, Constance smiled her last, and drew her final breath. Peace was upon her face, and it seemed as if the light of God's presence suddenly filled the room.

The Doctor checked her pulse for the final time, and pronounced that she had departed this world for a better place. All present wept at the pronouncement, some for the loss of our dear friend, some for our momentary loneliness, and some for the joy we knew she was now experiencing alongside her Lord.

A wire had been sent through the War Department to Amos regarding his mother. He would arrive a week later, in time for the final services.

Rebecca approached me as I left the room, where Constance now lay at rest, and spoke for the first time since arriving at the Stoltzfus residence.

"Miss Elizabeth, I am sorry for your loss. If it pleases you, let me stay on until this matter has been laid to rest, and we can decide my future at that time."

I looked at her through my tear filled eyes and thanked her for her willingness to assist me, and the family, in whatever way she could.

"Of course, my Dear, you shall stay with me as long as you wish. And thank you for your offer to help."

I took Rebecca to formally meet Lydia Ann, and the two set about making preparations for visitors and family. The Doctor had sent for the Undertaker, who arrived by midmorning to care for the body. The household was set into mourning for the next several days.

.

CHAPTER FIFTY TWO

Attired in mourning clothes, the family greeted friends as they came regularly to pay their respects. Isaac was inconsolable for the first few days, but slowly had begun to recover his usual spirited attitude toward life.

"Oh, how I will miss her, Elizabeth", he had commented several times.

The children were all present, as well as close family friends. Greta, Peter and Lars, along with Hetti, had traveled from Hagerstown, and were staying with me. Rebecca participated as if she had been with us for many years, although in truth we had met just the day before Constance died.

Many of the politicians and officials had also attended to Isaac and the family. Simon Cameron was most sympathetic, and offered the use of his servants for the care of the final arrangements.

I can not remember the last time I witnessed so many flowers in one place. Daily, bouquets of lilies, roses, daisies, and a host of other flowers arrived, with sympathies and cards of concern and care. It seemed as if all of Washington was in mourning for their Resident Bishop's wife.

Even Rose O'Neal Greenhow dared to make her appearance. Neither Constance nor I particularly liked the woman who seemed to have the inside ear of every politician and General in Washington. It had even been rumored as of late that she might have particular sympathies toward the South.

As Greenhow entered the residence, she immediately handed her cloak to Lydia Ann, and walked past her without saying a word.

"My Dear Isaac", she began. "Or shall I call you Bishop; I never know which is most proper? Do tell me, my Dear Sir, how are you ever managing in your grief at the loss of such a dear wife?"

Isaac acknowledged her presence and engaged in some small talk with the social hostess of the Washington elite. Caroline came to my side and began to complain about her presence.

"That woman only has one thing in mind when she comes around any man", Caroline stated with a sharp tongue.

"And what might that be, my dear?" I inquired.

"She just wants them to cater to her own vain sense of power, and to get them into bed with her, so she can manipulate them into whatever it is she desires at the moment. I cannot stand her." Caroline complained.

"Neither can I, nor could your Mother", I reminded the child.

"Anyway, she will be gone soon, but you must keep a watch out for her in the days ahead, lest she tries to snare your Father into her web of deceit."

On the day of the funeral, the services were held at Trinity Lutheran Church. James, assisted by Abraham, conducted the "Celebration of Death and Resurrection", as James had called it. He spoke eloquently about the life that Constance had led, full of joy and great anticipation of one day being with her Lord in Paradise. That day was now her present reality.

Many spoke throughout the service, giving great testimony to her love of family, friends, and of the Church. Many shared of her uncompromised belief that all were created equal, and that she believed in freedom for all of God's children, black and white, male and female.

Several spoke of her compassion toward others. Some shared of her spirit that engaged life to the fullest, wherever she went and whatever she did.

Greta, Peter, Hetti, Lydia Ann, all spoke of how she gave them a home and a sense that they were people of value and worth. Lydia spoke of being rescued from the jaws of enslavement and death, by Constance and her family. And all spoke how they never felt they were outsiders, but instead were made to feel like family.

Following the service at the church, we gathered around the graveside. I stood with Caroline at the head of the procession, and next to Isaac. James read scripture over the grave. "Who shall separate us from the love of Christ? Shall tribulation, or distress, or persecution, or famine, or nakedness, or peril, or sword?"

Constance had heard these words from Romans, chapter eight, earlier in life, sitting in the home of a Quaker family as the slave trappers came to the door. They had been etched forever upon her mind and heart, and she would often quote them when in the midst of danger. Today, these words brought comfort to those of us gathered to say farewell.

At the close of the service, starting with their youngest son, Andrew, and working through Caroline, then me, and finally

Isaac, we all threw a handful of dirt into the grave and upon the closed casket. I held Caroline close as we both wept. Isaac and his three sons walked together toward the waiting carriage. The others, along with James, followed.

I looked back and saw Lydia Ann standing alone, with dirt in her hand. Tears were streaming down her face as she looked into the grave. Caroline and I walked back and stood on either side of her, taking her into our arms.

Lydia looked for approval as she was about to throw the handful of dirt into the grave. Caroline and I smiled and nodded our heads in approval at the gesture. At that, the dirt fell from her soft, small hand into the grave, and the three of us walked to the waiting carriage that would transport us back to the Bishop's Rectory.

A gentleman whom I did not recognize was standing to the rear of the gathered crowd, with Rose Greenhow.

As Amos was passing by, he overheard the man say "Rose, when we have won the day, these nigger lovers will have no place in the new land."

Rose giggled softly.

"Sir, how dare you speak such insolence at my mother's funeral?" Amos spoke with fire in his breath at the remark.

"Sir, I meant no disrespect", the man stammered.

"Then I suggest you remove yourself at once and take this, this, southern harlot with you." Amos countered.

Before any further words could be spoken, Isaac came to his son's side and took him off to the carriage. The man spoke something to Rose Greenhow, and the two departed in a waiting carriage that drove them in the opposite direction of the rest of the funeral party.

The remainder of the day, Isaac and the children received various guests at their home, and maintained the proper decorum of mourning. The Church's business would have to wait until another day for Bishop Stoltzfus to resume his duties.

CHAPTER FIFTY THREE

By the week following the funeral of Constance, there was no longer time for mourning. Secession fever was beginning to take hold across the nation. Horace Greeley had wired, saying that he needed me to cover the Senate on the morning of January twenty-one.

Rebecca and I had spoken, along with Caroline, and the three of us reached an agreement that Rebecca would continue to stay with us as long as she wished. In exchange, Rebecca stated that she would tend to the care of the household duties, so Caroline and I could continue in our work. I agreed to provide room and board and a stipend for her personal expenses, in exchange for the work.

The morning of the twenty-first, Caroline and I went to the Senate chambers. The press box was already filled, but two seats were quickly made available for us near the front row.

Several southern states had voted for secession, with Mississippi being one of them. Five Senators, including Jefferson Davis, stood and made farewell speeches before leaving the chambers. Davis spoke with such eloquence, and it was apparent that he did not wish to see the Union come to this place.

Fearing no other choice, he sided with his State, stating concurrence "in the action of the people of Mississippi", believing secession was not only "necessary, but proper". Afterwards, it was reported by his wife that Mister Davis was so downcast over this course of action that he spent the night praying for peace.

Earlier in January, the "Star of the West", having been dispatched by President Buchanan, arrived in the Harbor of Charleston, South Carolina. The ship had been fired upon by guns in the harbor and was forced to turn back, failing to give Major Anderson any relief.

By the end of January, seven states had ratified articles of secession. Jefferson Davis, in his farewell speech, had decried the use of force by President Buchanan and urged a more civil and political compromise to the issue of states rights, particularly as they concerned the issue of slavery.

Several Federal properties had been overtaken by state militia forces throughout the southern states in secession. The President had firmly stated that Fort Sumter would remain a federal establishment and would be held by federal forces. It was not to be surrendered.

By the first of February, Secretary of State designate, William Seward, had been informed by the President-elect that he was inflexible in the thought of extending the rule of slavery in the Union. Lincoln was quickly being placed in the middle of the debate, even before his inauguration. The only question that remained was whether President Buchanan could offer any hope of resolution before the new President arrived in Washington.

Former President John Tyler convened the "Peace Conference", with the hope of reaching a compromise that would save the Union. Over one hundred delegates attended, from twenty-one states. None of the seceded states attended, but optimism for a resolution continued to run high among those in attendance. President Tylor stated that the "eyes of the nation" were upon the work they had set out to perform.

At the same time, the Montgomery Convention was meeting to form the provisional constitution and government of the South. Jefferson Davis was elected by the unanimous decision of the Convention to be the provisional President of the Confederate States of America.

I was daily attending briefings at the Capital and the War Department. Word had reached the White house of the formation of the new government in Montgomery, Alabama, and the election of Davis as its new President. President Buchanan was deeply disappointed in this course of action, and advised that he would continue to do what he could to preserve the nation for the next President.

I had contacted Horace Greeley, to suggest that I should travel to Montgomery for the story, but was informed he already had reporters there, and I was to remain in Washington for the time being. Caroline continued working closely with me, and was enduring her grief with the professionalism and dignity of a true newspaper woman.

Amos had remained in Washington, and was now working for old "Fuss and Feathers" in the War Department. He daily took dispatches between the War Department and the President, keeping both arms of the government informed as to the actions of the other. He had been promoted to full Captain at the urging of General Winfield Scott.

Mister Lincoln and his family were now making their way toward Washington for the inauguration. Horace Greeley sent Caroline to accompany the President-elect on his journey and to report on the attitudes and behaviors of the crowds. This was her first solo assignment.

After traveling for several days with the Lincolns, Caroline arrived back in the city, the morning of February twenty-fifth. The President-elect had received a death threat in Philadelphia and had traveled on with Allan Pinkerton and another agent by a revised route. It was not until the day following the President's departure that the press had been informed of the situation.

"Tell me, Caroline, how did you enjoy your first assignment without me?" I inquired of my young protégé.

"Oh Auntie Liz", she began. "It was absolutely marvelous. The other members of the press were most gracious to me, and I was able to file my reports to Mister Greely in a timely fashion.

"Everywhere we went, people just adored Mister Lincoln. Many called for him to go to war with the rebellious southern states."

"I read in one of your dispatches that Mister Lincoln suggested there was no need for blood-shed in this matter. Do you believe that he is correct in his assumptions?" I queried.

We talked on for hours about the assassination plot, the possibility of war, the sentiments of both Union and Confederate sympathizers, and the role we might be called upon to play in the unfolding drama. Caroline went on to talk about Allen Pinkerton.

"He runs the Pinkerton Agency out of Chicago. I don't know much about him, as he keeps very quiet regarding his role and as to why he is present. But I do know this, Auntie Liz. He is not a man you would wish to make angry. I believe he would rather just kill than have a discussion of facts."

I suggested that he might be a man we would want to keep our eye on, if he remained in Washington. Caroline agreed.

On March forth, in front of a gathered crowd of over thirty thousand spectators, Abraham Lincoln was sworn in as the President of the United States. Amos, in his new, sharply tailored uniform, and beside General Scott, was present on the platform. Others included Isaac Stoltzfus and several other prominent clergy of Washington.

Along with the General and Allen Pinkerton, Amos rode in a carriage just behind the President in the inaugural procession. It was a grand day, full of celebration and hope.

Caroline and I were invited, through Simon Cameron, to several of the inaugural balls that would take place throughout the evening. Andrew escorted his sister. Isaac, though still in mourning, escorted me to the various functions and dances. He insisted that his public appearance was expected as the Bishop.

For just one day, the conflicts and crisis of the nation seemed to be placed on hold. Even Jefferson Davis had sent word to the new President, congratulating him and suggesting that emissaries should be sent to formalize relations and avoid armed conflict in the matter. The dispatch went unanswered.

The commissioners that had been sent by President Davis to Washington attempted to meet with the new administration, by using their contacts in both houses of Congress. There was no success. Secretary of State Seward, under the direction of Lincoln, refused to grant an audience. Lincoln stated that he did not wish to give validity to the southern states and their proposed government.

Amos appeared to be somewhat downtrodden following the inauguration. He had stated that General Scott feared Fort Sumter might be lost, for there was no reasonable way to reinforce or supply the troops under the command of Major Anderson. He also shared that if war should break out, he would be called upon to fight against some of the very men he had attended West Point with and had served with during the Indian Wars.

"I really don't want to take up arms against my friends, Auntie Liz", he had stated on several occasions recently.

Washington was alive with speculators and politicians, all vying for the President's ear on the matter. Speculators were encouraging war with the south, assuring one another that profits are made in war. Politicians were urging for new peace and compromise initiatives, following the failure of the Peace Convention.

Simon Cameron had been made the new Secretary of War for the Lincoln Administration. I met with him briefly in March. He suggested that I move some of my funds to iron and mercantile ventures. He said his son would care for the redistribution, if I was agreeable. As always, I allowed Simon free reign over my investments.

"Simon, is there going to be war?" I asked.

"Dear Elizabeth, I can assure you that there will plenty for you to write about in the near future. I would suggest that you remain in Washington, close to the War Department. Amos is serving there, I believe? He can be your insider to the affairs of the men of Power and War."

Simon made his remarks with the smugness I had come to understand when he was about to make a shrewd business deal. I knew then that war was inevitable.

CHAPTER FIFTY FOUR

Washington was a flurry of activity. Soldiers were arriving almost daily, and the President seemed relieved at the sight of these men in blue coming to protect the Capital against a possible invasion by Southern forces.

The headlines in the paper had read "Fort Sumter Fired Upon". "Anderson Surrenders to Confederate Forces". "Call for Seventy-Five-Thousand Troops to Stop Rebellion". War was quickly coming, and it appeared that no one was able, or willing, to stop the approaching bloodshed.

Maryland had voted to remain in the Union, even with strong pro-southern sympathies in Baltimore and Annapolis. Virginia elected to secede with the other Southern states. However, the western part of Virginia remained pro-Union.

A delegation of Union supporters from Virginia met in Wheeling to form the Government of Restored Virginia. Francis Pierpont had been elected as the provisional governor of the new state. Now two Virginias existed, one Union, the other Confederate.

Lincoln had offered command of the newly organized Union Volunteer Army to Colonel Robert E. Lee. Lee, however, resigned his commission in the regular army and returned to his home in Virginia. He was now serving in the newly formed Confederate Army as a General.

War fever was everywhere. Most saw the coming conflict as some romantic adventure. Voices on both sides of the conflict shared that the war, should it come, would be short lived.

Many believed it was as if two brothers had a brawl. At the end of bloody noses, they would stand, shake hands and return home as brothers and friends once more.

Seasoned soldiers held a different view. Those who had seen the horrors of war before knew that pain, suffering, loss and defeat were the realities of any battle.

Andrew came to see his father early in June. He had been requested by the War Department to return to active duty, with the rank of First Lieutenant.

"Father", Andrew began. "Amos assures me that I will be assigned to the same command as he, and we will serve together.

Amos suspects that the war will be over within the ninety day enlistments Mister Lincoln has established to stop the rebellion."

"Where is Amos to serve? Does he have an assignment as of yet?" Isaac inquired.

"Amos has been assigned to General McDowell, as his adjutant. He says this will keep him close to command decisions and the War Department. General Scott wants Amos to be able to report back directly to him and the President as events unfold", Andrew responded.

"And what of your assignment?"

"I am to serve as Amos' assistant. Basically, Father, I will be an errand boy. I am afraid the assignment is not very glamorous or exciting. Anyway, this whole war business should be over even before it starts, and I can continue my law studies."

Father and son continued to talk for some time over the coming conflict. Andrew was assured of his father's blessings in the matter. Isaac knew that each of his sons, as well as his daughter, would do what their consciences dictated, despite any reservations or objections he might voice.

By the end of June, Andrew was back in uniform at the headquarters of General McDowell, alongside Amos. Amos had been promoted to Brevet Major for this new assignment.

Caroline and I attended daily to the briefings held at the War Department and the White House. The Senate chamber was housing newly arriving soldiers. The grounds of the mall were covered with white canvas, as a tent city of Union soldiers began to emerge.

Caroline and I often found it difficult to make our way though the web and congestion of the military machine. At times we were harassed by rude soldiers who felt it their duty to impede our progress. Officers, often recognizing this bad behavior, would intervene on our behalf and escort us through the maze of men and equipment to the meetings we attended.

This new army of volunteers Mister Lincoln had formed proved to be most undisciplined, lacking military bearing in their actions. I wondered how this undisciplined, all volunteer force would prove to be an advantage, should an actual battle occur. Amos expressed the same concern.

With the loss of officers like Robert E. Lee to the south, questions of even the abilities of the remaining officers to defend the Union were in question. Both Amos and Andrew were saddened to hear that their mentors and friends, Henry Heth and Thomas Jackson, had also resigned and joined the Southern cause.

Heth had met with Amos prior to resigning, to ask if Amos would consider joining him in the cause of states rights. Amos stated that he could not even consider supporting action to dissolve the Union or to continue the practice of slavery. Henry and Amos shook hands and promised to meet after the issue of secession had been settled.

On July fourth, the President addressed a special session of the full Congress. Caroline and I were in the press balcony as we heard the President state clearly that it was his intention to declare war on the Confederacy, in order to maintain the integrity of the Union. Mister Lincoln made a request for an additional four-hundred-thousand troops.

Congress overwhelmingly approved the measures the President outlined in his speech. The Government would fund the war machine of the Union, to end the rebellion.

Enthusiasm and excitement ran high, both in the Capital and across the Union, for war. Southerners were no less optimistic.

Horace Greeley insisted that I remain in Washington, along with Caroline. Our dispatches to New York went out daily, as new reports flowed into the War Department regarding the building of Confederate forces.

By mid-July, it was apparent that a major battle was taking shape around Washington. General McDowell was making war preparations with his troops and consulting daily with General Scott and the President. Andrew was living on horse back, delivering messages night and day between McDowell's headquarters and the office of the Secretary of War, Simon Cameron.

As Andrew came into the Secretary's office with one of his dispatches, I was just exiting the building.

"Andrew, it is so good to see you. You, however, look as if you have had little sleep of late. How are you doing, my little one?" I spoke to him much as his mother had.

Andrew greeted me with his usual kiss to my cheek.

"I am fine, Auntie Liz. But I must confess that it appears as if I am the only one able to deliver messages to Secretary Cameron these days. He has personally asked me to run these errands on his behalf."

"Simon has been a good friend for many years now, Andrew. I am sure he is just looking out for your well-being in these interesting times", I responded. "And how is Amos?"

Andrew went on to explain that Amos was working closely with Generals McDowell and Scott as they formed plans in the event of an attack by Confederate forces on Washington.

"And do you think the Confederate Army would dare launch such an attack?" I inquired.

"I am afraid I do believe it is possible. We have received word through Mister Pinkerton and his agents that the Confederates are massing for an attack around Blackburn's Ford, near Manassas. There has already been some fighting in western Virginia, with General McClelland in command. He successfully defeated the Confederates he encountered there, but that does not mean it will go so easy this time for General McDowell."

"I have heard of the conflicts in the western part of the state. General McClellan has already proved he is a capable commander, as I understand it from Simon. But with regards to Blackburn's Ford, I have been told that the Confederate Army is nothing more than raw recruits and should be easily defeated", I responded.

"Auntie Liz", Andrew offered in protest. "Have you not seen what our Army looks like at the moment? These soldiers, if you can even call them that, have no place on the battlefield, and will probably turn and run at the first sight of blood. I am afraid that if there is truly a battle of any magnitude, it will not go well for us."

With that, I kissed Andrew and bid him a good day. As I walked from the Secretary's office, a tear of sadness filled my eyes, with fear for the safety of both Andrew and Amos. My thoughts turned also to all the young boys who had been so eager for an adventure as to enlist for the ninety day period requested by the President. I prayed quietly that they would live through the present danger, to return home again.

CHAPTER FIFTY FIVE

By late afternoon on July nineteen, word came to Caroline and me though an aide to Amos, that General McDowell would be advancing on Confederate forces near Manassas. The aide advised that, should we wish to observe the battle, we might want to proceed at our first opportune moment to the area around Sudley Ford on the creek known as Bull Run.

I instructed Caroline to dress, as I would, in men's clothing, to aid in our ability to move rapidly and with little attention drawn to ourselves. I immediately wired Horace Greeley and instructed him that we were moving into the area, advised by an aide to Amos, in order to observe the opening battle of the Rebellion.

Earlier in the week, I had met with a number of junior officers from the War Department at the Capital Hotel for dinner. Also present was Alfred Waud, an artist illustrator now working for the New York Illustrated Weekly.

Alfred and I had met in London during my assignment to cover the Temperance Convention, in August of 1846. He had been a wonderful friend in those earlier days, and it was good to once again renew our friendship.

The young officers of the evening were eager to demonstrate in battle their particular skills at leadership and bravery. Most spoke of an early victory, leading to the end of the conflict after the first real battle. The rebels, it was promised, would be put to the run, and the rebellion would come to as quick and sudden an end as it had begun.

I reminded these young gentlemen that the issues around the rebellion had gone on for several decades, and it was my hope that the rebellion would not last that long. With that, the men raised hearty laughter and shared a toast to the success of the Lincoln administration and the Union.

As Caroline, Alfred, and I departed early on the morning of the twentieth for Sudley Ford, we noticed a caravan of Washington elite had already begun taking the highway toward Manassas. I inquired of Alfred where these fashionably dressed individuals might be heading, and remarked that neither of us was particularly dressed to join them in their adventure.

Alfred informed me that the elite were on holiday picnic to observe the battle. They had been informed by Secretary Cameron and other officials that the day would demonstrate a Union victory, with little or no bloodshed.

Officials promised much regal prancing across fields and hills of brightly colored flags and men in stately uniforms, driving the ignorant and uneducated rebels back to the south. Many went early, in hopes of obtaining the best view of the parade, as many were overheard referring to the coming fight.

"You are well aware, Elizabeth, as I am certain, that this will be no parade or regal observance", Alfred reminded me.

"Yes, my old friend", I countered. "I am afraid these poor fools will witness more than they are presently bargaining for."

Amos, Andrew, Abraham, James and Isaac had all made me promise, that if fighting did break out, I would keep both Caroline and myself out of danger.

"This will not be like covering Conventions or political rallies", Isaac reminded me.

James and Abraham were well aware of the dangers present concerning the rebellion. Abraham had recently returned from a secret trip to Richmond, where he was able to witness first hand the cruelty of anyone remaining in the south with pro-Union sentiments.

Two newspaper men with the New York Herald had been arrested and accused of spying on the Confederate movements and war preparations. They had been beaten, tried, and sentenced to life in prison in Richmond's Libby Prison. The editor of the Herald, James Bennett, had filed an official protest on behalf of his reporters, and, after paying a sizable ransom for their release, the men were expelled from the Confederacy and returned to the North.

"I do not want you and Caroline to fall into the hands of Confederate forces, Auntie Liz", Abraham had firmly stated.

"By the way, Liz, I really like your attire", Alfred said. "Although I am not sure if Alastair were still alive, he would approve."

I laughed at the thought of Alastair's reaction, and commented that he would probably have just considered it part of my nature to engage in the unexpected.

"And besides, Alfred", I went on. 'I am sure that in all honesty, Alastair would have preferred I wear nothing at all."

Caroline blushed at the thought and giggled lightly under her breath.

Then she commented, "I had all but forgotten the nice Mister Abercrombie, Auntie Liz. It seems as if that was a century ago that we were all in London together."

By late afternoon, we found a large hill overlooking the area of Sudley Ford at Bull Run. We set up a makeshift shelter for our comfort, and Alfred set a small fire in place. Caroline prepared a meal of salted pork and bread, with coffee set to the side.

Alfred commented that he would like to explore the area some and would return before night fall, if nothing of importance was occurring. We were able to observe Union troop movements and gatherings around the stone bridge, but had not seen, as yet, any Confederate soldiers.

By late in the day, nearly thirty-thousand troops, mostly new recruits with regular army officers in command, surrounded the area near Centreville, Virginia, at Bull Run. Some evidence, from our vantage point, began to emerge of a gathering of Confederate forces some few miles to the south.

The Confederates appeared to be well out-numbered. Perhaps the promise of a quick resolution and end to the conflict would prove to be true, after all.

All around us, spectators were filling in every conceivable vantage point to observe the festivities of the coming day. Many had ventured close to the lines General McDowell had formed. Even the pickets seemed to enjoy the attention they were receiving from the visitors.

Politicians from the Northern states, who had come with their wives to enjoy the spectacle, were freely engaging the soldiers and recruiting reelection votes from members of their constituencies. The scene looked more like a political rally or party than that of an army preparing for battle.

Alfred arrived back at our small camp just before dark.

"Liz, these people are fools. There will be a battle here tomorrow, and I can assure you, it will not be pretty or short lived."

Alfred spoke with great concern and was almost out of breath.

He continued. "I was able to advance close to the Confederate lines, and there are at least twenty-thousand soldiers massed ready for the attack. Beauregard has men at Manassas

Junction and more on the way. Not only that, but he is being supported by Jackson and Longstreet, two of his top officers."

"Yes, I know of Major Jackson", I responded. "Caroline's brother, Andrew, attended VMI while the major taught there. Andrew was deeply saddened when he heard that Jackson had gone to the south to fight for the Confederacy."

"Well, he is now General Jackson, and some say he is one of the best tacticians the south has. I would love to have the chance to draw his portrait during the battle." Alfred shared.

"Perhaps you will have your opportunity, my friend", I said.

At that, we decided we should get as much rest as possible. The next day promised to be full of adventure, as North and South would clash swords in the blazing light of the sun.

CHAPTER FIFTY SIX

As the sun was just beginning to make the morning dawn, around five o'clock on the twenty first, the Union cannons opened fire and began to assault the Confederate positions. The Confederates began their advance on General McDowell's position, but by noon had to fall back.

There was great cheering, and the carnival-like atmosphere surrounding the battle by the elite of Washington seemed to grow at the firing of each cannon, or the raised voice of an officer crying "advance". Suddenly, the Confederates, now pushed back, were reinforced by men under the command of Generals Johnston and Jackson.

The Confederate forces made a strong stand. Reinforced and holding, the Confederates forced back General McDowell's troops. A call was sent out for the Union forces to withdraw from the Confederate held position.

As the men in blue began their retreat, an explosion occurred in a wagon. The main road of retreat was suddenly blocked. Men began to panic and run, just as Andrew had suggested they might.

Many dropped their weapons and ran to the rear, leaving their friends and comrades to fend for themselves. Panic ensued among the civilians who had been enjoying the spectacle as if it had been a holiday adventure.

Chaos was everywhere. Soldiers were taking horses and wagons from politicians and citizens alike. Women were left alone and abandoned, as even their male escorts fled in terror.

The promise of an early victory had been shattered in one afternoon by a Confederate force nearly half the size of the Union advance. The cheers of the Confederates could be easily heard above the screams of fear from the Union forces.

Caroline and I had lost contact with Alfred early in the opening hours of the conflict. He had gone to another area, away from many of the civilian observers, in hopes of catching a better view of General Jackson.

"Auntie Liz, what are we to do?" Caroline stated with a look of horror in her eyes. "What of Amos and Andrew?" She asked.

I had been thinking the same. I was concerned for their safety in this rout of unprofessional, ill trained, and ill disciplined soldiers.

"First, we must make our way back to Washington without further delay. I think, though, we must avoid, if possible, the main highway. I am sure it will be cluttered with refugees and run-away soldiers. Also, I do not wish to take the chance of losing our horses to some thieving soldier." I stated.

Caroline agreed. "What of Mister Waud, though?" she asked.

I responded, "Alfred will be fine without us. We will see him again in Washington."

We gathered our supplies, and headed north through Centreville, toward Leesburg. We rode well into the night, making camp just south of Leesburg, Virginia.

At first light, we resumed our travels, crossing the Potomac near Poolesville, and then went on to Washington City, arriving late on the twenty-second. We encountered no resistance toward our return home, except for a brief episode near Centreville.

Earlier the previous day, near Centreville, we fought off a few soldiers who wished to commandeer our horses. I always carried the pistol that Amos had given me, in the event I needed to defend myself from personal attack. Even though I had not fired the weapon, the gun had come to our assistance on this adventure, to ward off the attacks. The soldiers, in their hasty retreat, had dispatched their rifles to some forgotten ditch.

Caroline and I were both exhausted as we arrived home. We handed the reigns of the horses to Jeremiah, the stable master. Rebecca was there to immediately greet us.

"Miss Elizabeth", she started. "I was so afraid that you might not come back. The whole town is in a frightful state, fearing the Confederates will march in and take Mister Lincoln to jail any day now. You think that will happen?"

I did not know if the Confederates would attack the Capital now or not. I was too tired to care.

Caroline answered Rebecca. "It was terrible, Rebecca, just terrible. I have never seen so much death and destruction in my life. I think that if the Rebels want to take Washington, they could easily do so. Our fighting men, if you dare call them that, will just run away."

Caroline and Rebecca continued to talk for some moments more, as I made my way to change out of my clothes. Rebecca called to me to assure that the bath would be ready in a few moments and that she had prepared a meal for us earlier, in anticipation that we would come home sooner or later.

"Miss Caroline", Rebecca went on. "I almost forgot. Your Daddy was here earlier looking for you. Says you are to send word as soon as you get home."

"Thank you, Rebecca. Any word yet about Amos or Andrew?" Caroline asked.

"Bishop Stoltzfus says he spoke with Secretary Cameron earlier in the day, and both his sons be fine. I guess, though, General McDowell might be fired for his mistakes and letting the Rebels off easy like."

Caroline came to my room to share the news of Amos and Andrew. We were both relieved that they were all right, at the moment, and safely back in Washington.

She called for a carriage and sent word with the coachman to Isaac that we were both safely home. Caroline promised a visit as soon as she was able to get away.

At that, we both had a bath and a light meal, retiring to our beds for the night. The next day meant we would have considerable work to do, in following up on the story of the opening of the War between the Union and the Confederacy.

CHAPTER FIFTY SEVEN

Following our return to Washington, I spent the better part of the next day preparing several dispatches to Horace Greeley. Those dispatches, safely sent by courier, would arrive within two days at the Tribune.

At first opportunity, I arrived at the War Department to speak with my old friend Simon Cameron. Simon was intensely involved in discussion with the President. It was obvious that their conversation was centered on the performance of the soldiers at Bull Run and the rout by the Confederates.

The President questioned Simon as to whether General McDowell would even be able to defend the Capital against an expeditionary force sent by the Confederates. Simon assured the President that he was evaluating the command of McDowell and would have a report prepared within two days.

On the twenty-seventh, just six days following the Union defeat, General McDowell was relieved of command, and General George McClelland was placed by the President as the overall commander of the Army of the Potomac.

Amos was furious at the decision. He had said that the failure at Bull Run had not been the doing of McDowell.

"The General had raw recruits to fight with." Amos had argued.

His other friend, General Scott, had reminded the young officer that McDowell was a casualty of war.

"Heads must roll, my boy", the General had stated. "And this time it is McDowell's. Next time, it will be mine."

Across the country, skirmishes and battles were taking place. The Confederate Army appeared to be more ready to fight than the Union soldiers. The Federal Army regularly suffered losses and defeats at the hand of the Confederates.

I had dinner with Amos and Andrew shortly after McClelland took command.

"Are you going to stay with General McClelland?" I asked.

"For the moment. We are assigned to his staff at the War Department. But our primary responsibilities are to look after General Scott." Abraham shared.

Amos continued, "I will be curious to see if "Lil' Mac", as the other Generals refer to him, will be able to advance the Army anytime soon. There is a lot of work to be done to get these raw recruits to act like soldiers."

Amos went on to talk about Ulysses S. Grant being given command as General in charge of Volunteers.

"He will undoubtedly enjoy this assignment." Amos stated with some sarcasm. "He has somewhat a reputation for enjoying his whiskey, Auntie Liz. With everything else going badly for the Union at the moment, all we need is a drunken General."

Andrew had defended General Grant, stating that the rumors were more designed to hurt the man, by jealous officers who wished the job had fallen to them. Amos just laughed, and stated that he would wait until Grant was engaged in real action to make up his mind as to the ability of the man.

"Why are the rebels doing better in battle than our soldiers?" I finally asked.

The response from both young men was the same.

"They have better commanders and officers to start with. And second, Auntie Liz, they have a cause they believe in."

We discussed the number of articles and editorials lately in northern papers, condemning the actions of the President and the War Department in fighting to preserve the Union. Many northern papers were calling for the Union to allow the southern states to secede without a fight.

As a result of the articles, the President had suspended the writ of habeas corpus from New York to the Capital. Several editors were arrested, and papers had been shut down by military authority. This action, in and of itself, caused much concern for the press.

"Auntie Liz, you will see much more than this in coming months, if the issue is not settled quickly. The President already has ordered the blockade of all southern ports, and the British are currently willing to receive commissioners from the Confederacy.

"If the British enter the war on the side of the Confederacy", Amos continued, "The Union will undoubtedly cease to exist as we know it today."

We concluded our dinner with the promise that we would regularly meet to discuss the war department efforts to bring a satisfying resolution to the conflict. As always, I promised not to use any information I gathered from the two men in my reports.

The next day, Caroline and I arrived early at the War Department. Simon was at his desk, and his secretary announced my presence to him. He immediately came out into the hall and invited us into his office.

"Simon, how did you know we were even here? I was not going to bother you today." I shared.

Simon responded in his usual warm manner. He stated that his secretary had instructions to always let him know when I was in the building, so we could speak if he were available.

We talked for several minutes about both Amos and Andrew, and Simon promised to keep them safe at the War Department as long as he was able. General McClelland was just entering the building as we spoke, and made his way into the Secretary's office unannounced.

"If you have time, Mister Secretary", McClelland started, "I have need to discuss some matters with you and General Scott."

"Yes, of course, General." Simon returned. "But first, I do not know if you have had an opportunity to meet Miss Fitzgerald and her associate, Miss Stoltzfus. Both of these lovely ladies are with the New York Tribune."

General McClelland acknowledged our presence, stating only that he had heard of me through reputation, but had not had the honor of a meeting.

"Then allow me, my dear General, to invite both you and Missus McClelland to dine with me and both ladies at the Capital Hotel, say next Thursday?" Simon went on.

"I will ask for your pardon in the matter, Mister Secretary. I do not care to engage reporters at this time. No personal offense, Miss Fitzgerald." McClelland said.

"No offense taken, General. But please, Sir, do not discount all of the press as enemies of the Union. We are just as loyal as you to the defense of the Constitution and the Nation." I remarked.

"We shall see, Miss Fitzgerald", was all the General was willing to state further.

He excused himself from my presence, and went to see General Scott and await Secretary Cameron to join them.

"My apologies for his rudeness and arrogance, my dear", Simon stated with some discomfort. "Will you be attending Missus Lincoln's ball next week?"

Caroline and I both assured Simon that he did not need to apologize for his commanders. We also confirmed that we would indeed be present for the ball and had already responded to the invitation. "And don't forget Simon, you owe me a dance at this event", I reminded him.

CHAPTER FIFTY EIGHT

On August nineteen, 1861, Caroline, escorted by her brother Abraham, and I, along with James, attended the party at the White House. The President and Missus Lincoln were properly dressed for the occasion. Missus Lincoln told how she had received her new dress, commissioned by a wonderful seamstress in New York, just for this evening's gaiety.

The dress was indeed stunning, with a square yoke neckline and pillow sleeves. The fabric was composed of rich silks in various shades of green, from dark emerald to light mint. Flowers adorned the dress along the hem line, and a wide sash in a dark forest green complimented her waist.

Sarah Hale said that my description of the dress in one of my letters rivaled most descriptions found in Godey's Lady's Book.

"As I have spoken to you many times before, dear Elizabeth", she had written, "You are capable of writing for me."

Throughout the evening, I danced with most of the men in attendance, including Simon Cameron. Many of the officers, led by General McClelland, were in attendance.

Over four hundred in all were present for the festive occasion. Some present had the audacity to criticize Missus Lincoln for her extravagance while our fighting men were busy reuniting the nation.

One of the more vocal protestors to the event was Rose O'Neal Greenhow. She often found fault with the Lincoln administration, and always with the Lincoln household.

I asked her why she came to the affairs at the White House if she was so inclined as to find fault with the extravagance, as she called it.

Her response was "You never know what useful information you might retrieve at the events, my Dear."

Rose Greenhow always made sure she spent time with the important figures of Washington and would eavesdrop on the President at every opportunity. Tonight was no different.

Early in the evening, I was approached by Mister Allen Pinkerton, of the newly formed Secret Service Bureau. Mister Pinkerton had requested that he be placed on my dance card, to which I graciously agreed.

At the appointed time of our dance, a waltz, Mister Pinkerton wasted no time in coming to the object of his curiosity. As we waltzed around the room, Mister Pinkerton asked what I knew of the southern sympathies of Missus Greenhow.

"I know that she is quite supportive of the Confederacy and makes no effort to hide her feelings", I responded.

"Do you agree with her position, Miss Fitzgerald?" Pinkerton asked.

I laughed at the suggestion, and stated with certainty that I did not agree with her, and in fact could barely tolerate the woman.

"I only maintain enough relationship with Missus Greenhow to have a good source, should I need it", I explained.

At the conclusion of the waltz, Mister Pinkerton thanked me for the opportunity to engage in dance and conversation, and promised that we would talk more in a day or so, with my permission. Permission was granted, and I promised to arrive at his office early on the morning of the twenty-first.

The remainder of the evening was filled with light conversation, and it seemed for the moment as if the war were non-existent. Missus Lincoln and I spoke for a few moments on her plans for redecorating the family quarters, and she asked if I would like to visit her there some time.

I assured her that I would be most honored to visit and to share a time of casual discussion. In the following months, I would often visit the President and his wife, and learned very quickly that Missus Lincoln was an extremely intelligent woman, well beyond her contemporaries in her ability to logically reflect and comment on societal issues.

In many ways, Missus Lincoln reminded me of Elizabeth Cady Stanton and Lucretia Mott. If she had not been the President's wife, I was sure she would have been actively engaged in both the Abolitionist and Suffrage movements.

As the hour struck past mid-night, the party goers began making their way toward home. Caroline, Abraham, James, and I had had a wonderful evening. We thanked the President and Missus Lincoln for the invitation and hospitality.

The President spoke briefly to James, thanking him for his work toward the freedom of the Negroes and suggesting that he might attend his services on some Sunday, even though he was a Presbyterian. James extended the invitation, and assured the

President that even Presbyterians were welcome at his table. The two men shared in laughter and shook hands before departing.

The carriage ride back to our home was quiet and peaceful. I drifted off briefly on James' shoulder, feeling safe and secure next to my old friend. Caroline and Abraham talked of adventures yet to come, promising that they would have more times like this evening, unless of course Caroline were to capture the heart of a handsome young officer.

In that case, Abraham assured his sister, "I will step back and only be there should I need to defend your honor, Sis."

The following day, Caroline spent time reviewing a story she was working on and began compiling her notes. I began writing the dispatch for Horace, covering last night's event at the White House.

Late afternoon, Isaac arrived at our home. Rebecca showed the Bishop into the library and then came to my private study to inform me he was waiting for me downstairs.

"Have you informed Caroline that her father is here?" I asked.

"No ma'am. He says he has come to speak with you today", she responded.

I went to the Library and greeted Isaac with a kiss on his cheek. He returned the symbol of the affection we felt toward each other.

"Elizabeth", he began. "I must travel to Richmond next week, to meet with representative clergy of the Lutheran Churches in the Confederacy. I am still trying to keep the church together."

"Will that not be a dangerous assignment, Isaac? What if you are arrested by either the Union or the Confederacy? How will you explain your reason for venturing south, other than being on a mission for the Church?"

I was, for the first time in some while, fearful of travel south into Confederate territories. Recent arrests had been made of Northern correspondents and Northern supporters who were found traveling near Confederate military camps. Those arrested had been accused of spying for the Lincoln war machine, and a few had been sentenced to hanging.

"Please, Liz, you are not to worry for my safety. I have a letter from the Council of Bishops, introducing my mission. Also, I have been in contact with some of the clergy from northern

Virginia who are in the process of organizing the meeting. They have assured me of my safety."

Isaac explained in detail the plans for traveling and arriving at the Capital of the Confederacy.

"I may even have the opportunity to meet with President Davis while I am there."

I inquired further as to what he would do about the issue of giving the appearance of support to the Confederacy.

"The writ of habeas corpus has been suspended throughout much of the Union", I reminded Isaac.

"Again, Liz, I have cared for the matter. I spoke with Mister Pinkerton and Secretary Cameron at the War Department." Isaac continued, "They have given me a pass to use to return north across Union lines, should I have need of the writ. And that brings me to the reason for my visit."

Isaac went on to share how he had been encouraged by both Cameron and Pinkerton to ask if I would join him. They suggested I could vouch for the legitimacy of his visit to the south, as well as perhaps find a good story in the process.

"So, in other words, Isaac, they hope I can give them information on the Confederacy that could be used in aiding their war effort", I suggested.

"I am not sure I would state it in that manner Liz. They are not asking you to spy on the south. They only hope that you will be able to write a meaningful story which will help win the sentiments for a quick resolution to the secession issue", Isaac explained. "And it would be a great comfort to me to have you come along."

Isaac and I continued to talk for some time. I assured him that I already had a meeting with Mister Pinkerton scheduled for tomorrow morning. Pinkerton, I was certain, knew about Isaac's plans and was going to make every attempt to enlist me in his network of secret service spies.

"If Mister Pinkerton is willing to grant me documents assuring my safety through the Union lines, then I will be most willing to accompany you south, Isaac", I assured my dearest friend.

CHAPTER FIFTY NINE

Early the following morning, I arrived at the War Department. Mister Pinkerton was standing in the open hall, along with General McClelland. The two were in soft communication, amidst the flurry of officers and couriers moving quickly about with the first reports of the day.

Upon seeing me, the General excused himself and made a remark that suggested it was best to not engage in conversation where a reporter might be found. I suggested to the General that he might find it to his benefit to trust reporters more, and his generals less.

With a slight bow, and no further exchange of words, the General departed for his office. Mister Pinkerton invited me to his.

Allen Pinkerton indicated that we would meet in his office down the hall. As we passed the communications room, I noticed the President sitting with the telegraph operator.

"Does the President often spend time here at the War Department?" I asked.

"Yes, Miss Fitzgerald. He is often found in the room we just passed, to hear first hand the early reports of the day, before proceeding to sixteen-hundred Pennsylvania Avenue."

Pinkerton was unusually forth coming with what little information he would give.

Pinkerton's office was a small room near the end of the hall on the main floor. There were no windows to let in either sun or fresh air. The room had the scent of men who had labored there for extended periods, with their cigars and lack of hygiene.

It contained one desk piled to overflowing with stacks of papers and files for review. Behind the desk was one leather, high back chair that had obviously seen better days. It appeared to be a left over remnant from an earlier administration in the City.

There were four additional chairs, all wooden with arm rests that wrapped around the body, to hold the one sitting in place. They were most uncomfortable.

Behind the desk, a picture of former President James Buchanan hung. Aside from this one adornment, the room was simply painted in a dirty white overcoat of diluted horse hair plaster. The hardwood floors creaked with every step.

Captain Lafayette Baker, along with Secretary Cameron, joined us in the small office.

"Let me come right to the point, Miss Fitzgerald", Pinkerton began. "The Secretary assures me that you are a most trust worthy and loyal member of the Union."

There was a long pause, as if somehow I should know to respond to his statement.

I finally said, "Are you asking me if the assessment is true, or telling me it is so, Mister Pinkerton?"

Simon laughed at my remark. "I told you, Allen, that she would not be taken in by you or your feeble ways of intimidating civilians."

Captain Baker immediately stepped in, "My Dear, we are not insinuating or remarking in a way as to challenge you or your reputation. It is just that in these troubled times, as I am sure you can appreciate, we must know where certain individuals stand, should the question of loyalty arise. Are you indeed a loyalist to the Union, or do you have some, even minor, sympathies toward the south?"

"Well, Captain, let me assure you and the Secret Service that I am loyal to the Union. I am also a correspondent for the New York Tribune and work for Mister Greeley, as I am sure you already know."

I went on to declare that I would always attempt to be fair and balanced in my reporting of events, and that my interest lay more with the events of a human interest nature.

"I intend to play no favoritism, nor to take sides in the matter. I shall only, to the best of my ability, report the events as they occur, with the greatest consideration to accuracy and neutrality." I said.

"Would you be willing to sign an oath of loyalty to the Union, Miss Fitzgerald?" Pinkerton asked.

"If that is what you require, in order that I may continue my work, certainly. I understand from Mister Waud and others, that they also have been required to sign loyalty papers, as well as a promise not to bear arms", I responded.

"Yes, that is true, my Dear", Simon continued. "But I have assured Mister Pinkerton and Captain Baker that there is no need for you to sign that type of oath. After all, Elizabeth, I can't imagine any woman taking up arms."

"Then Simon, you must not be aware of the pistol Amos gave me to use in my defense, should the occasion present itself", I countered.

The three men laughed at the prospect of anyone attempting to forcefully accost me and violate my person.

"Well, Miss Fitzgerald", Pinkerton continued. I have your press credentials that you will be required to carry on your person at all times. Should you be challenged and asked to produce these documents, you will be required to do so or face some detainment. And we both know that would be a very unpleasant experience for any person."

Despite the objections and proclamations of Simon regarding my bearing arms, I was asked by Captain Baker to place my left hand on the Bible and raise my right hand. I was asked then to swear allegiance to the United States Government and promise not to bear arms against any friend or foe of the government to which I pledged loyalty.

"Does this also require that I not raise the pen or take issue with the government in my reporting, as well?" I asked.

"I would exercise discretion, Miss Fitzgerald, in matters of criticism of the Government or the Army, unless you wish to have your credentials revoked and perhaps spend some time in the Old Washington Prison", Baker stated with an air that sent chills down my spine.

"I am quite unaccustomed to being censored, Captain Baker, but I shall remember your warning in the future." I stated, with my own air of contempt at the man.

I looked over the papers handed to me. They read:

Press Pass

> *This pass is hereby issued to Elizabeth Grace Fitzgerald and certifies membership of the press with the New York Tribune.*
>
> *Miss Fitzgerald has taken oath not to bear arms against any nation, foe, or enemy, and to report the news in fairness and without bias as observed during the events of the day.*
>
> *You are hereby authorized to allow Elizabeth Grace Fitzgerald free access to all fields of engagement, press meetings, officer calls,*

and other activities deemed necessary to the reporting of events. Any misconduct should be reported immediately to the nearest Commanding General and Provost Marshall.

Signed this 21ˢᵗ day, August, 1861.

The document was signed by the Secretary of War, Simon Cameron; Alan Pinkerton, Director, Secret Service; Captain Lafayette Baker, Chief, War Department; and Horace Greeley, Editor of the New York Tribune.

I was most surprised to see Mister Greeley's name on the document. He had given no evidence that such would be forthcoming. I asked Simon about the issue.

"There are some things that we do not discuss until the time is right, and Mister Greeley was informed to say nothing to you until we saw that you, indeed, were to remain loyal to the Union. I had no doubts, but my friends here trust no one, not even me." Simon said with some distaste.

Mister Pinkerton then handed me another document that gave permission to cross Union lines. The document further offered whatever service might be available from Union officers, and transportation to assist me in reporting the news, all, of course, favorable to the Union and the Lincoln administration.

I thanked Mister Pinkerton for his generosity, to see that I would have no difficulty covering the war should it continue much longer. To date, there had been little fighting since Bull Run. A few skirmishes occurred throughout the south, but nothing of significant magnitude.

"I wish to ask another favor of you, Miss Fitzgerald", Captain Baker started. "Your dear friend Isaac, I mean Bishop Stoltzfus, is planning a trip to the south for his church work. I suspect he has already informed you."

"Should he have?" I inquired.

"Yes, it was quite all right for him to do so. In fact I asked him to see if you would be interested in possibly accompanying him on the journey", Baker said.

"In order that I might spy on the south and report back to you, Sir?" I asked.

"I would not call it spying, my Dear", Simon interjected.

"Then, Mister Secretary, what would you call it?" I asked abruptly.

"What we are asking, Miss Fitzgerald," Pinkerton went on, "is that you merely write a story, should you find one, regarding the sentiments of the south towards the Bishop's endeavors."

"That I can most certainly do, and would have done none the less." I continued, "Let me be very clear, gentlemen. I am not in the least bit interested in the spy business. I am a reporter first, and foremost. Please do not presume to ask me to engage in some other activity. I have sworn allegiance to my Country, and my President, but please do not insult me with thoughts that I would also betray my profession for your vanity."

With that, Mister Pinkerton and the other gentlemen rose to their feet, suggesting our meeting was coming to a close.

"I shall assume no such thing, Miss Fitzgerald", Pinkerton stated. "I have appreciated our visit and look forward to reading your accounts of the war, as you have opportunity."

I once again thanked the gentlemen for their letters and passes. I further reinforced my previous statements of loyalty to the Union, with assurances that I would report any activity in the paper which I felt relevant and important, and that they could read my accounts and glean what they wished for their purposes.

Simon walked me from the room toward the entrance of the building. When he felt we were out of the hearing of Pinkerton and Baker, he spoke.

"Liz, please do not inflame these men. They are not to be trusted, and will make life very uncomfortable for you if they so desire."

"I will do my best to remain on favorable terms with the Administration as I am able, Simon, but I will be honest in my reporting and will not put my career and life in jeopardy for their vain sense of importance. Besides, I would not make a very good spy", I suggested.

"Don't sell yourself short, Liz. I have seen you go undercover as it were, to get a good story", Simon reminded me.

As we stood near the main entrance, the President slipped by us on his way to the White House. Mister Lincoln stopped and spoke briefly of the dance earlier in the week.

Simon and I continued our conversation. We enjoyed a brief moment of laughter and small talk before I gave him a slight kiss to his cheek and left the War Department for home.

It was nearly noon by the time I arrived back at my home. Isaac was already there, waiting for my return.

CHAPTER SIXTY

As I entered my home, I heard laughter and conversation coming from the kitchen area. I went in to find Isaac and Caroline, engaged in lively conversation with Rebecca. Before the three of them was a light lunch.

"I am gone for a brief time, and you think I may not come back?" I asked.

"Well, Liz", started Isaac. "You do have a reputation for going off in a hundred different directions at the same time. We were not sure if you would come home today, or not."

"Did you think I might infuriate Mister Pinkerton and Captain Baker to the point of being placed under arrest and sent to the Capital Prison?" I jovially inquired.

"There was that possibility, Liz", Isaac remarked.

Rebecca placed a bowl of beef soup, along with fresh bread, on the table for me to enjoy.

"Thank you, Rebecca. The soup smells absolutely wonderful, and I am a bit hungry following my encounter at the War Department."

Caroline immediately asked me to share what Pinkerton and his "Hench Men", as she called them, wanted to know.

"First of all, Pinkerton's Hench Men were not present. Unless, of course, you include Captain Baker and Simon Cameron in the list."

I went on to share the content of our meeting and showed the credentials Pinkerton issued to me.

I continued, "I am sure, Caroline, that you will be also be called in before long. Most likely, when your father and I are out of town. In any event, remain neutral and calm, and agree to their oath of loyalty. Do not claim any southern sympathies, should you have any."

"Now, Auntie Liz, you know I do not have any sympathies toward the southern cause." Caroline shared, "But that Rose Greenhow sure does. And she makes no apologies for them. Why do all those Congressmen and Union Officers keep attending to her so? Now, that is where Pinkerton and Baker should be spending their efforts. Not on decent families like ours."

The conversation continued for the next several moments, as I consumed my mid-day meal. I shared seeing the President at the War Department's communications room and that I was told by Simon of Lincoln coming daily to receive the early morning reports first hand.

Following the meal, Isaac and I excused ourselves from Caroline and Rebecca and retired to the library. We had much to discuss.

"Liz, did Pinkerton talk about my trip to Richmond?" Isaac asked.

"Yes, we discussed the possibility of my going with you. I made it clear, though, that I would not become one of their spies. Isaac, please do not ask me to engage in work that I do not believe in or have a talent for", I pleaded.

"Liz, I would never ask you to go against your principles. Nor would I ask you to do anything in which you had the slightest hesitation. If you would like to go with me, I will be honored to have you by my side. Otherwise, I understand, and will go alone."

Isaac appeared almost as a small boy with his eyes full and wishful of a positive response.

"Isaac, I would be honored and delighted to go with you. I have only one concern. Do you think it is too soon following Constance' death for you to be seen so publicly with another woman?"

I was never concerned regarding my own reputation, but fiercely defended that of Isaac and the other members of the family.

Isaac protested "I am not concerned about the propriety of mourning, Liz. This war is going to last a long time, despite what the politicians and Generals say. And the Angel of Death is going to visit every house and home across the nation before it is over."

The look of sadness and gloom suddenly came over his face. I became acutely aware of his fear that, in addition to losing Constance, he feared even more the loss of his children.

"Liz, I have two sons in the Army already. Fortunately, Abraham has not indicated his desire to fight. He is still a man of peace. For that I am grateful."

I tried to assure Isaac that Simon promised to look after Amos and Andrew.

"I know, Liz", Isaac continued. "But Simon Cameron will not be Secretary of War forever. There is even some talk that he might be asked by the President to resign."

"Whatever for?" I queried.

"He is being accused of incompetency and corruption in the War Department. If the charges prove correct, he will be discharged, and then, what of the rest of us?"

Isaac was certain that both Amos and Andrew would be assigned to units in direct conflict at some point of the war.

We spent the next hour discussing the future of the war and that of Simon Cameron, should the charges hold true. Finally, our conversation turned toward Richmond.

"When do you intend to go, Isaac?" I asked

"If arrangements can be finalized by the middle of September, it is my desire for us to travel south by the end of September or the first of October, at the latest." Isaac responded.

He went on to explain that we would be able to take the train as far as Fredericksburg, if Union forces were still in control of the region. If not, then we would go by train as far as possible, and coach the remainder of the way. Once in Confederate territory, Isaac had been assured of safe passage and arranged transportation to the Confederate Capital.

"Do you anticipate any difficulties going through either the Union or Confederate lines, Isaac?"

"No. I have received passes from both governments, allowing us to move freely between the two countries, as long as we are on a mission of mercy and peace."

Isaac continued to state that we might encounter delays, and possibly modes of transportation that might not be as comfortable as we preferred, but that we would arrive in Richmond in one piece.

Isaac returned to his residence, with the promise to keep me informed as to the coming arrangements for our trip to the south. I promised to remain prepared to go at a moment's notice.

As he walked onto the outer porch, Isaac stopped and spoke.

"Liz, you will never know how much your coming on this trip means to me."

I touched his lips with my fingers and quieted his words.

"I know, Isaac. It has not been easy for you these many years. You loved Constance very much, but I also know you have never stopped loving me. Constance would not wish you to live with guilt over the matter. It was her desire that you should continue loving, as you had previously done."

Moisture filled Isaac's eyes and a tear fell from his cheek.

I continued, "Isaac, I love you. I have always loved you. But it would have been unfair to both of us should we have allowed that love to bring us together so many years ago. I would not have been a good wife to you, as Constance has been. But I trust I have been a good friend, and I promise that I shall endeavor to remain a good friend."

Isaac took me into his arms and spoke, "Liz, I do love you. And yes, you have been and continue to be not only a good friend, but my best friend. I am not asking you to be my wife. But, please, don't leave me ,either."

We kissed long and hard. Then Isaac withdrew from the porch without a further word.

I went back to the library and sat in my chair. Caroline came in and asked if her father had left without saying goodbye. I nodded that he had.

"Auntie Liz, you are all flushed and have tears in your eyes. Is everything all right? What has happened to you? Did Father hurt you? If so, I will give him a piece of my mind."

Caroline was often protective of me, as much as I was of her.

"I am fine, child. Your Father is a wonderful man and did nothing to harm me", I shared in return as I regained my composure.

Caroline sat across from me and looked deep into my eyes.

"You are in love with Father." She spoke with tenderness.

"Oh, Caroline, you know I have always loved both your mother and father", I shared with a slight smile.

"Yes, but not like this. You are actually in love with Father. How absolutely marvelous. Will you marry Father? May I start calling you Mother now, instead of Auntie Liz?"

Caroline could still act as a small spoiled child from time to time.

"First, your Father has not asked me to marry him, and I doubt that he ever will. Second, I am not the marrying kind. You know that. What an absolutely horrid wife and mother I would make. I would always be running off to catch another story and leaving the dishes piled for Rebecca or someone else to care for", I stated with my objection to marriage.

"You do that now, Auntie Liz. When was the last time you washed a dish, or even fixed a meal for yourself? I imagine you can not even remember", Caroline taunted.

"Well, there are other things a wife does for her husband, in which I have no experience or even desire. So, end of discussion", I firmly stated.

Caroline left the room, with her childish giggles and laughter about romance and flirtations. The late afternoon sun was streaming through the open windows, and I ascended to the top of the stairs and sat at my writing table.

I began writing, "Dear Horace…"

CHAPTER SIXTY ONE

I dispatched my letter to Horace Greeley at the Tribune, early the morning of the twenty third of August. I informed him that I would be going to Richmond with Bishop Isaac Stoltzfus, to cover his meetings with the Lutheran Church in the South and Isaac's attempt to keep the Church united.

Late that day, Andrew arrived with a dispatch for Caroline. It was requesting her presence at the War Department, to meet with Pinkerton and Baker on the twenty-forth, at nine in the morning.

I met briefly with Andrew, and he spoke that this was merely routine for all those who were working as correspondents. He assured me that I did not need to be present, and that he and Amos would both look out for their sister.

"Also, Auntie Liz", Andrew continued. "Did you hear about Rose Greenhow?"

"Hear what, my dear Andrew?" I asked.

"She has been arrested by Pinkerton, and placed on house arrest."

Andrew was quite excited about the events.

He went on, "She, and several pro-southern congressmen and Union officers, have been detained. It has been reported that her dentist tried to escape south, but was also apprehended. He apparently was most instrumental in passing messages sent by Rose to General Beauregard, prior to the battle at Bull Run.

"According to Pinkerton and Baker, Rose managed to tell just about every detail of McDowell's plans for the battle, through various members of her acquaintance, to Beauregard. The Confederates knew before we did what was going to happen, thanks to that southern harlot."

"What will they do to her?" I asked.

"Probably just keep her under arrest at the moment. There is talk that she may be sent to the Capital Prison."

"What about her daughter, Andrew? Little Rose is too young to be sent to prison with her mother, or to be left alone."

I worried about the child, thinking all along that her mother's influence was not a positive one in her young and impressionable life.

"So far, she is with Rose at home. Beyond that, I am not sure."

Andrew continued, "What they should really do with the woman is hang her for espionage and spying. But I don't believe it will come to that."

We continued to talk for some time, regarding the consequences of Rose's actions and of those who were also accused of assisting her in spying for the Confederacy. The total depth of her involvement was yet to be realized. Nor did anyone take into consideration that Rose Greenhow could continue her work of supplying the Confederacy with information regarding Union plans, while under arrest.

She continued to receive visitors from both government and military at her home. She was also cared for by a staff of assistants, who provided her with adequate food for her personal use as well as for her entertaining of regular visitors.

Abundant materials for dress making and quilting were at her disposal. Her influence and inner sanctuary among Washington City's elite continued, in spite of her arrest.

Caroline returned from her appointment at the War Department late morning the next day. She spoke how Pinkerton and Baker, along with Amos, had been present. Little had been said to her regarding her loyalties, and she was given the oath, which she took. Pinkerton, as he had accomplished with me, presented her with credentials to carry out her work reporting the war.

"He said that he knew I worked more as your assistant than on my own." Caroline said.

She was somewhat annoyed that neither man, aside from her brother, recognized her own growing abilities as a correspondent.

"However, Auntie Liz, Baker did ask me to take on one assignment."

Caroline went on to describe how Captain Baker asked her to meet with Rose Greenhow for an interview and to report what, if any, information she might gain regarding those involved in the conspiracy.

"I informed Captain Baker I had no desire to ever speak with the woman again, and that to use me to spy against her would violate my role as a correspondent."

Caroline reminded me that "you must protect your sources at all cost; otherwise they will no longer be your sources."

By mid-October, Isaac and I were on our way to Richmond on an errand of mercy. Isaac was hopeful that the Confederacy would not interfere with the mission of the Church. This he saw as maintaining the universality of the church's work over the temporal condition of nations and governments.

We were able to make most of the trip by train from Washington to Richmond. The Union Pickets near Fredericksburg stopped us for a brief moment, but a young Lieutenant came to our assistance and allowed us on our way.

Upon arrival at the depot in Richmond, the delegates from the Church met us. Reverend George Brinkerhoff led the delegation.

"Bishop Stoltzfus, thank you for coming. We have all been looking forward to your visit, in the hopes of resolving the differences that threatened the unity of the Church. We desire this as much as I am sure you do, and are praying and hoping."

Introductions were made of all parties. Reverend Brinkerhoff then escorted us to our accommodations at the Richmond Strand Hotel. The hotel stood only blocks from the Richmond "White House" and was one of the finest hotels in the city.

Meetings with elected clergy and the Bishop would begin in earnest in the morning. The hotel staff had provided a banquet room to accommodate the clergy in their work.

Throughout the next two weeks, I was able to explore Richmond, with one of the clergy wives assigned the task of escorting me each day. I attended luncheons and fashion shows, as well as teas too numerous to remember.

The spirit throughout the south was one of expectancy and exuberance for the success of the Confederacy. No one believed the Union would prevail in the final hour. The Generals were praised for their commands and the men who fought were honored for their bravery.

After two weeks of negotiations, Isaac asked if we might meet for dinner alone. I agreed and the women attending to me suggested that he might wish to have some intimate moments with the woman he loved.

I reminded them that we were merely friends, with no romantic involvement.

"You are most certainly a Yankee female, then. If I had a man as attentive to me as the Bishop is to you, my dear, I would have him in a moment for a night of passion", one of the clergy wives suggested.

I had often found the south to be most hospitable, and their values somewhat different from mine. But I could not conceive of the idea of an intimate moment with a man merely for my pleasure, to then cast him off for another, should the need or desires arrive.

Isaac and I enjoyed a quiet moment over dinner, as I told him of the suggestions of his clergy wives.

"Isaac, I think you should preach a sermon against loose morals before we return home", I suggested.

Isaac found it all amusing, and assured me that he was not as uncomfortable at the idea of a romantic entanglement as I appeared to be. I blushed at his comments, knowing how easy it really would be for me to find myself strongly held in his arms.

Throughout the evening, Isaac shared how the desire of the Lutheran clergy remained steadfast in keeping the Unity of the faith and church.

"All they have really asked for is that we might agree that we shall not be agreeable on the issue of slavery", Isaac explained.

"What of the General Convention, Isaac? How do they stand on the issue?" I asked.

Isaac explained that at the General Church and among the Council of Bishops, there was division on the issue of slavery.

"Up until now, Liz, the position has been non-interference by the Church. But of late, the Northern Bishops are calling for a decisive ruling of no allowance for slaves, while the Southern Bishops express their sentiments that, should that happen, they will divide the Church."

"So why are you here, then?" I asked.

"Both the Northern and Southern Bishops see me as a moderate, and are hoping I can keep peace among both sides, until the issue of secession is finally resolved." Isaac continued,

"No one wants to split the church, but I fear it will happen anyway. There are too many hot heads within the ranks of clergy and membership, calling for the split along the lines of the Union and Confederate States."

Later that evening, we attended a party held at the residence of the Richmond Bishop. He and his wife were wonderful hosts, and refused to allow any to speak of Church business. Over fifty clergy and their wives attended.

Bishop Francis Caldwell, Richmond's resident bishop and colleague of Isaac, shared that the Confederate President, Jefferson Davis and his wife, Varina, had extended an invitation to us to attend a ball at the Richmond White House on the fifteenth of November.

Isaac and I thanked the Bishop for the kind offer and accepted. Bishop Caldwell also stated that the President was most open to an interview with him, if I so desired.

I expressed my deep appreciation and stated most enthusiastically that I would very much appreciate the opportunity to speak with Mister Davis. I also asked if there was any possibility of meeting a few of his Generals anytime during our visit. Bishop Caldwell assured me that he would make every effort to secure the appointments, if possible.

As the evening came to a close, Isaac and I were taken by carriage back to our hotel. It was now into November, and the nights were cool and damp, with overcast and grey skies.

The next few days saw little change in the meetings Isaac held. The parties agreed to a brief recess of three days, allowing Isaac and me time to relax and see sights together.

CHAPTER SIXTY TWO

Early the next morning, Isaac and I met for breakfast, then headed for a stroll through the heart of Richmond. It was not long before we came to Libby Prison, where a few Union soldiers were still held captive following Bull Run.

Isaac approached the sentry at the main entrance and asked if we might have a moment with the Warden. We were turned away, and told that if we wished to visit, we needed to make arrangements through the War Department.

"Which one?" Isaac asked.

The sentry shoved Isaac back and swore a few words regarding Yankee scum. Isaac and I left quickly and returned to the main street.

Over lunch we noticed the atmosphere was still one of joyful anticipation for a Confederate victory. The one obvious sign of the war, beside the number of men clad in grey uniforms marching through town at all hours of day and night, was the lack of certain supplies and goods from the shelves of the Richmond stores.

"Isaac", I began. "The wives of the clergy tell me it is becoming more difficult to find certain food supplies and other materials just to keep the household going. The Union blockade is having its desired effects on the availability of goods to the region."

"I understand, Liz. The clergy were saying similar things to me."

Isaac went on, "It has been only a few months since the blockade went into effect. Can you imagine what it will be like for these people, if this continues for a year or more?"

We talked for a long time regarding the position of the people, especially the poor, should the war continue and the blockade remain.

Isaac stated, "It is always the poor who suffer the most, Liz, always the poor."

Isaac was correct. The wealthy were able to buy what they needed from the blockade runners, even if the prices were heavily inflated. But the poor, and their children, had little resources beyond what they could normally afford. Already, there were signs of refugees living in slums and begging for bread, while the wealthy continued their parties and balls.

In every war, it seemed as if the wealthy always profited at the expense of the poor. It was the poor man's son who usually fought in the ranks, while the rich man's son commanded, often from a distance.

There is no fairness, or even justice, in war, only pain, grief and sorrow. It seemed as if I was becoming a cynic in my brief exposure to the ways of men and their fights.

It was as if little boys grow up to become only bigger boys, demanding their right to bigger and better toys. Instead of playing with their toy soldiers cast in lead and painted with bright colors, they now dressed up other boys in brightly colored uniforms. Weaker boys than they became the new soldiers of their play. These bigger boys now placed into the hands of their new "toy" soldiers the means of death and destruction, unleashing their power and fury upon any who would stand in their way, hindering their desire for even more power and bigger toys.

"Isaac", I finally blurted out from my trance. "Take me away from here. Take me home and let us run away from this war. It is madness, sheer madness, my love."

I was now quietly sobbing, with tears freely flowing across my face.

Isaac took my hands and brought comfort to me. We talked about my feelings, and he was in agreement with my perspective.

"And that is why we can not run away, Liz. We must stay and correct what we can and report the rest, so that perhaps the world, and future generations, will avoid the horrors that are yet to be unleashed upon the face of the nation."

Isaac dried my tears, and we returned to our hotel. We sat together in the lobby for hours, talking of love, life, gentler days, and simpler times. We reminisced about our early days and adventures with Constance. We talked about our hopes for his children, and prayed that God would mercifully spare all sons and daughters in the conflict.

As the evening came to a close, Isaac escorted me to my room, which had been his custom since our arrival. This night, however, I asked Isaac to kiss me once again. He had not ventured to do so since the night in August as he was leaving my home.

263

He took me into his arms and gently pressed his lips to mine. I had not felt such release and abandonment since the night so many years ago, when Alastair had taken me into his arms and pressed me close.

"Isaac", I spoke beneath my breath. "I do love you. Stay close to me forever. I fear, more than at any other time, that my time left with you will be so brief. Do not leave me, Isaac. Promise me."

"I promise, Liz. I am not going to leave you ever. Marry me, Liz. Marry me this very night." Isaac spoke with such conviction of his feelings.

I pushed back, and regained my senses.

"Isaac, you know that I can not. I love you. I will always love you. I have not known any man, and my desire is for you. But I can not marry you, not yet. I still have my work to do, and, as you said earlier this evening, we must, I must, report the horrors and tragedy of this war. I must show the human cost to victory, or defeat."

"I understand, my love", Isaac stated.

"I have been fortunate in having the love of two women. But I am also experiencing the tragedy of having only one to call my wife."

I went on. "Isaac, it is not to say that I shall never marry you. I just can not at the moment. Give me some more time, Darling. I promise, I will not deny you forever."

Isaac held me in his arms and reassured me of his love. He promised to be near, should I need, or desire him. And he promised he would not press me further for a time of proposal.

I kissed him goodnight upon his sweet lips and said goodnight, as I entered my room and closed the door for the night. This time I did not sob, as I had for Alastair. I knew that Isaac and I would become one together in the future, as soon as assignments were completed, and the war was over. Oh God, let the war end soon, I prayed that night.

CHAPTER SIXTY THREE

By the evening of November fifteenth, Isaac had concluded his business with the clergy representatives of the south. An agreement had been reached, as the southern clergy leaders promised to work in cooperation with Isaac and the other Bishops, to maintain the unity of the church in the midst of the conflict that now divided the nation.

The promise was based on Isaac's assurances that the Church would not interfere in the politics of the current state of affairs concerning the rights of the states, unfair trade and tariff restrictions, and the never ending question of slavery. Isaac encouraged the ministers to focus on the spiritual needs and eternal issues of their congregants.

As a result of the compromise, Jefferson Davis issued a Presidential Proclamation to his military commanders, requesting that no military action, including firing upon any member of the clergy, should occur. Further, President Davis declared that ministers from both North and South should be permitted to pass without hindrance in their work of mercy, peace and compassion.

Isaac replied to the President of the Confederacy with his appreciation of the proclamation, and assured the President that he would do all in his power to stop any action by Northern or Southern Clergy under his care to disrupt this proclamation. Isaac had stated that he was looking forward to this night's ball at the Richmond White House, to personally thank President Davis for his support.

"You are sounding as if you have become sympathetic to the southern cause, Isaac", I had remarked as we prepared to go into the evening's activities.

"No, Liz, I am just trying to be as diplomatic as possible, to maintain the unity of the Church. It will be difficult enough to rebuild the nation once this war is over, without also having to rebuild the Church", Isaac explained.

Isaac went on to discuss how rebuilding the nation without malice toward the southern leaders and people would be essential in the end for the well-being of all the people, north and south. He added that the war, in his view, would continue on for some time, and that there would be a great deal of healing needed in the end.

"And the Church will be integral in the process, Liz", he stated.

We arrived at the White House shortly before eight in the evening. We were accompanied by Bishop and Missus Caldwell. Guests were arriving by carriage regularly, and it appeared as if there were well over five hundred in attendance.

The portico was brightly lit, and servants, dressed in their finest attire, greeted each guest by attending to their wraps and whatever other need they might have. It was difficult to accept the hospitality, knowing that each of the freshly dressed Negro attendants was considered the property of someone in the household. I prayed under my breath that the day of "Jubilee", as I had often heard Frederick Douglass talk of freedom, would someday soon come to these poor souls, as well.

Upon entering the house, we were immediately greeted by President and Missus Jefferson. The President's wife looked so youthful and bright, full of optimism and fanciful joy on this occasion. Varina Davis was dressed in a magnificent gown with layers of lavender silk, giving no appearance of the shortages now commonly seen in the south.

"Bishop Caldwell, Missus Caldwell, how delighted we are to have you join us this night." President Davis was most charming.

Bishop Caldwell began, "Mister President, Varina. Allow me to introduce my friend and colleague, Bishop Isaac Stoltzfus from Washington City."

Isaac and the President exchanged a few words and then Isaac introduced me as well. "You may remember Elizabeth, Mister President, from your days in the Senate."

"Yes, quite so. Miss Fitzgerald, it is so very good of you to come this evening. My wife and I have been looking forward to seeing you once again."

I thanked the President for his kind words, and stated that it was indeed my pleasure, to see them once again.

"Bishop, your companion was one of the few reporters who expressed words of kind sentiment upon my retiring from the Senate to return to my home in these troubled times." Mister Davis continued, "I shall always be grateful that she did not take me to task, as many others did."

With that, the President kissed my hand, Varina and I spoke briefly, and we then continued through the receiving line.

The President assured me that we would talk again before our leaving for Washington. He further indicated he was looking forward to a dance later that night.

As I collected my dance card for the evening, I noticed that President Davis had already listed me as his partner in the Grand March, and Isaac was to partner with Varina Davis. I felt much honored to be asked to accompany President Davis in the introductory dance of the evening.

Throughout the evening, I had the opportunity to promenade with a number of Davis's Cabinet. Following our waltz together, Judah Benjamin, Secretary of War, invited me to sit with him for a few moments in the private study.

"Miss Fitzgerald", the Secretary began. "It is a delight to meet you first hand. I remember you from my brief time in the United States Senate."

I thanked the Secretary for his remembrance, and immediately asked if there was a particular reason he wished to speak privately with me.

"My Dear, I only wished to have a few moments to reminisce of past events and explore my hopes for the future. Off the record, of course."

"Of course", I responded.

Judah Benjamin never engaged in small talk without some deeper purpose. I was certain that I would know that purpose shortly.

The Secretary of War for the Confederacy shared at length his frustration over the criticism that he was receiving almost daily. There were many who blamed him directly for the slow advance of military action guaranteeing the right of secession.

"Generals Beauregard and Jackson seem to think that their lack of success is directly my fault", Benjamin stated in frustration.

"The Union blockade makes retrieving war supplies from Great Britain and France almost impossible at times", he went on to explain.

"So have Great Britain and France finally agreed to recognize the government of the Confederate States?" I asked.

"Not yet. But as I am sure you know, it is only a matter of time. If Secretary Hunter is able to work through the matters of State with her majesty Queen Victoria's representatives, then I am sure Great Britain will join our cause."

Benjamin was almost enthusiastic at this point, compared to his relative frustration moments ago.

Judah Benjamin went on to share that two of the Confederate commissioners to Great Britain had been seized from the British frigate Trent just a few days prior. Great Britain had already filed an official protest with Washington.

"If Washington does not release the Commissioners soon to the care of the British Minister to the United States, then Britain must declare war on the United States. You can clearly see how this will advance our cause and assure our right to form our sovereignty as a nation."

Queen Victoria had ordered, through her Prime Minister, the recall of their Minister to the United States in one week, if the Commissioners were not released. Lincoln was attempting to stall as long as possible, to aid in bringing a quick resolution to the Rebellion.

To withdraw the British Ambassador would be paramount to ending diplomatic relations with the United States. Surely the British would seize the opportunity to go to war once again with the Nation.

"Will Lincoln comply with the terms and demands of the Queen, Mister Secretary?" I asked.

"We are praying he does not."

Benjamin had a most cynical look in his eyes that made one want to run away.

"What is it you wish me to do with the information you have shared? I assume that is the reason for this private meeting", I stated with as much boldness and arrogance as I could manage.

"I merely wish you to report in your paper that the people in the sovereign states of the Confederacy are most excited about Great Britain entering the war on the side of the South. Report that the support of Great Britain and France will ensure our victory", Benjamin concluded.

"In what way will my reporting this information bring it about?", I inquired.

"My Dear Miss Fitzgerald, it will boost the morale of every southerner and revitalize our Army to read this in a northern paper. And hopefully, it will harden even further the hearts of the wicked in Washington", Benjamin concluded with small, self-amusing laughter.

I promised to write a report of my travels to the south in fairness and with accuracy. How he, or anyone in either the north or south, interpreted my articles was entirely up to them.

The Secretary of War rose to his feet and escorted me back to the main party. Isaac was waiting for me, concerned for my well being, as I had been away for nearly an hour.

"Did he hurt or threaten you, Liz?" Isaac asked quietly in my ear.

"No, my Love. I am quite fine. We will talk later."

With that, I kissed Isaac on the cheek, and was immediately taken off by one of the young officers for another dance.

Throughout the remainder of the evening, I was able to briefly engage the Secretary of State, Robert Hunter, in conversation, as well as a number of Confederate officers. They all were inquisitive as to whether I held sympathies to the southern cause, or was I merely there to accompany Bishop Stoltzfus and report the stories I found. I assured each one that my loyalties remained with my work, and that of reporting stories with fairness and accuracy, to the extent possible.

President Davis remarked to his statesmen and officers, "Miss Fitzgerald is as much a politician as she is a reporter, gentlemen. You will not get a straight answer from her on any subject. And don't play poker with her; she will take even the pants you are wearing, before the night is out."

With that, the men all enjoyed a hearty laugh. Several of the men invited me to accompany them into the library for a cigar and brandy, having heard of my reputation for enjoying these vices as much as they. I accepted.

The evening came to a close, and by the time we were back at our hotel, it was nearly three in the morning. Isaac escorted me to my room, and we kissed goodnight.

Isaac asked, "Did you have a good time tonight, Liz?"

"Yes my Darling. I had a wonderful time. How sad, though, to know that none of this will end well. The pain and suffering yet to come is beyond any reasonable person's mind to grasp", I responded.

I went into my room, closed the door, and prepared for bed. We would leave for Washington within the week. I still hoped for a meeting with General Lee, and perhaps General Jackson, before going home.

CHAPTER SIXTY FOUR

Two days later, I was summoned to the Confederate War Department by Judah Benjamin. I arrived early in the afternoon, and was immediately greeted by his undersecretary, Mister Hiram Blackstone.

"Miss Fitzgerald, the Secretary wishes for me to extend his apologies that he can not meet with you. He has summoned you here, however, to meet with one of his Generals, General Thomas Jackson. I believe you know each other."

"Yes, we do." I responded.

As Mister Blackstone escorted me to a small conference room, I was too excited for words, at the chance to once again converse with Abraham's favorite instructor at the Virginia Military Institute.

"If you please, Miss Fitzgerald, wait here and General Jackson will be with you momentarily."

I stood by a window overlooking the gardens that had been full of beauty and life only a few months earlier. They now lay barren and dead, with only remnants of the previous season's glory.

"I, too, often look upon the garden and wish for brighter days, Miss Fitzgerald."

General Jackson had entered the room as I was lost in my own thoughts.

"My Dear General. How wonderful to see you once again. How is your family?" I inquired.

General Jackson kissed my hand and invited me to sit with him. He shared that he had only a few moments before he needed to return to his duties. He was leaving within the hour to attend to his troops located near Harpers Ferry.

"I believe it was near Harpers Ferry that we last met, General", I recalled.

"Yes. I was there with the duties of security in the execution of Mister Brown. How is your nephew, Andrew, these days?" Jackson asked.

I shared that Andrew was well and assigned to the War Department in Washington.

"He runs errands and dispatches throughout the day for General McClelland and the President", I stated.

"He has expressed that he still respects and honors you, Sir. He wishes you were fighting for the Union. He is of the opinion the Union might have a better chance at victory, if that were the case."

"Andrew thinks too highly of me, Madam. I would have been honored had he decided to join me in the south. I, however, understand that a man must follow his convictions and conscience in these matters. Let us pray that neither of us will be the instrument of death for the other."

There was certain sadness in the General's voice as he spoke those words.

We went on for several minutes, exchanging memories, and asking about various acquaintances. I promised to deliver a note the General had written to Andrew, and give it to him in private.

Finally General Jackson stated that he must be off, and offered to pray for all of us before taking his leave. He took my hands into his and spoke a most treasured prayer, asking for Divine intervention in protecting all from the coming horsemen of the apocalypse. He prayed for victory in death as in life, and shared his joy at the coming resurrection.

At the conclusion of his prayer, he looked up into my eyes filled with tears.

"Do not cry for me, or any soldier, my Dear. Cry only for the loss of innocence our children will experience."

The General spoke with great tenderness. It would be several months before I would have the opportunity to speak to the General again.

I took my time returning to the hotel. Isaac and I were to be joined by Bishop Caldwell and his wife for dinner at seven, in the hotel dining room. I was ready to return north to my own home.

The evening concluded on a note of optimism and hope. I shared with the Bishop and his wife my conversation with General Jackson earlier in the day, and the remarkable way he prayed.

Bishop Caldwell commented that Jackson was a man of deep faith who believed that he would not depart this earth until his time had been completed. Jackson's only prayer, according to the Bishop, was that he might enter into glory on the Sabbath.

The next morning, Isaac and I began our journey north. The day was overcast and threatening snow. The train was filled with soldiers on their way toward Fredericksburg, and then on to points not discussed. Isaac and I were required to take seats in the baggage car for part of the journey.

The train rumbled on for what seemed eternity. Stops were made frequently, to add more soldiers to our already crowded accommodations. Twenty miles south of Fredericksburg, we were ordered off the train, along with all other civilians, as the soldiers took over what seats were vacated.

Isaac found a mule and a small wagon to accommodate us further toward Washington. Confederate pickets stopped us near Fredericksburg, to inform us that the lines had been closed north, and we would have to return to Richmond.

Isaac presented his papers to the sentry, who merely stated that orders were orders. Then Isaac asked to speak to the nearest commander, and we were escorted into a camp where a young Captain was reviewing maps and orders of the day.

"I am Captain Basil Evans, 24th Virginia, Company D, at your service. How may I assist you?"

The young officer, smartly dressed in his new uniform, looked no more than in his late teens.

Isaac showed the Captain his travel papers and passes, issued by Richmond, and asked for safe passage and clearance to the north. The young officer saluted Isaac and asked for a few minutes time to sort out the request.

Within ten minutes, the Captain had returned and informed Isaac that we were granted permission to continue. Isaac inquired who had granted the permission, and we were informed that General Longstreet had authorized our passage.

I was inclined to ask the Captain if we might have a few minutes of the General's time for an interview. Isaac, already sensing my desire to speak, quickly thanked the Captain and asked that he extend our appreciation to the General. A sentry led us back to the main road and allowed us to pass the pickets without further delay.

We were just north of Fredericksburg, as night began to close in around us. Now in Union controlled territory, we found lodging at a small hotel near Stratford and decided to stay the night. The Inn Keeper informed us he had one room remaining. Isaac accepted the offer.

Our bags safely in the room, we enjoyed a light meal before retiring. The Inn Keeper asked if Isaac were a clergyman and if I were his wife. Isaac responded that he was, and that, indeed, I was his wife.

"Well, I was hoping so. It wouldn't look right if you be sleeping in the same room as a lady if she were not your wife, you being a man of God and all", the Inn Keeper stated.

Isaac and I laughed and held hands across the table. It would indeed be awkward to have someone discover we were not married, but enjoying the same bed. Suddenly, the thought occurred to both of us at the same time; we had never before shared the same room, let alone the same bed to sleep in. We ate the remainder of our meal in quiet.

We entered the room together, and Isaac apologized for his carelessness in placing me in this situation.

"Nonsense, Isaac. We really had no other options. Besides, James and I have shared a room before, so I am not afraid to be here with you", I said with an assurance even I was not certain was true.

"Yes, Liz. But you were not in love with James", Isaac stated.

I assured Isaac that it would be all right, and that we would honor each other in the night's rest. I promised I would remain on my side of the bed, if he remained on his.

We both dressed privately for bed, and crawled in next to each other. Isaac gently kissed me goodnight, and extinguished the lamp. I could hear him breathing softly in the night, and my desire for him continued to grow. How I longed for him to take me into his arms and caress me into oneness with him.

Instead, I turned away from him, and drifted off to sleep. My night was filled with dreams of romantic adventure with the man who lay beside me. Isaac had remained the perfect gentleman throughout the night.

Early the next morning, we arose, dressed for the day and proceeded down the stairs to the dining area. We ate our breakfast of eggs, bacon, sausage, ham, potatoes and toast. After consuming two cups of hot coffee each, Isaac paid the Inn Keeper and thanked him for his hospitality.

We left the mule and wagon at the stables, and arrived at the train depot in time for the morning train to Washington. With our passes, the Union officer in charge of transportation provided us with seating in the forward coach, and we arrived in the City by early afternoon, with no further delays or complications.

It was good to be home, and Isaac promised to call on me in the next few days, after he settled into his work at the Rectory. I would spend the next few days writing about my adventures in Richmond and sending the dispatches to Horace Greeley.

CHAPTER SIXTY FIVE

By early December, the Union had recruited nearly six-hundred and fifty thousand men into its ranks. It was the largest Army ever assembled on American soil. Congress was now meeting, to consider a number of bills designed to bring an end to slavery in America, particularly in those sates now considered to be in rebellion.

Delegates from Virginia had met in Wheeling late in November and had adopted a constitution calling for the creation of a new state, West Virginia. The President ordered General McClelland to secure the gold at the Bank in Weston, Virginia, a sum of some thirty thousand dollars, to be held in reserve. These funds were to be used to reward Virginia legislators for their signature in assuring that West Virginia would become a Union state.

Word arrived in Washington that Prince Albert, husband to Queen Victoria, had died on December fourteen of typhoid. The Queen and her household were now in mourning.

The British Prime Minister, Lord Palmerston, had continued to push for the immediate release into British custody of the Confederate Commissioners, Mason and Slidell, now held in the prison at Fort Warren, in the Boston Harbor. Lord Lyons advised Washington to surrender the Commissioners, or face war with the United Kingdom. Lincoln continued to delay the decision, looking for a way to keep both Mason and Slidell from establishing any kind of relationship with Britain.

Christmas Day arrived, and Isaac, Caroline, and all three boys, as well as James, attended the festivities at my home. Rebecca and Caroline had furnished the family with a wonderful feast.

Lydia Ann, who had been an attendant to Constance for a number of years, had remained on with Isaac following the death of Constance. She had continued to regularly attend all affairs of the holiday with Isaac and the children until this year.

Lydia Ann had recently met a young correspondent from England, and had fallen in love. The two were married just before the first week in December, and she had set sail the following week with her husband, for England.

Isaac stated that he had received a wire from Lydia Ann informing us they had safely arrived in Liverpool. She promised to correspond as she was able, but for now was looking toward her future in this new land.

Andrew shared that he had received a letter of a congenial nature from General Jackson. General Jackson reported that he, too, was going to enjoy Christmas at his home, if possible, and invited Andrew to attend to him whenever they were close at hand.

"All I have to do is be granted permission from my commanding officer, and proceed under a flag of truce", Andrew reported.

Amos agreed that this was a more common practice than most realized, and that he, too, was thinking of meeting his old friend and Commander, Henry Heth, in the same fashion.

"How is it that you can be in the process of trying to kill one another one moment, and then the next, go under a flag of truce and enjoy tea together?" I asked.

"You have to understand camaraderie, Auntie Liz", Andrew stated.

Caroline talked about going south, to look for a story on the human cost of the war so far. She said that reports were coming into the War Department that morale in the mountain areas was low, and that already desertion on a wide scale was occurring.

I reminded Caroline that she would need permission first from Horace Greeley, and then the War Department, to make such a trip.

"But, Auntie Liz, we already have the passes from the War Department", she reminded me.

"They may not be valid much longer, Sis", Amos broke in.

He explained that charges of corruption were growing with Simon Cameron.

"It looks like Edwin Stanton might actually be behind it all."

"What do you think will happen to Simon, if the charges prove valid?" I asked.

"I really do not think it will come to that. Rumor has it, however, that Mister Lincoln may ask Simon to resign after the first of the year. Right now, though, the President has his hands full with the Trent affair."

Amos appeared more concerned over the issues of war and state than I had seen before.

The President was to meet on Christmas Day with his Cabinet, to make a final decision regarding the disposition of the Confederate Commissioners held at Fort Warren. He was being pressed by Simon and Secretary of State Seward to release the men into British custody, to avoid further entanglements with her majesty's government.

"If the President remains adamant against the release of these men, Auntie Liz, we shall be at war with Great Britain within six months."

Amos stated his thoughts with the sound of death.

Isaac and James turned, as they could, the conversation toward brighter discussions. James reported that the work he and Abraham were doing was rewarding, and Isaac stated that it appeared the Church would remain unified for the time being.

The day following Christmas brought news that the President had relented. He called for the immediate release of the two Confederate Commissioners, and they were handed over to the British consulate in Boston.

This ended the possibility that the United Kingdom would enter the war on the side of the Confederates. It would, however, take gentle diplomacy for the remainder of the War, to keep Great Britain from entering into a forceful agreement of providing arms and supplies to the Confederates.

The end of the year brought sad word that Hetti had passed away, from pneumonia. She was nearly eighty at the time of her death. Greta and Peter asked what they should do about arrangements.

Caroline, Isaac, and I traveled to Hagerstown to care for the funeral concerns, on the thirtieth of December. Hetti was buried on New Year's Day, in the Colored section of the Rosehill Cemetery. The only mourners were the three of us, along with Greta, Peter and Lars.

Isaac made arrangements to transfer ownership of the house over to Peter and his family.

"I have no need for the home any longer, Liz", he stated.

I assured him that he was well within his rights to do with the house as he chose. Peter and Greta were most appreciative, and promised that we were welcome any time to visit and stay with them. The next day the three of us returned to Washington City and our responsibilities.

On January eleven, 1862, Simon Cameron resigned under charges of general incompetence and fraudulent actions. Although the charges were never proven, the shadow of doubt lingered over Simon's ability to carry out his responsibilities. As a consolation, the President appointed Simon as the Ambassador to Russia.

Within four days, Edwin Stanton was named by the President as the new Secretary of War. As it was, Stanton and McClelland were good friends, and it had been rumored that the two sought the demise of Cameron.

General McClelland was unable to attend the ceremonies to swear Mister Stanton into office. The General was recovering at home from typhoid fever, and would be unavailable for several more days.

Throughout January and February of 1862, McClelland did little to move the Army of the Potomac into action. In the meantime, General Ulysses S. Grant continued to advance his army in the western theatre.

On February sixteenth, Grant took Fort Donelson near Dover, Tennessee. Southern casualties were high in the fighting. Over twelve hundred Confederate soldiers surrendered, and over fifteen hundred were wounded or killed in the fighting.

Caroline returned from a trip she had made into Virginia early in February. She had obtained permission to go to Richmond, to report on the morale of the average citizen. Abraham had accompanied her.

"Auntie Liz, it is absolutely amazing. The general populace has practically nothing to even eat, and yet, the aristocracy of Richmond acts as if there is no need among the people", she explained.

Caroline went on to describe meeting Mary Boykin Chesnut.

"You may know already her husband is Colonel James Chesnut. He was one of the men responsible for the surrender of Fort Sumter."

Caroline continued, "She is a very intelligent and enlightened woman of about forty, Auntie Liz. Missus Chesnut shared some of her writings with me, and she is most remarkable at recording events.

"This is what she wrote of Grant and his action in the west. 'He don't care a snap if men fall like leaves fall; he fights to win, that chap does'."

Caroline and I talked at length about her experiences, and whether she desired to return south any time soon.

"The next time I go south" she stated, "you will have to go with me."

"So you will go again?", I asked.

"Yes", was her reply.

CHAPTER SIXTY SIX

During the early part of 1862, the war continued, with skirmishes and battles throughout the south. General Henry Halleck, along with Grant, Pope, and other field commanders, were winning significant victories in the western theatre.

General McClelland, ordered by the President to move on Richmond, had launched the Peninsula Campaign, as it came to be known, and moved within ten miles of the Confederate Capital. With over one hundred thousand men at his disposal, McClelland, however, was unable to take the Capital and capture the heart of the Confederacy.

Finally, by late summer, McClelland was ordered to advance the Army of the Potomac toward positions held by General Pope and reinforce the Union Army of Virginia, confronting General Thomas "Stonewall" Jackson. Defeated at the Battle of Second Bull Run, General Pope retreated toward Washington.

In a letter to the President, Pope complained that General McClelland was tardy in his response and left Pope's Army without proper support. The President made a surprising move, as he dismissed Pope and placed General McClelland in charge of both Armies. The General consolidated the Union Army of Virginia into his Army of the Potomac. McClelland was now ready to confront Lee and Jackson.

Word had reached the War Department that dispatches from General Lee concerning his advance into Maryland had fallen into the hands of General McClelland. McClelland was now advancing on Frederick and Antietam, Maryland, along with Harpers Ferry, Virginia.

Union troops defending Harpers Ferry were unable to hold against General Jackson's Confederate Army, and nearly twelve thousand Union soldiers surrendered. Lee was strategically placed at Antietam near Sharpsburg, Maryland, as McClelland advanced his army.

Andrew arrived at my house early on the morning of September fifteenth. Rebecca answered the pounding at the door.

"Where are Auntie Liz and Caroline?" Andrew asked without hesitation.

"Caroline recently left for the War Department, and Miss Elizabeth is in her private study, Master Andrew", she responded.

Before an invitation could be extended, Andrew bounded up the stairs to the second floor and entered my room abruptly and unannounced.

"To what do I owe this sudden intrusion, Andrew?" I asked, still dressed in my morning coat and slippers.

"Auntie Liz", he began at once. "There is no time for proprieties. McClelland is advancing on Lee near Antietam, and I must be off within the hour with dispatches from Secretary Stanton and the President for him."

Andrew continued, "I have an extra horse, if you can be ready in the next half hour to travel with me. There is going to be a major battle, and possibly the end of the war."

"Yes, indeed, I will go with you. Let me dress quickly. Ask Rebecca to join me at once in my room. Dear Andrew, thank you for coming for me", I said with a light touch to his cheek.

"I would not have allowed you to miss this for the world, Auntie Liz", he stated.

Rebecca came at once, and within twenty minutes I was dressed in male traveling attire. I had adopted this manner of dress from my days of reporting on run-away slaves with Constance. Male clothing made traveling by horseback through rugged terrain more easy.

As I gathered my supplies and writing materials, along with a few items of comfort for the journey, Rebecca packed food supplies for Andrew and me.

"Master Andrew", she stated. "Here is some salt pork, jerky, and hardtack. The hardtack I made fresh last week, so there should not be any insects in the biscuits."

Andrew thanked Rebecca and, along with freshly filled canteens, loaded the pack of food upon his horse. I secured my pack upon the horse provided by Andrew, and we set off immediately for Frederick.

It was shortly past noon when we stopped and received fresh horses from the Union stables established days earlier by General McClelland. Andrew signed the required papers, and we were once again off toward Hagerstown. It was nearly nightfall as we arrived at General McClelland's headquarters near Boonsboro, Maryland.

Andrew handed the pickets his orders, and we were immediately escorted to the General's tent. General McClelland was dressed in proper military attire, as was his custom. Andrew entered the tent, as I stood near the opening. With a smart salute, Andrew greeted the General and informed him of his mission.

McClelland looked over the dispatches and summoned one of his aides. He exchanged a few words and handed a dispatch to be carried to General Burnside at once.

General McClelland escorted Andrew from the tent, and asked if he was intending to remain for the next few days, or was he to return to Washington.

"With your permission, Sir, I wish to remain and observe the battle", Andrew responded.

The General was gracious, and granted permission.

"You may wish to remain near headquarters, though, Lieutenant", McClelland responded.

At that, Andrew introduced me to the General, although we had met previously.

"Miss Fitzgerald, you are welcome in my camp, as long as you channel your reports through my headquarters before sending them to Mister Greeley."

I thanked him for his hospitality, and thought how he had softened toward the press over the past several months. It did help, I was certain, that he and my editor, Horace Greeley, were somewhat friends.

I was offered the opportunity to share a tent with Miss Clara Barton. Miss Barton was attached to the Army of the Potomac as a nurse. In previous battles, she had demonstrated her unique ability to attend to soldiers upon the field of battle, even before the fighting had stopped. Miss Barton demonstrated courage that even some seasoned soldiers lacked.

"Miss Barton", I began. "I am Elizabeth Grace Fitzgerald of the New York Tribune. I am told I may share this tent with you for the next day or so."

Clara graciously invited me to place my things on the open bunk and offered me some tea.

"Have you eaten as of late, Miss Fitzgerald?" she inquired.

"I have managed a few biscuits and some jerky the last several hours", I replied. "I think, though, I am too exhausted from today's ride to eat anything else."

However, I discovered that, with my tea, I was able to consume some light sandwiches that Clara had reserved from the evening's meal. We spent the next hour talking about my journey from Washington City, and my impressions of the Secretary of War.

"I find it difficult to request the supplies I need for our fighting men in the field", Clara remarked.

I promised that, upon my return to the City, I would do what I could to assist her in the work she engaged. Soon I found myself falling off to sleep, even as we talked. Clara covered me with a blanket, and assured me that I could sleep until I was well rested.

Early the next morning, I was awakened by the sounds of reveille and the movement of the troops. Officers and sergeants alike were shouting orders to the men to prepare for the day.

Clara was already up and sitting at her desk.

"Will there be fighting this day?" I asked.

"No, I do not think so. General McClelland, however, wishes to advance some of his forces near to the Antietam Creek and the stone bridge. He is hoping to cut off any advance General Lee may try to make toward Harpers Ferry and Washington", was her response.

I dressed and went toward the mess tent for breakfast. The officers and enlisted men alike were gracious in accommodating me with a bountiful supply of food, even though they poked amusement at my attire.

As I sat eating, I recognized Alfred Waud walking toward me. I immediately rose and went to greet him.

"Liz, the last time I saw you was at Bull Run. I thought you might have been killed or something, but then I have read your stories in the Tribune and knew you were stuck in Washington."

Alfred appeared genuinely glad to see me.

He continued, "I see you are still wearing men's trousers."

We exchanged ideas and stories for some time. Alfred stated that he was going to attempt to move near the Confederate position just north of Sharpsburg, to gain a better perspective.

"Come with me, Liz. This promises to be one heck of a fight."

I agreed, and after collecting a few of my writing materials along with my passes, we proceeded toward what Alfred believed would be a spot near the Confederate center. He assured me the center was usually safer, as most Generals, McClelland being no different, would try to fold the flanks first.

As we approached the Southern lines, we were stopped by Confederate pickets, and challenged. We were then taken without delay to the headquarters of General Jackson. The detaining sergeant reported to Jackson's aide that he had arrested two spies, one a woman dressed as a man and stating that she was a war correspondent.

The young officer looked at me and made an amusing remark to the sergeant. He entered General Jackson's tent and within moments I could hear the laughter coming from inside the canvas home.

General Jackson came out and, with laughter in his voice, said, "I was sure it was going to be you, Miss Fitzgerald. And who is your friend?"

I introduced Alfred to the General, and we were invited to sit and dine with him. Over the next hour, we spoke of our work and desire to capture the battle from the Confederate position. Alfred asked if he might sketch the General as we spoke, and Jackson graciously agreed.

"How is Andrew these days, Miss Elizabeth?" Jackson asked.

"He is doing well. He still works at the War Department. In fact, he is right now observing with General McClelland. As soon as this whole affair is over, we will return to Washington City together", I responded.

"Perhaps we will join you upon your retreat to the City, Miss Elizabeth, and pay our own visit to the War Department and Mister Lincoln", Jackson stated with some amusement.

"Perhaps, General", I said.

By the time we finished our brief conversation, Alfred had completed his sketch of the General. Jackson's aide presented us with passes, and told us to report to General D.H. Hill at the Confederate Center. He assured us that there would be plenty to report on in the next twenty four hours.

As we arrived at General Hill's command, we were told to stay with Virginia units that would occupy the area around the sunken road, later to be called "Bloody Lane", following the battle. A young Captain provided us with shelter and food. The remainder of the day was spent talking with various soldiers about home and family.

CHAPTER SIXTY SEVEN

Before dawn on the morning of September seventeenth, cannon fire erupted and disturbed the process of morning's gentle awakening. The ground shook beneath my feet, and the sound of more than a hundred cannon deafened the shouts of officers and men alike.

The buglers and drummers began their task of sounding commands that could be heard above the noise of battle. Men hurried to assume prearranged positions of defense.

Alfred Waud and I followed quickly, as Virginians took position in and around the sunken road. We found protective cover a mere twenty feet or so from the Confederate line on their immediate right. The young Captain assigned to watch over us assured our safety as best he could, before leaving to attend his men.

As the sun rose, the advance of McClelland's Army seemed more than enough to overwhelm the forces that Lee and his Generals had amassed for this day's fighting. The Confederates, however, had been outmanned before and had managed to seize the day. I wondered if this would be more of the same.

The fighting grew more intense by the moment. Soldiers were falling faster than replacements could be brought forward. Alfred was sketching as furiously as the soldiers were attempting to fire their weapons.

A young Rebel private, standing near me, was shot through the head. Blood and flesh from his wounds now covered my clothing. I rose, to try to help him, but Alfred stopped me, saying the man was already dead.

For the moment, I became sick and lost my meal from the previous evening. As balls of fire from Union guns raced past my head, one striking the hat I wore upon my head, I cowered deeper into the cover provided by dirt and fence rails. There was no time for being sick.

The fighting continued on throughout the day. Union troops finally broke through our position with the Confederate Army. Success, however, was not nearly as great on other parts of the field.

General Burnside, who only days before was assuring everyone of a quick and final victory, had been defeated at the stone bridge by General A. P Hill's forces. The battle seemed more a draw than a conclusive victory for either side.

As I wandered the field of battle, I came across many young men who, just the night before, I had spoken with about home and family. They now lay motionless, hopes and dreams dashed to the depths of death itself.

Clara Barton was attending many of the wounded. We saw one another, and fell into each other's arms. She saw the stains and remnant of battle upon my clothing, and noticed the hole in my hat where a Minnie ball had passed only hours before. I saw the stains upon her, as well, and noticed the hole in her sleeve where a ball had cleanly traveled.

Holding each other's hands, we stood back, looked and laughed. We were alive.

"Union or Confederate?" she asked of the hole in my hat.

"Union" I replied. "And you?"

"Confederate" was her answer.

Clara went on to tell how she was attending a fallen soldier on the field as the ball passed through her sleeve, striking the young lad in the chest, instantly killing him.

"It was not his day to live", she had said with melancholy in her voice.

Young drummer boys and old veterans lay dead. Many more were screaming in pain, as the surgeons lay their knives across their limbs to remove arms and legs, before infection could settle in. I wanted to be sick once again, but there was no time.

I returned to my tent as night fell. Alfred and I had parted at the end of the day's fighting, with the promise to look for each other in the morning.

I took off my attire and as best as possible, brushed the dirt and filth of the day from my clothing. I washed in the basin left by Clara, and sat by the light of the lamp to begin recording my dispatches.

Skirmishes and fighting continued the next day with less intensity, as General Lee began to withdraw his Army into Virginia. I looked for Andrew near McClelland's headquarters, but was told that he had not been seen since early the day before. He reportedly had gone to observe General Burnside's action near the stone bridge.

As I was making my way though the hospital staging areas, I found an aide who reported that Andrew had been wounded and was recovering at the rear hospital. I went immediately, to see how serious his injuries were.

I found Andrew resting comfortably on a litter. He was surrounded by at least a thousand other men, clad in both blue and grey.

I knelt down beside him and took his hand in mine.

"Andrew, how badly hurt are you?" I asked.

"Auntie Liz", he responded as he opened his eyes. "I was worried you might have been injured or killed in the fighting yesterday."

"I am fine, my dear. What happened to you? How severe are your injuries?" I asked.

We talked for some time. Andrew told how he had been observing the battle, when it appeared the Confederates were about to make a break through their lines. The Captain in charge of a company had fallen, and the men were in disarray. Andrew had immediately moved forward to take up the line once again, and proceeded to make an orderly advance to hold the position.

In the end, he needed to yield to the advancing Confederates and, in doing so, had been injured in both his right leg and left arm, with shot from a cannon. The men in blue carried him to the rear.

"I am told by the surgeons that the wounds are clean and went straight through, Auntie Liz. It looks like I will recover and keep both limbs", Andrew stated with his usual smile and confidence.

I told how I had been on the Confederate side when the fighting broke out. I also shared how I had spent a few moments with his old mentor, General Jackson, prior to the fighting.

Andrew was to be transported back to Washington City, to recover at the hospital there. I stated that I was going to Hagerstown to visit Greta and Peter, before returning to Washington City. I promised that, as soon as I was home, I would come for a visit.

Early the next morning, I said my goodbyes to Clara Barton and Alfred Waud over breakfast. I made my way to Hagerstown, and found Greta at home with her growing son, Lars. Peter was away, working on the rail lines near Cumberland, and would not return for several days.

Greta offered me the use of my old room to write my dispatches and send them to Horace Greeley. By the morning of the twentieth, my work had been completed and I was off, by train, to Washington City.

CHAPTER SIXTY EIGHT

I arrived home late in the day. The train had been heavily laden with casualties of the previous day's fighting. The most severely wounded were transported first to the staging hospitals around Washington City, and then to other hospitals for recovery, or death.

The streets were filled with newly arriving family members in search of their loved ones. Hotels and boarding houses filled to overflowing, many weary travelers found only side streets and bridge coverings for shelter.

Rebecca prepared a bath for me, as was her custom upon my return. The soothing warm waters graced with scented oils made me feel as if I had been living a dream, or more rightly, a nightmare, the past few days

As I lay quietly soaking in the prepared luxury, with my eyes closed and my thoughts in far off places of happier days, Caroline entered the room.

"Auntie Liz", she began almost in a whisper.

"Are you all right?"

I opened my eyes and looked upon her face, filled with concern. "Yes, my Dear", I responded.

"I am just recovering from my travels and adventures of the past week. Have you heard of Andrew?" I asked.

"Yes", was her reply. "We received word from Amos. Andrew is to be back in Washington the day after next, and will be taken to Union Hotel Hospital."

"Is there any word yet as to the number of casualties?" I inquired.

"Amos says that the final count is not yet completed, but it is believed to be more than twenty thousand from both sides", was her response.

With her voice trailing off and her head slightly bowed, Caroline left the room while I completed my bath. I sat, still numb from the experience. I had seen fighting at Bull Run and other places, but nothing quite as horrific as Antietam.

At night, I still could see the shattering of the skull and the flying blood and tissue from the young Confederate soldier who died only feet from me on the first day. My dreams were filled with the screams of dying soldiers. And no matter how much I bathed or perfumed, I could not cleanse my nostrils from the odors of dying and decaying men.

I dressed in my wrapper and slippers and went to the kitchen, joining Rebecca and Caroline. We ate together, a meal of beef in broth with vegetables and bread, in silence.

After several minutes, I finally asked, "Can we bring Andrew here to recover?"

Rebecca at once stated that she had already spoken to Master Amos about that possibility and reported that, indeed, Andrew could come. Caroline stated that she would make arrangements to bring Andrew home straight from the train station, upon his arrival in the city.

"Father also said that he will come and stay until Andrew is healed, if it is all right with you, Auntie Liz", Caroline stated. "I told him that you would have no objection."

I responded, "Of course it is all right. Rebecca, let's put Andrew in the guest room at the top of the stairs. We can fix a bed for your father in my private study."

The final preparations were made. On the twenty-fifth, Andrew arrived by train in Washington. Rebecca, Caroline, and Isaac met him there and, with orders from the War Department, took Andrew by Coach to my home.

I was out for most of the day, attending to meetings at the Capital with various members of the Senate. Much of the discussion centered on General McClelland's lack of advance on Lee's army following Antietam. Senator Benjamin Wade from Ohio stated that he believed McClelland should be fired for his lack of aggressiveness.

"I was present at Antietam during the heavy fighting, and I can assure you that the task you are asking is not small, Senator", I stated.

"That is precisely why we don't have women in the ranks. You women are too timid and weak, my Dear, for such matters", the Senator had said with his usual air of superiority.

"Senator, I have met women with more backbone than most of the politicians in this city. And I will clearly state that I also found two women who died in battle wearing Union blue. Will you now tell me they were too timid to live?" I countered.

The good Senator mumbled a few more words and abruptly excused himself from my presence. Others were more sympathetic to the outcome of the battle and the responsibilities that General McClelland faced. Others from Massachusetts were now calling for a company of Negro men to be recruited. Frederick Douglass was adding his voice to the growing number of those calling for the Negro to fight along side the white companies.

I arrived home later in the day, to find Andrew already resting in bed, and Isaac by his side. Rebecca was continuing in her care of the household, and Caroline was at work at her writing table.

"Andrew", I began at once. "How are you feeling, my precious Dear?"

"I am fine, Auntie Liz", he stated. "The train was overflowing with the wounded. It is a terrible sight. I am sorry you had to see it all."

Isaac rose, and we greeted one another. It was the first I had seen him since my return to the City from Antietam. We embraced, and Isaac kissed me with his usual tenderness.

"Liz, I am so glad to see you. I am sorry I could not come as soon as you returned home."

"Isaac, my love", I responded. "There was no need. You knew I was safe and unharmed."

"No, Liz, I should have come at once. Andrew has been telling me what you saw and experienced in Antietam. Clara Barton filled him in on what you failed to share."

Isaac continued. "There is no way you could have come away from Antietam unharmed. Rebecca tells me she hears you crying out in the night with horrible dreams."

"She tells too many stories, Isaac", I said. "The dreams will pass in time, as they always do."

We spent the next several minutes listening to Andrew tell of his adventures and the retreat of Lee's army into Virginia. General McClelland was regrouping, in order to make another attempt to advance on General Lee and Richmond by winter.

Later that evening, Amos arrived, and all of us joined in a meal of trout, potatoes, vegetables and bread. Rebecca had managed to buy some rare and expensive coffee, which we enjoyed with some light pastries for dessert.

Following the meal, Amos spent a few minutes alone with Andrew, and then departed for his quarters. The remainder of the family retired, as well, for the evening, with the promise of more conversations in the coming days.

CHAPTER SIXTY NINE

As the Christmas of 1862 approached, Andrew was all but healed from his wounds suffered at Antietam Creek in September. General McClelland had been relieved of his command, and General Burnside, now in charge of the Army of the Potomac, moved on General Lee's forces in Fredericksburg, Virginia.

On Christmas Day, Isaac and his three sons, along with James, gathered with Caroline, Rebecca and me for dinner, early in the afternoon.

"Liz, you look radiant", Isaac shared as he entered the kitchen area.

"Nonsense, Isaac", I replied. "I am an utter mess. You are not due here for at least an hour. Now you see me at my worst."

Caroline and Rebecca both laughed at my protest. They knew that I hated being in the kitchen, and that I enjoyed cooking even less. It was, however, my habit of at least offering some support during the gathering of the family over holidays.

"Father, as you can see, Auntie Liz is well into preparing the biscuits for this evening's meal", Caroline offered. "I think, however, she has managed to put more flour on her face and clothes than in the bowl for mixing."

"Miss Elizabeth, you run now and get yourself fixed for the rest of the family. Caroline and me will take care of the rest of things on our own." Rebecca spoke with firmness as she chased me from the kitchen with her broom and youthful laughter.

I went to my room and poured fresh water into the basin. After washing my face and hands, I dressed in a Christmas frock made for me by Greta some years earlier. It had been a Christmas present from her while she worked for Constance and Isaac. I had worn the dress every Christmas since, and always my thoughts turned toward her and Constance in brighter days.

Properly attired for the evening, I arrived in the parlor, to once again be greeted by the men of the Stoltzfus household.

"Andrew, you are looking much healthier these days", I remarked. "Any thought as to when you shall return to your duties?"

Andrew did appear recovered from his wounds, but the experience had aged him considerably. He was even showing signs of prematurely turning gray in his red hair.

"I am ready to begin my work again, although I am not sure what that will be", Andrew responded. "Since General Burnside's defeat and the loss of over twelve thousand men at Fredericksburg, there is now a need, more than ever, for officers at the front. I may be reassigned soon."

Along with Amos, we talked for some time about the progress of the war. Burnside was to be relieved, and rumors had surfaced that General Joseph Hooker was to be the next General in command of the Army. Neither Amos nor Andrew particularly liked General Hooker. He had a reputation of spending too much time with the ladies, and not enough time with his men.

As our thoughts turned toward Amos and Andrew, Abraham, the middle son of Isaac and Constance stated he had an announcement to make.

He began, "Father, Auntie Liz, I have already spoken to Uncle James, Amos, and Andrew about what I am going to share with you. Please hear me out before you speak, especially you, Auntie Liz. I know how you are with your never ending questions."

Abraham went on to share how he had been approached by Frederick Douglass, regarding the formation of a Colored Regiment to serve alongside white regiments. The Governor of Massachusetts had authorized the new unit as the fifty-fourth Massachusetts, under the command of Colonel Robert Shaw.

Abraham shared that the Negroes would be able only to be enlisted but that it was a start toward their emancipation. The officers were to be white, and he had been selected to serve as one of the Chaplains for the new unit. Colonel Shaw had asked for him by name.

"The Colonel feels that with my past experiences working with the Negro, I might be of assistance in helping the men adjust to the rigors of military discipline", Abraham explained.

He was to leave for Boston after the first of the year, and, from there, join Colonel Shaw and the newly formed regiment. I looked toward Isaac as he listened, waiting for the response of a father to his son, before I would speak.

In the eyes of Isaac, I saw so much pride in his son, the man of peace. I also saw fear. Fear that he might somehow lose this precious child to the war. He had already dealt with one son coming perilously close to death's door. He did not wish that experience again. But he also knew in his heart that he could not avoid the experience for himself, while so many others faced it each day.

"Son", Isaac finally spoke. "You go with my blessing as your Bishop, but, more importantly, as your Father. I am so very proud of you. I am proud of all of you. Your mother would be just as proud of all four of her children, as well, should she be here to witness this day."

I took Isaac's hand as a tear streamed down his cheek.

"Abraham", I started. "I do have many questions, but this is not the time for them. Today we celebrate life, family, faith, and all that is good. And your calling is good, my precious one."

At that, Amos and Andrew both congratulated Abraham and encouraged him toward his work. Caroline reminded all of us that, in just a week, Mister Lincoln's Proclamation of Emancipation would go into effect, and that she was certain Colonel Shaw would indeed raise an entire regiment by spring.

The remainder of the evening was spent in merriment and playing of parlor games. Caroline defeated Amos five games in a row at chess. She would often remark that she was a better tactician than he.

The evening came to a close, with the men returning to their quarters and Isaac, James, and Abraham returning to their homes. Caroline, Rebecca, and I worked together to return the house to a somewhat respectable condition, before retiring.

New Year's Eve came and went with the usual celebration at the White House. Isaac and I attended and met Mister Douglass once again. He was as delighted to see me as I him. We discussed the issue of raising a Colored Regiment, and we talked about Abraham serving as one of the Chaplains.

As the midnight hour struck, there was great cheering in the streets by the colored members of the City, as the Emancipation Proclamation went into effect. Tears flowed freely down the face of Mister Douglass, as he rejoiced in this day. Freedom for his people was now at hand. He stood on the portico of the White House and prayed that the day of Jubilee would be recognized throughout the land, and that the war would soon be won. Those of us listening, in unison, said Amen.

CHAPTER SEVENTY

By spring of 1863, Abraham was serving along side the other officers and men of the Fifty Fourth Massachusetts, as one of their Chaplains. Nearly a thousand men of the Negro race had enlisted. Their training was going well, and they had been ordered to South Carolina to continue their training and to engage, where possible, the Confederate Army.

Abraham had written often of the men and their pride in wearing the blue uniform. Most were former slaves. Some had been freed or been born free. Most could not read or write. He was working with other Chaplains to correct this problem.

In the South, the black flag had been raised against the Black regiments. Any colored man caught fighting for the Union would be sent back into slavery, or killed. The white officers were seen as inciting treason and riot among the colored troops. Any caught would be executed. Abraham reported that, even with these threats, the men were eager and ready to fight.

Meanwhile, General Joseph "Fightin' Joe" Hooker had taken command of the Army of the Potomac, and General Burnside had been sent to the western theatre. Andrew was now serving in first Corp as a captain, in charge of a company of men.

General Hooker had advanced the Army near Chancellorsville, Virginia. He was preparing to engage General Lee's Army once again, and felt he had the upper hand. It was not to be so. As Hooker's army lay stretched along a wide line, General Jackson's forces came around the Union left and attacked in the late afternoon.

I was at General Hooker's headquarters, along with Amos, who was now serving as an aide to the General. Word of the attack came almost at once. The Union Army was quickly retreating from the surprise and advance of the Rebel Army. The lines were crumbling.

General Hancock, of Hooker's command, finally was able to rally his men to make a stand. By nightfall, it appeared as if the Union lines might hold for an organized retreat. Skirmishes and firefights continued throughout the night. Neither the Rebels nor the Union forces knew exactly where the others were.

By the next day, General Hooker ordered the withdrawal of his Army to the North. Word arrived early in the afternoon that

General Jackson had been wounded the previous night and was not expected to live.

Amos sent for Andrew at once. It was within the hour that Andrew arrived at headquarters.

"Captain Andrew Stoltzfus reporting as ordered, Sir", Andrew announced with a sharp salute, as he stood at attention before his older brother.

"Relax, Andrew. You know you do not have to salute me", Amos responded.

"I know, brother. But it is proper military protocol, and you never know who might be watching. I do not wish to undermine your authority with the men", Andrew stated, with great respect for his brother.

"Please, Andrew, sit down."

Amos went on to explain that he had received word of the fate of General Jackson.

"We do not know for sure the extent of his wounds, but are informed they are serious. He may not live."

Andrew's eyes filled with tears. "Anything we can do for him?" he asked.

"Not at the moment. The Army is in disarray, and we are retreating. I have, however, been authorized to give you a pass through the lines, if you wish to try to see the General. I know how fond you are of him", Amos offered.

"Yes, thank you. I would like to go at once", Andrew said.

"Auntie Liz has agreed to accompany you. You will have only seventy-two hours to make the attempt and return to me here", Amos stated with firmness.

"Time is short, Andrew, and we will be miles north of here by the time you get back. Wait too long, and you may not get back. I do not wish to see you a prisoner of the Rebels for the duration of this war, my dear brother", Amos said with tenderness.

Andrew and I left for the Confederate lines almost immediately. We had no difficulty crossing under a flag of truce. Andrew was relieved of his sword and side arm, and the two of us were escorted to the hospital tent where General Jackson lay. Doctor Maguire, Jackson's personal physician, greeted us and informed Andrew of the General's condition.

"He has lost his left arm and suffered several less serious injuries", the Doctor stated. "If we can keep the infection at bay, I believe he may survive. Time will tell."

Andrew asked, "Do you know which company from the Union is responsible?"

"Does it really matter?" the Doctor asked.

"Yes, it does. I was engaged with Confederate forces in the night. I pray it was not I who did this horrible thing to my old mentor and friend", Andrew stated with sadness in his eyes.

The good Doctor held Andrew's shoulder as he said, "No, Captain, it was not you. It was Confederate shot that caused the injuries."

Andrew wept.

Andrew regained his composure as quickly as he lost it. We were escorted to the bed side of General Jackson, who, still drugged with chloroform and laudanum, was able to recognize his once young protégé.

"Andrew, my dear boy", Jackson spoke in a whisper. "You have finally come to join the cause?"

Jackson coughed and laughed a little, as he tried to poke fun in the midst of the suffering.

"And I see you have brought along your lovely Aunt to see me as well. Miss Fitzgerald, you will pardon me if I do not rise to my feet at the moment. Doctor Maguire insists that I lie here and rest."

"No, General, I do not mind", I said with softness. "It is I who is privileged to rise to my feet for you."

General Jackson and Andrew spoke for a brief time, before Doctor Maguire insisted that the General rest. We gave our leave, and I kissed the General on his forehead.

The Doctor was most sympathetic and supportive. He immediately arranged for our return to Union lines, with the promise that he would write as he was able, to report on the progress of the General. I gave him my personal dispatch routing to use. This would assist in expediting correspondence to me in Washington City.

On Monday, the eleventh of May, word arrived by courier that General Jackson had died of his wounds. Jackson was to be transported to Lexington, and services were to be held at the Virginia Military Institute. I immediately made arrangements to attend the services, and left for Lexington that same day.

CHAPTER SEVENTY ONE

The funeral for General Thomas Jackson was a most solemn occasion. Nearly two thousand people turned out and lined the streets of the procession. Andrew tried to get leave to attend, but was still engaged with General Lee's Army, near Fredericksburg, Virginia. There had been little fighting in the past several days, but General Hooker remained steadfast in his conviction that he would be able to confront Lee at this place and time.

I returned to Washington by the first of June, and settled in to write my dispatches. To report on the death and burial of Thomas Jackson had been one of my most difficult assignments. I believe I loved the dear man as much as anyone. I had come to appreciate his humor, tenacity, resolve, and integrity over the past few years. His death, like so many others, had brought to a premature close the life of this man.

Once again I left Washington City, on the fifteenth of June, and traveled to Wheeling, in western Virginia. The western counties of Virginia had remained loyal to the Union, and had been granted acceptance as the thirty fifth state in the Union. The inauguration of statehood would occur on the twentieth, in a ceremony to be held at Wheeling, now West Virginia.

I joined others, as we traveled by train from Washington, through Baltimore, on to Cumberland. We arrived, late on the fifteenth, in the small town of Mannington, West Virginia.

The Army held a presence in this small mountain town, to secure the rail lines from Wheeling through to Cumberland, Maryland, and on to Baltimore. The Baltimore and Ohio Railroad provided a vital link for both supplies and men from the Ohio Valley.

In Mannington, we found adequate lodging and food, provided by some of the townspeople. Once settled for the evening, I began to explore the camps around the town, and talked with the soldiers. They had seen little action, but performed a variety of duties in maintaining the rail lines.

I had also remembered that Ella, the daughter of David and Florence Foote from Hagerstown, had married and moved to this town many years before. I made several inquiries of her whereabouts, and finally an elderly lady remembered her and her husband. They had owned and operated the feed store for a while, and also the post office.

According to the lady, Ella and her husband had fled the area shortly after the start of the war, having declared their loyalty to the Confederate cause. Mannington, like much of the area, was supportive of the Union and Mister Lincoln's policies. She did not know where they had relocated, but suspected that it was in the eastern part of Virginia.

Early the next morning, we boarded the train again for Wheeling. Arriving by midday, I made my way to the Wheeling Hotel, and checked in to my accommodations. The town was alive with excitement and dignitaries for the festive occasion.

The morning of the twentieth, I gathered with other members of the press near the platform, as Governor Francis Pierpont, along with his wife, Julia, took the stage. As he ascended the stairs, the crowd erupted in thunderous applause and cheers.

Throughout the hours, many gave speeches of loyalty to the Union, and hopes for prosperity to those who supported Mister Lincoln in the War of the Rebellion. Governor Pierpont thanked those who had supported the decision to remain with the Union, and gave an eloquent speech concerning the future of all free men, as the Union would one day reunite and move ever westward, expanding the territories. West Virginia, he reminded his listeners, would play an important role in providing the coal and natural gas so needed by the nation to fuel its expansion.

That evening, several celebrations, balls, and dances were held throughout Wheeling and other areas of the new state. The next day would see me once again on the train east.

As I traveled toward Washington City, I decided to take a side trip north into Pennsylvania. After arriving in Hagerstown, Maryland, I spent two days with Greta and Peter. Lars was growing so big now and had become a regular little boy, full of energy and mischief. Greta was expecting her second child in the fall. Peter was working hard on the rail lines, continually repairing the damage caused by Confederate raiding parties.

I continued by train from Hagerstown to Chambersburg, and on to Gettysburg. I arrived on the twenty-seventh of June at an old friend's home. Reverend Schumacher of the Lutheran Seminary, along with his wife, was quick to greet and welcome me. I told them that I was due back in Washington City for the forth of July celebrations at the White House.

"Did you have any trouble from the Confederates on your way here, my Dear?" asked the good Reverend.

I stated that I did not see or encounter any activity, but that I had heard rumors of General Lee's advance into Maryland. Reverend Schumacher explained that only the day before, General Early had passed though Gettysburg and was on his way toward Harrisburg. Also, it was reported that General Lee's Army was now in Chambersburg.

"I believe you may have just made it through, Elizabeth", stated Missus Schumacher with much concern.

I immediately wired Horace Greeley, at the Tribune, for instructions. His reply, "Stay in Gettysburg for now".

The Schumachers provided me with lodging, and made me promise I would stay with them until it was safe to proceed on to Washington City.

"If there is going to be a fight in Pennsylvania, I want to be here to cover it", I assured my host.

I went quickly into town and acquired some men's clothing to wear, should a battle ensue. This had become my manner of dress whenever I had the opportunity to be near a battle. Not thinking I would need such clothing on my trip to Wheeling, I had left all my other items usually worn at home.

CHAPTER SEVENTY TWO

Late on the thirtieth of June, Union Cavalry arrived near Gettysburg, commanded by General John Buford. Just to the west of the Seminary, General Buford established his lines, in preparation for an encounter with Confederate forces. The Seminary was taken over by the General and his staff, to be used as his headquarters.

Early the next day, Confederate forces, commanded by General A.P Hill, engaged Buford's cavalry west of Gettysburg, on the Chambersburg Pike. Word had been sent by Buford the preceding evening, advising his commander, General John Reynolds, of the situation.

By mid-morning, General Reynolds was on the scene with First Corp and the Black Hats, as they were known. The Black Hats had gained the reputation of being fierce fighting men, and were the envy of every commander.

However, within moments of his arrival, General Reynolds had been mortally wounded and removed from the field. General Buford's forces were forced to pull back through the town and make a stand near Cemetery Ridge. By the early evening, John Buford's Cavalry had sustained numerous losses, but had been able to hold the Confederates from making an all out assault, allowing General Meade, now in charge of the Army, to bring up his reinforcements.

The Seminary was the scene of much suffering, as the building used for studies had now been turned into a hospital. Union and Confederate surgeons worked through the night, side by side, caring for the men who had fought so valiantly during the day.

As I made my way through the wounded, I came across Andrew. He had been wounded again, only this time with greater severity. A surgeon had removed his left arm and he had bandages on his legs and right arm. He was weak from significant blood loss, and lay in a state of unconsciousness. A surgeon nearby spoke to me, saying that he doubted the young Captain would live through the night.

I immediately went to see Reverend Schumacher. Together, we moved Andrew to his home, and Missus Schumacher set about the work of caring for the young soldier.

As morning broke on the second of July, Andrew was still alive. There were no doctors available to tend to him, so the Schumachers and I did the best we could. We changed his bandages, as instructed the night before by the surgeon.

Missus Schumacher made a broth soup to nourish him. She had stated that she knew it was important to keep him hydrated, and the broth would also provide healing nourishment.

Over the next two days, the fighting was more intense than previously experienced. The towns people remained locked in their basements. Word arrived of a civilian casualty on the south side of town near the Cemetery.

By July fourth, the fighting had all but ended. I had ventured out from time to time during the past two days and had encountered Confederate soldiers around the Seminary. General Lee's headquarters were a mere five hundred yards from the Schumacher home.

I sat, on the evening of July second, for a brief time with General Longstreet and General Armistead. General Armistead asked me if I knew how General Hancock was these days. I informed him that I believed him to be well, and that he was at the other end of town.

We talked for some time of happier days and the loss of several good men. I spoke of knowing General Jackson, and that I was truly sorry for his loss.

I spoke briefly to General Lee, who appeared very tired earlier in the evening. I asked General Longstreet about his commander, and the General informed me that Lee was not well at the moment.

"He appears to be suffering from a heart ailment, along with mild dysentery", was the General's answer.

By the fourth, the Confederate Army was beginning to withdraw from Gettysburg. General Lee was having some difficulty in finding Henrietta, his prized pet chicken, and refused to leave without her. The hen was eventually found, already in her traveling cage home, aboard General Lee's supply wagon.

The carnage in and around Gettysburg was horrifying, with over fifty thousand casualties. Limbs were piled as high as the second and third story windows on most public buildings used for hospitals. Surgeons from both north and south remained long after the armies had left, continuing their care of the wounded and dying.

Andrew was showing signs of slight improvement each day. The only fear was of the possibility of pneumonia. Missus Schumacher made Andrew sit up in bed each day and do deep breathing. She said this would exercise the lungs and help with preventing the pneumonia. With each breath, Andrew would wince in pain, as he coughed and wheezed with the exertion.

Throughout the town, the stench of death was overwhelming. The quiet Adams County community was flooded with families seeking their loved ones.

I had wired Isaac with the news of Andrew, as soon as the fighting had ended. Amos had come to see his brother, as well, before leaving with General Meade's staff toward Hagerstown in pursuit of General Lee.

Word arrived on the seventh of July that Vicksburg had fallen on the fourth, to General Grant. The Mississippi River Valley was now totally under Union control.

Isaac arrived on the ninth to be with his son. Daily, Andrew's health showed improvement, and by the twentieth, he was laughing and talking at length about the first day's battle.

The joy of Andrew's improving health was overshadowed by a letter from Clara Barton. Abraham, serving with the fifty-fourth Massachusetts in South Carolina, was dead.

According to Miss Barton's letter, Abraham had been tending to fallen soldiers on the sandy beaches around Fort Wagoner, when a shell from a Confederate cannon exploded near him, killing him almost instantly.

"He did not suffer", she wrote, "and now rests peacefully in the arms of his Savior."

Clara had made arrangements to have his body shipped home. He would arrive around the twenty-fifth.

Isaac maintained his composure, as he did not want Andrew to know of the loss of his brother while he was still so fragile.

"I will tell him after Abraham is safely home, and before we lay him to rest next to his mother in Hagerstown", Isaac had stated.

I returned to Washington City and, along with Rebecca and Caroline, made arrangements to receive Abraham's body. I promised Isaac that as soon as I knew for sure when the body would arrive, I would wire him.

On the twenty-fourth, Abraham's body arrived in Washington City. James met the train and, with Caroline and me, traveled to Hagerstown, escorting Abraham. Isaac met us in Hagerstown on the twenty-seventh, and Abraham was laid to rest the next day along side his mother. Isaac finally gave in to his grief, for the first time since hearing the news.

"Did you tell Andrew?" I asked.

"Yes", was Isaac's response.

Amos arrived late in the day. He had just received word from General Meade of Abraham's death, and was given leave to return to his family.

We gathered at Greta's and Peter's home for the next two days. Amos inquired as to the health of Andrew, and was assured that he was improving daily.

"How goes the pursuit of General Lee?" I asked Amos.

"Not well", he responded. "Lee has crossed back into Virginia, and Meade does not wish to pursue him at this time. He says our army is too scattered and broken, following the clash at Gettysburg."

Isaac, along with James and Caroline, returned to Gettysburg to be near Andrew. Amos returned to his duties with General Meade's staff. I returned to Washington City and my responsibilities. There was so much sorrow and loss that it left little time or energy for mourning. Will this insufferable war ever come to an end?

As the fall colors began to change across the mountains of Maryland, Pennsylvania, and Virginia, the Union Army continued its pursuit of Rebel forces, with a mixture of victories and defeats throughout the Confederacy. Nearly a year following Antietam, the Chickamauga Campaign was under way in the western theatre.

After two September days of bloody fighting at the creek known as Chickamauga, which means in Cherokee, "River of Death", the Union Army was once again forced to withdraw without a decisive victory. The field of battle saw nearly thirty four thousand Union and Confederate casualties.

Amos was still with General Meade, on the Eastern front, near Culpeper Court House in Virginia. Exhausted from constant courier and dispatch duties, he arrived at my home late on the fifteenth of September.

"Auntie Liz, do you mind if I find some rest and refuge here for a few hours?" he asked.

At once, Rebecca and I took him in and prepared the guest room. Rebecca prepared his bath, while I attempted to make a satisfying meal of leftovers.

"I have a dispatch from the President for General Meade, but I must rest first", Amos stated. "I will have to be off at first light."

Amos explained that the President was pressing Meade to attack at once against Lee at the Rapidan.

"Sometimes I think the President does not totally understand the strength and abilities of Lee's Army. It seems as if he knows what we are going to do, even before we do, Auntie Liz."

"I understand that supplies and man power in the south are failing quickly, Amos" I commented.

"Yes. This war will not go on much longer, if the South does not receive help from foreign powers. At least I do not know how it can", Amos said.

He went on, "However, the Confederacy has shown its ability to fight, even against all odds, so who knows how much longer this can go on."

We continued to talk after Amos had his bath and a small meal that Rebecca had taken charge of preparing, following my feeble attempt. I shared that Andrew was doing well at the Capital Hospital and was allowed to leave each day for a short walk.

"He has even met a wonderful nurse by the name of Louisa May Alcott", I shared.

"Is it love?" Amos asked.

"I think he wishes it might be, but I think it is only friendship on her part", I answered. "And she is a writer, as well."

"That is all we need. Another writer in the family", Amos groaned. "You and Caroline offer enough adventure as it is."

I also told how, during her visits to the hospital to look in on Andrew, Caroline had met a young officer who had smitten her heart.

"He is a Captain with the sixty-third Pennsylvania. He, too, was wounded at Gettysburg, and has lost his right leg", I shared. "Caroline seems not to notice, though. She says his heart is pure and his face radiant with life."

We laughed together as we thought of Caroline, strong willed and independent, being smitten.

"All I can say, Auntie Liz", Amos continued, "is that we shall pray for the poor devil, that he is aware of what he has hold of in my sister."

As morning broke, Amos was already dressed and ready to depart for Culpeper. He took the food prepared by Rebecca, and kissed me goodbye. I assured him that I would let both Caroline and his father know he had been in for a short visit.

As the sun broke over the horizon, Amos sped off on his steed for more adventures. Rebecca and I returned to the house, and I dressed for the day.

By nine o'clock in the morning, I was off for the War Department. Caroline was due back from her trip to Philadelphia later in the day, and I wanted to be home in time to ask of her adventure.

As I entered the War Department, Mister Lincoln was reclining near the telegraph operator's desk, which had become his usual practice over the course of the war.

"Good morning, Miss Fitzgerald", the President spoke.

"Good morning, Mister President", I responded. "Any news yet from the Rapidan?"

"News travels fast among the Correspondents", the President replied.

"I do have friends in low places, Mister President", I stated with laughter in my voice.

We spoke for a few brief moments about Amos and Andrew. The President was happy to hear that Andrew was recovering well, and might be back at his post, now at the White House serving as the War Department's liaison.

"I do promise, Elizabeth, that I will not send the young Captain into harm's way again", the President said reassuringly.

I thanked the President for his concern, and promised that Isaac and I would be at the White House Ball the end of the month. I went into the office of the Secretary and asked to speak with Mister Stanton. I was then informed that the Secretary was indisposed, but that General Baker was available if I wished to see him.

General Baker rose to his feet as I entered his office, once occupied by Allan Pinkerton.

"Miss Fitzgerald, how nice to see you this day. Would you like to be seated and chat for a moment?" he asked.

"General, I really am not here on official business. I came to thank you for the assignment you gave Captain Andrew Stoltzfus", I stated.

"No thanks is necessary, my Dear lady", the General responded. "He is a heroic young officer, and I wish to keep him on in service to his country. I understand that he wishes to return to the study of law following this war, and who knows, I may someday need a good lawyer for myself."

I again thanked the General and stood to make my way toward the Capital.

"Miss Fitzgerald", the General started. "Before you go, may I inquire as to whether you intend to make another trip south anytime soon?"

I responded, "Caroline and I have thought of going to Florida after Christmas, to enjoy the warmer climate. But we have not finalized our plans yet."

"Well, should you decide to venture south of our lines, please check in with me before hand. I may have a request for you", he stated.

I never liked it when Lafayette Baker "requested" anything. He always had ulterior motives, and demanded much, without offering much in return. Like his boss, Edwin Stanton, he could not be trusted to protect his own mother, if it affected his advancement.

CHAPTER SEVENTY FOUR

As fall moved into early winter, the air grew colder by the day and the leaves had all fallen from the trees, as they were entering into their winter slumber. Washington seemed colder than usual, as the fighting continued throughout the south.

Andrew was doing well, and had returned to light duty at the White House. He would spend his mornings at the Military Liaison Office located on the first floor, preparing reports and shuttling papers between the Secretary of War's office and the President's office. In the afternoon, he would venture to my home and rest the remainder of the day.

Andrew stated that couriers actually took the papers around to the various offices and the people who needed them. He, in the meantime, sat working at his desk and entertaining the numerous visitors who came seeking an audience with the President concerning Military matters.

Early in November, the President received a special letter from Mister David Wills, an attorney from Gettysburg. The President, upon reading the contents, signaled he wished to talk with Andrew immediately.

Andrew arrived in the early afternoon of November tenth, eager and excited to talk.

He began at once, "Auntie Liz, I have wonderful news for you. I am sure Horace Greeley already knows about this, but you need to know and request that you go."

"What are you talking so excitedly about, Andrew?", I inquired.

"Gettysburg!" He stated with excitement. "There is a group of citizens in Gettysburg who have formed a cemetery to bury the Union dead. They are going to dedicate the ground on November the nineteenth, as a National Cemetery, and have asked President Lincoln to come and say a few words."

"Is he going?" I asked

"Yes", Andrew replied. "He said that he will not be the keynote speaker. That honor will go to Edward Everett."

"So then, when will the President speak, and what is his official role?" I questioned.

Andrew went on, "He will follow Mister Everett and pronounce the dedication of the Cemetery as a National Cemetery. He is asked to take no more than a few minutes."

I said, "I know Mister Lincoln will go, but he can not be pleased by the request. I would think the people would rather have the President as the keynote speaker."

We discussed for some time the request and the ceremonies planned for Gettysburg. I would inform Horace Greeley at the Tribune that I would go in my official capacity as the Washington Correspondent.

Andrew was also going to attend. The President had asked him to accompany him, along with others from the War Department. Secretary Stanton had declined the request, since he was not asked to speak.

The nineteenth of November arrived, and I found myself standing among a crowd of fifteen thousand gathered for this solemn occasion. I had arrived in Gettysburg three days earlier and was staying once again with Reverend and Missus Schumacher. Andrew was also staying with them and enjoying the hospitality they always provided.

Mister Everett was finally introduced, after several hours of preliminary remarks, music, directions and miscellaneous notations that always seem to accompany such events. As Edward Everett took the podium, the crowd fell quiet for the first time.

Everett spoke for a little more than two hours of the battle that had taken place, just a few months earlier. He highlighted the events, talked of significant moments, and commended the men who had fought, and died, so bravely.

The longer he spoke, the colder and more overcast the grey November sky seemed to turn. The wind was blowing from the north and seemed to add an exclamation point to the words Everett spoke, as he enumerated the losses.

The signs of the horrendous fighting that had taken place in July were still abundantly evident. The civilians, left to attend to the clean up and bury the dead, had done a remarkable job, but there was still much to do.

My mind drifted back to those days in the July heat, as Confederate and Union forces met and clashed here. I thought back to how we were not sure that Andrew would live following his injuries. Now he was here again, on the platform with the President.

I thought of how Abraham would have enjoyed being here this day, as well. I was certain, though, that he was here, watching alongside all the soldiers who had given their lives on this ground in defense of their cause.

At the conclusion of Everett's speech, the crowd applauded politely. Some around me commented how eloquent the speech had been, and how it would be remembered for all of time. Others said that he rambled on too long, like all politicians.

Then the President was introduced. He came to the platform, wearing his usual attire of black suit and beaver skin tall hat. The President had aged terribly since coming to office, and looked exceptionally weary this day, as he stood before the crowd.

He removed his hat, setting it on the table near him. From his coat pocket, he removed a piece of paper he had used to inscribe his notes. As he looked over the crowd, the gathering once again was in complete silence.

The President began in his high, monotone manner,

"Four score and seven years ago, our fathers brought forth on this continent, a new nation, conceived in Liberty and dedicated to the proposition that all men are created equal.

"Now we are engaged in a great civil war, testing whether that nation, or any nation, so conceived and so dedicated, can long endure. We are met on a great battlefield of that war. We have come to dedicate a portion of that field, as a final resting place for those who here gave their lives that that nation might live. It is altogether fitting and proper that we should do this.

"But, in a larger sense, we can not dedicate...we can not consecrate...we can not hallow this ground. The brave men, living and dead, who struggled here, have consecrated it, far above our poor power to add or detract. The world will little note, nor long remember what we say here, but it can never forget what they did here. It is for us the living, rather, to be dedicated here to the unfinished work which they who fought here have thus far so nobly advanced. It is rather for us to be here dedicated to the great task remaining before us—that from these honored dead we take increased devotion to that cause for which they gave the last full measure of devotion—that we here highly resolve that these dead shall not have died in vain—that this nation, under God, shall have a new birth of freedom—and that government of the people, by the people, for the people, shall not perish from the earth."

Following the President's remarks, the crowd remained silent. I wept. His remarks had touched my very heart. I would never forget his words or this moment. Mister Everett's words had already begun to fade from my memory, but Mister Lincoln's were burned into my soul.

As I looked around me, others were silently shedding tears as well, and no one was yet speaking. The silence continued for some time, until Mister David Wills, who had invited Mister Everett and Mister Lincoln, took the podium and concluded the ceremonies.

Later that evening, Andrew shared with me and the Schumachers that the President felt his remarks had been a failure, due to the lack of response from the crowd.

Andrew continued, "Mister Everett told the President on the platform that no one would remember what he had said beyond this day, but that the President's two minute speech would always be remembered. Mister Lincoln does not agree. Mister Everett insisted that the President said more in two minutes than he had said in two hours."

The following days, the press was unkind to the President regarding his remarks. Some had accused the President of avoiding the issue of the war completely, and of minimizing the tragedy of the battles that had occurred in Gettysburg.

On the other hand, many praised the statesmanship of Edward Everett and called him the true hero of the dedication. I wrote that the President had made the defining speech of his Presidency, and that his words would endure long after his office had ended.

CHAPTER SEVENTY FIVE

As the year came to a close, our lives were once again scattered in different directions. Andrew, James, and Isaac attended the Christmas celebrations at my home, along with Rebecca and me.

Caroline was in Philadelphia, and would be with Sarah Hale for the holidays. She had resigned from Horace Greeley in the fall, and had taken a position with Sarah at Godey's.

Caroline realized following Gettysburg, with Andrews's injuries and the death of her brother, Abraham, while serving with the Fifty-Fourth Massachusetts, she had had enough of covering the war. In addition, her brief affair of the heart with the young officer from Pennsylvania ended when Caroline discovered he was already married and was simply using her for his amusement.

Godey's Lady's Book had refused to enter into the war coverage, claiming that women needed at least one source that would give them a reprieve from the tribulations facing the nation and their families. Godey's provided that, and Sarah was a good friend for offering Caroline that reprieve, as well.

Andrew was now well recovered, and would start spending full days at the White House in the New Year. His friend, Louisa May Alcott, had returned home earlier in the year to continue her writing.

Louisa had shared with me prior to her departure the notes she had kept regarding her experience at the hospital. She had hopes of one day publishing them into a book.

Amos was still with General Meade in Virginia, and would not be home this year. His duties were taking him further from home in many ways, not just in distance.

On his last visit some weeks prior, Amos had refused to discuss the progress of General Meade and the Army of the Potomac. He appeared exhausted, and often drifted off into a silent gaze that seemed to take him some place far away.

Amos had shared that he was having more and more nightmares of late, in which he fell off his horse in the mist and fog and could not find his way back to his lines. His horse would run away and in the mist, he would see both his Mother and Abraham calling to him to follow them.

"I do not believe I will survive the next major fight", he reported to his Father.

Isaac assured his son that he would be fine and that there was no need to worry. Isaac said that he had prayed, and felt God would spare his children in the remainder of this war. Amos felt little, if any, comfort.

Isaac and I attended the President's and Missus Lincoln's New Years Eve party, which had become our custom. We danced through the evening and enjoyed lively conversation with many of the guests.

At the stroke of midnight, fireworks were launched from the White House lawn, and several made toasts to the ending of the war, with Union victories throughout 1864.

The Richmond Examiner, following a year of Confederate setbacks, reported on the last day of 1863, "Today closes the gloomiest year of our struggle". The paper went on to say that the "superior manpower and material resources of the North have begun to tell, and the Union Army is soon to prepare for the first time a unified strategy for the final conquest of the ailing Confederacy".

I had been privy to a meeting earlier in December, in which the President met General Grant and some other key officers in the sleepy hamlet of Bedford, Pennsylvania. I had been invited by Mister Lincoln, with the understanding that I would not report the meeting, but would record the event for future use, should the President feel it advantageous to share it.

The meeting concluded with the assurance that General Meade would remain in command of the Army of the Potomac, but that General Grant was being given command of the armies in the field. Mister Lincoln's instruction to Grant was specific, "Win the War at all costs this year." Grant understood the order and agreed.

The beginning of 1864 was filled with extreme cold in both the North and the South. The Confederacy was beginning to suffer in ways no one could have imagined at the start of hostilities.

President Davis of the Confederacy had ordered General Lee, in desperate need of food and supplies for his men, to take from the civilian population of Virginia whatever provisions were needed. This order did not endear Davis with the civilian population, and General Lee was hard pressed to put the order into action.

Lee understood how badly the civilians were already suffering in the cold of winter, and to deplete their supplies placed the civilians in even greater peril. However, Lee's men also needed food and supplies, if they were to continue the fight. Reluctantly, he gave the order to acquire as much food as was needed, wherever it could be found. Lee's army was nearing its end, along with the entire Confederacy.

CHAPTER SEVENTY SIX

By early spring, General Ulysses S. Grant was poised to take command of the entire Army. The President had been looking, for the past three years, for a commander who would fight and engage the Rebels at all costs. He found his man in Grant.

Grant arrived in Washington in early March, to receive his commission as Lieutenant General, and to take command of the Army. General Meade was relieved, and was placed in command of the Army of the Potomac, at Grant's request.

A formal ceremony, conferring the new command, was held on March ninth, 1864, at the White House. Brief remarks were made by both the President and Grant. The two retired to the President's study for more conversation.

I went into the White House to speak with Andrew. He looked so handsome this day, as he had thoroughly cleaned his uniform and polished the brass buttons, in anticipation of meeting the new Chief of the Army.

"What are your initial impressions of the man?" I asked Andrew, as I entered his office.

"A bit unkempt, Auntie Liz", he responded. "I thought he might be more formal in his bearing, meeting the President for the first time in Washington."

"Yes, Andrew", I responded. "I, too, was somewhat amused by his demeanor. I hear from the other correspondents, though, that he is willing to win at all costs."

"That will be the first time we have had a Commander willing to do that", Andrew said, as he stood and walked to a stack of papers sitting on the table across the room.

"The others have been more concerned with public opinion than their victories. Victory at little to no cost is what they want. But you can not win a war that way, and Grant knows it", Andrew stated.

We talked for a few more minutes, as more and more officers and couriers entered the room where Andrew worked, seeking a few moments with the new Army Chief. Andrew politely directed them to a room full of hard, straight backed, wooden chairs, and instructed them to wait there while he would see what could be arranged.

I stood, placed my bonnet neatly upon my head, and gathered my writing materials.

"I shall take my leave, dear Andrew. You have much to do. Shall we see you tonight for dinner?"

Andrew acknowledged that he would be there around eight in the evening, and would enjoy whatever Rebecca could find to prepare a meal for him. He kissed me softly on the cheek, and we bid good day as I walked out of the office.

Later that evening, Isaac and Andrew joined me for a late supper. Rebecca had prepared a lovely meal of boiled lamb, with potatoes and cabbage.

We sat by the small fire in the drawing room. Isaac sat near me on the divan, and Andrew took his usual seat in his favorite, overstuffed arm chair nearest the fire.

Andrew explained that General Grant was proceeding at once into the field to meet with his senior officers.

"General George Meade is most excited about Grant's promotion and taking command of the Army. Meade believes this is the best decision the President has made concerning the war, up to this point."

"What of the other officers?" I asked.

"You know most of them, Auntie Liz. They are, for the most part, capable men, but there is, of course, some jealousy among a few of the officers. I suspect that Grant will quickly replace them if they do not follow his orders", Andrew responded, as he sipped his brandy and drew a long drag of his cigar.

Andrew held the smoke for some time, and then slowly allowed the blue hue to escape into the air. He looked thoughtfully at the rolled tobacco he held in his fingers and smiled briefly.

"I always enjoy southern tobacco, Auntie Liz. Thank you for retrieving these for me."

Last fall I had taken a trip south into Virginia, to the town of Harrisonburg. I had told no one of the adventure. Lafayette Baker would have questioned me intolerably upon my return, and I wanted to make this trip purely for personal, and not professional, reasons.

A few years earlier, I had met a wonderful woman who had cared for James and me following an incident with some slave trappers. James had been shot, and we were left stranded. Ella had been at home when we arrived on the porch of her small farm house, and immediately took us in, caring for both of us until

James was well enough to be on his way. She had used a variety of homemade remedies to care for his wound, as well as any other needs we had.

I had been suffering for some time with a heart condition that only my physician was aware of. I had not told even Isaac, for I did not want him to worry. I also did not inform Horace Greeley, as I did not wish for him to limit my travels and work.

Doctor May had prescribed a tonic that was to help regulate my heart and relieve the pressure that occurred in my chest from time to time. The elixir, however, often made me sleepy and irritable, neither of which I appreciated. I was certain that if Ella were still alive, she would have a remedy.

After traveling by train to Winchester, I took the loan of a horse and made my way through the southern pickets to Harrisonburg. A few miles out of town, I came to the small farm house that had greeted me once before.

As I traveled toward the small dwelling, I could see smoke rising from the chimney, and an old black gentleman working at the wood pile to the side of the house. The man stood up and stopped his work, holding the ax at his waist. He stared at me, as I made my way toward the house.

Arriving at the front, I dismounted and, holding the reigns in my hand, asked if this was still the home of Miss Ella. The strong, large framed, elderly man, still holding the ax as if he intended to use it, should the need arise, simply said, "Yes 'em." Then he added, "Don't I know you, Missy?"

I responded with a smile on my face, "Yes. You are Mister Sam. We met a few years ago, and you and Miss Ella helped me and my friend."

"I remember you, Missy. You that newspaper woman, and your man was the preacher fellow, who'd been shot."

Sam almost seemed excited at this point, and put down his ax. He went running toward the door shouting, "Miss Ella, Miss Ella. Come quick. We got company." He lumbered up the steps of the porch, yelling and grinning, showing what few teeth remained.

Miss Ella came out of the house, asking Sam what all the fuss was about. He merely pointed in my direction. Drying her hands on her apron, she pushed her long gray hair back from her face. She squinted hard and, standing motionless, looked at me for what seemed eternity.

"My Lord", she began. "It ain't you, is it, Elizabeth?"

317

"Yes, Miss Ella, it is I", I responded softly and with a smile. Tears were beginning to fill my eyes as I realized she had remembered me. I knew at once that my journey south would not be a wasted one.

Immediately, she and Sam beckoned me inside. Sam took my horse to the barn. He said it was not good to leave animals in the open, as you never knew when one of them starving soldiers were to come and just take it away.

I thanked him for his concern and care. I had been informed that if I lost the horse and did not return it to the stables in Winchester, I would have to forfeit my seven hundred and fifty dollar deposit. I assured the stable master that I would return in a few weeks with his precious horse.

The house and friendship was just as I had remembered it from my previous stay. The warm fire still burned. The cozy cabin had not changed. The comfortable rocker, though slightly more worn, was still by the kitchen fire. I was once again commanded to my place, wrapped in its strong, wooden arms.

The fresh odors of baking bread filled my senses. Ella apologized for not having real coffee, as it had become harder to acquire since the war began. Instead, we had a refreshing herbal tea.

Ella and Sam explained over the next few days how first Rebel, and then Yankee soldiers, would frequently come through and take whatever they desired, and could find. Ella assured me that she was much wiser than the soldier boys, and knew where to hide her stock and supplies, so as to prevent thievery.

On more than one occasion, both the "blue bellies" and the "gray backs" had tried to take old Sam away. The Rebels wanted to return him to slavery, but Ella always produced her bill of sale, proving her Sam belonged where he was. The Yankees always wanted to take Sam away for his freedom, and to serve in the Union Army. Sam would protest and refuse to go.

During my few days with Ella, she prepared an elixir of herbs that she assured me would be better than anything the doctor could give.

"I knew when you were with me the last time, you would be prone to heart troubles", she said. "Good thing you never married and tried to have children. You would not have lived, I am sure of that."

I left with the promise of returning, if possible, some future date and thanked her and Old Sam once again for their care. Before riding off, Sam handed me a small package and stated that he had been given the items inside by an officer on General Longstreet's staff.

"The officer told me that the General, himself, liked to smoke these. Give 'em to your preacher friend from Old Sam."

I stepped off my horse, wrapped my arms around his huge shoulders, and kissed him on the cheek. I placed the tobacco into my bag and rode off toward Winchester.

"If I have the opportunity to go south again this year, Andrew, I promise I will do my best to retrieve as many cigars as I can get, just for you", I said with delight.

"Please, don't", Isaac protested. "You know how I despise those things."

"You did not always feel that way, Isaac", I countered in playful banter. "I recall a time before you became Bishop that you enjoyed a good cigar, and your pipe tobacco."

"Auntie Liz, you know that was before Father became too high and mighty for the rest of us", Andrew joined in with the banter.

Isaac blushed a little, and said with a smile, "I guess I have become too wrapped up in my own importance. You don't, by any chance, have an extra one of those lovelies I can share?"

I pulled from my private stock, two well made Cuban cigars I saved for special occasions, and the three of us continued into the evening, enjoying a good smoke and a glass of brandy.

CHAPTER SEVENTY SEVEN

By late April, General Grant had the entire Union Army poised to engage the Confederate forces on several fronts simultaneously. It was as if the General had drawn a large noose around the neck of the Confederacy and was about to begin drawing it close around its intended prey.

Grant had issued but one order to General Meade and the Army of the Potomac. "Where Lee goes, you go" Grant had said with a severe intensity in his eyes that told General Meade that failure to do so would have resulted in Meade's immediate dismissal. Grant further indicated that, until further notice, his headquarters would remain in the field, with General Meade.

Grant also gave orders for General Sherman to begin his "march to the sea". The Shenandoah Valley Campaign had been ordered, along with the Mississippi Valley engagements. The restructuring and details of Grant's plans were now carefully laid, with the understanding that all commanders would initiate the strategy on or about the fifth of May.

In the early light of May fifth, the Union Army began its assault on the Confederacy. Meade advanced the Army of the Potomac toward General Lee in the wilderness, near Spotsylvania and Rappahannock.

The area, so dense with forest and underbrush, was virtually uninhabitable. General Grant, however, felt that the terrain, along with easy access to water transportation at the junction of the Rappahannock and the Rapidan, would be of valuable usefulness in supplying the Army as it advanced.

In Washington, the President was now spending almost all his time at the War Department. He remained in the communications room, resting on a small bed placed in one corner for his use.

Mister Lincoln insisted that he wanted first hand accounts of the advances of Grant's army, and insisted on regular updates. Almost immediately, as the plans of Grant were implemented, the telegraph began to click away with reports.

For nearly ten days, the clicking of the key continued without rest. The operators were exhausted from the reports flowing in. The President was weary from lack of sleep. He had not left the War Department for these many days.

On May sixth, word arrived that General Lee had lost his most trusted friend and General, James Longstreet. Longstreet had been severely wounded, and was now taken out of action. His injuries had occurred near the place where General Jackson had been mortally wounded almost a year earlier.

May eleven reported that General Lee had now lost his most valuable Cavalry commander, General J.E.B. Stuart. General Stuart had been mortally wounded at Yellow Tavern, Virginia.

The Confederate Army of Northern Virginia under General Lee had begun to unravel, with the pressure Grant was applying. This was not, however, without cost to the Union Army.

On June first, Grant ordered the start of the Shenandoah Campaign and, with reinforcements, once again confronted General Lee. This time, General Grant would move against Lee at Cold Harbor, Virginia.

Following three days of fighting, Grant was forced to withdraw his Army, after suffering immeasurable losses. General Grant began the battle at the wilderness with nearly one hundred thousand soldiers. A month later, following battles in the Wilderness and Cold Harbor, nearly half had been wounded, killed, or captured in the fighting.

Reports were flowing in to the War Department regularly from both telegraph and newspaper. One reporter wrote that Cold Harbor represented a horrible failure on the part of the Federal generalship. Another wrote that the groans and moaning of the wounded and dying, all Union soldiers who were stranded between the lines, were heartrending.

Nearly seven thousand men lay dying or dead between the lines. Grant refused the request of his subordinate commanders to retrieve the wounded under a flag of truce. For three days, they lay waiting, crying, begging, pleading, and dying. After the fighting had ended, and the stretcher bearers entered the field, only two were found alive. The rest had died of their wounds, starvation, and dehydration.

I waited, along with the President and others at the War Department, for the reports. As they were read aloud to those gathered in the small office, I wept for the first time openly before the President and the Secretary of War.

"Elizabeth, I am sure Amos is fine", Mister Lincoln said as he placed his arm around my shoulder.

I responded, "How can any man be fine; Mister President, after witnessing and engaging in such atrocity?"

I dried my eyes, put on my bonnet, gathered my writing materials, and left for home. That was the last time I visited the communications room of the War Department.

Arriving home, I freshened myself, packed a small bag with essentials, changed into my traveling clothes, and headed for Harrisonburg, Virginia. I wanted to see Ella and Old Sam once again, and escape the war for a few days.

The trip took nearly a week on horse back. Communications and rail lines had been disrupted once again. I regularly encountered both Confederate and Union pickets, often being detained while my official documents were examined.

Lodging was increasingly more difficult to find, as one army or the other was commandeering most of the resources of the civilian population. Many nights, I simply found a small resting place, and would sleep for a few hours before proceeding.

I arrived at the gate leading on to Miss Ella's small farm. The gate had been torn from its hinges and lay, broken and splintered, on the ground. As I looked toward the house, all I could see was the stone fireplace and chimney standing where the house had once stood. The barn was gone, as well.

In horror, I rode at full gallop toward the remains, certain that I would find Ella and Sam standing nearby. As I came to the front, where the porch once stood, I realized they were gone.

Two mounds of dirt and gravel with small markers were placed near the front of the small cabin. They read, "Here lies the woman" and the other "And her slave". Who ever did this did not even know their names. I sat on my horse and wept bitterly for some time.

The cabin and barn had been reduced to burnt rubble. The garden, once so neatly cared for and arranged so that it produced the finest herbs and vegetables for Ella's remedies, now laid bare and stripped. No other signs of life remained. What could be taken was, and the remainder destroyed.

I took out my writing materials and fixed the markers.

I wrote, "Here lies Miss Ella, Friend, Healer, Saint of God".

For Sam, I wrote, "Here lies Mister Sam, Faithful Servant and Friend, a Freeman, belonging only to God".

I packed up my belongings and mounted my horse. I began a slow ride to Harrisonburg, with the hope of finding lodging and, possibly, someone who knew what had happened to Ella and Sam.

Just outside Harrisonburg, I came across an old tavern I had lodged at previously. I went in and found accommodations for the night.

The room was poorly furnished, and most of the pieces of furniture and decorating had been removed. The bed was worn out, and the coverings and linens were thread bare. Only one small, straight back chair and one small candle remained. The wash bowl was cracked and dirty.

I unpacked my personal belongings. I had brought a few items for Ella, along with some federal money for her, in case she would have need. I looked at the few items, and wept for her and Sam.

How could any Army be so inhumane as to treat civilians in this manner, if, indeed, it was the army? I was daily growing weary of the inhumanity of this war, and had contemplated leaving, as Caroline had, joining Sarah in Philadelphia.

I refused, however, to give in to the temptation, and would continue with my work until the completion of hostilities. I prayed at that moment for Amos, who was still with General Meade, somewhere in Virginia.

"God", I prayed, "bring Amos home safely to us."

I refreshed my face, and went down for the evening meal. The Inn keeper apologized for the lack of a good dinner. All he could offer this night was bean soup and corn bread. There was no coffee to be had anywhere in the south now.

I assured him that the soup would be sufficient and then handed him a small bag of coffee I had brought with me for Ella and Sam, from home.

"Lordy, Miss, where on earth did you get this?" the Inn keeper asked.

"It is probably best that you not ask", I suggested.

"Quite right, Miss", he responded. "If the Yankees come and see it, they will just take it. But if the Rebs come, they will accuse me of spying. I'll just say I got it from some Yankee woman that come through and used it for a night's lodging."

"I agree. You can always tell that story", I said.

Following the meal, I asked the Inn keeper if he would sit with me for a few moments, as I had some questions to ask. He agreed, but suggested that we not talk too loudly as there were always other ears listening in.

I asked him about Ella and Sam, if he knew them, and what had happened at their farm.

"Yes, Miss, I knew them both", he stated with some sadness in his voice. "They were fine people. Miss Ella, the old witch, had freed Sam some years back. Old Sam had remained on with her and got along well."

"I went out to see them today, and found their graves and the farm burned out", I stated.

"Yes, terrible business, this war", he started. "Yankee cavalry came through about a week ago. They were boasting that they would take anything they wanted and burn the rest. They pretty much cleaned me out as well, but left the Inn stand, saying they would be back and would not burn me out if I had some more Rum for them when they returned."

"What about Ella and Sam?" I pressed.

"Well, one of the soldier boys was bragging how they came upon a farm outside of town", the Inn keeper continued. "He said that when they rode up, this old nigger was chopping wood and some old crone came out of the house with a shotgun, threatening to shoot the first one who got off his horse and tried to come in.

"The soldier boy said that one of the men started to step down, when Ella pulled the trigger on her shotgun and injured the soldier. That was when the soldiers opened fire on both Ella and Sam and killed them on the spot. They took what they wanted and burned the rest."

After the Inn keeper finished, we sat together quietly for some time, nursing the coffee that he had prepared for us. I took his hand in mine and looked into his face. With tears flowing down my cheek, I simply said, "Thank you".

The next day, I packed my belongings and prepared to make the journey home. I left the money I had for Ella with the Inn keeper, along with a few other items. He insisted that it was too much and not necessary.

I assured him it was my pleasure to leave the items with him, reminding him that not all Yankees were as cruel as the men in blue he had recently encountered. We parted with the promise that, should I travel this way again, I would always have a room at his Inn, providing of course, the Yankees did not burn it down first.

The early morning sun was already warming the earth, and I could tell it was going to be a hot day. I decided to travel back through Winchester, as I had heard other travelers at the Inn the previous night state that Winchester was now back in Union hands.

CHAPTER SEVENTY EIGHT

The mid June sun was high in the sky, indicating the time was about noon. There were no clouds, only the bright blue hue of the crystal heavens and the piercing intensity of the ball of flaming gasses that illuminated each day.

I had just passed through New Market, Virginia, hoping to make Edinburg by night fall. I knew of a small Inn there that would provide me with lodging and a good meal, provided they were still in existence after the fighting that had recently occurred in the Valley.

Without warning, a shot was fired from somewhere among the trees just ahead and to my right. I cried out in pain as I fell from my horse, feeling the hot piercing lead enter my left shoulder.

I tried to pull myself behind a clump of trees for protection. The pain was intense, and the blood was pouring through the wound, causing a deep crimson stain upon my blouse and riding coat.

Almost immediately, two Confederate soldiers, not much older than their early teens, arrived by my side and ordered me not to move. They held their rifles at my chest, threatening to shoot if I did not obey.

"Why did you shoot me?" I asked, almost breathless and becoming more lightheaded. I felt as if I might faint at any moment.

"Jethro", the older of the two lads began to say. "You done and gone shot yourself a woman."

"Samuel, what am I gonna' do now?", the young soldier replied. "The Captain's gonna' kill me over this."

"May I suggest that you bind up my wound to stop the bleeding first", I suggested.

Samuel took from his haversack a small rag and immediately placed it over my wound, applying pressure to stop the bleeding. About this time, a seasoned Captain appeared on horseback. He stepped down and asked the young private what had occurred, and why did he fire upon me.

The private stood at attention, while explaining that I had come upon them unexpectedly and surprised him. He shot before he had thought to command my halt.

"Jethro, I should have you shot for this, and maybe I will", the Captain sputtered. "But for now, retrieve her bags and see what you can find in there to tell us who she is and where she came from. Now git."

Jethro raced across the path toward my horse, which was now standing near a small stream refreshing herself. He reached in the side bag and produced the satchel with my credentials and writing materials. He immediately returned these to the Captain.

In the meantime, the Captain spoke to me. "What is your name, Miss?"

"I am Elizabeth Fitzgerald, a War Correspondent with the New York Tribune", I responded. "Captain, may we attend to my wound before I bleed to death?" I stated with annoyance.

"In a moment, Miss Fitzgerald", he said matter-of-factly.

"Captain, here are her papers", Jethro said as he handed the satchel to his commander.

"I see your papers are in order", the Captain said after taking his time to review the information.

"Sam, take her horse and ride back to get the stretcher bearers", the Captain shouted.

"Please don't steal my horse from me", I protested. "She is the only means I have of getting home."

"Where is home?" the officer asked.

"Washington City", I replied.

"Well, don't worry about your horse. You are not going to see Mister Lincoln today", he said with a hint of kindness and amusement in his voice.

In a few moments, Sam had returned with the stretcher bearers and they were placing me on its hard, canvas surface. I was jostled and dropped twice on the carry back to the Confederate Camp.

Upon arriving at camp, the stretcher bearers placed me on a table in the surgeon's tent for an examination of my wound. The tent was full of injured soldiers from the battle of New Market that had taken place in mid May.

"All right, now let me have a look at this shoulder, Miss", the surgeon was saying.

I thought I recognized the voice, when the surgeon suddenly stopped and looked deep into my eyes.

"Miss Fitzgerald, is it really you?", the surgeon inquired.

"Yes, Doctor McGuire. It is indeed I", I responded softly and with a sincere appreciation that he not only recognized me, but would also be attending to me.

"Miss Fitzgerald, I must open your blouse and examine the place where the bullet entered the chest. Do I have your permission?"

"Yes, Doctor. Do what you must", I said. "I have full confidence in your abilities. And please, call me Liz, as all my closest friends do."

Doctor McGuire began his examination as gently as possible. He removed the bandages and with a small probe, located the shell. I winced several times with the pain of his work, but remained as quiet as possible, not complaining, knowing he was doing his job in the best fashion possible.

"Liz", he began. "The shell is still in your shoulder and will need to come out. I will give you some chloroform to make you sleep, so I can work without hurting you more than is necessary. May I proceed?"

"Yes, Doctor, do what you must", I said.

The assistant placed a brass cone over my face and encouraged me to breathe deeply. The room began to swim, and I drifted off to horrendous dreams I can not now recall.

Some hours later, I was awake, resting on a hospital cot near the opening to the tent. Nightfall had occurred, and the sounds of the woods, with its chirping and grunting, were everywhere. In the distance, I could hear soldiers laughing, singing, and talking.

Doctor McGuire came to my side and sat by my bed.

"How are you feeling, Liz?"

"As if I have been kicked by a mule in my chest. Thank you for taking care of me."

McGuire began, "I am so sorry that I had to take care of you at all. What were you doing out alone in these woods?"

"I had gone to visit an old friend near Harrisonburg. I had to get away from Washington and the war for a few days, and look at me now. Here I am, a casualty of that very war", I said with some disgust at my circumstances.

"Did you find your friend?" he asked.

"Yes, but she and her farmhand had been killed earlier by Union soldiers."

Doctor McGuire said nothing. He sat for some time, holding my hand and checking the site of the wound. Finally he spoke.

"The shell came out with no problems. I did notice, though, you have a heart problem. Is anyone attending you for this?

"Yes. I have a Doctor who is supposed to be a specialist in the area of heart care", I answered. "His name is Kenneth May. Have you heard of him?'

"He is indeed a pioneer in the field, and I am sure will help all of us understand more, in time", McGuire shared. "You are in good hands with his care, Liz. Now, you rest, and we will talk tomorrow."

With that, he rose and took his leave. I consumed some broth the orderly had prepared for me. In a few moments, I drifted off to sleep, forgetting about the journey home, or what would happen next.

Doctor McGuire checked with me daily, to observe my progress. We often spent a few moments talking about current events and the progress of the war.

"Liz", he began one afternoon. "I do not know how we can continue this struggle much longer."

"Amos tells me that the south is being overwhelmed by Northern resources and, unless a foreign power intercedes, the Confederacy will simply run out of men and supplies before long", I responded.

"Amos is quite correct", Doctor McGuire shared. "How are he and Andrew these days?"

"Amos is with General Meade and is part of his staff", I shared. "He is now a Major. Andrew was badly injured at Gettysburg and lost his left arm. He is still in the Army as a Captain, and is serving at the White House as the Military Liaison between the War Department and the Lincoln Administration."

"What of their brother, Abraham, I believe, was his name?" McGuire inquired.

"He was serving with the Fifty-Fourth Massachusetts as a Chaplain, in South Carolina", I responded. "He was killed while the Fifty-Fourth was engaged at Fort Waggoner last July."

"Liz, I am so sorry", Doctor McGuire said with great sadness. "This war has taken the lives of so many good men."

"Indeed it has", I responded with a sigh.

Doctor McGuire added, "I have some good news for you, anyway. I have arranged to have you to be transferred to a Union Hospital near Winchester for your recovery. You should be well enough to make the journey in a couple of days."

"If it is all right with you, Doctor, I would just prefer to stay here until I am well enough to travel home myself", I protested.

"I would enjoy that, Liz, but unfortunately, I will be moving the remaining wounded to Richmond in the next few days. We will close this camp, and will be moving on", the Doctor stated.

Doctor McGuire left my side and returned to duties elsewhere. I asked the orderly where my horse was, and if she was doing all right.

"Yes, Miss Fitzgerald", the orderly replied. "She is fine and well fed for the moment."

I later learned that one of the officers rode her daily in the performance of his duties and had decided to keep her, giving me his worn out stallion instead. I protested at this news, but it was already too late. The officers unit had moved out, taking my mare with them.

Ten days following my injuries, General John Imboden entered the hospital tent and came to see me.

"Miss Fitzgerald", the General began. "It is indeed an honor to finally meet you. Allow me to introduce myself. I am General John Imboden, of the Confederate States Army."

With that declaration, he removed his hat and made a slight bow.

"May I sit down?"

"Please, General, make yourself comfortable", I replied.

"I have been informed that you suffered injury from one of our young privates", he said.

"It is really nothing, Sir", I replied. "Only a minor shoulder wound."

"Doctor McGuire tells me it was very near a significant artery, and, had the man been a better shot, would have killed you", the General went on.

"I think Doctor McGuire is over exaggerating the point, my dear General", I answered.

"None-the-less, I wish to ask if you desire that the young man be punished for his crime against you?" the General asked.

"Not at all", I protested. "He was just doing his job as best he could."

"He is a soldier and must be held accountable for his actions", the General insisted.

"General. As a favor to me, please do not harm the young lad", I asked in petition.

"Offer him advice. Give him more training. Father him, if you can. But do not punish him. He is only a boy and is being asked to grow into a man overnight. Let him grow up, for my sake, and the sake of his family."

"But what of your injuries?", the General asked.

"They will heal in time, and I will be none the worst for it", I replied.

.

The General thanked me for my time and allowing him to speak with me. He promised no harm or discipline would come to the boy, at my request. He ordered himself, and bid me good day as he left the tent.

A few days later, Isaac arrived. Most of the wounded had now been transported to Richmond. Doctor McGuire was readying his supplies and equipment for transport to the next engagement.

"Liz", he began at once. "We received word only three days ago of your whereabouts and injuries."

"I am fine, Isaac", I said. "Only a little sore and some stiffness from lying around on this hard cot."

"I have spoken with Doctor McGuire", Isaac said at once, "and he says I can take you home. James is waiting outside with the carriage for us."

"James is here, as well?" I said with a joyful voice. "How wonderful! I have not seen him for several months now."

Doctor McGuire gave us some last minute instructions on the care of the wound, and made me promise to take life carefully for the next several weeks.

"No chasing the story for at least two months, Liz", he said with firmness.

I replied with a childish grin, "You know me, Doctor. I always do as I am told."

Isaac and James loaded my belongings, which were still intact, into the carriage. The old stallion that had been left for me was brought over to be tied to the carriage.

I looked at the old face of the worn out horse and spoke with Doctor McGuire.

"I think I will leave him here with you. Perhaps one of your wounded can use him to make it home or to Richmond."

Doctor McGuire thanked me, and assured me that the old stallion would not become dinner for the men. I reached up and kissed the good Doctor on the cheek, and assured him that when the war was over, we would again meet on happier terms.

With the help of Isaac, I stepped into the carriage. Isaac sat on the same side as me. James sat across from us. The driver, hired along with the carriage in Washington City, began to pull from the Confederate camp, with the appropriate passes safely tucked inside his waistcoat. It was good to be going home again.

CHAPTER EIGHTY

The journey home consumed the better part of two days. We spent the night of the first day in Amissville, Virginia, before proceeding to Washington City the next day.

James and Isaac talked throughout the entire journey of their work and the possibility of strengthening the Church following the close of hostilities. James appeared more optimistic than Isaac.

"You are well aware, my dear Brother", James was saying, "that the southern churches will be in great need of support and financial assistance, following the final battle and the surrender of the Confederacy."

Isaac responded, "I agree on the need for assistance, but I fear the pride of many of the southern clergy and congregations will forbid them to seek that assistance from the Church in the North."

The debate continued throughout the trip.

I had settled in next to Isaac, and was resting peacefully against his shoulder. He had prepared for my comfort, as best he could, under the circumstance.

With his arm around me, he attempted to brace me against the constant bumping and jarring of the carriage, as it sped along rutted and shell pocked roads. The pain had been tolerable at the hospital tent under the care of Doctor McGuire, but now the intensity was becoming almost unbearable from the travel.

The carriage, late in the day, hit a rather large hole made by previous shelling during some engagement or another. All three of us were lifted from our seats, and I cried out for the first time, in pain.

Isaac called for the driver to stop for a moment, as he retrieved some elixir Doctor May had provided to help ease the pain. Isaac had called on my personal physician, to inform him of my wound, and the good Doctor had suggested the tonic as a supplement to any pain medication the Confederate surgeon might have available.

I took a drink of the bitter brew and quickly followed the medicine with a drink of whiskey from a small flask in my valise. James examined the wound and found some fresh blood on the bandages.

"I do not like the look of this", he explained. "I think that last jarring we endured may have reopened the wound."

I gave my permission for him to more closely examine the bandages. He placed fresh linens over the wound, wrapping them once again as Doctor McGuire had demonstrated.

"The wound does not appear to be torn open, Liz", James shared. "It does appear that there is some superficial bleeding at the site, though. We will watch it closely for the next several days, to make sure."

"Thank you James", I said. "When we arrive home, I shall call for Doctor May, and he can look in on my wound as well."

The carriage driver slowed the carriage, somewhat, for the remainder of the afternoon. We arrived at the small Inn outside Amissville, and settled in for the remainder of the evening.

The three of us engaged in a meal of meat and potatoes. The Inn keeper apologized for the lack of creativity and selection, accusing the Confederate Army of relieving him of most of his supplies.

"I notice you are having a bit of trouble with the meat, Miss", he stated.

"No, I am just trying to figure out what animal the meat came from", I stated matter-of-factly. "Is it deer?"

"I do not think you would wish me to divulge the source of tonight's fare, Miss", he said with a wink in his eye.

At that, he left us alone to continue in the process of downing what was probably the worst meal I had ever attempted to devour. After a few more attempts, I asked the Inn keeper if he could just bring me some broth and bread. He went to the back kitchen and, within a few moments, returned with a large bowl of meat broth and hard bread.

I made a half-hearted attempt to consume the meal, but eventually pushed it aside. James pulled from his satchel a small bag containing tea, and ordered hot water to be brought to the table.

"Liz, perhaps you will find this more to your taste", he suggested.

Isaac also retrieved a small parcel and removed some provisions that Rebecca had given them for the journey. He removed some of her bread, which was still fresh and edible, along with butter and jelly.

As the inn keeper arrived with the water, he spoke, "Where did you get the tea, and the fresh bread, and jelly?"

It was difficult to determine if he was excited or annoyed at our good fortune.

"Miss Fitzgerald's housekeeper provided them for us, prior to leaving Washington", Isaac responded.

"You would not have any to spare, would you Sir?", the Inn Keeper asked.

Isaac looked at me, and then James. Finally, James answered. "We would like to leave you with what we have, if you will wait until the morning when we continue our journey. We wish to insure we have adequate provisions for our friend and the remainder of the journey."

"Thank you, Sir", the Inn keeper responded. "I will be happy to acquire anything you might have."

The carriage driver, because of the color of his skin, was not permitted to enter the Inn. He was required to remain outside with the carriage, and could rest in the stable with the horses, if he so wished. His meal was provided at the kitchen door.

James added to the conversation.

"I have but one request for our provisions. You allow our carriage driver to have a proper bed inside the Inn."

"But that just ain't right", said the Inn keeper. "Darkies…"

"Negroes", James interrupted.

"Negroes", continued the man. "Negroes are not allowed in here, by law of Virginia. If I got caught, I could go to jail."

"I understand your plight, Sir", I finally interjected. "James, if you will move my belongings to the stable, I shall spend the night with Jeremiah."

I had learned shortly before leaving Doctor McGuire the coachman's name, as he wished to be called.

"Yes, please, then move all our bedding to the stable", James agreed.

"Now, just wait", the Inn keeper replied. "I will make room for your dar…, I mean coachman in the Inn. Just let me wait until nightfall."

"It is dark now", I answered.

"Yes, Miss. Quite right you are" responded the Inn keeper, now frustrated and somewhat annoyed by the three Yankees sitting at his table.

Before long, Jeremiah was placing his haversack, with his few belongings, in a small room at the rear of the Inn. James went to assure he was well cared for. The strong coachman thanked him for making this possible.

On the trip to find me in the Confederate Camp, the three men stopped by the roadside, and had spent the night sleeping under the carriage. It was good for all three of them to have a bed this night.

We finally retired to our rooms. James rechecked the bandages, and assured me that the bleeding had stopped.

Isaac informed James that he would take the first watch and would arouse James around two in the morning for the next. They were determined to sit outside my bedroom door throughout the night, to insure that I would not be interrupted in my sleep or accosted in any form.

I offered protest, but to no avail.

"Liz, with your injuries, you are not strong or capable at the moment of defending yourself, should the need arise", Isaac had responded.

I closed my eyes, thankful for the wonderful friendships and the good men who were a part of my life. No woman could ever be as fortunate as I had been over the years, to be a part of their adopted family.

CHAPTER EIGHTY ONE

As the sun was beginning its morning ritual of breaking forth a new day, we climbed, once again, into the carriage. Jeremiah had risen earlier, to prepare the horses and load the luggage atop the sturdy coach that would transport us back to Washington City.

As promised, we left what supplies and provisions we could with the Inn Keeper. He was grateful for the small sampling, especially the tea and coffee James provided.

The remainder of the journey home was uneventful. Aside from a few rough places along the highway, the road had begun to smooth somewhat as we came closer to Washington City.

Rebecca greeted us as we entered my home, late in the afternoon.

"Miss Elizabeth", she began. "You look almost as pale as a ghost. And weak too."

"How many ghosts have you seen, Rebecca?" I inquired.

"You know what I mean, Miss Elizabeth", she responded. "Now let us get you settled and into bed."

"I am not going to bed this instant", I protested. "I wish to sit in the study for a period. James, would you be so kind as to take my belongings to my room for me? Isaac, I believe I will take a little of Doctor May's pain medicine. It does help. And Rebecca, please prepare me a cup of tea, if you would be so kind."

All three responded immediately to my requests and set at once to comply. In a few moments, James had returned to the study, and Rebecca entered with tea for the three of us. Isaac poured a little of the elixir for pain into a small glass and placed a glass of sherry next to it, to assist in disguising the bitter aftertaste.

"Why do medicines that help all have to taste so poorly?" I asked.

Isaac laughed at my reaction to the concoction. He said that I made a face that was extremely contorted and seemed to belong to a child expressing deep disapproval over a reprimand.

"I will have dinner ready to serve in a few moments, Miss Elizabeth", Rebecca announced.

"Thank you Rebecca. You indeed are a good friend and caretaker", I said with softness in my voice.

I was truly appreciative of her care. I could leave home for days at a time, returning at a moment's notice, while Rebecca would carry on as if I had never left. She always seemed to have everything I needed, without my asking.

James, Isaac, and I sat at the table for a meal of fresh trout, garden vegetables, and freshly baked biscuits. Honey, retrieved from the market just a few days prior, was placed next to the basket of bread, along with freshly churned butter.

Rebecca had also made her mint tea, heavily sweetened with sugar. The white sugar had become harder to find these days. I sipped the cool drink slowly, thinking of days before the war when I would enjoy this refreshment on hot, summer days, in Georgia and South Carolina.

Following the meal, we retired back to the study for a short time. Rebecca brewed fresh coffee and served it along side a blackberry cobbler she had made earlier in the day.

I was quite weary, and, before long, excused myself to retire to my room for the night. Isaac, James, and Rebecca had encouraged this earlier, but I had resisted, stating that I was capable of deciding when I should go to bed and get up.

Rebecca assisted me in preparing for the night. James examined the bandages once again and pronounced that there did not appear to be any additional bleeding. Isaac administered another dose of pain medication to assist me in sleeping, and the three care takers left me to rest.

James stated that he would return to his home and in the morning, would summon Doctor May to my side. Isaac was determined to stay with me until I was healed and back on my own. I assured him that was not necessary, but he would have no thought of doing otherwise.

Rebecca prepared the guest room for him, and laid out extra linens and whatever else he requested to make his stay comfortable. I was well cared for by my merry band of friends.

Early the next morning, before I had a chance to rise and prepare myself, Doctor May entered my room, along with James, Isaac, and Rebecca.

"I understand you have had quite the adventure, my Dear", Doctor May spoke with his usual gentle voice and fatherly care.

"Not too exciting, Doctor", I countered.

"I was simply doing an investigative report on what it felt like to be shot by a Rebel", I continued with laughter in my voice.

"I have tried to warn you about being too adventuresome with your heart condition", the good Doctor now slightly reprimanded.

"Nonsense", I said. "You know how I enjoy life, and I absolutely refuse to take it sitting down."

"Well, true enough", Doctor May said. "And now, let me have a look at the wound."

Rebecca opened my bed clothes enough for the Doctor to examine the wound. He cleaned the area with a solution of water, soap and salts.

Upon redressing the area, he said, "The wound actually appears very good. There are no signs of infection. The Confederate Doctor who took care of you did a fine job."

"His name is Doctor McGuire", I shared.

"Doctor Hunter McGuire?", Doctor May asked.

"Yes, that is the one. He is with the Confederate Second Corp of Jackson's Brigade", I said. "Do you know him?"

"He is a fine surgeon and doctor. No wonder the wound is so cleanly cared for, and the site well prepared", Doctor May stated with great admiration.

"I met him previously, when General Jackson had been injured", I said. "Fortunately, he remembered me and immediately set out to take care of my injuries in a most professional and kind fashion."

"You were extremely fortunate that it was he who attended you and not some barbarian posing as a doctor", Doctor May said with finality.

"Now, Elizabeth", May continued. "I will check in daily with you. In the meantime, you are to remain in this bed, only rising for what is absolutely necessary. Do you understand?"

"I have my work", I started to say.

Doctor May interrupted, "No work for now, only rest. Your heart needs the rest, as well as your body and the shoulder where you were shot."

Then turning to Rebecca and Isaac, "I expect the two of you to ensure she remains in bed, resting. Perhaps, Isaac, you should notify her editor that she will be unavailable for the next two months."

"I have already informed Horace Greeley of Elizabeth's injuries, and he has responded that she is to take as much time as needed to recover", Isaac stated.

"I assume it is the intention of all of you to take charge of my life", I protested. "Do I not have any thing to say in the matter?"

"NO!" responded all four of my care givers simultaneously.

At the abruptness of the response, I looked at them wide eyed and pulled the covers over my head. "Ugh!" I shouted from beneath my hiding place.

CHAPTER EIGHTY TWO

Over the course of the next several weeks, Doctor May would visit me daily. Isaac refused to return to his own home, insisting that he would tend to me until I had healed well from my wound.

Around the early part of July, word reached us that the Confederate Army had launched a raid on Washington City. Panic was in the streets, and Isaac, along with James and Andrew, spoke of taking me to a safer place, possibly Baltimore.

"I will have nothing of the kind", I had insisted of my care givers. "If General Early wishes to attack the City, then I intend on witnessing the act, even if from my bed."

As the event unfolded, General Jubal Early with his forces made an attempt on the City, but to no avail. By July the thirteenth, the Confederates had made their retreat into the Shenandoah Valley, and would not threaten the City again.

Shortly following the Confederates' attempt on Washington City, my editor, Horace Greeley, arrived at my home. Isaac knew of his coming, but had chosen not to inform me.

"My dear Elizabeth", he began at once, upon entering my room. "You look exceptionally well."

"Horace, what on earth brings you here?" I asked.

"I could not stay away a moment longer", he replied. "I was afraid, my Dear, that I was going to lose my best Correspondent."

"Nonsense, Horace. You did not think that a Confederate Enfield would stop me, did you?" I said.

"It was not the Confederates or their weapons that concerned me, but your heart", Horace remarked tenderly.

"My heart! I don't have a problem with my heart that a little tea does not care for", I said with some disgust.

Isaac had written Horace to inform him that Doctor May was concerned with the pace I had been maintaining from the start of the war. Doctor May stated that the intensity of my assignments could be detrimental to my health.

"Horace, you know how many in the past have tried to call for my retirement from this business", I objected. "Certain individuals are convinced that a woman has no place as a

Correspondent, and would discredit me, and others, given the opportunity."

"Elizabeth, my dear", Horace went on. "I do not believe that Doctor May, or any of your friends, would dare to entreat me on your behalf in such a fashion. I believe in you, as they do, as well as I believe in all my female Correspondents."

"I know, but..." I started.

"But nothing, Liz" Horace continued. "Your friends wish only to look out for your well-being. Therefore, and I will have no argument from you, I want you to rest, as Doctor May has insisted. You may write from your bed as you hear news, but NO field work for the next two months, or until Doctor May gives you his approval. Understand?"

"Yes, Horace, but...", I responded.

"NO BUTS", Horace stated forcefully.

We spent the next few days discussing the war and my experiences so far. After about one week in my home, Horace returned to New York, to resume his duties there.

It had been good to see him, and even though I disliked being confined to bed and home, it had been good to visit with him once again. I always enjoyed his intellect and humor, as well as his conversation on a wide range of subjects.

Mister Lincoln also visited, along with his wife, Mary, while Horace was present. The President and Horace had known each other for a number of years and were somewhat good friends, despite the fact that Horace often disagreed with the President's policies concerning the war.

The visit was somewhat short and cordial. Missus Lincoln insisted that they not stay more than a few minutes, in order to allow me my rest.

"If we stay more than a few minutes, my Dear", she was saying to me, "my husband will begin telling one of his many long-winded stories, boring all of us to death. And you have been close enough to that doorstep already, without his help."

We all laughed at her statements, knowing how correct she was.

"Well then, Mother", the President said. "We shall return to that oversized cabin they call our home at sixteen-hundred Pennsylvania Avenue, and allow our dear friend her rest."

The President and Horace, along with Isaac, left me, as Mary remained behind for a moment.

"My dear Elizabeth", she began. "Please do recover quickly. I do not wish to lose another dear friend in the midst of this present suffering and tribulation. I fear that there is much more loss that awaits me in the near future. Please say that you will not add to that burden."

"I promise you, Mary" I said as I took her hand in mine. "I will recover, and soon shall be back to my normal routine. Besides, I refuse to miss your Harvest Ball in the fall, or any other adventure that might lie before us all."

"Then I shall look toward that day with glad anticipation", she responded. "I will come back for a visit soon, my Dear, without Father."

"I will look with great delight for that visit, my dear friend", I said.

Mary Todd leaned over my bed and embraced me as she prepared to take her leave. With a hint of a tear in her eye, she waved goodbye as she exited my room.

I was once again in the quiet of this imposed retreat. I closed my eyes and rested, for even short visits with many at one time consumed much energy, and were somewhat exhausting to me.

CHAPTER EIGHTY THREE

"Auntie Liz", Caroline greeted me as she burst through the study door. "I am so glad to see you awake and sitting in a chair. I was afraid you would still be too frail to be out of bed."

Late in July, Caroline, along with my dear friend, Sarah Hale, arrived at my home for a visit. Both had been busy with their work at Godey's Lady's Book in Philadelphia and had, for the most part, removed themselves from the war. Sarah insisted that the women of the Union needed a respite from the daily agony of the war, and that her magazine was the one place they could turn and hear nothing of the conflict.

Louis Godey encouraged Sarah and Caroline to take some leave from their responsibilities and visit me. Arrangements were made, and they arrived safely to spend the next two weeks with me.

"I am recovering quite nicely, Caroline", I said. "Now come, give me a kiss and an embrace, as you always do."

"How bad is the injury?" Caroline inquired.

"It is really nothing at this point", I said. "Doctor May and your father still insist that I remain at home and rest. They even solicited my editor's support in the matter."

Sarah Hale arrived in the room with Caroline and me, after a brief visit with Isaac in the downstairs parlor. Isaac had taken the opportunity to make Sarah aware of the restrictions placed upon me by the good Doctor.

"Liz", she began as she entered the room. "I am so glad to see you up".

Sarah and I embraced, and the three of us cried together, as we enjoyed the visit that had been too long in coming.

"Forgive my emotional tears", I pleaded. "It is simply too wonderful to see you both again. How I miss being together on a regular basis."

The three of us sat for some time, telling stories and recounting previous adventures. Sarah told of their work at Godey's, and Caroline spoke of the social life she was enjoying in Philadelphia.

"Mister Godey makes certain that I am introduced to the most influential people in the city", Caroline stated with some pride. "He is determined that he shall find me a proper suitor before the war is over."

"Is that what you wish for yourself, my Dear?" I asked.

"Oh, Auntie Liz. You know I have no interest in a husband at this time", she went on. "I do, however, truly enjoy the festivities and social engagements. And there are a number of eligible and handsome young men in the city."

"I would have thought they had all gone off to war", I said.

"Not the truly rich ones, Auntie Liz. They were able to buy someone else's service to take their place." Caroline shared.

"And you are all right with this practice?" I asked.

"Not at all. That is why I would never consider any of them as suitable for marriage." Caroline continued, "In marriage, they would simply continue their elitist attitudes by hiring someone else to do their work in the relationship, so they could continue in their irresponsible ways."

"Then why bother to even see any of them?" I questioned.

"For the fun!" was her answer.

I knew that Caroline had seen and been touched by the war in ways that most of the other young women also had. But Caroline had had to report on her observations, which deepened the impact. Her new cynical sense of playing with the affections of men was troubling for me, and yet I found I was unable to challenge her on the subject.

After some time, Caroline excused herself and went down to the parlor to spend some time with her father. Sarah and I talked then for some time, regarding Caroline's behavior.

"She is just a young woman with fanciful ideas of what true romance should be", Sarah insisted. "Besides, I see much of you, at that age, in her."

"No, Sarah", I challenged. "I did not toy with the affections of men. I was always honest about my work and the need to remain focused on my assignments."

"Not true", Sarah countered. "You often used your female ways and flirtatious behavior to get what you wanted, when it came to the story. And I am certain that has not changed over the years."

As the afternoon wore on, I grew more tired, and decided I needed to rest before the evening meal. Rebecca had provided

Sarah and me with tea and fresh cakes, but now I needed to return to my bed for a short rest.

Sarah helped me into bed, and made certain that I was quite comfortable. Her act of kindness reminded me of an earlier time, nearly fifteen years prior, when I arrived at her house following my journey to Great Britain.

While abroad, I had fallen in love, and then rejected the desire of my heart for my work. He had been killed just prior to my leaving London. I was heartbroken, and Sarah took me in to help me recover from the loss.

"Thank you, Sarah", I said.

"For what?" she asked.

"For being my friend all of these years", I said.

CHAPTER EIGHTY FOUR

Word arrived on the morning of July thirtieth that Belle Boyd had been arrested outside Washington City and was being held at the Old Capital Prison. I asked Caroline to visit the prison, to see if she might gain access for an interview. She agreed.

Caroline reported that she first went to see her brother at the White House, and received a pass from him for the Old Capital Prison. Upon arriving at the prison, she was escorted to a small room, where she waited for the Confederate Spy to be brought in for their conversation.

Caroline reported that she waited for nearly an hour, after which a young officer entered the room to report that Miss Boyd had refused to meet with the reporter from New York.

"The officer informed me, Auntie Liz, that Miss Boyd had nothing to say to the Yankee press", Caroline apologized.

"It was well worth your efforts, Caroline", I said. "We do not always have the success or the results we wish, but thank you for trying. Perhaps another day, she will feel more like having a visitor, even if it is Yankee press."

The Old Capital Prison was no place for a woman to be confined. The walls were thick and dirty. The windows to the cells provided little room for light or fresh air. The privies stank and were not well tended to or limed regularly. The food was better served to the hogs than for human consumption.

Since Rose Greenhow had been arrested and detained at the Prison early in the war, conditions had deteriorated significantly. Rose had been treated with kindness, and given every consideration. She had, however, taken advantage of her keepers, and had managed to continue to pass secrets on to Richmond.

Now, civilians accused and arrested as spies were treated with cruel contempt. They were isolated from the population and kept from open windows. Under constant guard, they were escorted to and from the privies and were forced to eat their meals in isolation in their cells. Women fared no better than men in this situation.

The next two weeks passed quickly, and before long, Sarah and Caroline were preparing to return to their duties in Philadelphia. Their final evening with me brought Isaac, James, and Andrew for dinner. It was such a joy to have them with me once again, around the dining room table.

Caroline promised to return at Christmas, if her responsibilities would allow for the journey. Sarah assured her that they would, and plans were made.

Andrew stated that he felt the war might be drawing to an end soon, and that perhaps Amos would be able to come home this Christmas, as well. It had been nearly three years since we were all together at that special time of year.

Isaac took Caroline and Sarah to the train station, early the next morning, to begin their journey toward Philadelphia. Rebecca had prepared a basket full of food and drink, for them to enjoy on the train.

Sarah objected, reminding us that the trip to Philadelphia would take only a little more than five hours to complete. Caroline said that they would be able to eat in Baltimore, during their short layover.

"Never you mind, Miss Caroline", Rebecca said. "You never know when them trains are gonna be late or run afoul."

Rebecca was correct. During the past several months, train service often became unreliable, as the lines were used more for supporting Grant's troops in the south and less for regular public transportation. Passengers were known to be put off the trains at any given stop, if the cars were needed for troops.

"Promise to wire as soon as you have arrived", I insisted of Caroline and Sarah.

"Please do not worry, Auntie Liz. We WILL be fine on the journey to Philadelphia", Caroline protested.

Isaac arrived back at my home a short time after the train had departed. He reported that the women had boarded safely, and were on their way.

"By the way, Liz", Isaac began. I saw Secretary Stanton and General Baker at the depot this morning. They inquired as to your well-being."

"What did you tell them?" I asked.

"Just that you were recovering nicely, but were still confined to rest at home", Isaac reported. "General Baker asked if he could pay you a visit soon."

"I am not ready for his egotistical and accusatory ways in my home, Isaac", I stated firmly.

"I understand, my dear, but he will speak with you, sooner or later", Isaac said.

"Then let it be later", I countered. "I do not wish that snake in my home, if I can avoid it."

General Lafayette Baker was one of the most despicable men I have ever known. He was always suspicious of everyone, and often accused individuals of acts of treason without reasonable proof.

He had been responsible for arresting several of my colleagues and holding them for some time, merely for publishing stories that he felt were not supportive of the Union or the Lincoln Administration. I was certain that he would have arrested me several times, had I not been good friends of the Lincolns.

"Baker informed me that he was certain he could arrange an interview with Belle Boyd, should you desire it when you are feeling better", Isaac quickly added.

"Yes, but at what cost?" I asked.

CHAPTER EIGHTY FIVE

The next few weeks passed quickly. Several old friends came for visits, and to share their war adventures with me.

By mid-October, the fall weather had settled in, and the trees were alive with the autumn colors. Harvesters were busy in the fields, retrieving the final crops of the season.

Mister Lincoln's Army was advancing on all fronts, and the end of the Rebellion seemed inevitable at any time. Grant had cornered Lee's Army of Northern Virginia near Petersburg, and a standoff was in process.

The end of October, Isaac and I attended once again the Harvest Ball at the White House. The usual guests, approximately five hundred, were present.

It was only minutes from my entrance into the grand hall that my dance card filled completely. Mary Todd Lincoln, the first to officially greet me, was warm and charming. She apologized profusely for having failed to visit more than once during my recovery. I assured her there was no need for concern in the matter, and promised that I would soon visit her, now that I was about my regular responsibilities.

As the Grand March began, Secretary of War Stanton came to escort me to the dance floor. He was the first on my dance card, and I was relieved to be free of further obligation to dance with him, so early in the evening.

As the music began and we moved in time to the music, the Secretary inquired as to my well-being. I assured him that I was fully recovered, and that he would see more of me at the War Department.

As the dance concluded, Mister Stanton suggested that we would talk soon, regarding my experiences at the Confederate Hospital. I assured the Secretary that there was really little to talk about.

"I was shot, the Surgeon removed the bullet, and Isaac and James came for me", I said. Adding, "There is little else to tell, Mister Secretary."

"Perhaps you are correct, Elizabeth", Stanton replied. "But we shall speak at a later time none-the-less".

His words sent chills down my spine, as they always did. I did not like this man, or his Chief of the Federal Detectives, Lafayette Baker.

"One more thing, Elizabeth", the Secretary added. "I do apologize that you were unable to gain an interview with Belle Boyd while she was, shall we say, our guest at the Capital Prison. The prisoner exchange occurred before we could finalize your time with her."

"That was quite acceptable to me", I stated. "I was not particularly anxious to speak with her, or anyone, at the prison. I have had enough of those circumstances and conditions to last me a life time."

"Then let us pray that you shall have a long, very long, life-time, my Dear", Stanton replied as he graciously kissed my hand.

Isaac came to my side as soon as he saw the Secretary move from me.

"I need to wash the slime from my hand, Isaac", I said at once.

"Now, Liz, it can not possibly be that horrific", Isaac stated with a hint of laughter.

"No, Isaac, it is not that bad, it is worse", I responded playfully.

Throughout the evening, I danced with a number of officers and dignitaries. Isaac and I enjoyed a waltz together and, aside from this, spent most of the evening entertaining, and being entertained, by any number of adoring and warm associates.

Mister Lincoln and I danced near the end of the evening, and the President was charming and delightful. He, too, apologized for not visiting since early after my arriving back home. I assured him that no apology was necessary, as he had greater responsibilities to be concerned with.

"I do have one question for you, Mister President", I stated. "Do you see the end of the conflict in sight?"

"Now, Elizabeth", the President began. "I can not, I dare not, speculate on a time or place for the end of the hostilities between our peoples. I can and will, however, say that my Generals assure me of a suitable end within the next few months to the death and dying that is occurring on a daily basis."

With that, I thanked the President for his friendship and kindness over the past four years. I curtsied as he released my hand and departed, making my way to Isaac for the final dance of the evening.

The evening drew to a conclusion well after the mid-night hour. The air was cool and crisp, and I suggested that we should walk back to my home, rather than take the carriage. Isaac agreed, after a brief protest, and informed the coach driver to follow a short distance behind us. This was, according to Isaac, in the event I should tire and need to finish the journey by carriage.

We arrived home and made our way to my study. Rebecca was awake and waiting for us, and assisted me with preparing for bed.

"How was the party at Father Abraham's tonight, Miss Elizabeth?" Rebecca asked.

"We had a wonderful time, Rebecca", I responded.

"Did you dance all night?" Rebecca inquired. "Was there beautiful women in their pretty dresses and all?"

"Yes, Yes, and Yes", I said. "Rebecca, I think the next time we are invited to the Lincoln home for a party, I shall endeavor to secure an invitation for you as well."

"Oh lordy, Miss Elizabeth", Rebecca said. "That ain't no place for me. I wouldn't know how to behave in a place like that. I be just a servant girl, not rich folk, like you and Mister Isaac."

"You belong there as much as anyone, Rebecca", I insisted. "After all, the White House belongs to the people, not just the Lincolns or any President who resides there."

"I don't know 'bout that, Miss Elizabeth", she responded.

Isaac and I sat near the fire in my study, enjoying the tea Rebecca had prepared for us before retiring. The small cakes she added to the silver serving tray were the final treat of the evening. Isaac and I did not speak, allowing instead our thoughts to flow silently into the night air.

After thirty minutes or so, I finally spoke, and thanked Isaac for a wonderful evening. Isaac assured me that it was even more wonderful for him. At that, we went to our separate rooms and retired for the night.

CHAPTER EIGHTY SIX

I did not awake until nearly mid-day, after enjoying a long and restful sleep. The previous evening had been a delightful experience, even with the necessity to dance with Secretary Stanton and his henchman, Lafayette Baker. I never understood why Missus Lincoln tolerated her husband's insistence that they be invited to every affair at the White House. Isaac assured me that protocol dictated nothing less than their presence.

I dressed in my morning gown, and proceeded to the kitchen area by way of the back stairs. Rebecca was busy at work, preparing an apple pie for the oven. She looked up as she heard me enter the kitchen, and spoke.

"I was thinking you might sleep 'till tomorrow", she said.

"I don't believe these weary bones of mine will allow me to stay in bed that long. They begin to ache if I lie too long", I protested.

"That be the rheumatism that come with age, Miss Elizabeth", she responded.

I inquired, "Where is Isaac this afternoon?"

"He be in the study workin' on his papers", she said. "He done had three visitors already today. Some preacher men."

I took my leave from Rebecca, and proceeded to the down stairs study, where Isaac regularly worked when he stayed at my home.

"May I come in?" I asked.

"Of course, my Dear", Isaac said, as he stood and walked to greet me.

Isaac took me into his arms, and pressed his lips to mine. I reciprocated and then laid my head on to his chest, as he stood there holding me for the first time in what seemed an eternity.

Finally, I stepped back, and held his hands in mine.

"So what brings this sudden show of affection, Isaac?" I asked.

"You know that I love you, Liz, and just want to be with you", he stated firmly.

"We have had this conversation before, Isaac, and I love you, too", I stated tenderly. "But we promised not to discuss these feelings until the war is over."

"I know, my Darling, but I don't wish to wait until the war is over", He stated, almost in tears. "Liz, I almost lost you in Virginia when you were shot. I do not want to wait until the war is over, fearing every time you go off on one of your adventures that I might never see you again, alive."

"I will live through this war, Isaac. I promise", I said.

"Marry me, Liz. Marry me right now", Isaac insisted.

"No, Isaac. Not until the war is over. And that is final", I said with firmness. Then I added with tenderness, "Ask me when this war is over, and I will say yes. I promise."

"I only pray you will live long enough for me to ask you and then to be married, my love", Isaac said, with some sadness in his voice.

I wanted to cry at his words and thoughts. I could almost see the desperation in his eyes at the thought of losing me. He had lost me before to another lover, my work. He did not want to lose me now to death, and I understood him. He had already lost to death two whom he loved, Constance, his wife, to fever, and Abraham, his middle son, to the war.

And now I was causing him pain again, with the fear of losing me. I felt certain that the war would not take my life. But I could make no promise beyond that. I did not wish to be a source of further pain to this man with whom I had fallen in love many years earlier, and now loved even more deeply.

I left Isaac standing in the study, as I returned to my dressing room to prepare for the remainder of the day. The hour was past three in the afternoon, and I wished to attend to the War Department to see if there were any new activities to report.

By four-thirty I arrived at the War Department. I stopped in to see the chief telegraph operator, and inquired if there had been any significant news.

"Only word is that Sherman is making his way into Georgia and Grant still has Bobby Lee on the run", Mister McPherson stated with a hint of glee in his voice. "Mister Lincoln finally has a General in command of the Army that ain't afraid of fighting and spilling a little blood from time to time."

"I understand", I said as I thanked him for the report and commentary.

Secretary of War Stanton and Lafayette Baker had already left for the day. I was relieved that I would not encounter either of them.

As I prepared to leave as well, Andrew came bounding up the stairs and into the reception area of the War Department.

"Auntie Liz", he began. "How wonderful to see you back here in these stench filled halls of the War machine."

"My Dear Andrew", I responded. "Why so cynical today?"

"Later, Auntie Liz", he said. "I'll come for dinner tonight, if it is all right with you."

"Andrew, you know you are always welcomed at my table. You do not need an invitation. Would eight o'clock be acceptable to you?", I asked.

"Eight is fine. I may be there earlier, if I can get away", Andrew responded. "Tell Father hello."

"You can tell him for yourself. He is still staying with me", I said.

Andrew kissed me on the cheek and took his leave. Mister McPherson hollered out through his open door, "He is a fine young man, that one is."

I thanked Mister McPherson and expressed my agreement of his assessment. I placed my bonnet on my head, and hailed a coach to take me home. I usually walked, but today felt more tired than usual. It was probably the after affects of last night's party.

CHAPTER EIGHTY SEVEN

Later that evening, Andrew arrived in his freshly pressed uniform, looking very mature and worldly. His adventures, as he called them, had aged him considerably over the past few years, since the start of the war.

"Good evening, Auntie Liz", he said, as he greeted me with his usual kiss to my cheek. "How are you and Father this evening?"

I escorted the handsome young man to the library, where his father was working on church business and correspondence. Isaac immediately stood and greeted his son, as the two men embraced.

Rebecca announced almost immediately that dinner was ready and would be cold if we continued to delay our arrival at the table. Andrew reminded Rebecca in his jovial manner that she was always exaggerating in her estimations of when the food would grow cold. Rebecca dismissed the young officer with a tilt of her head as she turned and walked away, murmuring just loud enough for us to hear but not know what was said.

The three of us gathered around a meal of fresh pot roast purchased earlier in the day at the local market. Surrounding the center piece of the meal were piles of cooked carrots, boiled potatoes and baked onions. Rich, brown gravy, thick as molasses, sat steaming in the serving boat. The table was complete with the addition of fresh baked wheat bread served with butter and honey.

Rebecca was enjoying the same fare in the pantry with her new friend, John. John Mason was a young Negro worker at the Capital Hotel. His responsibilities included purchasing fresh produce from the local farmers market when available. It was on one of his assignments a few weeks prior that he met Rebecca, and the two became instant friends.

Rebecca had asked permission to allow him to come and call on her from time to time. I assured her she did not need my permission, and that any friend of hers was always welcomed in my home. John soon became a regular visitor.

Rebecca regularly ate at the table with me, when the two of us were alone in the house. She said, though, that she did not feel comfortable sitting at the table when others were present, including Isaac and his sons. I tried on occasions to entice her to join us, but learned after a short while to respect her desires in the matter.

After the meal was completed, the three of retired to the drawing room for the remainder of the evening. Andrew took his silver cigar case from his breast pocket and removed a beautifully made Havana from its sleeve.

"This is for you, Auntie Liz", he announced with much pride. "These arrived today from Amos, courtesy of General Grant."

"Where on earth did Grant get these?" I asked.

"Who knows?" Andrew responded. "Probably off some blockade runner, I would suspect. And one for you as well, Father. Oh hell, I think we should all three enjoy one", he added.

"Andrew, your language", Isaac gently rebuked his son.

"Don't be so prudish with Andrew", I defended. "Where do you think he learned to talk like that in the first place, the Army?"

We all laughed at that moment, realizing that Andrew, as well as his brothers and sister had all learned a little "sailor language" from me in their childhood. Isaac also reminded us that it was I who had taught his children to enjoy a fine cigar and a little brandy from time to time.

As the three of us sat smoking and drinking brandy, Rebecca came to announce that she and John were going out for a while. She inquired if I had need of anything before she left. I assured her that we were fine and could care for ourselves in her absence, and wished her a fun filled evening.

Rebecca took her leave and assured me she would return before the late evening hour. I reminded her she could enjoy the evening for as long as she wished and had no curfew with me.

"Just be sure to take necessary precautions", I suggested with a wink as she left, blushing from the exchange.

"Liz, you really should not torment her so with your teasing of such intimate issues", Isaac rebuked.

"I think it is rather funny, and I truly believe that Rebecca enjoys the banter with Auntie Liz", Andrew defended.

"Don't encourage her, Andrew", Isaac protested.

"Well, it really does not matter what you say, either of you, for you both know that I always do as I please, anyway", I stated with laughter.

357

The two handsome men seated in my home joined in the amusement, and we continued into the night with conversation.

"Andrew", I began. "You sounded a bit cynical earlier today, when I saw you at the war department. What is going on?"

"That is why I wanted to come and have dinner with you and Father this evening", Andrew started. "I have something I wish to discuss."

Andrew went on to explain that he had decided to request a transfer to General Meade's staff, to be with Amos in the closing months of the war.

"This war will be over soon and I want to be there when it ends", Andrew explained.

"But what will your duties be?" Isaac asked.

"Essentially the same as here in Washington", Andrew explained. "I will be a courier between Generals Meade and Grant."

"Will you see action?" I asked.

"Probably not", Andrew responded. "My responsibilities will keep me to the rear, and along with the fact that I have only one arm, I am not permitted to command a company, as I had in the past."

"I can not imagine, though, that you will not somehow find your way to the front", I said with firmness.

"That may be the case, Auntie Liz", he sharply responded. "But I must do what I believe is right for me, just as you have always done, and taught me, as well."

"Now, both of you", Isaac interjected, "stop this at once."

"I mean no disrespect, Father, Auntie Liz", Andrew said with softness.

"Neither do I, Andrew", I said. "I just worry about you on these adventures, as I know that you and your father worry about me on mine. We are wonderfully and fiercely independent and must choose our paths as best as we can."

Then I added, "I will respect and honor any decision you make in the matter. You go with my love and blessings, Andrew."

"Thank you, Auntie Liz", Andrew said. "And what about you, Father?"

Isaac sat silent for a few moments, drawing from his cigar and letting the blue smoke exit and float about his head as he exhaled. Finally he spoke.

"You know my heart, Andrew" he began. "I love you and will support your decisions. I place you completely in the care of our loving God. May His will be done in all matters. Go, my Son, in peace and love."

We continued to speak of the matter for some time. Andrew explained that he would not leave for Petersburg, Virginia, where General Meade was at the moment, until after the first of the year. He also assured us that he would be with us for Christmas, and, if possible, Amos and Caroline would also be joining us this year.

"That is a wonderful dream, Andrew", I said. "Let us pray that it, indeed, comes true."

CHAPTER EIGHTY EIGHT

Christmas Eve arrived and, as promised, Caroline, Amos, and Andrew were all present, along with Isaac and James. Caroline had arrived two days prior, and Amos came through the door late in the evening, accompanied by his Uncle James.

As was the custom of his brother Abraham, while he was living, Amos had attended the Christmas Eve services with James, and then came to my home for the remainder of the festivities. It was good to see them all.

Rebecca, Caroline, and I had finished the preparations of holiday treats earlier in the day. All was ready.

A knock came at the rear door, and John entered at the bequest of Rebecca, He had been instructed to use the front door, as there was no need in this house to observe the custom of the colored men using only the servants' entrance, but John found it difficult being treated with any dignity by a white family.

The table was set with delicious treats, cold hams, and other assorted meats and breads. Isaac offered a word of thanks to Almighty God for bringing his family safely together once again.

James offered a toast to John and Rebecca, who had announced they would be married and jump the broom handle the first of the year. John had asked if Isaac would perform the ceremony, and, of course, he had agreed. My home was to serve as the chapel for the event, as well as the center for the following reception.

Everyone was in a gay mood as the evening began to unfold in merriment. Suddenly, there was a loud knock at the front door. John immediately wanted to excuse himself from the room and return to the pantry, so as not to cause me any difficulty, should someone other than the family find him in the proper living quarters.

Isaac placed his hand on John's shoulder, and assured him there would be no difficulty for any of us with his presence. John stood still, and waited.

James had gone to see who was arriving at such a late hour, and happily returned with his late arriving guests. Greta and her family walked into the lively lit room filled with friends, and immediately embraced all of us. Rebecca took their wraps, as they were introduced to John, who bowed slightly at the introductions.

Isaac, holding Greta's hand in his said, "Liz, did you know that Greta and Peter and their children were coming?"

"Of course I did, Isaac", I responded. "Greta and I decided, though, to keep it a secret, and make it a special treat for all of you."

"And your children, Peter", Isaac continued, "They are beautiful, and growing so fast. Why, Martha (she was Greta's and Peter's youngest child, now two), you are becoming quite the young lady."

Martha hid behind her father and sucked her thumb. Peter apologized for her, and said that they had awakened her as the train pulled into the station, only a short while ago.

"Well, we must get these little ones settled right away, as Santa shall certainly be here soon", I stated.

"Will he be able to come down the chimney, Auntie Liz?" Lars inquired.

"Yes, indeed, my little man", I said. "Rebecca and I have put out the fire in the largest fireplace in the house, so Santa will have no problem bringing you treats when he arrives."

"But first, my Darling", said Greta to her son, "You must go to sleep quickly, so as to not miss Saint Nicholas."

"But Mother", Lars protested. "I can stay up with you and Papa and still not miss Father Christmas."

Rebecca, Greta, and I took the children to their room and safely tucked them in for the remainder of the night. Returning downstairs, we found Caroline entertaining the men with her stories of adventures in Philadelphia with Sarah Hale.

"Sarah certainly knows how to entertain, and she is always finding me a new male companion to escort me throughout the city", she was saying.

"So, have you found anyone of particular interest?" I asked as I came into the parlor.

"No, Auntie Liz", Caroline said. "I am just having fun at the moment. I do not think that I shall ever marry, unless I am like you and wait until I have had my fill of career, and can find a man like Father."

"You shall never find a man as good as me", Isaac stated with a twinkle in his eye.

"You are correct, Father", Caroline agreed. "Auntie Liz, you let Father get away once. Don't risk that again. At least for my sake, please marry the man", she almost pleaded.

I sat by the fire and blushed, as I said nothing. I knew, as did Caroline, that Isaac was determined to marry me as soon as I would accept. And I had promised to accept, should he ask me after the war was over.

The remainder of the late evening, we sat around the parlor, enjoying cigars and brandy. John was finally beginning to relax in our presence, as Greta and Peter told how we had all become friends. Rebecca shared with John how she, too, had been invited into the family, and how wonderfully accepted she felt. He would learn to be comfortable here in time, as well.

Just prior to early light, the presents had been laid neatly under the tree, and the children's stockings had been filled with wonderful treats. Everyone had finally retired, knowing the children would have everyone up in a few hours.

I sat by the fire, sipping the last of my brandy, observing the room, filled with toys and gift wrapped packages. How wonderfully full my life had been to this point.

I closed my eyes and prayed, thanking God for His richness in my life throughout the many adventures I had undertaken over the past thirty or so years.

"But most of all, Dear God, thank you for my friends and family. Amen."

CHAPTER EIGHTY NINE

Christmas Day was a delight for the children, as well as the adults. The joyful and excited faces of Lars and Martha as they explored the gifts left for them by Father Christmas were a source of wonder and joy for all of us.

"I truly hope that our children will never face the tribulations we have endured these past few years with the war, Elizabeth" ,Greta had commented as she watched her children in Christmas delight. I understood her desire.

It had been truly a joy to have small children in my home for Christmas once again. This had been the first time, since Isaac's and Constance's children had grown into young adults.

Before we knew, the time had come for Greta and Peter to return home to Hagerstown, with their little ones in tow. The parting was one of joy and sorrow, as I watched them pull from the station toward their destination. The visit was entirely too short, and I had promised that we would again be together, as soon as the war was over and life had returned to normalcy, whatever that now meant.

New Year's Eve arrived, and with it the usual gathering at the Lincoln Mansion. This year promised to offer a special sense of gaiety, with the knowledge that the Confederacy was collapsing under the weight of the Union war machine. The war promised to be over by summer.

I had obtained invitations for both Rebecca and John to accompany Isaac and me to the White House for the Presidential Ball. Mister Frederick Douglass was also to be there, and I looked forward to seeing him once again.

The evening of New Year's Eve, Rebecca looked absolutely stunning in her new ball gown. John was handsome, and appeared in every way the perfect gentleman, in his evening attire.

Caroline had taken Rebecca shopping for the dress just before Christmas, and they were able to find a nearly perfect fit, with the need for only minor adjustments. The dress was a combination of deep reds and winter whites, flourished with lace throughout. The square yoke dropped ever so slightly from her shoulders, revealing her beauty.

John was dressed in one of Isaac's formal suits. John stated that he felt more like a preacher man in the outfit, than an escort to a ball. Isaac assured John that he was perfectly dressed for the occasion, and that he would gain the admiration of all who witnessed his attendance with Rebecca.

The four of us, along with Caroline, Andrew, and Amos, arrived promptly at eight o'clock by coach on New Year's Eve at the main entrance to the Executive Mansion. The servants took our cloaks and escorted us to the main hall, where we were greeted by the President and Missus Lincoln.

"Mister President, Missus Lincoln", Isaac began. "You already know Miss Fitzgerald."

"Yes, we certainly do", said the President. "And how are you this wonderful evening, Elizabeth?"

"I am well, Mister President", I responded with delight.

Mary Todd Lincoln and I embraced and kissed one another on the cheek, which had become our custom.

"Who do you have with you this evening?" Missus Lincoln inquired.

Isaac introduced Rebecca and John and informed the President and Missus Lincoln that they were to be married shortly after the first of the year.

"I shall have the honor of officiating at the service", Isaac stated proudly.

As Mister Lincoln took Rebecca's hand in his and kissed the back of it ever so gently, the President stated that he and Missus Lincoln would be honored to receive an invitation to the joyous event. Rebecca stood with her mouth open, unable to speak.

"The President sometimes has the same effect on me, Rebecca", I said with a slight giggle in my voice.

Immediately, Rebecca closed her mouth and thanked the President for his kindness. Missus Lincoln shook the hands of both Rebecca and John, and we moved through the receiving line toward the great hall.

Inside, Rebecca stated many times that she could not believe she was actually in the President's home and accepted as a guest, rather than a servant.

"Tonight, my dear, you shall be waited upon with just the whisper of a command on your part", I reminded her.

"But what if I don't know what to do, Miss Elizabeth? What then?" She said, almost pleading.

"Just remember what we spoke of before coming", I reminded her. "Stay nearby Isaac and me, and give the signal if you need help. We will come right away to your side."

Isaac and I had prearranged a signal that Rebecca was to use, should she become confused or unsure how to proceed or behave in any given circumstance. All she had to do was use the signal, and we would be by her side in moments, to assist her.

Within the half hour of our arriving, both Rebecca's and my dance cards were full. First on her list was Frederick Douglass, who asked for the honor of the Grand March. Isaac was to escort Missus Douglass across the dance floor, and John would dance the March with me.

This had been agreed upon, as I would be able to assist John, and Mister Douglass would be able to help Rebecca feel comfortable for the first time on the dance floor at the White House. As the dance began, and we were escorted by our appointed partners, all began to relax and have a merry time.

The end of the evening arrived much too soon for the young couple. I was, however, exhausted and ready to return home and find my bed for the remainder of the night.

Upon our departure, Rebecca thanked the President and Missus Lincoln for making the evening a most memorable occasion for a former slave girl.

"I never dreamed anything as wonderful as this would have ever happened to me", she said with tears in her eyes.

"Missus Lincoln took Rebecca's hands in hers and kissed Rebecca on the cheek. With a smile that was warm and genuine, Missus Lincoln said goodbye to her guest and thanked her for coming.

Arriving home at nearly three in the morning, Caroline assisted first Rebecca, and then me, in preparing for bed. Caroline said that Rebecca could not stop talking during the moments they were together, assisting each other out of their evening clothes, and preparing for bed.

"I am so glad, Auntie Liz, that you were able to get invitations for Rebecca and John", Caroline stated. "You gave them a gift they will never forget."

"Nor I, my child", I said as I retired to my bed for the remainder of the night.

As I lay on my pillow, drifting off to sleep, I thought of the young couple as they entered into the evening, afraid and timid, and then exited from the magic of the evening, excited and alive. It was indeed a grand evening for all of us.

CHAPTER NINETY

The first of the year brought more news that the Confederacy was collapsing. Jefferson Davis had sent an envoy to meet with Secretary of State Seward, to discuss plans for peace.

The President, however, made certain that Seward understood that peace was acceptable only if the south would lay down their arms and reunite with the rest of the nation. The envoy returned to Richmond, having made no progress on terms acceptable to the Confederacy.

Grant's Army had laid siege to Petersburg, Virginia, and Sherman had begun moving through the Carolinas from Savannah. General Lee had been made General in Chief of the entire Army of the Confederate States of America, and had begun to make contingency plans for the relocation of the Government in Richmond, should the need arise.

The south had now been divided into four major areas, each effectively isolated from the other by the Union Army. Virtually all the ports in the south were now controlled by Federal troops and naval forces. The noose that Grant had put in place earlier the prior year had begun to close around the neck of its intended victim. The end was in sight and would come in a matter of time.

On January twentieth, 1865, John and Rebecca were married at my home. The Lincolns had been extended an invitation, but were unable to attend, due to prior commitments. They did, however, send a lovely wedding gift to the couple that included a standing invitation to attend all future balls and galas that might occur during such a time as they might be available.

Over one hundred guests attended the wedding and celebrated the event with the young couple. Isaac performed the ceremony in his usual graceful manner, assuring the couple of God's blessing upon their lives.

Caroline had already returned to Philadelphia, and Amos was back in Petersburg, Virginia, with General Meade. Andrew attended the event and represented his brother and sister.

Toward the later part of the evening, Rebecca and John were taken by carriage to Isaac's home. They would spend their wedding night together at the Bishop's residence, with his house servants tending to their every need. Isaac had given them this gift.

He had wanted to make arrangements at the Capital Hotel for them but there was, as he stated, "no room for them at the Inn". Instead, he made the arrangements for them to be treated as royalty at his residence. James also assisted in the arrangements, to ensure they would have a memorable occasion and a fine start to their new life together.

The following morning, Andrew announced that he would be leaving the first of February to join Amos in Petersburg. His orders had finally been approved by General Meade, with the one stipulation that he was to find a man capable to serve as his orderly and attend to his needs as may occur in the field.

The General had expressed concern that Andrew might find it more difficult to care for some of the more routine items of daily grooming, without some assistance. The General had also expressed his concern that he did not have immediately available an enlisted man who could attend to the responsibilities, since Andrew held only the rank of Captain. To have a personal orderly would require the rank of Major, at the minimum.

"Where will I find such a man, Auntie Liz, on such short notice?" Andrew lamented. "I am going, with or without, a man to assist me."

"No, you can not do that, Andrew", I stated. "Meade will only send you back. We will find someone. I promise."

Andrew seemed satisfied with my response, and remained optimistic throughout the next few days. Isaac stayed with me for the next two days, until Rebecca and John returned to my home.

By the time they were back, I had managed to redecorate the living quarters of Rebecca, to make them more accommodating and comfortable for the couple. Rebecca was exceedingly pleased and cried, laughed, and cried some more, in appreciation. John remained silent, almost afraid to believe what was happening to him.

"How can I ever thank you, Miss Elizabeth?", John said almost in a whisper.

"No thank you is necessary, John", I stated. "It is my privilege to do this for you both."

Later in the day, Isaac and I sat with Rebecca and John in the kitchen, drinking a cup of tea and enjoying left over cakes from the wedding. John had been quiet for some time when I finally asked him if he was all right.

"Yes 'em, I be fine, Miss Elizabeth", he said. "But I does have some business on my mind I wish to talk about."

"Please, share what you wish with us", I said as I took his hand into mine.

"I knows Master Andrew is going off to fight the Rebs again, and you and Master Isaac is afraid of him goin' alone. Is I right about that?" he asked.

Isaac said, "Well, John, we have our concerns. But what does this have to do with you?"

"Well, Sir", John began. "Rebecca and I was talking last evenin', and she was saying to me that maybe I should go along and help Master Andrew and all. I don't want no money, only a place to sleep, and some food for the hunger now and then."

"John, thank you for your kind offer, but that would be up to Andrew to decide", I said.

I was having a difficult time holding back my tears of gratitude that our prayers had been answered without having yet advertised for the need. Yet how could I ask Rebecca to let her new husband go off to war with Andrew, not knowing if or when he would return?

"Then you talk to Master Andrew and lets me know" John stated, with a sense that it was already decided that he would be going.

I finally asked Rebecca, "Are you sure you are in agreement with this?"

"Yes, Miss Elizabeth", she said with determination. "It is the right thing to do. And if you taught me anything, it is to always do the right thing, no matter the pain or cost."

Isaac assured John that he would speak with Andrew as soon as he arrived later in the day, and a decision would be made before night. John seemed genuinely pleased with the prospect of going with Andrew and said he would wait patiently for Isaac to give him an answer.

Isaac retired to the Library to work on his correspondence. I went to my private study to read, while John and Rebecca remained to enjoy each other's company in the kitchen for the remainder of the afternoon.

CHAPTER NINETY ONE

Spring was beginning to emerge, as March unfolded. On March fourth, 1865, Abraham Lincoln was sworn in for his second term. As he stood at the podium on that cold, blustery, March afternoon, the President appeared weary from the past four years.

Mister Lincoln once again spoke with firmness, inspiring confidence and hope within the hearing of those present. With his vision firmly focused upon the future and the pending end of the hostilities with the states still in rebellion, Abraham Lincoln spoke words that demonstrated his view of a proper peace.

"With malice toward none; with charity for all; with firmness in the right, let us strive on to finish the work we are in; to bind up the nation's wounds; to care for him who shall have borne the battle, and for his widow, and his orphan – to do all which may achieve and cherish a just and lasting peace, among ourselves, and with all nations", concluded the President in his brief inaugural speech.

I shall always remember that day. I believe this was one of the finest speeches Mister Lincoln ever made. He seemed almost prophetic in his tone and holy in his presence.

I, along with most of those gathered this day, listened in silence as the President spoke, rarely applauding or commenting, as was the custom at such events. It seemed to all of us that we were being visited at that moment by something more pure and holy than we could have imagined.

A colleague, Noah Brooks, and I spoke after the occasion. Noah asked if I saw the clouds that had obscured the sky throughout the day, part, allowing the sun to radiate upon the scene, filling the platform with golden beauty. I said that I had, and thought how God was setting His divine seal upon the moment.

Throughout the speech, the sun shone upon the faces of the gathered crowd. One could see moist eyes and tears flowing from faces of both men and women, as the President concluded his remarks. Somehow we all knew at that moment that the end of the war was truly at hand and the process of healing had already commenced, as far as Mister Lincoln was concerned.

The following days were filled with constant reports of the advances of the Union Army on all fronts. There were still a number of skirmishes and small engagements, but the intensity and magnitude of battles like Antietam and Gettysburg were now of the past.

In early April, Andrew had written that there were rumors that Robert E. Lee might be ready to talk terms of surrender with General Grant. Details were still sketchy, but the possibility was now very real.

The Confederates under Lee's command were running dangerously close to having little ammunition and no provisions of food or clothing available to them. Several of Lee's Generals were encouraging him to abandon the strategies of the past and to divide the troops that remained into small guerilla fighting units.

According to Andrew's letter, this strategy would obviously continue to disrupt the lives of many for possibly several more years, without resulting in the formation of the Confederate Sates as a legitimate government.

"Lee", Andrew said, "probably understands this better than anyone and is not willing to engage in a lost cause for much longer."

Word had reached the War Department communications room on April fourth that Davis and his Cabinet had fled Richmond. Lee was engaged with Grant near Appomattox Courthouse. In Andrew's letter, he suggested that if I wished to witness the surrender of Lee, I should travel at all speed toward Appomattox. Andrew's letter had arrived on April the seventh.

I spoke briefly with Isaac about going south to be near Andrew as Grant closed in on the Confederate Army. He was not in agreement with me on this subject, fearing that I might once again be caught in the cross fire of a desperate army. I assured him that I would remain on the Union side and not venture toward the fighting.

The morning of April eighth, I left for Appomattox Courthouse, with James along to escort me. We were able to take the train as far as Five Forks, Virginia. From there we were accommodated with horses to proceed to the Union headquarters of Generals Meade and Grant, arriving in the early hours of April ninth.

I proceeded immediately to Amos' tent and found him there, still preparing for the day.

"Auntie Liz", he exclaimed as he saw me. "It is good to see you, and Uncle James, you, as well."

We embraced, and Amos told us how General Grant had offered terms of surrender to General Lee yesterday, but that Lee had not accepted the offer yet.

"Do you think he will, Amos?" I asked.

"I don't see how he can not accept", Amos responded. "Lee's army is surrounded. He has no provisions left. His men are starving."

"Will Grant offer good terms?" James inquired.

"He already has", Amos said. "I just hope Lee accepts soon, before our Army is forced to essentially destroy what remnant is left of the Confederate Army."

"We noticed on our way here, just how devastated the land is from all the fighting", James concluded.

The three of us sat for a few quiet moments, as Amos contemplated what he should do next.

Finally he spoke, "Well, I have to report to headquarters. Andrew is already there. If you wish, you can get some food at the quartermaster's tent and then join us at General Meade's quarters."

"That will be fine, Amos, and thank you", I said.

Amos left James and me at his tent. The two of us headed to find some breakfast, before going to the morning briefings that would occur shortly. I noticed several other Correspondents in camp as well.

I spoke briefly with Alfred Waud and Thomas Nast of Harpers Weekly. We caught up on our current activities, and Alfred commented that he was glad to see me back in the field, after hearing I had been shot last fall.

"It was only a minor flesh wound", I said as I dismissed the memory.

By noon, word was coming in that Lee had attempted to break through the Union lines, without success. Under a flag of truce, General Lee had sent word he was ready to meet with General Grant, to discuss terms of surrender.

General Grant met General Lee, along with numerous staff officers, in a farm house just outside of town, to discuss the terms. General Lee was dressed in the freshly pressed and cleaned uniform of a General. I believe that this was the first time I actually witnessed the General dressed so.

He usually wore his grey frock coat with Colonel Insignias on the collar. I once asked him about this, and he responded that he had held the rank of Colonel in the Union Army and never felt quite correct in wearing anything indicating a higher rank of office.

I watched as the man stepped from his horse, Traveler, accompanied by his aides. He walked to the top of the steps on to the porch and looked back for a moment, before entering the house where General Grant was waiting. His expression seemed to be one of relief that the end was now at hand.

Some time later, the two men emerged from the house. They stood and shook hands. General Grant, with his cigar in his mouth and dusty frock coat, appeared worn and tired. He, too, had the look as though to say, "enough is enough".

General Lee pulled on his gauntlets and strode down the steps to his waiting horse. He mounted, saluted General Grant, who returned the gesture, and began riding toward his men.

As General Lee arrived to his waiting men, he said, "Go to your homes and resume your occupations. Obey the laws and become as good citizens as you were soldiers."

I stood, held in the arms of James, and wept. My tears were of gratitude that the fighting was ending. My tears were of pride at the character of General Lee and the generosity shown by General Grant. My tears were of sorrow for those who would not see the return of their loved ones.

James and I left the next day for Washington City, after having dined with Amos, Andrew, and John. They promised to return home as soon as their duties would allow them. John asked me to tell Rebecca that he would return in a few days with Andrew, and they could be together again, never to be separated by war or slavery.

CHAPTER NINETY TWO

April fourteen, 1865. It is difficult to believe the war is over, for all intents and purposes. With the surrender of Robert E. Lee and the Army of Northern Virginia to General Grant just five days ago, the remainder of the Confederate Army should be disbanded within weeks, if not days. President Lincoln has promised that, during his second term, he will begin to rebuild the nation without malice or vengeful thoughts toward the southern states. His actions will perhaps ensure the future development of the nation, as the citizenry pushes ever westward into the expanse that lies ahead.

Isaac has promised to take me to Ford's Theater this evening, to see "Our American Cousin". It has been several weeks since we were at the theatre, and I am promised that this will be a special time for us. Isaac and I have grown closer over the past four years, since the death of Constance.

The War has been painful for the entire nation. Over one million men, women and children have lost their lives due to the ravages of the fighting. Families have been torn apart and destroyed, the land has been left in burned out ruin, and disease has crippled and killed more than the bullets and shells. Now is the time for healing, returning home, new romance, and beginning to live again.

As I sit in my study at my home, I begin to think of all that has taken place and where I am now. I am appreciative of Simon Cameron. At the start of the war, Secretary of War Cameron had encouraged me to invest in the iron and mercantile industries. He had shared that, with the coming need for supplies of weapons, clothing and ammunition, these would be patriotic industries to support with my funds.

Trusting him, I took what funds I had available and invested as he directed, to do my part in supporting the nation during this time of tribulation. The return was more than I could ever have anticipated or planned for. I am now a very wealthy woman, with considerable means for my future.

At the start of the war, I had made Reverend and Missus Isaac Stoltzfus both the beneficiaries and the executors of my estate, should something happen to me while I was reporting on the events of the war. I have survived, and have now left everything I own to Isaac for his ministry and care. Should I precede Isaac in death, he will be handsomely cared for.

I know that Isaac is coming, not only to take me to Ford's Theater, but also to ask me to marry him. We have been such good friends for so many years now. I know that he loves me, and I him. Marriage had been considered when we were both young and foolish, but I refused, knowing I had other plans for my life.

Now I am growing old, and have accomplished a great deal. Aside from Isaac's children, we are both alone in the world, and it seems only fitting that we should make a new start, becoming one, just as the nation is now making a new start and becoming, once again, one nation.

It is nearly four in the afternoon, and Isaac will attend to me around seven. I went into the parlor and met Rebecca there, tending to her chores. I asked her if she would be so kind as to assist me in preparing for the evening, with a new dress I purchased just for this occasion. She immediately agreed, and we both went to my room.

The satin dress is a lovely shade of lavender, with a darker shade of purple in the trim. It is probably the most elegant and feminine evening dress I have ever owned, and I feel as if I were twenty once again, as I climb into the layers of sophisticated fashion. I am sure that Isaac will be surprised at the extravagance of this dress. He knows that over the past several years, I have been very prudent about clothing, acquiring only what I needed to effectively do my life's work.

He has, also, over the past four years, grown accustomed to seeing me in men's attire, as I often dressed this way to travel into the lines and report the battles from the ranks of the soldiers. No woman would ever have been allowed to do what I did in gathering and reporting the news of the war, and so my disguises had become ever more convincing over time. It is now time to put those clothes to better use, by donating them to charity for the many returning soldiers who have little or nothing left.

After dressing for the evening, I suddenly feel so very tired and weary. The heaviness in my chest occurs more often now, and I have used the last of the brew that Miss Ella gave me so long ago. Perhaps after Isaac and I are married, I will consider returning to the medicine which Doctor May prescribed for my heart. It will no longer matter, then, that I will need to nap from time to time.

For now, though, I have asked Rebecca not to disturb me until Isaac arrives to take me to the theater. She offered me something to eat and drink, but I refused, knowing that we will be dining out this evening.

I have retired to my study, closed the door, and am sitting at my desk to write a little in my journal. I am, however, so very tired that I shall, instead, sit here with my eyes closed and rest, until my love comes for me, and carries me off into this glorious and eventful night.

Six Months Later...

EPILOG BY REV. DR. ISAAC STOLTZFUS

I arrived shortly before seven, that evening of April fourteen, 1865, to take my dear friend and love to the play at Ford's Theater. Rebecca answered the door and let me in. She said that Elizabeth was in her study and that she would announce me, if I wished to wait in the parlor. I thanked her but said that I would be happy to go into the study and gather Elizabeth up for the evening.

Rebecca and I shared a few moments together before going in. She asked me if this was the night I would ask Miss Elizabeth to marry me, and I assured her that it indeed was. I could barely wait, for the excitement grew in me at each passing moment. I shared with Rebecca the story of the first time I met Elizabeth, and how I knew then that I wanted to marry her, but she was too stubborn and independent to be a wife.

Now, though, with our advancing years, I assured her that we could be together at last, and enjoy a fine time together. Elizabeth had indicated that she was now receptive to the idea, and had talked about retiring from her reporter's work. She had been writing her life's story. She had hopes that it might inspire other young women to break out of the traditional mold and engage life to the fullest.

I quietly slipped into Elizabeth's private study on the second floor, so as not to suddenly disturb her. I could see her sitting, ever so peacefully, in her favorite chair, resting, with her eyes softly closed. The flicker of the fireplace, now burning low, was reflecting off her gentle and lovely face. Her lips were red, as if ripe for the kiss of a lover. On her desk lay her opened journal, with her glasses beside the leather bound volume of daily notes.

I moved gently to her side and knelt down, taking hold of her hand. It was then that I realized for the first time, that Elizabeth was not breathing. I shouted for Rebecca to call the doctor, but I knew it was already too late.

Her heart had been troubling her for some months now, and she refused the medication the doctor had prescribed, saying that it made her too sleepy. She relied, instead, on a brewed cup of an herbal tea that had been given to her by a southern woman she had helped some time ago, on one of her trips south.

Once again, it seemed as though I would be denied my love for Elizabeth. She had always been running off for the next story, the next adventure, the next...

I was alone. My children were now grown and off on their own adventures. My first wife, Constance, had been taken by typhoid at the start of the war. And now Elizabeth had succumbed to the stress of long hours, hard travel, disease, and even a wound she received from a Confederate Enfield Rifle. Her heart had had enough, and had now given up.

Later that evening, we were to learn of the tragic death of our beloved President, Abraham Lincoln. President Lincoln had fallen at the hands of a coward. An assassin's bullet had found its mark. The nation mourned its loss of the President. But few even noticed that one of the truly remarkable women of our times had passed on, that same evening.

Elizabeth was laid to rest next to her father, mother, and brother, with only a few close friends present, in the small cemetery at Cranbury, New Jersey. She was both a giving and forgiving woman, with a positive word for everyone she met.

Elizabeth believed in the best of people. When others found fault or used angry words, she saw something good, and spoke peace. When she criticized or condemned anyone, it was always because she had discerned a genuine character flaw. Even then, she treated them with courtesy.

She was always trying to fix the wrongs of the world, and was constantly in search of the truth. She will be missed, even by those who knew her only a little. For those of us who loved her, her loss is immense.

Elizabeth made certain that those she loved were well cared for after her death. She left me in charge of her estate, and had penned a letter to me some years earlier, directing me to distribute her funds, first for the care of myself and family, and then to the care of others as needed.

She also made sure that upon her death, Rebecca, her friend, faithful servant, and companion, was to be cared for. She left her home in Washington City, all of its contents and a sizable portion of her funds, to be placed in trust for Rebecca. Rebecca and John were to have an income and be allowed to live in the house until their death. I was to see that it was so.

The remainder of her funds, she left in my care. She said she wanted me to be comfortable in old age, and I was to use whatever funds I needed to insure that this would be the case. Elizabeth had acquired a sizable fortune prior to her death. I would be cared for, thanks to her love and generosity.

There was one additional request. I was to use funds that remained to establish a scholarship at the Wilson School for Women in her name, to support young women who desired to go into journalism.

I was able to provide such an endowment of well over five hundred thousand dollars. I also set up a trust fund for my care and future needs as may arise, with the balance of those funds upon my death to be distributed to the Seminary at Gettysburg, for the education of future ministers.

As I go into my twilight years, I shall forever remember Elizabeth and her love for life. I shall look to the day when we shall be reunited in the eternal Kingdom of Almighty God, never to be separated again.

Elizabeth's father wrote one time, long ago, to her,

"Lizzy was a little lamb, whose heart was pure as snow.
And everywhere the story went, Lizzy was sure to go."

Somehow I think Elizabeth knew that Mister Lincoln was about to go into eternity, and that there would be a wonderful story to tell. She always wanted to be the first to tell any story, and she always wanted to tell the human side.

I would like to think that she decided that it was all right to go after that story, and to engage in the next adventure, full of life. May God bless you, Elizabeth, as you have blessed all of us.

Book FIVE

a time for peace...

.

Dear Reader,

It is my privilege to add this letter of introduction to the following materials.

As I have been going through Auntie Liz's personal belongings, assisting Father in his work to finalize her estate, I have come upon several clippings of her writings during the War, as reported in the New York Tribune.

I have also discovered a few of her letters, editorials, and miscellaneous articles I believe might interest you, and assist you in discovering a little more about my Aunt.

As you have already discovered in her story, she was a wonderful and remarkable woman. I count it an honor and a privilege to have known her so well and to have been able to call her for my entire life, Auntie Liz.

She was a role model, a friend, a source of inspiration, and above all else, she was, and shall always remain, my Auntie Liz.

With all sincerity,

Caroline Stoltzfus

May 28, 1862
Gettysburg, PA

REPORTERS ARRESTED, TRIED AS SPIES

M. J. Farnsley, War Correspondent, New York Herald and C. C.
Rowe, War Correspondent, Alexander Gardner Photography
Studios, were arrested late last week and charged with passing
information to the enemy in the South. An expedited military
tribunal was set in motion in which formal charges were presented
to the military court in Gettysburg. The court, under the care of
local Judge Joseph Kerrigan, heard charges of conspiracy to assist
the enemy though the relaying of military information through the
reporting efforts of both reporters. Presenting the charges to Judge
Kerrigan was Colonel Roy Smith of the Washington War
Department.

Colonel Smith argued that both reporters had relayed vital military
information to the Confederacy by placing misleading and
counterfeit articles relating to certain social engagements that were
code for military movements. In addition, Colonel Smith informed
the court that these reporters also visited the south on several
occasions, using their press passes and credentials to move freely
across enemy lines to take information to several Confederate
Generals, particularly Gen. James Longstreet and Gen. Thomas
Jackson. Gen. J.E.B. Stuart supposedly also benefited from the
information supplied.

As part of his argument, Colonel Smith presented the courts with
detailed articles published in the New York Herald as well as
several Pennsylvania and Maryland papers with their byline, and
demonstrated how these articles were indeed in code.

Farnsley and Rowe argued that they had only written articles of
fact and that there was no code, secret or otherwise, in the written
materials. They also gave testimony that they were in full
compliance and within their rights to report the news and that if
those in Washington City and elsewhere wanted to read more into
their articles than was there, they could do so at the peril of the
reader, not the author.

After short deliberation by a panel of military officers, the recommendation by the panel to the judge came and stated that the correspondents were reportedly to be detained for the duration of the war in a federal prison located in Washington City.

However, in a last minute development, a Pinkerton Agent stepped forth to give new insights to the particulars of this case. Judge Kerrigan allowed for the new evidence to be presented before passing sentencing.

The Pinkerton Agent stated that Colonel Smith had been under investigation for certain irregularities in the War Department and found Colonel Smith to have plotted the discredit of several members of the Army. The plot was designed to disrupt the command structure of the Army of the Potomac, to give the Confederacy the upper hand in logistics. It was also revealed that Colonel Smith was in the process of forming a plan and recruiting various members of the General staff to assassinate President Abraham Lincoln. Further, the Agent reported that both Farnsley, and Rowe, a distant relative of General John Reynolds, were in fact working to assist the Pinkerton Agency in the performance of their duties in uncovering this plot. When both reporters were asked why they did not reveal any of this during the trial, they offered the explanation that they did not wish to disrupt the Pinkerton investigation and that, if imprisoned, they knew it would be only a matter of time before they would have been freed and vindicated by the Pinkerton Agency.

At this report, the tribunal offered their apologies to the reporters and freed them. Colonel Smith was immediately taken into custody and later attempted to escape. During this attempt, he was mortally shot by guards. The investigation continues to determine who else, if anyone, may be involved in this plot.

September 19, 1862
Sharpsburg, Maryland
Elizabeth Grace Fitzgerald
War Correspondent
New York Tribune

Sharpsburg –

September 17, 1862, may be recorded as one of the bloodiest days in the history of this Nation. Opposing forces engaged in the fields, woods and mountainsides of this rural, southern Maryland soil, located just a few miles from the Virginia border, north of the Potomac River. It is estimated that over 20,000 men, in both gray and blue, lie dead in the heat of the day. Many a young man shall never again see the faces of home. Many have lost their innocence this day. Many a boy has suddenly and unexpectedly become a man. Many a wife has become a widow, many a mother will sit in excruciating grief, and many a child will become an orphan, never to be held in the loving arms of a father again.

The following report is filed by this reporter, as witnessed, first hand, on the day of this bloody atrocity near a creek called Antietam.

The Union Army, under the command of General George McClellan, engaged the Southern Army, commanded by Robert E Lee, on the outskirts of Sharpsburg, Maryland, near Antietam Creek. Under the clear, sun filled fall sky, the two armies clashed in the most horrific and thunderous manner, set upon the task of destroying, nay, annihilating one another, thus bringing to an end this terrible conflict of hatred.

A few days earlier, I had the opportunity to engage General Ambrose Burnside. He said that as soon as the Army caught up with General Lee, the conflict would be over, and the men of his command would find themselves home for Christmas. This day would find General Ambrose' Division almost destroyed under the heavy barrage of Confederate Cannon fire, under the command of A. P. Hill, CSA.

Early on the morning of September 17, 1862, General Joseph Hooker, USA, launched an attack on General Lee's left flank. The fighting was immense, with attacks and counter attacks on both sides. The Confederates eventually made a stand at the Sunken Road, and seemed to hold for some time. The Union forces eventually broke through the Confederate lines, and the forces under Lee had to withdraw.

General Burnside launched an attack near the bridge at Antietam Creek and was initially successful, but with General A. P. Hill's counter attack, was driven back. Hill reclaimed the real estate briefly commanded and controlled by Burnside.

I found myself pinned under protective cover at the sunken road, along side Alfred Waud, artist for Harper's Weekly, as we were reporting the events at the time. Both Mister Waud and I were approximately ten feet from the Confederate right flank.

The Union encountered the Confederates in the afternoon sun at the Sunken Road, now called by the soldiers of both forces as "Bloody Lane". Hostility and death poured forth from both sides. Men in Blue stood only a few yards away from the men in Gray, as volleys of hot fire poured in from both sides, ending the life of many good men. Casualties were such that the blood of the fallen flowed like a river through this narrow patch of ground.

It appeared for a brief period that the Confederates had won the day, as the Union forces advanced and then retreated, repeating this action several times. As men were carried off the field of battle, Confederate sharpshooters took careful aim at the ones tendering aid to their fallen comrades, thus mortally wounding the soldier, leaving the rescuer and the rescued fallen, rendering both men incapable of continuing the fight. This barbaric action would be carried out over and over by both armies.

With each fallen Union soldier, Confederate yells and cheers were heard, sending chills down the spine of this correspondent. The hatred of the men from the south toward men of the north was never more prevalent than on this day. It could be seen in their faces, upon their posture, and in the very tone of their voices.

The fire power from both sides seemed to go on for eternity, its power of destruction relentless, as thousands from both North and South lay dead and rotting under the sun. The smell of sulfur in the air could only be compared to that which Dante writes in his "Inferno". Hell itself can not be more hideous than the sights of this day's action.

Camp followers, women who stayed with their husbands or sons, stood helplessly by as the screams from the "field of glory" rose into the noonday air. Their cries only barely heard above the sounds of battle, carried towards the heavens in desperation, asking only for mercy.

This correspondent gained advantage to the devastation from the side of the Confederate forces. I was so close to the fighting, that several balls of fire screamed past my ear, one penetrating the very hat upon my head. I have experienced and witnessed conflict and fighting before, but nothing of this magnitude.

It seemed after two major assaults by Union forces against the Confederate position had been repelled, that the fighting had ended, but a third Union assault began almost as suddenly as the previous one had ended. "How could this level of intense fighting continue?" was my thought. "How can this go on? How many more innocent lives shall be destroyed this day?"

This third assault seemed as if it was a desperate action by General McClellan's forces. It was a third attempt to move the Confederates from this vantage point, where so many had already died. As I lay just twenty feet from the nearest Confederate soldier on the right flank, the desperation of both sides, the Union to overtake the Confederates, and the Confederates to hold back the Union, was abundantly evident.

Soldiers were falling faster than before. I found myself stained with the blood and flesh of the closest soldiers, as balls of destruction easily sliced through their frail and vulnerable bodies of flesh and blood. Soldiers once filled with dignity, hope, adventure, optimism, desire, love, now lay dead and lifeless, dreams once held close and dear, now dashed and forgotten. The air, once filled with the fragrance of autumn's harvest and warm, sun filled days, now was filled with the smell of death, sulfur, suffering, and cries of agony and defeat. Smoke, not from kitchen fires preparing the meals for the workers, or the canning fires of the harvest, but smoke from decaying carnage, cannon and musket fire, now filled every nostril within miles of this horrific place.

The Confederate Army finally yielded this ground as the Union forces seemed to overwhelm the day. The Union Army was victorious in men and fire power to overtake the disadvantaged forces of Robert E. Lee. Out numbered nearly two-to-one, the Confederates this day held as long as possible, but in the end, were able only to deliver a devastating and critical blow to General McClellan's Army, not total defeat.

September 18 saw more action by both sides, as skirmishes between the Union Armies and Lee's retreating Armies took place. Robert E. Lee has begun to withdraw his troops to the south, across the Potomac and back into Virginia. The question remains, will General McClellan advance his entire Army at this time and pursue Lee in an attempt to bring a quick end to this horrific conflict, or will "Lil' Mac" hold back, allowing Lee to regroup and refit his Army for future action against the North?

September 20, 1862
Sharpsburg Maryland
Elizabeth Grace Fitzgerald
War Correspondent
New York Tribune

Sharpsburg-

I have already sent the initial report of the Battle at Antietam Creek, near Sharpsburg Maryland. This is a supplement to that report. As I have already reported, General Burnside reported that he believed this would be the decisive battle and end the conflict once and for all. With nearly 20,000 dead, it would seem that this has not happened. General Burnside suffered immense losses and defeat to General A.P. Hill.

It would also seem that General McClellan has no desire to pursue General Lee into Virginia at this time, claiming he has lost a third of his Army on this blood drenched ground.

Prior to the start of this action, I was able to visit with some of the union troops and I met some of the young men who serve as the "drummer boys" for the units. These brave lads, who do not carry weapons, but only their drums, are some of the bravest I have ever met. They stand at their post, giving with great accuracy the commands that can only be heard through their beats and tempo upon the instruments of war they gallantly carry. Leading the armies into battle, initially at the head of the columns, along side the officers, they count off the cadence of step. Then, at the appropriate time, they change their tempos to reflect a new command: attack, retreat, left flank, right flank, and so on. The yells of the commanders cannot be heard over the cries of other men and the sounds of fire power, but these drums can and are heard. The men in rank and file rely on this means of communicating commands to coordinate their actions. By their presence and exposure, these lads are often the target of snipers and sharpshooters, and many have already fallen.

I met a young lad from the 14th NY. He was proudly dressed in his uniform and carrying his drum. He had not yet seen the elephant. This was his first battle. I asked him if he was afraid. He said no, his mother had given him a medal to carry that was supposed to protect him from harm and danger. He said he knew his job and would be all right in the end. His commander had promised him that he would be near him, and, keep him safe as well.

After the battle's end, I was walking through the fields of death, and found him face down in the dirt. He had been killed, I was told, during the second assault on the sunken road. His small, frail body already bloated, he was holding in his right hand the metal his mother had given him. His legs were missing, and his Captain's body lay next to him, with a large hole which his chest once occupied. I was told that a cannon shell exploded very near them, killing the officer instantly and mortally wounding the young drummer boy.

I learned his name was Samuel Axelrod from Brooklyn, New York. His mother and father are still at home. I will send a letter with the metal his mother gave him for protection and a lock of his hair to them, as soon as I am able. Sam, as he was called, is now out of harm's way, safe in the arms of God. May he rest in peace from this day forward.

The women who follow.

It seemed as if hundreds of women; wives, mothers, daughters, sisters, stood helplessly by, watching and waiting, hoping, praying, longing for word of a loved one on the field of battle. Many were standing, with terror in their eyes and tears streaming down their dirt stained faces, hoping their men would return unharmed in physical and mental stature.

Laura Scott and her eight year old daughter, Katherine, had traveled from Pennsylvania, in hopes of catching a glimpse of their husband and father. They found him in a hospital tent, suffering from wounds and amputation, not sure whether he would live or die.

I met Nicholas, age five, and Abigail, age eight, along a fence row where they were told to wait for their mother and father. They had been there four days now, with nothing left to eat and little water. I was told their parents were with a Pennsylvania unit and that they were sure their parents would be back for them soon. Alfred Waud of Harpers Weekly helped me take them to a shelter. They are no doubt left as orphans from this horrific encounter of forces set upon the destruction of one another.

Jennie Bush and her daughter, seven year old Emma, were waiting for their husband and father. There was no word. Jennie works as a wash woman for the New York unit for which her husband is a Sergeant. Jennie tells me that they are refugees. The fled from Harpers Ferry, Virginia, at the start of hostilities, to her parents' home in New York, hoping to avoid the coming conflict. Her husband, however, decided to join the Union Army. She feels she can not go home to Harpers Ferry, and she has no funds to return home to New York.

A side note: As I was walking with Alfred Waud, we came upon two Union soldiers who were killed. As we looked upon them, it became evident that these were indeed women, dressed as men, in blue, Union uniforms. We had heard that this was occurring, but, at last, I have seen it for myself. I do not know who they were or where they came from, and we could find no information upon their persons or in their possessions. They will become part of the unknown dead at Antietam.

January 11, 1863
Washington City
Elizabeth Grace Fitzgerald
War Correspondent
New York Tribune

Washington City-

News in Washington at the War Department is once again most disturbing, and, at the same time, most hopeful. Major General Ambrose Burnside has been replaced by Major General Joseph "Fighting Joe" Hooker, following General Burnside's defeat at Fredericksburg.

The Union Army, under the command of General Burnside, suffered horrendous casualties in futile frontal assaults on December 13, 1862, against entrenched Confederate defenders on the heights behind the city, bringing to an early end their campaign against the Confederate capital of Richmond. The Union Army has once again pulled back to position themselves for a future assault, this time with yet another new commander.

General Joseph Hooker has been described as a man of great courage and fortitude and somewhat questionable morals. However, General Hooker promises that he will refit the Army of the Potomac and move aggressively against General Robert E. Lee and the Army of Northern Virginia at his most opportune appointment.

Can this, yet another change in the command structure of the North, provide the necessary will and conviction to bring about the end of this terrible conflict? Only time will tell.

General Lee and his lieutenants have also vowed to end this terrible atrocity, with the defeat of the Union Army. According to sources, the victory at Fredericksburg has given them the impetus to advance once again against Union forces, possibly moving into Maryland or Pennsylvania as early as May.

General Hooker has already issued orders to refit his army and to prepare to march into Virginia as early as April, thus cutting off

Lee and his men from advancing further. General Hooker is hopeful of removing Lee from his entrenched position around Fredericksburg, Virginia, forcing the gray fox to retreat. The Union General states that he will eventually win the day, and the war, with a Union victory in Richmond.

As General Hooker continues his plan, the War Department will do everything in its power to insure a Union victory at this most crucial time in the war. Another Union defeat such as recently suffered in Fredericksburg, as well as the Union stalemate at Antietam Creek near Sharpsburg, Maryland, this past fall, would likely lead to a Confederate victory of the entire war. This would undoubtedly end not only the present fighting, but all hopes of forever preserving the Union.

The New York Tribune
An editorial by
Elizabeth Grace Fitzgerald
War Correspondent
June 3, 1863

I had the privilege last month of attending the Association of New York Clergy Prayer Breakfast at the Metropolitan Methodist Church on 44th Street, NW. In attendance were a number of distinguished pastors, ministers, priests, and theologians. Several of the guests made reference to the Children of Israel wandering in the desert for forty years after being led out of the bondage of Egypt, before arriving at the Promised Land. Others referenced the forty days and nights of rain upon the land in the story of Noah and the Ark.

After the meeting, I queried a couple of the theologians on the meaning of these passages, why they were referenced, and did the number forty have any significance in the Scriptures. I was told that these particular passages had significance in the sense of the current struggles of the nation to define itself. Further, they have significance in the fight for freedom against slavery. The Negro looks to God as the great deliverer, just as the children of Israel looked to God for deliverance from the tyranny of Pharaoh. The number forty holds significance in that God takes "as long as necessary" to accomplish His will. Forty in the Bible means literally "as long as it takes".

The great struggle we are currently in seems to be taking, to some, longer than necessary. To others, the conflict is still in its infancy. The reasons for the conflict are also as varied and many as are the opinions of the conflict itself. The one question, though, that is always on the lips of those we encounter is, "How much longer will the fighting go on?" There, of course, is no simple or reasonable answer to this question. We know that it will go on, and that it will take as long as it takes. Forty years? Forty days? No one has that answer. Or perhaps we do.

The current administration in Washington City has made it clear that the current policy is to pursue an end to this war only after the Confederacy has been totally destroyed and the southern states have reunited as part of the Union. According to Mr. Lincoln, there will be no peace until the south lays down its arms. But what are the costs, the price, and the profit of such a policy? What would the cost, price, and profit be of a different policy?

Let us look briefly at the cost. So far, we have seen a number of significant defeats of the Union forces. To date, over 400,000 men, both from the North and South, are dead. The rights and civil liberties of the citizens of both the North and South have been eroded, perhaps never to be reclaimed, following the end of these current atrocities. Bankers, financiers, and politicians appear to be making a sizable profit through this war on both sides, while the middle class and poor appear to be losing ground economically, emotionally, and spiritually.

Civil Liberties, once believed to be sacred and protected, have been eroded. The writ of Habeas Corpus has been suspended, in order to quiet those in dissension with the current Washington Administration. Anyone seen remotely as "sympathetic" to the southern cause is immediately imprisoned without reason, without recourse, without expeditious hearings, without representation.

The draft has been imposed, forcing the working class into the fight, while the wealthy are able to "buy off" their sons' service for Three Hundred Dollars, sending the poor to fight in their place.

The press is constantly under scrutiny and slander by the Washington elite, who wish that only materials from the "minister of propaganda" were allowed to be published, while the first amendment is trampled under foot, editors and reporters are accused of spying and unpatriotic sympathy, if anything of the truth is published which goes against the current sentiments of the Administration.

War atrocities occur daily, as homes and communities are burned, supplies and stores are raided, consumed or destroyed, civilians are treated as soldiers, shot, arrested, beaten, children are left fatherless, and in many cases, motherless as well. Orphanages are being formed daily and, even then, are bulging at their very seams with the unwanted and abandoned children who are the real victims in this war.

The rich continue to become rich at the expense of the poor. The factories of the North, and their owners, are increasingly more powerful, wealthier and more wasteful of the human spirit, as well as the daily commodities needed for survival, let alone prosperity.

The South is ever more isolated from the world, and the North, leaving little promise of a brighter tomorrow. England and France, to date, have agreed to remain neutral and stay out of the conflict, thus further isolating the South. The blockades of the Union Navy have totally disrupted the trade and commerce of the South, leaving it with no way to expeditiously sell its cotton and other commodities, leaving the South virtually bankrupt in its need to fund the war machine. Some say this is a good thing. But is it? What will the ultimate cost be when peace is restored? And will there ever be peace?

I believe there will peace again and the Union will be preserved, just as Mr Lincoln and his cabinet have designed, unless there is a change in the Administration next year. The war will continue as long as it is able to be profitable to the banks, the factory owners and the politicians. When there are no more profits to be made, the North will sue for peace.

The reality is that the War Machine of the North is far superior to that of the South. Prior to the war, I had the opportunity to travel extensively throughout the south and I can tell you this: there are no significant factories in the south. Without factories, there can be no manufacturing of weapons and other necessities for war. Since the war, and as recently as April of this year, my travels into the south proved once again the lack of resources needed to sustain a lengthy war.

I saw soldiers who were barefoot and dressed in rags. I saw farms, homes, entire communities in disarray, devastated by the presence of both armies. I saw wounded without medical care, suffering and dying. I saw homeless mothers and their children, begging for any piece of food that may be available. I saw the elderly, waiting for their turn to enter into the "promised land".

I saw the Negro, still praying and hoping for the coming of the Jubilee and the Deliverance of Father Abraham. I saw fear, hopelessness and devastation on the faces of many. I also saw arrogant pride and sense of honor to the homeland and a fierce determination to fight on, "as long as it takes".

If there is no change in Washington City next election year, the War will come to an end. The Union will be reunited, the south destroyed. The rich will become richer off the sufferings of those who will have lost everything they had worked generations for.

When will the end come? I do not know. But it will come. It will come because the resources of the North are endless, compared to those of the South. The War Machine in the North continues to grow, while the few resources of the South dwindle away, irreplaceable due to the blockades.

The pain and suffering will continue as long as profits can be made, as long as political agendas can be realized, as long as people are willing to do whatever their government demands of them.

This war really is not about states rights, or slavery, or even about the preservation of the Union. This war is ultimately about Greed in the North and misinformed Honor, Loyalty and Pride in the South.

The one remaining right that each of us has is the right to vote. Next year, we will be asked to cast our vote for one of two candidates for the Presidency of the United States. It is a precious thing, our vote. In this nation, the people have the right to decide who will lead us, who will establish the policies that will guide us into the future, who will best represent the interests of all the people, not just the wealthy, or the political. It is not too early to begin thinking who will best deserve your vote. For, whoever is elected to the Presidency of the United States will determine the final outcome of this war and the future of the South.

It is my desire, and I believe the desire of most Americans, to see the end of this war come quickly. I believe it is also the desire of the people of this land, in both the North and the South to see the government once again be about the people. It is to be a government "of the people, for the people and by the people..."

And it is time for that government to be restored. It is time for the greedy of the North to acknowledge they have enough wealth at the expense of the common man, and it is time for the prideful of the South to humble themselves and seek a peaceful solution to the present conflict.

As a theologian friend of mine stated recently, "What does God require of thee, O man, but to do justice, love mercy, and walk humbly with thy God?" It seems as if this would be a good place to start on the journey toward healing.

Gettysburg, Pennsylvania
July 2, 1863
Elizabeth Grace Fitzgerald
War Correspondent
New York Tribune

Gettysburg-

I find myself caught in the midst of much angst and tribulation in the sleepy Pennsylvania town of Gettysburg. Traveling here from Charleston in Western Virginia just a few days earlier, I arrived here to visit my old friend, Reverend Schumacher, of the Gettysburg Seminary. It was within two days of my arrival that news came of Robert E. Lee's Army of Northern Virginia having been sighted near Chambersburg, with possible movement toward Harrisburg. Also, news reached us that General Jubal Early, CSA, had taken York, Pennsylvania, on the 28th of June. I was told by my Editor, Mr. Horace Greeley, to delay my departure to Washington City and await further developments in the region.

On June 30, news that Lee had advanced near Gettysburg had reached us, and we were notified that Gen John Buford, USA, and his Cavalry were near by and would attempt to engage the Confederates as soon as practical.

On July the 1st, General Buford engaged the Confederates just west of the Seminary on the Chambersburg Pike, and the conflict began. Fierce fighting, with what appears to be heavy losses on both sides of the conflict, has already occurred. The Seminary has been turned into a surgeons' butchering house. The limbs of helpless lads are piling up on all sides of the building. Both Federal and Confederate troops are cared for here, or left to die on the slopes of the grounds. Federal and Confederate Surgeons work side by side to crudely care for the injured. The smell of death, and the cries of the dying are already every where throughout the town, but none so much as here in this place of the sacred and the profane.

Word has reached us that General John Reynolds, USA, fell in battle not far from this place, in the fighting of July 1st. General Buford held the ground as long as possible, before being ordered to withdraw to the Cemetery on the south side of the town. Now the town and Seminary are in the hands of the Confederates, yet the Federal Surgeons continue on in caring for the wounded, from the North and South.

The sounds of weapons, artillery, horses and wagons, charging, fighting, dying men can be heard though out the entire town. Civilians are huddled in their basements, or have fled to neighboring town and farms, in hopes of avoiding the catastrophe at hand. Additional word has been received that there is already a civilian causality of one Jennie Wade, killed this morning by a sniper's bullet as she was tending to her sick sister in the home on the edge of town, near the Federal Lines.

I have attempted to venture toward the center of town with little success, constantly stopping to avoid being run over by racing horses pulling Confederate artillery toward the Cemetery. It seems to me that a Cemetery is a strange place, indeed, to hold a defensive line by the Federals. I am told that this is good ground, however, because of its height and advantage to see over the entire area of Confederate advance.

As of yesterday, Generals Winfield Scott Hancock, John Buford, and John Reynolds were commanding for the Federals. General Reynolds is reported dead, General Buford has been pulled to the rear for reserve, and General George Meade has arrived on the field to take command. General Hancock remains by General Meade's side. Who else is here we do not know, but we have been able to decipher that as many as 40,000 Confederates are here, along with as many as 50,000 Federal troops. More Federal troops appear to be arriving as the day wears on.

General Lee is commanding the Confederates at this time, with General Longstreet and others by his side. How many Confederate commanders overall, we do not know.

As this day is drawing to a close, the fighting continues, and death remains a constant. The stench of death is already rising high above this town, and the heat and humidity of July presses in with oppressive heaviness. There appears to be no advance on either side, and the bloody contest will continue when the sun rises over Pennsylvania in the morning.

As darkness falls on these killing fields, the fighting has at last, if only for a small respite, stopped. Yet the cries of the fallen, wounded, and dying can still be heard from the place where they fell. Will this place ever hold peace again for those who reside here? Will the fallen of battle find their eternal peace in this place? I think not.

Gettysburg, Pennsylvania
July 3, 1863
Elizabeth Grace Fitzgerald
War Correspondent
New York Tribune

Gettysburg-

In my attempt to move about the town and to find what information I could as to the advance of the battle underway, I engaged a civilian pair within the Union camp at Cemetery Ridge, south of Gettysburg. They were there seeking a pass from the provost to pass through Federal lines towards Washington City, in hopes of avoiding further conflict and encounter with Confederate troops.

The gentleman was Reverend Josiah Young of Boston. Reverend Young had traveled to Gettysburg, arriving with his traveling companion, Missus Cora Hatch, also of Boston.

Reverend Young had traveled to this small Pennsylvania town to start a new congregation for the AME Zion Church. He found that many of the Negroes had already fled north as a result of Confederate raids earlier in June that had taken approximately forty Negroes back to Virginia to be sold as slaves. Most of the 200 colored residents of this town had fled, leaving behind their homes and work, for safer refuge. Reverend Young, a freeman, expressed to the Provost concern for his safety and that of his traveling companion, who proclaims herself a spiritualist and abolitionist, in hopes of obtaining the required travel documents allowing them safe passage to Washington City.

The Provost advised Reverend Young that no passes were being issued at this time, due to the engagement of the Confederate Army, and that no passes would be available until the outcome had been decided. With no safe place to go, Reverend Young stated he would remain within the confines of the Federal Lines.

At this time, there appears to be a short respite from the fighting. The heat and humidity of the July sun has apparently taken its toll on both Armies. General Hancock feels that there will be little if any fighting this day, as both Armies rest and prepare to continue the massacre of sacred lives on the 4th, Independence Day. Should that occur, many a soul will find its eternal independence on the 4th, and Missus Hatch will have ample opportunity to display her abilities for grieving families.

Gettysburg, Pennsylvania
July 4, 1863
Elizabeth Grace Fitzgerald
War Correspondent
New York Tribune

Gettysburg-

The citizenry of Gettysburg are rejoicing this day, as Confederate forces have begun to withdraw from the town and countryside under orders from General Robert E. Lee, CSA, to retreat back into Virginia following the devastating loss of life during the third day of battle.

At approximately 3:00 pm on the 3rd of July, under the command of General George Pickett, about 12,000 Confederate troops began a massive assault on the Federal position at Seminary Ridge, hitting the Union center. The Union, under the immediate command of General Winfred S. Hancock, USA, sustained significant bombardment from Confederate cannons, and then a rousing assault by General Pickett's Brigade. The Union was able to repulse the attack. Confederate forces were decimated in the attack, while Union casualties were not nearly as severe.

During the attack, General Hancock was seriously wounded and taken from the field after the fighting had concluded, for care. His condition is believed to be fatal; however no word has been received, as yet, to the extent or outcome of his injuries. Union losses are believed to be less than two thousand men.

Confederate forces suffered nearly fifty percent casualties. Among those are several principle officers, including Generals Armistead, Garnett and Kemper, Trimble and Pettigrew. Pickett's three brigade commanders and all thirteen of his regimental commanders were casualties during the assault on the Union center.

There is speculation that these losses will undoubtedly be the end of the Army of Northern Virginia, and that the Confederacy will not be able to recover after this devastating loss. Rumor has it that Mr. Lincoln will seek to bring an end to the war, pursuing a policy of reestablishing the Union through peaceful negotiations with Richmond.

General Meade has ordered a pursuit of Lee's army into Maryland and into Virginia, if necessary, to end this bloody conflict. All prayers are with the Federal forces, in hope that this defeat of the Confederate Army will now bring with it a swift conclusion to these hostilities and a restoration of the Union and peace for all people.

Elizabeth Grace Fitzgerald
War Correspondent
New York Tribune
New York, New York
Washington City
July 9, 1863

Washington City-

I had the distinct pleasure of meeting with one of the heroines of the present conflict, while present in this government city. Her name is Miss Clara Barton, and she is a true angel of mercy upon the field of valor. I wish to share with you some of my impressions of Miss Barton and the work she is doing. Perhaps in doing so, her story will inspire other women of the Union to avail themselves of similar, sacrificial offering, for the eventual settlement of the present hostilities that are gripping this nation.

Miss Barton is extremely reticent to tell her story, and much of what I have learned and gathered has come from sources who know Miss Barton and have the utmost respect for her work.

Miss Barton is a quiet woman, with a great deal of personal strength, courage and determination. She attributes her educational achievements to her family. The youngest of five siblings, she was taught much from her older sisters and brothers. Her family, strong abolitionists, encouraged her in every endeavor. Her interest in caring for the injured, sick, and less fortunate has been instilled in her from her early childhood, by the reports of her great-aunt, Martha Ballard, an exceptional midwife Miss Ballard reportedly served in Hallowell, Maine, and delivered over one thousand infants.

Miss Barton states that her father taught her: "As a patriot, serve your country with all you have, even with your life if need be; as the daughter of an accepted Mason, seek and comfort the afflicted everywhere; and as a Christian, honor God and love mankind."

Today, Miss Barton is continuing to care for our wounded soldiers and meeting their needs on the field of battle. She readily collects and supplies the much needed materials to care for the wounds and illnesses that are befalling our fighting men. She carries her materials and wares directly to the front, where they are most urgently needed, often getting through when and where the Army cannot.

Miss Barton has established an agency to obtain and distribute supplies to wounded soldiers, and has received a pass from Army Headquarters to ride in army ambulances to provide comfort to the soldiers and nurse them back to health. She has obtained permission to travel behind the lines, reaching some of the grimmest battlefields of the war.

During the Battle of Antietam Creek in September, 1862, Miss Barton was nearly killed when a bullet passed through the sleeve of her dress, killing the wounded man she was attending. Although lacking medical training, at the insistence of a wounded soldier, she extracted a bullet from his cheek, using only her pocket knife.

In April of this year, Miss Barton traveled to Hilton Head, South Carolina, in preparation for the anticipated bombardment of Charleston. While there, she was able to join her brother, Captain David Barton, an Army Quartermaster, and her fifteen year old nephew, Steven E. Barton, serving in the military telegraph office.

In May, she met Mister Frances D. Gage, and has assisted him in the care and education of former slaves and freedmen. At this present time, Miss Barton has begun to develop an interest in the growing cause for equal rights among women and the Negro.

At the time of our meeting, Miss Barton has been in Washington City, attempting to procure more supplies for the Army in South Carolina, as well as materials to be used in the education and care of the newly freed Negros. She states that she shall return to the South within the week, and hopes that many will respond to her request and needs.

Miss Barton is indeed an extraordinary woman, who has placed herself in unselfish service to her neighbor and stranger alike. The men on the battle field find great comfort when they look up and see her approaching in her Navy blue dress, bonnet, and bright red bow.

You may contact Miss Barton through regular Army channels, by addressing correspondence to her at "Miss Clara Barton, War Department, Washington City." Donations of cloth, medicine, and food may also be sent, in care of the Army, to Miss Barton.

Washington City
July 9, 1863
Elizabeth Grace Fitzgerald
War Correspondent
New York Tribune

VICKSBURG FALLS.

Word has arrived at the War Department that the Confederate City of Vicksburg fell on July 4, 1863, the day following the Confederate defeat at Gettysburg, to the hands of Federal Troops under the command of Major General Ulysses S. Grant. Grant began his blockade of Vicksburg in late March and has laid siege to the city for almost sixty days. Daily bombardment of the city resulted in numerous casualties of Confederate troops, with minor casualties of Union soldiers, according to Secretary of War Edwin Stanton. Confederates surrendered to Grant's Army after exhausting their resources. About ten thousand Confederate troops are now in the custody of the Federals.

Approximately fifteen hundred civilians had remained in Vicksburg, after General Grant had offered the civilians free passage to safety prior to the siege. Vicksburg had completely exhausted all its resources as well, including food and medical supplies. Many of the remaining residents were forced from their homes to find shelter in surrounding caves, due to the intense and regular bombardment of the city. General Grant reportedly states that he will offer amnesty to all civilians who will pledge allegiance to the Union. The Union Army has made the city its new headquarters in the Mississippi delta region.

Washington City
July 15, 1863
Elizabeth Grace Fitzgerald
War Correspondent
New York Tribune

Washington City-

According to Secretary of War Edwin Stanton, the Confederate Army returned to Virginia, through Maryland, following their defeat in Gettysburg this past week. Several skirmishes have occurred in and around Hagerstown, Funkstown, and Williamsport, Maryland. The Confederate Cavalry has been harassed by Federals in pursuit of Lee's Army of Northern Virginia. Reports indicate that the majority of Lee's army was held in check at the banks of the Potomac River in Williamsport, Maryland, unable to ford the river, due to the high amounts of rainfall over the past several days and the swollen river conditions.

Union forces reportedly engaged Confederates in withdrawal on July 4th and 5th, near Fairfield and Monterrey Springs, Pennsylvania. Several additional Federal losses were reported to the Union Cavalry, with several fighting men wounded and reported prisoners of the Confederates.

On July 6, Federal units once again launched an attack on the Confederate positions near Hagerstown, Maryland. Reports indicate that as soon as the attack was commenced, the Federals once again retreated, fearing additional losses. Reports are that Federal losses were as high as ten to one against the Confederates.

From July 7 until July 13, cannonading and small skirmishes continued throughout the region, with Confederate forces pinned against the swollen Potomac in Williamsport.

If the Union Calvary could have kept the Confederates in check, perhaps General George Meade would have been able to advance his infantry troops toward Williamsport and again engage the defeated Confederate Army, ending the bloody conflict that has been ripping at the heart of the Nation. However, General Robert E. Lee and his Army of Northern Virginia have escaped back into

Virginia and the south, thus slipping the hounds of the Federal Army, to fight another day.

General Meade has not yet given an answer to Secretary Stanton as to his slow response to the Confederate withdrawal. It appears that the will of the Union Generals to fight and win this war has once again been challenged.

Elizabeth Grace Fitzgerald
War Correspondent
New York Tribune
New York, New York
August 7, 1863
Gettysburg Pennsylvania

AFTERMATH OF A BATTLE

It has been a little over one month since the Union and Confederate Armies clashed in horrific conflict over the sacred farm lands surrounding this sleepy Pennsylvania community. Over 100,000 soldiers gathered on both sides of the conflict, to slaughter and annihilate one another in bloody pursuit of victory. Each was hoping to bring an answer to the question of whether the Southern States have the right to independent rule and sovereignty as an independent nation. After three horrific days of battle, the question remains largely unanswered. But in its wake, lie more than 50,000 casualties, and the destruction of a quiet community.

I have returned to this small Pennsylvania town, just north of the Mason-Dixon Line, to observe the effects of such a battle on the citizens who remain here. I wish that I had not returned, for the sights, sounds, and smells of the past atrocity still vividly remain; and the suffering is more than any person can, or should, endure. The heroic folks of this community are, however, enduring. They are surviving, reconstructing, tending to the wounded left behind, and burying the fallen, despite their own losses and suffering.

Everywhere I go, the bodies of fallen soldiers are stacked, some ten to twenty feet high, waiting for a proper burial. Others are tossed into shallow graves, unmarked and unknown, where they fell. The carcasses of dead animals, mules, horses, dogs and a variety of farm animals lie in heaps waiting to be destroyed by fire. The stench of death is so strong in the August heat that there is no escaping it anywhere within fifty miles of Gettysburg. Civilians everywhere wear a mask scented with lavender or other fragrances, attempting to counter the rotting odors of decaying flesh.

Children scurry along the battle grounds, looking for keepsakes left behind by the fallen and retreating soldiers. There is the sound of an occasional explosion, which brings the heartbeat of every mother to a standstill until the child, just killed by a previously unexploded shell, has been identified. So far, over twenty children have lost their lives in this fashion since the fighting ended.

Disease is beginning to take its toll as well. The rotting flesh of man and animal has attracted disease carrying rodents and insects to this town. Many have already succumbed to the effects of dysentery and fever. The local cemetery is reaching its maximum capacity, and efforts are underway by a local attorney to secure property for a national cemetery in which to bury the Union dead.

Every public building, church and school alike, is still being used to house the injured soldiers who have thus far survived. Surgeons from both the Union and Confederacy have remained to care for the wounded. Rumor has spread that these dedicated men will be leaving soon, as more of the soldiers are moved to Washington City to continue their recovery. The process is slow, however. Confederate soldiers, now prisoners of war, will be removed to Union prison camps in Maryland and Ohio as soon as possible. The surgeons will be leaving as well, leaving the remaining care, which will be quite significant, to the local physicians, too few in numbers to be of considerable value. The towns' people will be left to care for one another as best as they can.

There have been no church services since the battle began on July 1. All of the churches are being used to house and care for the wounded and disabled. Services will not resume until well after the last casualty has been properly cared for and removed to better quarters.

I spoke briefly with Reverend Schumacher of the Lutheran Seminary here in Gettysburg. He stated that the classroom building used from the first day as a hospital is still in use, and that classes may not resume until late in the fall. He further stated that the amputated limbs, piled as high as forty feet around the building, continue to be a source of great concern, attracting undesirable varmints from the countryside. Rats, raccoons, skunks, wild dogs, and birds have descended upon this once holy and sacred ground.

Families of the fallen are arriving daily, in search of their loved ones. Visitors and refugees alike arrive in a steady stream, seeking help, lodging, and information. The town's resources seem stretched beyond the breaking point, yet these simple folks continue on, rebuilding and reclaiming their community. The tears, cries, and wailing are beyond any description. The suffering of a broken heart and dream most likely should not to be compared to the suffering the soldiers endured in the brutality of this war. Yet, the suffering of loved ones is equal to, if not greater than, the suffering of the fallen soldier. For the loved one often must sit alone, emptily and helplessly, as their loved one suffers and either lives, or dies.

It is my hope to return to Washington City within the week and leave this place of devastation, destruction, and sorrow behind. Will this town ever recover? The local residents say that it will. Life continues on, in spite of the tragedies encountered. Is life the same as before? Absolutely not, for nothing remains as it was; and everyone, for better or worse, is forever changed by the circumstances of war, and of life. I shall forever more appreciate the daily gift of life, the glory of a sunrise and the majesty of a sunset, the joy and laughter of a small child at the surprise of life, the robin on winged flight, the petals of a new flower, the first frost and the purity of freshly fallen snow, the joy of birth and new life, and the rejoicing of a life, lived fully and wonderfully, as the soul enters into the heavenly realms.

The madness of the present conflict will eventually come to an end. Order will be restored, both across the nation, and in the many small towns, like Gettysburg, that have already suffered the hardships of war, or who will yet encounter the scourge of the war machine. May the end come quickly, before more destruction, devastation, and sorrow are thrust upon the populace of this nation.

Brooksville Florida
January 19, 1864
Elizabeth Grace Fitzgerald
War Correspondent
The New York Tribune

Brooksville-

Early on the morning of January 16, a column of Federal soldiers marched into this small southern community, in order to rid the population of any Confederate defenders. At first, it appeared that the small band of 150 Confederates under the command of Lt. Col. Robert Neipert, CSA, were of no match to the vast and seemingly endless number of Union soldiers quickly moving into the region.

Col. Neipert, however, was able to send immediate word to General Michael Hardy, CSA, seeking reinforcements. General Hardy responded without delay and straight away sent over 1000 Confederates into the foray to confront the nearly 2000 Union troops. By late Friday, January 16, the Confederates were well reinforced and ready to engage the Union threat.

Early on the morning of January 17, lines had been clearly drawn between Confederate and Union. An attack was launched by the Union, and the Confederates instantaneously found themselves in the defensive position. Several times, the lines broke and the Confederates had to pull back and regroup.

Around noon, there seemed to be a brief ceasefire while the Union soldiers regained their footing and rations were delivered. The Confederates took advantage of this situation to regroup and organize their lines once again.

Fighting again broke out around two in the afternoon. This time the Confederate lines held and began the hard task of driving the Union back. The Union thus began a slow retreat, and the Union Colonel in command had to order the withdrawal of his men back to the other side of the town.

By four thirty in the afternoon, the guns were once again silenced. The Union had regrouped on the far side of town, entrenching at this point as best as possible. The Confederate Army once again occupied the town itself. Aside from a few small skirmishes around the perimeter of the community, both Armies took their leave of the field of battle, to attend to the care of their men and prepare for another day.

As the evening wore on, both Armies quickly recovered as much equipment and rations as available. The men were told to rest as much as possible in the hours ahead, ready for the next day's engagements, which were surely to come. Neither Army seemed prepared or ready to make an offer of peace, withdrawal, or surrender.

As the night faded away into the morning light, the sight and smells of a camp ready for action were clearly seen. The sounds of troop movements, both on horse back and on foot, were heard from both the Union and the Confederate camps. Cannon rumbling in the distance were clear. There was no doubt by man or beast that action would be seen this day. As the Sunday morning broke calm, clear, and crisp, the men of both Armies were clearly on the move with the intent of not gathering for worship this day, but instead of sending one another to meet their maker in person.

Yesterday saw the casualties small in numbers in comparison to previous battles observed by this correspondent, but there was a smell and electricity in the air this day that gave one the sense that more blood than any would desire would be spilled on the battle field.

Shortly after noon, the first cannons could be heard lofting their deadly fire into the Union lines from the Confederate stronghold just to the west of town. The Union advance at first seemed slow, almost nonexistent, but then, as slowly as it began, the Union advance quickened, and, before long, the Confederate lines were fully engaged in close combat with overwhelming numbers of blue uniforms. Within a span of just a few short hours, the Confederate lines had broken, and a full retreat of the Army of the South had begun.

Soon the sounds of cannon and musket fire had ended, and the remaining sounds were of wounded and dying men crying out for mercy and help. The local angels of mercy began their tedious task of tending to the wounded, both in blue and gray, and the surgeons knife and saw began its cruel task of amputating limbs that had been shattered in the situation.

Soon the Union forces were organized and prepared to move against Confederate positions further to the east. Little more seems to be left for the south to gain, here in the swamps and heat of the Florida everglades and country side. Perhaps Richmond will order what is left of this Southern Army to retreat into the North, in an attempt to bring relief to Robert E. Lee in Virginia.

Everywhere one looks, there seems to be little hope now that the government in Richmond can endure much longer. Surely it must entreat the Washington government for peaceful settlement to the current conflict.

January 17, 1864
Brooksville, Florida
Elizabeth Grace Fitzgerald
War Correspondent
The New York Tribune

Brooksville-

During the lull between engagements on this warm Florida evening in Brooksville, I had the opportunity to engage the Confederate Commander, General Michael Hardy, at his headquarters. My impressions of General Hardy are not particularly flattering at this first time meeting the gentleman. Given that the circumstances of our meeting were following a difficult day of battle with a superior force, I shall excuse his lack of polish and shortness of speech to the stress he undoubtedly experienced at the time, and shall look forward to the possibility of speaking with the General at some future date, under more favorable conditions.

I did have the opportunity to talk with the General about a few issues and shall attempt to share some of our discussion. The General's views, as expressed to a Northern Correspondent, were refreshing, if somewhat short.

I asked the General how he felt with regard to the Negroes being recruited and armed in the North. He responded that the colored are no match for the white man when it comes to arms and fighting. He further stated that the black man will drop his weapon and run at the first sign of engagement. I asked if it were true that the South was arming some of its slaves to fight, and he stated that not under his command would any Negros hold a weapon.

I then inquired if he knew that General John Buford had died in Washington late in December, and he said that he had not heard that, but that it was good news to hear of another Yankee General gone to his maker.

In reference to the question of General McClellan running against Mr. Lincoln in this year's election, his only response was that anyone would be better than the Ape that currently resides in

Washington City, and that McClellan would undoubtedly sue for a peaceful end to the butchery currently practiced by the North.

Finally, I asked if he had heard that General Grant may soon assume the command of the Army of the Potomac, to which he replied that Grant is too drunk most of the time to win a card game, let alone a battle.

General Hardy then excused himself and withdrew from the interview. The Provost gave us a pass to see us safely through their lines to the Union position, where we retreated forthwith and found safety, as well as hospitality.

Within the next few days, we shall attempt to return North to the safety of the Union and the gaiety of Mrs. Lincoln's parties.

January 20, 1864
To the Honorable Horace Greely
Editor, The New York Tribune
New York, New York

Dear Mister Greely,

*I am taking this opportunity to share with you a dispatch
from Brooksville, Florida, where I have observed the engagement
of Union forces against a less superior Confederate Army. We
came upon this engagement quite by accident, not expecting to run
into Confederate and Union soldiers at all on our journey to this
warm winter respite. It was, as you are aware, my desire to escape
for a few weeks the turmoil I have witnessed over the past two
years. This has turned out to not be the case.*

*We left Washington City about Mid December by train
and traveled to Roanoke. There we met up with a small Union
division comprised of Negroes with their white officers. They were
somewhat disorganized, or so it seemed at first. After a short
while, though, I began to see their organization and discipline,
and was most favorably impressed by their abilities.*

*They invited us to join them further south, as both rail and
coach were unavailable at this point. I was informed upon my
inquiry that they were a unit from the 54th Massachusetts, under
the command of one Lieutenant John Price, and they were to
return and report to the 54th sometime after the first of the year.
They said they could accompany us as far as South Carolina, and
then we would be on our own. I greatly appreciated their escort,
as there were no more means of public transportation at the
moment.*

*We arrived at a small town in South Carolina, and took
our leave with two horses supplied by Lt. Price. We were very
grateful for this wonderful gift and for having had the opportunity
to share Christmas and New Years with these happy souls on their
way to defend the freedom and the Union that had sent them
Jubilee, just a year earlier.*

*We arrived near Tallahassee, Florida, around the 10th of
January, and immediately had our horses confiscated by a band of
Confederate ruffians. We then continued our journey on foot and
an occasional ride in a wagon from local farmers, until we arrived
near Brooksville on the 15th. Hearing that both Confederate and*

Union soldiers were in the area, we made ourselves the guests at the local Inn, and stayed to see what might transpire. That is how we were able to attend to and send these dispatches.

The Confederate General offered us two mules, to replace the horses taken by the ruffians in Tallahassee. We thanked him, but have been able instead to find public transportation suitable for our travels. We have been told that, once we arrive in St Augustine, we shall be able to board a ship going north, and may be able to go all the way to Williamsburg Virginia.

As soon as we are able to reach anywhere in the north occupied by Union forces, we shall send immediate word of our presence and make further reports as deemed appropriate. If possible, please forward expenses to our office in Washington City, to be assumed by me upon my arrival there.

I will look forward to our meeting again soon.

With much fondness, I remain,

Elizabeth Grace

My Dear Elizabeth,

Florence has insisted that I send you my editorial regarding the current state of affairs our nation is facing.

We are both doing well at this time. We have heard from our dear Ella in western Virginia that her husband is demonstrating sympathies for the southern cause. We pray that they will remain safe and out of harm's way should violence erupt.

Please come and pay us a visit when time allows. Florence says she misses your expeditions for shopping to Baltimore.

With warmest regards,

David

The Right to Secede Does Not make it Right to Secede

By

David Foote
Editor
Hagerstown Weekly Dispatch
April, 1861

It is the undeniable right of any state to secede from any superordinate government under which it may exist when that state believes it can no longer serve its people's best interests by remaining under the jurisdiction of that government. Certainly the people of a state, in considering the extent to which they believe other rights have been violated by the government, may at some point decide that they can no longer accept conditions as they are and must act to regain those rights.

Yet, doing so inevitably invites the potential for a considerably worse situation, as the government also has a right to take whatever steps it believes are in the best interests of all the people under its jurisdiction, including to retain the separate states within its union, and is likely to possess or be able to command resources well beyond those of any one individual state or group of states that it may use in accomplishing its purposes.

Thus, while it is the *right* of a state to secede, the unlikelihood of success in doing so, coupled with the potential for substantial loss of resources consumed in the attempt and the potential for great bloodshed throughout the land make the practical implementation of this theoretical right untenable at best. Surely, no government will allow one or more of its member states to simply withdraw without conflict.

Accordingly, we believe the best interest of Maryland's citizens is to avoid such a conflict if at all possible. Maryland's responsibility to its own citizens, as well as to its fellow states, is to find that course of action that best maintains the peace. We must work far into the night of this dark time to find some peaceable means of resolving the issues now so troubling to our southern neighbors. Maryland must not join its fellow states in secession, but also must not ignore the desires of its fellow states and should do everything in its power to see that those desires are fairly considered in developing an acceptable compromise. If other states persist in exercising their right to secede, Maryland should remain neutral as much as possible, neither seceding itself nor objecting to those states that do so, for that is the course of action that best serves the welfare of its citizens.

Still, there is one issue on which we cannot agree with our southern neighbors, and that is the emancipation of the Negro. This union, now threatened with dissolution, was built on the belief that "all men are created equal." Nowhere in our founding documents is it stated that all men *except the Negro* are created equal. Those who would argue that the Negro is in some way inferior to whites ignore the truth of this statement and, indeed, the truth of nature, for it is plain to see for those who would look that the Negro differs not from the white except in his outward appearance. Despite its all-too-frequent manifestation in the history of mankind, it has always been detestable for one man to enslave another. While there is no question that keeping the Negro enslaved offers limited financial benefit to his owner, no pecuniary advantage can be considered worthy of the moral and spiritual indignity allied with this institution.

The morality of this institutionalized depravity aside, on a purely economic basis, and contrary to the loudly voiced arguments of the proponents of slavery, the situation is such that greater pecuniary advantage might well be achieved, on the large scale, if the Negro were emancipated and given the opportunity to contribute his efforts to the national welfare. If the Negro was paid for his work and, in turn, paying for his existence by buying others' goods, the net accrual may well increase the region's (and thus, the nation's) economic outlook rather than diminish it.

There is, unfortunately for proponents of slavery, little credibility to their arguments in favor of keeping the Negro under their collective thumb; there is, on the other hand, every reason, with the full credibility of nature, of God, and of history, to emancipate the Negro. The sooner we achieve such a purpose, the more compelling will be our national dignity, the stronger our national unity, and the more upright our moral standing in the eyes of our allies, our enemies, and our God.

Near Gettysburg, PA

July 6, 1863

Dear Miss Elizabeth Grace Fitzgerald - New York Tribune,

I am Capt. Henry H. Bingham, Aide De Camp to Gen. Winfield Scott Hancock, and am writing to let you know the general has not perished.

I was with him all through this campaign and at his side at the Angle at the stone wall that was being hotly contested, when a bullet shattered his saddle, driving wood and nails into his upper thigh. I saw to it that he was aided immediately to the rear. Before they took him away, he pointed toward the cannons at the Angle and said "go there, see to him. He is a fellow Brother". (We are all Masons, it turned out.) There were other words, but they were lost in the dying fight.

I rode over in that direction and found a Confederate officer being put in a blanket stretcher between several privates. I ordered them back, but they replied that they had an important prisoner, and they designated him as General Longstreet.

The suffering general looked up at me and said "I am the son of a widow ..." an indication he was a Mason. I dismounted my horse and inquired of the prisoner his name. He replied "General Armistead of the Confederate Army". Observing that his suffering was very great, I said to him, "General, I am Captain Bingham of General Hancock's staff, and if you have anything valuable in your possession which you desire taken care of, I will take care of it for you".

He then asked me if it was General Winfield S. Hancock, and, upon my replying in the affirmative, he informed me that General Hancock was an old and valued friend of his and he desired for me to say to him, "Tell General Hancock for me that I have done him and done you all an injury which I shall regret or repent (I forget the exact word) the longest day I live."

I then obtained his spurs, watch chain, seal, and pocketbook. I told the men to take him to the rear, to the 11th Corps hospital at the Spangler farm, which was the closest one I knew of.

Unfortunately, though his wounds were not fatal, Gen Armistead passed from this world yesterday. I suspect it had to do with his completely broken spirit and exhausted state. I had to take this sad news to Gen. Hancock, and it moved him to tears. The surgeons have told me Gen. Hancock will be spending some months in the hospital recovering. He is in much pain, but is bearing it well. With the general out of action, I expect to be transferred back to my original unit, the 140th Pennsylvania Volunteer Infantry.

Truly yours,

Capt. Henry H. Bingham
Aide De Camp to Gen. W.S. Hancock
2nd Corps, Army of the Potomac

In the field Williamsport-Martinsburg- Winchester
July 25, 1863
To: Elizabeth Grace Fitzgerald
New York Tribune

My Dear Miss Fitzgerald,

I am writing to let you know not to listen to the politicians or some of the political generals on making your judgments on what happens in the field. I am a West Point graduate and career officer. I have trained cavalry and served out West in the Navajo War before the present blood letting. This government is sadly fighting a war within the war.

The Radical Republicans in Congress and in the president's cabinet are all living under a terrible naïve, near childish, view of war. They think the armies must make grand head-on assaults in Napoleonic fashion, and that this war can be won quickly in one great battle. They think they know more than the generals, on how to run a war.

We have suffered two years of their interference in sacking good competent officers from regimental to army command level, who are Democrat, in favor of those who support their political views, or they become too impatient for victory and thus can not keep a commander of the Army of the Potomac in the field for long. You can not win a horse race by constantly changing the rider.

The Radicals know nothing of logistics, supply, tactics and strategy, or even the basics of the every day maintenance needs of a regiment in the field. I have seen this all first hand and been a victim of it. I saw the terrible result of meddling politicians on the Peninsula all too clearly.

Washington, and not McClellan (a fellow Democrat), was responsible for that fiasco. They would not let him have the troops he needed because of their irrational fear Washington City did not have enough defenders. They bled troops away from the campaign and did not order the navy to go through with joint support as planned.

I brought the Union its first cavalry victory at Kelly's Ford, yet recently I seem to be one of the very political Gen. Hooker's "scape goats" for his performance at Chancellorsville. I was relieved of my command in the AoP cavalry for supposedly poor performance and was sent this past May 23 to West Virginia, as sort of a punishment to turn infantry to cavalry and create a semi-independent command that is now designated the 4th Separate Brigade, with which I am to take a major part in ridding the new state of the Confederate presence. In May, I converted the 2nd, 3rd, and 8th West Virginia Infantry to mounted infantry, basically in forty-eight hours, by mounting them on green horses. I have always been short on supplies, especially horse shoes, and horses can not travel over the rugged roads of this region without shoes, without breaking down very soon. I am also plagued by the lack of ordnance stores and often widely scattered detachments. Men and horses must be, and are, continually drilled in between long patrols of the region.

During the recent Gettysburg campaign, after the battle, while out in the field below the Winchester area in Greenbrier or Pocahontas County, I received an urgent dispatch to cut off Lee's retreat toward Williamsport, that recent rains had flooded the Potomac to such an extent that he was trapped and could not yet ford the river. I headed my brigade northward by train and a forced march. It was my hope to find and join up with Gen. John Buford, whom I admire as probably the only great cavalry leader this army has.

But as often happens in war, what you hope for evaporates like water in a hot frying pan. As much as we hurried, we missed Lee by just a little less than twenty-four hours. I knew Buford and my command could have held them till Meade arrived to finish him. Now we are involved in marches and counter marches, keeping an eye on the Confederates in the area as they continue South.

I expect the Radicals in Washington will want Meade's head on a platter for "not destroying Lee". But these dolts will not realize that an army as hard fought as the AoP does not recover over night, let alone for an immediate chase of a retreating army.

Those units that I have seen are exhausted, ill supplied, yet pushing on. Supplies have not caught up, and, without supplies, an army slows to a crawl or stalls. The politicians do not understand that an army on the defensive has its supplies right with it, or at least a shorter line of supply than an army on the offensive pushing after it with a long and vulnerable supply line. Most of Virginia's farms have been ravaged by both armies, so even living off the land is not much of an option. This makes the pursuit slow.

I am beginning to wonder, at this point, if I will ever be adequately supplied so I can carry out my duties in this back water if the AoP is having so much trouble with their own. About the only advantage I have is the farms here have not suffered as much as those in the Old Dominion and many of the boys are excellent hunters, but that just covers food.

We need horse shoes, fodder, ammunitions, and to replace a lot of the Enfield's with Sharps or Spencer carbines, more proper weapons for the cavalry. But I suspect the AoP will get more of the same from these Radical meddlers. They will expect miracles, and their ranting to the Press will make the general public want miracles, while remaining willfully ignorant of the reality of modern warfare. I suppose I should consider myself lucky now to be mostly beyond the Radicals' reach in the mountains of West Virginia, in a semi-independent command with only Gen. Benjamin Kelly to answer to.

Your Obedient Servant,

Brig. Gen. William Woods Averell
4th Separate Brigade
Commanding

*An Editorial Response by Elizabeth Grace Fitzgerald to Brig.
Gen. William Woods Averell*
July 30, 1863
Washington City

My Dear General Averell,

*I have received and read your letter of July 25, 1863 with
much interest. I have heard the same arguments from other
leading officers that you make here, regarding the attitudes of the
politicians of Washington City. I wrote an editorial on June 3,
1863, reflecting some of what I believe to be the real motivation
and attitudes of our illustrious politicians regarding this present
unpleasantness. Unfortunately, most of the more competent
Generals are relegated at this time to positions of ineffectiveness
in bringing about the end of the conflict. As I stated in my
editorial, when profits are no longer to be made off the war
machine by greedy bankers, financiers, and politicians, then the
right men will placed in the position to bring a just and quick end
to the hostilities.*

*If it were not for the war policy of the present
administration and Mister Lincoln's insistence on the use of force
to end the "rebellion", then we would not have Virginia and much
of the South decimated by any army. It would seem that the War
machine of Washington City has caused this present suffering
more than any army. It would seem to this writer that this present
hostility is in every way a violation of the very Constitution that
the present administration has sworn to uphold and defend.*

*I have stated in prior articles and correspondence that the
way to have settled the argument over secession and slavery was
not through armed conflict, nor through an Army of the Federal
Government marching on its citizens to force the will of the
Administration, but to seek direction through the Justice
Department and the United States Supreme Court.*

*It is not Washington who should seek the heads of its
Generals following the losses and inability to end the conflict. No,
my dear General, it is the citizens of the nation who seek the
impeachment of the government for its unlawful actions in
violation of the Constitution. Unfortunately that process will, and
has already been, made impossible by the violation of our
Constitutional rights by a government in armed conflict with its*

citizens. To seek any action against the government at this point in time would result in the immediate arrest and imprisonment of the person initiating such action. With the suspension of the Writ of Habeas Corpus, there is little recourse for the citizens. My writing this very letter of response to you endangers me to that process. Even the press is no longer immune, as the First Amendment has been challenged by this Administration.

Having said all of this, my desire is to see the Union reunited, slavery come to an end, and peace be restored once again, but at what cost?

I truly wish for you, and all our men, a quick end to the conflict, so that all men may resume a peaceful existence with one another.

I remain your humble servant,

Elizabeth Grace Fitzgerald
War Correspondent
New York Tribune

Dear Miss Fitzgerald,

    I have just returned from Lambertville, New Jersey, seeking donations of supplies for our boys in blue. I only recently was able to catch up on my correspondence, having just this moment read your very fine article.
    I was indeed humbled by your generous praises of my efforts in helping our dear boys. I am not the heroine. Indeed I feel that the true heroines are the fine, patriotic women who have donated their time and talents in providing me with the necessities which I am then able to give to the soldiers. I have oft been told that the field of battle is much too dangerous a place for a woman to be. My response to that is "if it dangerous for me, it is just as dangerous for a man, as well!"
    My patriotic duty is to serve my country in whatever way I can, and, as long as I am able to do so, I will be where "my boys" are. Here in South Carolina, it appears that my services are not much in demand, and I find myself homesick for the great Army of the Potomac.
    Your kind and generous words have given me the strength to continue doing God's will, and, with the support of our ladies at home, I am able to provide for our "boys in blue."

Very Humbly Yours,

Miss Clara Barton

Allegheny Mountains, WV
Aug. 4, 1863

My Dear Miss Elizabeth Fitzgerald – New York Tribune,

It was with great interest that I read a copy of the New York World given to me by my aide and found your response to a letter I sent. As much as I am dissatisfied by politicians and those who wish to prolong the war, two facts must be realized and accepted. This present unpleasantness is a true Civil War, and it was started by the southern states the moment they decided to take Federal property in the form of various garrisons, forts, and armories. Several did this before they committed the illegal act of secession, Georgia, Louisiana and Florida in particular. Fort Sumter was just the straw that broke the camel's back, as the old saying goes.

From my observations at West Point when I was a cadet, I noticed the southerners' tendency to go off half cocked. Many of the southern cadets were from a class you could only describe as American aristocracy, used to getting what they wanted when they wanted it, and with the bullying habit of wanting to start a fight with anyone who disagreed with them. If dueling had not been outlawed earlier this century it would have happened, I am sure, at West Point. Debates off academy grounds often came to blows. I remember writing to my family about these goings on. But, I digress here.

These two facts - this being a true Civil War and started by the southern states - have been swept under the rug it seems - especially by the press. Having many friends in the military all over this country and on the frontier whom I corresponded while at home in Bath, New York, recovering from a broken leg as a result of a wound I received in the Navajo War, I must add that I heard first hand about these acts of war. One of these friends was a Lieut. Meade, who was stationed in Ft. Sumter and kept me informed of a South Carolina military build up which he was witnessing.

I do not expect you to understand the rules of war. However I must say that, to end Civil War, a government often must temporarily take away rights in order to restore order. I am confident that

Constitutional rights will be restored, once the Federal army is victorious. Remember, I took an oath as an officer to defend the Constitution, as did all my fellow officers and every man in the many volunteer units that make up the Federal army; and we will not allow the Constitution to be permanently "violated", as you complained in your response. If you have ever ridden down roads and been bush wacked by local guerilla units of the enemy who happen to be fellow Americans, you would understand why local farms, etc. must be searched without a warrant, and why the military must have a free hand to do so. I do not allow my troops to burn out or otherwise molest innocent civilians, unless there is due cause, and I would consider due cause as being shot at first or chasing bushwhackers right to their home. This kind of incident is quite common in West Virginia and parts of Virginia. And, by the way, West Virginia is that part of the Old Dominion that chose to stay loyal to the Union and my West Virginia cavalry regards itself somewhat as freedom fighters, having been taxed, and all monies gone east to the counties of rich planters. The Confederacy calling West Virginia illegal is about like the pot calling the kettle black.

As to the freedom of the press, that freedom must be curtailed if they are giving information on troop movements, maps of fortifications, etc. in general articles, for this can be considered aiding and abetting the enemy. General Lee, for whom I have great respect, as he was the superintendent at West Point during my years there, has stated to the closely guarded Confederate press that his best information comes from the Northern Press.

In closing, I do want to mention that I wish to see an end to this conflict, but fear we will not very soon, because of the sheer prideful bull headedness of the South, they refuse to see that they have no chance against a Union with more of a population and industry providing new weapons. Meanwhile, I will do what I can to put an end to this rebellion.

Your Obedient Servant.

Brig. Gen. William W. Averell
4th Separate Brigade
Commanding

An Editorial Response by Elizabeth Grace Fitzgerald to Brig.
Gen. William Woods Averell
August 6, 1863
Near Gettysburg Pennsylvania

My Dear General,

You seem to miss the point of my original discussion, and that is that the issues of Constitutionality, be it secession, the first amendment, or any other issue, should be decided by the courts and not by war.

The present administration has seen fit to ignore the Constitutional role of the Justice Department and preferred to exercise the role of the Military in these matters. Undoubtedly, the motivation is greed, as I have already stated previously, supported by Military men whose primary desire and role in life is to wage war. Since we have no foreign power threatening our sovereignty at this time, the military men must assist in creating opportunity to keep their jobs, by waging war on their countrymen.

As for your assertion that I may not understand the rules of war, you are implying that either I am an incompetent fool because, one, I am a female, or two, I am not a military man. Sir, I am quite capable of reading and understanding with much comprehension, the military manuals you read and studied at West Point. I have in fact, already read many of the texts of study which you and your fellow officers engaged in at West Point. I am quite capable at mathematics, science, history, philosophy, grammar, and military tactics, the latter, of course, only through reading and through discourse with many military men. Therefore, I am quite certain that I fully understand the "rules" of war, perhaps even better than you, sir.

So my original suggestion of several correspondence's ago is simply this, allow the courts to decide the Constitutionality of Secession, both for the Southern States as well as for Western Virginia. Disengage, or at least suspend, the immediate action of hostilities until the courts can decide what is constitutionally correct.

But you and I know that that will not occur, as there are still profits to be made, and in the words of Great Britain's King

George during the American Revolution, "There are the Rebels to be punished."

I remain your humble servant,

Elizabeth Grace Fitzgerald
War Correspondent
New York Tribune

Letter to Miss Elizabeth Grace Fitzgerald
War Correspondent
New York Tribune
New York, New York

Dear Miss Fitzgerald,

I read with great interest your articles and the responses from the various Union defenders, and, while I am privy to most of the information contained within their borders, I do gleam some items of import on which I am able to make worthy decisions.

In a recent dispatch from General Averell I found it interesting that he speaks of Virginia in its ravaged condition. I can only feel remorse for it's having been subjected to such torturous interference, by a government that boasts of offering government of the people, by the people and for the people; when in actuality it has stripped its citizens of free speech, freedom of the press, and habeas corpus, to mention a few.

I look to Providence for an end to this unpleasantness and a return to normalcy; when those people will return to their homes to plow their fields and we, in turn, can do the same.

With appreciation for your attentiveness to just journalism I am

Respectfully,

R E Lee

17th May, 1864

Dear Elizabeth,

I am sorry I have not written sooner. It is hard to find time to write, between helping mother and being in a finishing school. I have finished my studies in that horrible one roomed school house, and am finally attending the ladies seminary. We help with the war effort a lot, doing fundraising and writing letters to soldiers, as well as studying art and literature. The headmistress teaches us to be respectable young women. I like the headmistress; she is a lovely woman, and very caring. She reminds me much of you. She likes writing, literature, and is very involved with social issues.

The Seneca Falls meeting is somewhat familiar to me. We talk about it sometimes during our quilting sessions. That and the war effort seem to be the main topics we young ladies discuss during our quilting sessions. I try to imagine the impact these women who fight for our rights will have on my life in the future. They truly are heroines of the generation.

We stay off the topic of slavery, as some of the girls are from the south and still trying to adapt to northern thinking styles, but Mr. Douglass is a very familiar name. He seems to be mentioned a lot around this time by some local politicians. The newspapers either praise him or hate him, but I like him. I like how he helped start the first colored unit in Massachusetts, the 54th, if I'm not mistaken. They must be brave, fighting against the men who previously "owned" them.

Rachael says hello and she misses you as well. She is still in the school house, and has more studying then I do. She is still in primary school, learning the basics of grammar and arithmetic, but I have more learning to be a respectable young woman aware of social issues, well educated in art, history and literature.

I shall be sure to answer sooner next time. I hope to see you soon.

Love, from your dear friend,
Tillie

Appendix – Student/Teacher Guide

Your Mission: Be a Civil War News Correspondent
by Abigail Elizabeth Reynolds

Student/Teacher User's Guide

In the midst of battle, somewhere on an American battlefield, the war correspondent was surrounded by danger and death. His or her mission was to report on the events of the day, but as the battle ensued they realized that getting the story to press depended upon their very survival. Here, on the battlefield, survival seemed a matter of fate, not only for the soldiers engaged in the fighting, but for anyone caught in this humanly contrived storm. Armed only with pencil and paper, the correspondent went about the job of recording the news of the day – an observer of the battle as well as a brave participant.

A war correspondent is a person who risks personal safety by going onto the field of battle to record the events that occur there. The American Civil War was one of the first wars in history in which reporters filed stories from the field. With bullets whizzing by, a correspondent's only weapons might have been pencil and paper. Yet, with little regard for the dangers of battle, these brave reporters wrote first hand accounts for eager readers back home.

As you and your family visit the historic battlefield sites of the Civil War, you might want to actually become a Civil War correspondent. Do you think you can handle the job? You must be a brave and accurate observer, willing to do what you must to report on the war. You will need to patiently await the start of battle, and then quickly write about and sketch all that you see. You will want to interview soldiers and officers, as well as civilians in the local towns. Their stories will be a vital part of the story you write.

This is an important job - your readers will depend upon you and your pencil alone, to tell all that has occurred. The stories you write will need to include *who* was in the battle, *where* the battle took place, *when* the battle occurred, exactly *what* happened on the battlefield, *why* the battle took place, plus the interesting and exciting details that you will surely witness.

If you think you may be ready for the challenge, welcome. As you visit the battlefields and perhaps see reenactments, take along your book and pencil and begin doing one of the most important and dangerous jobs of the war – being in the line of fire as a Civil War correspondent.

Good luck and best wishes as you report on the war!

Introduction

At the start of the American Civil War, which began in (circle the correct year) '1812' '1917' '1861' , there were 2,500 newspapers being published in the United States.

Many of the news stories that were printed were sent from far off locations using a relatively new invention called the 'magnetic', more commonly known later as the (circle the correct name) 'telephone' 'telegraph' 'television'.

The magnetic was used to send messages through wires over long distances, using a special code invented by (circle the correct name) 'Samuel Morse' 'Alexander Graham Bell' 'Thomas Edison'.

The code is sometimes still used today, and is comprised of a series of dots and dashes.

At the start of the war there were nearly 100 war correspondents, sometimes also referred to as 'special correspondents'. Their pay was about $27 per week. Most of the correspondents were white males, but there is evidence of at least a dozen women and one African American reporter during the war. Later, as the intensity of the war heightened, nearly 500 correspondents were filing stories from the field – about 350 for the north and 150 for the south.

A war correspondent's life was not an easy one. There were long periods of inactivity between major battles. During these times, the correspondent might look for human interest stories –

interesting stories about the people affected by the war, like the soldiers and officers, or the civilians in towns where battles may have occurred. It was a constant challenge for the special correspondents to find warm and dry places to sleep and adequate food to eat. Not only was there danger from the obvious hazards on the field of battle, but there was also the danger of being captured by one side or the other and charged as a spy. During any war, information (also called intelligence) is crucial – correspondents who gathered information were sometimes viewed with suspicion.

To help one another with the challenges and hazards of reporting on the war from the battlefields, a social and working organization of correspondents and artists was formed, called the Bohemian Brigade. This band of brave reporters shared the many challenges of writing stories from the field of battle. Among the more difficult problems was actually getting the stories to press. The telegraph was a new and amazingly fast means of communication, but its availability was not always assured. Not only were telegraph lines controlled by the military, but the competition with other reporters wanting to transmit stories was fierce. It was a long and arduous journey for the news of the war to travel from the correspondent's pad on the battlefield to the printed page of the newspapers. But the stories *were* recorded by the brave war correspondents stationed out in the field for their audience of readers around the world.